TIGER, TIGER, BURNING BRIGHT
THE BETRAYALS
OF PANCHO VILLA

Book 3 of
"The Vanishing" Trilogy

Sundowners
A division of
Treble Heaat Books

Tiger, Tiger, Burning Bright
The Betrayals of Pancho Villa
Book 3 of "The Vanishing" Trilogy
Copyright © 2011 W. Michael Farmer
All rights reserved.

Front Cover Design
Copyright © 2011 Lee Emory
All rights reserved.

Painting of Pancho Villa
Courtesy of
J.D. Trolinger
Copyright © 2011

SUNDOWNERS
a division of
Treble Heart Books
Sierra Vista, Arizona
Published and Printed in the U.S.A.

ISBN: 978-1-936127-87-0
1-936127-87-3
LCCN: 2011943644

Other Books by W. Michael Farmer

Conspiracy:
The Trial of Oliver Lee and James Gililland

Hombrecito's War *

* Book 1 of "The Vanishing" Trilogy

To Razy
Good [?]!
all the best
Michael

Cast of Characters

Fictional Characters

Camisa Roja (Guillermo Camerena)
CPT Sinolo Gutierrez
Doctor Henry Grace
Doctor Oñate
Gamberro
Jesús Avella
Jose Soto
Juanita
Lupe
Magritte
Marco Guionne
Marta
Moon On The Water
Juan
Pelo Rojo
Persia Peach
Quentin Peach
Redondo
Roberta Gonzalez
Rooster
Runs Far
SGT Sweeny Jones
Yellow Boy

Historical Characters

Bunk Spencer
C. R. Jefferis

Candelario Cervantes
COL Nicolas Fernández
COL Slocum
Commandante Macario Bracamontes
Doctor Miller
Doctor Thigpin
E. B. Stone
Edward Wright
Father Abelino Flores
Frank Hayden
GEN Francisco Villa (Also known as Pancho Villa)
GEN Funston
GEN Pershing
GEN Rodolfo Fierro
GEN Urbalejo
George Carothers
Henry Fountain
Hughs Slater
Hipólito Villa
Johnnie Wright
LT George Patton
LT Martin Shallenberger
MAJ Frank Thompkins
Mariana Fountain
Maud Wright
Sam Ravel
Sara Hoover
Susan Moore
Texas John Slaughter
Will Hoover
Zack Cobb

Dedication

For Corky,
My Best Friend, My Wife

Acknowledgements

I have been supported and encouraged in this work by many friends and associates to whom I owe a debt of gratitude and I thank them. There are several who deserve special mention.

Bruce Kennedy's invaluable review, commentary, and knowledge of the southwest have made an outstanding contributions to this story. I thank him for his support and guidance.

Robin Smith and Barbara Warren provided editorial reviews and many helpful suggestions and comments to enhance manuscript quality. They are much appreciated.

Reviews by Jean Thomas and Ruth Austin saved me from numerous textual and typographical errors. I thank them.

Pat and Mike Alexander have graciously opened their home to me on my return visits to New Mexico for research and book tours and provided company on long back roads along the US-Mexico border. I'm in their debt.

Jim Trolinger is the fine artist who provided the cover art. His image emblazons the story and I thank him for his skill and patience.

There are many histories and stories about Pancho Villa. The ones I found most helpful are provided in Additional Reading at the end of the story.

Table of Contents

PART I

PART II

Prefatory Note

"The pursuit of truth, not facts, is the business of fiction."
Oakley Hall, Prefatory Note to *Warlock*

In 1910 Pancho Villa dreamed of a Mexico where the peons had rights and privileges, and were much more than serfs for the wealthy to use or abuse. Charismatic, often brilliant, sometimes shortsighted to the point of blindness, narcissistic and stubborn, he wrote his name large on the history and legends of Mexico and the American southwest. Admirers called him a great hero, a man of the people. Enemies called him a murdering bandit who bathed Mexico in blood. The men and women who followed General Francisco Villa through years of hard-fought battles, marching and suffering across burning deserts and freezing mountains, feeling his fire and knowing his crouching, cat-like energy, understood his demand for loyalty and his brutal, mafia-like revenge for a betrayal. They called him *El Jaguar Indomado*— the untamed jaguar, *El Tigre*—the tiger, *El Centauro del Norte*—the centaur of the north, *La Fiera*—the fierce one. They loved him, but mostly, they feared him.

In the early morning hours of 9 March 1916, Pancho Villa attacked the small Army camp and town at Columbus, New Mexico, three miles north of the United States border with Mexico. Villa's raiders killed eighteen American civilians and eight soldiers, wounded many others, burned a hotel and several businesses, and stole as much as they could carry in their arms or stuff in their shirts and raggedy pants pockets.

A week after the Columbus raid, much to the anger and embarrassment of the Mexican government led by *El Presidente* Venustiano Carranza, a United States Army division led by Brigadier General John J. Pershing crossed the border on an uninvited Punitive Expedition against Pancho Villa. The Expedition's stated mission was to pursue and disperse the Columbus raiders, but no one doubted its true purpose was to catch or to kill Villa and destroy his army.

The American Army stayed in Mexico eleven months. Most of its fighting was against Carranza government soldiers, not the Villa army raiders who attacked Columbus and scattered south in small groups, to parts unknown. The Punitive Expedition achieved its stated mission in less than two months but failed to catch or kill Pancho Villa. It was the first major American military operation using trucks for carrying supplies, automobiles for transport, and airplanes for reconnaissance, and the Army's last major horse-mounted cavalry operation. The Columbus raid and the Punitive Expedition marked the end of the classical Old West and prepared America for entry into World War I.

During the six months before the Columbus raid, Pancho Villa saw his army of over twenty thousand men, *División del Norte*, and his dreams of just treatment for peons destroyed by his inability to effectively counter European-style trench warfare, a lack of supplies, and American treachery. His downfall began in the spring and summer of 1915 with his defeats in three major battles with a former turkey farmer, General Álvaro Obregón, who had learned trench-warfare tactics from German advisors and had studied Villa's tactics in the 1910 Revolution.

After his defeats by Obregón, Villa regrouped *División del Norte*, and, in the fall of 1915, moved an estimated ten-thousand-man army with few supplies, starving and thirsty, across the Sierra Madre and up the Bavispe and San Bernardino River Valleys for an attack on Agua Prieta, a small village he believed was lightly defended and easy to take, just across the border from Douglas, Arizona.

The march across the Sierra Madre was an accomplishment admired even by Villa's enemies. But, after attacking Agua Prieta and failing, and then attacking the capital of Sonora, Hermosillo, and failing, *División del Norte* was essentially destroyed, and in December of 1915, its few survivors staggered back across the snow-covered Sierra Madre toward their homes in Chihuahua. To a rational mind, it was the end of the war between Venustiano Carranza and Pancho Villa. In early 1916, the Carranza government told Americans they were safe to return to their properties in Mexico. The war with Villa, it said, was over. Yet, in spite of devastating losses, Pancho Villa refused to quit fighting, refused to believe he was defeated, refused to surrender.

Described in today's vernacular, the Pancho Villa of 1915/1916 was a terrorist. After Woodrow Wilson betrayed him at Agua Prieta, Villa, once a sworn ally who protected American citizens and property in Mexico during the 1910 Mexican Revolution, vowed to kill any American and destroy any American-owned business he encountered in Mexico.

The attack on Columbus and the Punitive Expedition response nearly brought the United States and Mexico to war, and some historians believe that was Villa's objective. Understanding how Pancho Villa, once a strong friend of the United States and hero of the 1910 Mexican Revolution, became an enraged enemy can teach Americans much about border relationships and the significance of personalities and honorable dealing in the asymmetrical wars in which we become entangled.

The historical record of the marches and suffering for Pancho Villa and *División del Norte* in 1915/1916 is spotty and often apparently contradictory. I have endeavored to make this story as historically accurate as possible by using known and undisputed facts with close study of the lay of the land and the personalities involved and describing marches and events accordingly. However, the reader is advised to remember that the objective of this story is to pursue the truth and not necessarily the facts. This is the context of *Tiger, Tiger, Burning Bright*, a story of friends becoming enemies, of betrayal, of betrayed and betrayer, of the fire that produces madness in a time of blood and steel, and of the deaths of dreams. It is a story of the end of the Old West, a time that lives still in our myths and legends and in our hearts.

W. Michael Farmer
Smithfield, Virginia
October 2011

X

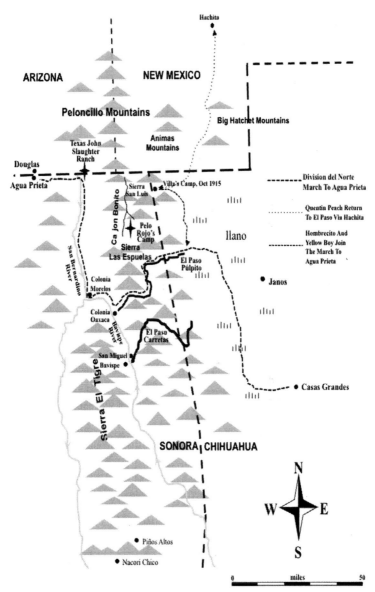

The March to Agua Prieta

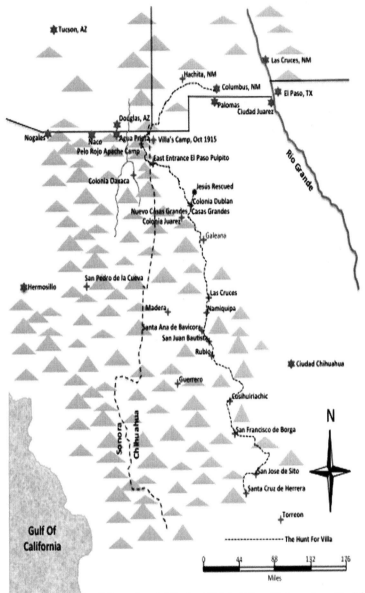

On the Trail of Pancho Villa in 1916 After Columbus Raid

PART I

PROLOGUE

The Fountain murders remain one of the great mysteries of the American West. Albert Fountain and his eight-year-old son, Henry, disappeared in the winter desert near White Sands, New Mexico, 1 February 1896. Their bodies were never found. The ranchers accused of the murders were found innocent in a famous 1899 trial. To this day, it is generally believed no one knows what truly happened to the Fountains.

In the winter of 1951, Dr. Henry Grace, an aging, highly respected general practitioner in Las Cruces, New Mexico, told a shocked and skeptical Roberta Gonzalez, his office nurse for over twenty years, that he was the long-lost Henry Fountain. His story described how an Apache cavalry scout, Yellow Boy, found him, near freezing to death, as he hid from his father's murderers. Fearful of being accused of Albert's murder, the Apache carried Henry to an old rancher,

Rufus Pike, who lived alone in the Organ Mountains. Under the care of Rufus, Henry grew to early manhood.

Trained by Yellow Boy to survive in the desert and fight like an Apache, and taught to be a phenomenal marksman with a Sharps rifle by Rufus Pike, Henry and his mentors destroyed the men Henry saw murder his father. Their destruction cost the life of Rufus, and still unable to tell his mother he survived his father's murder but couldn't save him, Henry disappeared into Mexico's Sierra Madre to live with Yellow Boy among bronco Apaches.

The years with the Apaches saw Henry become friends with the bandit Doroteo Arango, battle notorious killers like Apache Kid, and fall in love with and marry Rafaela, an American captive taken in the Geronimo wars. Killed during a raid on a *hacienda*, Rafaela left Henry mourning her for the rest of his life. In 1906, Henry left the Apaches and returned to New Mexico to settle accounts with the man he believed paid for and was behind his father's murder, and to a long-delayed, joyful reunion with his mother, who helped him enter college and medical school.

Hearing the telling of his story, the once incredulous Roberta sensed its truth, and Henry realized the long-denied love he had for her. He spoke shyly of his feelings, and she, secretly loving him since her first days in his office, was overjoyed. They were married in San Albino Church in Mesilla, New Mexico, and held their reception on the plaza on a fall evening in 1951.

Tiger, tiger, burning bright
In the forests of the night,
What immortal hand or eye
Could frame thy fearful symmetry?

—Excerpt from, *The Tiger,* a poem by William Blake

"Wisdom sits in places. It's like water that never dries up. You need to drink water to stay alive, don't you? Well, you need to drink from places. You must remember everything about them. You must learn their names. You must remember what happened at them long ago. You must think about it and keep on thinking about it. Then your mind will become smoother and smoother. Then you will see danger before it happens. You will walk a long way and live a long time. You will be wise. People will respect you."

Pisago Cabezón to his son Cochise as written by Peter Aleshire in *Cochise: The Life and Times of the Great Apache Chief*

1. THE MAN IN THE RED SHIRT

Mesilla, New Mexico, 1951

Feral fire, inexplicable and uninvited, burned in her new husband's eyes, confusing Roberta, even frightening her a little, and she held on to Henry's powerful hand as much to restrain him as for reassurance he was the same man she had just married.

Henry's brow focused into a hard frown, his jaw muscles rippled over clenched teeth as he aggressively stared at the creased, brown leathery face of a Mexican, tall and lean, sinew tough, his white hair combed straight back to the edge of his bright red shirt's collar. He was respectably dressed for a fiesta and wore a large, finely done silver and turquoise belt buckle and pressed jeans with perfect, straight creases running all the way to the toes of his shiny, black boots.

Bowing to them like an aristocrat, elegantly swinging his hand, fingers slightly curled, across his waist, and then standing straight, the old gentleman thrust his chin defiantly forward and locked his gaze on Henry's eyes. A lifetime seemed to pass, the men locked in a bond that surrounded and encapsulated them in a memory so focused and powerful Roberta didn't even exist and she knew it.

Speaking with a smoker's throaty growl, Red Shirt smiled and said in near perfect border English, "*Buenos noches,* Hombrecito. I have traveled many miles through the dust of Chihuahua to attend this fine *fiesta* and to wish you well. I offer my heartfelt congratulations to you and to your bride. May an old man have the pleasure of a dance with your lady?"

Henry, lips forming a thin straight line, said nothing.

Roberta, seeing Henry's first pink blush of surprise turning dark, angry red and feeling her fear recede, snapped her hand from Henry's and grabbed the old man's calloused, arthritic one to sweep him away in a grand ballroom swirl. Henry watched them swing through a few steps of a waltz and then returned to their table, leaving only them on the dance floor.

She looked into the old man's eyes and searched her memory, but found nothing except a certainty that somehow she ought to know him.

"You have me at a disadvantage, *señor*. I do not recall meeting you. You called my husband *Hombrecito*. Few know him by that name. You must know him from the days of his youth."

"*Si, señora*, I know him from those days. He has not told you of the *vaquero* in the red shirt, Camisa Roja?"

The old man felt her tense in his arms and knew he was no stranger.

"*Si, señor*. My husband told me the story of a *vaquero* in a *camisa roja* killing his wife and unborn child. You are that *hombre*?"

"*Si*, beautiful lady. I am the man."

"How is it my husband came to spare and know you instead of killing you?"

He shrugged his shoulders and lifted his brushy white brows.

"He came to know me by way of his *amigo*, General Francisco Villa. I served General Villa in the *Revolución* and ... in later times."

"My husband was in medical school during the *Revolución*. So you knew him in the later times?"

"*Si*, in the later times."

Roberta frowned.

"When were these later times, *señor*?"

Camisa Roja grinned, his teeth bright against his brown skin in the golden lantern light.

"Ah, that your new husband must tell you, *señora*. I will not."

Nothing more was said as he gracefully swung Roberta through a few more rounds before the music ended. He escorted her back to Henry, and handing her hand to him, bowed to them once more.

"*Muchas gracias*, beautiful lady and Hombrecito. I wish for you a long life together and much happiness. I hope you know now, Hombrecito, life dealt you a good hand. You more than broke even. *Buenos noches, and adiós*."

Leaving Henry and Roberta staring after him, he turned and disappeared into the darkness beyond the lantern light. Roberta slid her arm inside Henry's, and leaning next to him, she whispered in his ear:

"You owe me a story."

Smiling once again, Henry kissed her cheek and nodded.

Months passed. Henry never mentioned Camisa Roja.

One night a juniper-wood fire crackled on the adobe hearth, filling their house with the sweet odor of burning cedar. Outside, a wild January wind swirled and moaned across the desert, shaking the creosotes and mesquites and sailing tumbleweeds into fences and *arroyos*.

Sipping pinot noir, Roberta and Henry slumped together in the middle of their big sofa and stared at the fire, stocking feet resting on a reddish-brown, cowhide ottoman and pointed toward the hearth's toasty glow.

Roberta put an arm around Henry's shoulders and gave him a hug. Her question came out of nowhere, holding him to a promise implied but never spoken. He had hoped she would forget about the man in the red shirt, but he had not yet learned the lesson most men married a while know: wives never forget anything their husbands say or imply.

"You promised to tell me about Camisa Roja. Why won't you?"

Henry raised his brows and shrugged.

"I don't know. He's from a dark time I'd rather forget, a time I almost killed a friend who betrayed me, and an innocent man came close to being killed because I betrayed him. I made promises and swore oaths I did not keep, and I came to know things about my true self I wished I'd never learned…It was a time when I suddenly learned my choices in life weren't black or white anymore; most were shades of gray. Camisa Roja is lucky to be alive. It's a miracle I didn't kill him. I tried. The last time I saw him I promised him I'd kill him if I ever saw him again and he knew I meant it. He shouldn't have come to the wedding." Henry took a sip of wine, stared at the fire, and muttered, "He shouldn't have come."

"Oh, come on, don't be so hard on yourself or him. He probably traveled hundreds of long miles to wish us long life and happiness. He danced once with me and left. What's so bad about that? Tell me how you came to know him and what happened." She chuckled. "You know I won't let you rest until you do."

Henry stared at the flames playing hide-and-seek in a stack of glowing embers. He slowly shook his head and grinned. *I knew I should have read the fine print in that marriage contract.*

He looked at her, winced, and sighed.

"All right, I'll tell you. Better yet, after the spring winds die down, I'll show you the country where it all happened while I tell you the story. We'll go down to Mexico, rent a jeep in Casas Grandes, and drive the trails where it all took place. How does that sound?"

Roberta slowly nodded.

"Wonderful. It'll be our first vacation since we married, and I'd love to see the country where my folks were born. I've never been to Chihuahua."

"Pour us some more of that pinot. It lifts the burdens of the day and warms the heart…for better things…than telling stories."

She raised an eyebrow and smiled. "You don't need pinot for that Henry Grace and you know it."

He smiled and stared at the garnet-colored pool of liquid in the long stem glass as long forgotten memories awoke and reached for him through the cage where he'd kept them for the past thirty-five years.

2. TELL THEM ALL

El Paso Púlpito, The Sierra Madre,
Chihuahua, Mexico, 1952

"Why did you stop?"
Lost in another time, another life, Henry's knuckles grew white as he gripped the steering wheel and studied the old wagon road winding between rugged cliffs painted in black shadows. Old memories, set free months earlier, played before his eyes like scenes from a movie.

Campfires, giving an eerie orange glow against the black horizon, string out for miles down the trail to Casas Grandes and into the canyon …

Villa, a pistol in his hand, sleeping in the desert, hidden away from his soldiers, his blanket-covered black outline lying in the cold darkness at the feet of his big, black stud…

Jesús, Marco, and Jose…so young, so eager to fight, so eager to be men, so eager to die in Villa's war…

Wagons sliding off the trail's edge, dragging struggling, braying mules with them, the drivers screaming in terror as they twist and turn in the long fall to boulders far below...

So cold...so thirsty...so hungry in the dust-covered, falling snow...

The dream...the fire... el tigre comes...

He wanted to leave, to walk away from the past, to forget what was before him, but the canyon pulled at him, holding him transfixed, unable to move, unable to turn away. He remembered his mentor, Yellow Boy, and his words.

"We Apaches know wisdom is in places. Remember everything about those places. Fill your mind with their long-ago times. Drink them in like cool water in the desert country. Drink them in and let their voices smooth your mind. Then your words will be wise and true."

"Henry?"

Roberta rested her hand on his shoulder and gave him a gentle shake, her voice a distant comfort intruding on the canyon's power. She studied the profile of his brown, weatherworn face showing scars from a lifetime of battles with two-legged enemies and four-legged predators, and she wondered what images played before his mind's eye.

His black, marble eyes turned to see her face and he heard the concern in her voice. The canyon's spell broke and his grip on the jeep's steering wheel relaxed. He puffed his cheeks and blew the tension away as he leaned back against the seat.

His mumble was so low, she barely heard him say, "What hand dares seize the fire?"

"What?"

"Sorry. Just a line from William Blake's poem, 'The Tiger'."

She saw the stubborn thrust of his jaw and the sadness in the downward slope of his squint.

"It's okay if we go back. I don't—"

"No, we'll stay. Do you still want to see her cairn before we drive on across the pass?"

She hesitated, wondering if it were better to retreat in the morning light or to enter the canyon's dark shadows where the story of the man wearing the red shirt waited, the man from Mexico, the man who turned Henry's happy, wedding day smile into a thundercloud frown.

Her curiosity stiffened her wilting resolve. There could be no return to Mesilla and Las Cruces, no return to their staid lives of doctor and nurse in the dusty, New Mexico town until he told her about the man in the red shirt.

"Yes, please. Yes, I do want to see it."

Henry's squint narrowed as he nodded and pushed in the jeep's clutch, searching the gears, grinding and scraping until the World War II relic, its dusty, dented body filled with bullet holes, some locally made, gave an unexpected lurch and charged down the sand-filled ruts leading into the canyon. Wheels slinging brown dust in the still air, the jeep bucked over stretches of packed, washboard caliche, sailed off big flat rocks, and roared and clawed out of the low, sandy places. Jamming her feet against the floorboard and locking her knees to brace herself against the thinly padded seat, Roberta mentally cursed the curiosity that brought her to Mexico and El Paso Púlpito.

Stopping at the entrance to a canyon branching north off the wagon road, Henry turned off the engine. Silence lay thick and palpable, no breeze shook the junipers, no birds twittered, no small animals crept through the gourd vines and weeds.

Sand and gravel carried by flash floods spread out around them in the shape of a partially open fan, its pivot point at the beginning of the wash disappearing into junipers up the canyon. They walked arm-in-arm up the wash in the cold, early morning air, the sun not yet high, their boots making little grinding crunches against the sand and gravel.

A cloud of cactus wrens in a burble of squawks, tweets, and frantic flutter of wings, burst out of the junipers. Startled, Roberta flinched and grabbed Henry's supporting arm with her free hand. He gave the wrens a casual, knowing glance and her hand a warm, reassuring squeeze. Further up the canyon, complaining crows cawed and snarled at attacking jays and the sharp, snapping clicks of a hunting roadrunner added to the hallelujah chorus of morning rising.

As they approached a tall cliff on the canyon's eastside, Roberta saw a shiny ribbon of black down two-thirds of its height. Drawing closer, the ribbon morphed into a thin seep of water trickling into a jumble of rocks near the wash. Beyond the seep, fifty feet above their heads, a ledge protruded from the cliff face. From a distance, it appeared to be a smooth slab of stone held up by giant fingers pushed through the cliff wall. Roberta, able to see the top of a pile of scattered rocks collected on the shelf, wondered how long it had taken for such a big pile to accumulate there rather than bouncing into the talus at their feet.

Henry nodded toward the shelf. "She's up there."

Roberta realized the pile of stones was a perfectly camouflaged cairn. She stared at it, and nodding, crossed her arms and hunched her shoulders as if shivering in a winter wind.

"It's so strange to see the grave of a woman for whom

your memory kept us apart all those years. Until you told me about her last year, I had no idea she even existed."

He pulled her close, wrapping his arms around her, and, drawing the cold morning air deep into his lungs, smelled the cactus-flower perfume caught in the twist of her black hair. Feeling the morning's chill on her arms, he gently rubbed them and whispered, "I'm so sorry I was blind to what I felt for you and you for me all those years." She hugged him but said nothing; her body, warm and comforting, said all he needed to hear.

They found where the seep collected into a naturally formed, reddish stone tank at the bottom of the cliff, and drank their fill of the icy water. Sharing body heat against the morning's chill, they sat side-by-side on a bench formed by a boulder reclining in the rocks. Sap oozing from trunks of huge, primeval junipers filled the air with a clean, pungent cedar scent as they savored the morning. Henry, content, sat thinking in the silence. Roberta's curiosity gnawed at her until she nodded toward the high shelf.

"She's been up there a long time."

"About forty-five years."

"Do you think of her often?"

He reached down between his boots, broke off a straw of gra'ma grass and chewed on it as he leaned back on his elbows to stare a hole in the deep blue sky. Finally answering, he spoke in a soft voice filled with memory.

"Sometimes... I dream about her. I see the sun on her face and the sparkle in her eyes, remember the love we had and the love we made...and...and then..." He sighs, sounding bone-tired weary, "I've washed her body and I'm struggling to carry it up to that ledge where Yellow Boy and I work nearly all night to put the stones over her…" He shakes his head and his voice fills with relief. "But those dreams don't come around much anymore."

Staring into his eyes, Roberta caressed the scar on Henry's cheek and her fingers smoothed his trim salt and pepper mustache, touching his lips like a butterfly on the petals of a flower.

She whispered, "Tell me the memories you have here."

He smiles. "Tell them all?"

She pushed a few stray tendrils of her hair away from her face, looked in his eyes, and gave his hand a warm squeeze. "Tell them all. I want you to tell them all."

Henry slowly chewed on the gra'ma grass straw and looked off down the canyon toward the pass road where the jeep was parked. Wrapping his arm around her shoulders, he drew her close, listened to the water murmuring into the tank, and with her, watched the line of shadows on the mountains creep toward them as sunlight flooded the *llano*, the great dry plains behind them, and advanced down the rugged mountains before them.

At last, his memories spoke.

"The same day the university gave me my degree in 1915, I headed for a train to New Mexico. I'd been gone over six years and a lot had happened. New Mexico had become a state; Las Cruces was lighted by electrical power; automobiles stirred up dust on the roads; the ring of telephones was becoming common; the *Revolución* in Mexico had started, stopped, and a civil war had begun; and, my friend, Doroteo Arango, also known as Pancho Villa, had become one of the *Revolución's* most important generals."

Roberta frowned.

"Why didn't you come back to visit your mother and Yellow Boy once in a while?"

"There was a big empty place inside me missing Yellow Boy, my mother, and the land. But I thought of coming back as a reward for finishing what I set out to do. I couldn't come back to visit my mother without my brothers and sisters sniffing around to find out why my mother had such an interest in a stranger and he in her. They were certain I was some kind of scam artist still after her money, even after she passed away. Yellow Boy was a force of nature. He lived life one day at a time and he knew I'd be back when it was time for me to come back."

Massaging Henry's shoulders, Roberta shook her head. "I know you told me that you never told your brothers and sisters who you were because you believed you failed to protect your father from being murdered. But Henry, you were eight years old when you believed that. You were a grown man in 1915. Your mother begged you to believe Albert's murder wasn't your fault. Why didn't you just accept that as true and tell the rest of your family who you were?"

"They didn't know me and I didn't know them. I didn't think they'd ever believe me. I just couldn't make myself reopen that wound. Sometimes your reason makes it's easy to know what's true and what you ought to do, but it's impossible because of fears and heartaches buried deep in your soul."

As Henry spoke he sounded more and more intransigent. Roberta decided to change the subject and talk more when he was ready to listen.

"Had Cruces really changed that much when you came back?"

"Oh, it was still a dusty desert town, but it had grown and it looked strange to my memory." He smiled and shook his head.

"Returning to the Las Cruces land-of-mañana from California's hurly-burly was like stepping back in time, like returning to those golden days when, as a young man, I finally told my mother who I was…"

3. COMING HOME

Las Cruces, New Mexico, 1915

Darkness creeps in from the desert as the train stops at the Las Cruces station platform. I take my bags and hoof it down to the Rio Grande Hotel where room, meals, and corral space are two dollars a day.

After supper, I rent a horse and ride over to my mother's place. There are several buggies and a couple of cars parked out front, and electric lights glow in every room. I assume my brothers and sisters and their families are visiting, so I stay back in the shadows, smoke my pipe, and wait for them to leave. An hour later they're all gone and I knock on the door old Marta opens.

She studies me for a moment, her eyes beady, birdlike. Recognition floods her wrinkled face, and unlike the first time I appeared, six years earlier, she's glad to see me.

"*Señor* Grace! You are back from the university. *Bueno.*

La Señora speaks of you many times. *Por favor*, come in, come in. You are a doctor now, *si?*"

I have to grin. It's the first time I tell anyone I know from the old days that, yes, I am, in fact, a physician.

"*Si,* Marta. I'm a doctor with a university degree and I've come back to practice in Las Cruces."

She smiles. "*Bueno, bueno.* You are needed here."

Marta leaves me in the parlor and heads for the back of the house to get my mother. Little has changed since I left for California. My heart aches when I look at the picture of my murdered father over the mantle. As I look around the room, I recall the tears and warmth in our souls when I first returned to my mother who, for ten years, believed I was dead. After I returned, I stayed with her for several months as I tried and failed to get into a university, all the while putting up with my brothers trying to find out who and what I was and how I was trying to scam their mother out of money or land. I wanted to live somewhere else to help dissuade them of that notion, but she wouldn't hear of it.

As shy as she was, she still pulled political strings with my father's former associates to get me an opportunity to interview at Leland Stanford's university. The rest, as they say, is history. I wrote her often and told her of my struggles to survive in the university. It was hard, but believe it or not, all those years in the mountains and desert with Rufus and Yellow Boy's tough warrior training were good preparation for my university studies. The strain of study and the snobbery of elite gentlemen, who looked down their nose at anyone not as wealthy and as well connected as themselves, was nothing in comparison to what I'd already survived. My mother's letters were always an inspiration. She told me to stay there until I finished and then come back to her, and I did.

Marta is gone no more than a couple of minutes before I hear the swish of long skirts and the rapid thump of a cane down coming down the hall toward the parlor. I turn toward the door just as she pushed it open.

"*Mi Dios!* Henrique. At last, you return."

"I'm stunned when I see her. She looks so frail, so many more wrinkles, her once brilliant black hair now filled with gray, and she has to walk pounding about leaning heavily on a cane. But her eyes sparkle with joy and I'm sure mine do too. We sit together and talk a long time. She wants me to stay with her, but I tell her that it's better I don't, and that I'll visit her every day.

Letting me out the door, she whispers, "I understand you need privacy, my son."

A couple of weeks pass before I can go to Mescalero and visit Yellow Boy. I first have to look for office space and stay around long enough to reassure my mother that I'm not going to run off and leave her again. Finally, I tell her I have to go to Alamogordo on business and will be back in five or six days. She isn't happy about it but says she understands and for me to hurry back as soon as my business is done.

I take the train down to El Paso and then to Tularosa, where I hire a horse and ride up the winding trail to the reservation.

Yellow Boy, his wives, Juanita and Moon-On-The-Water, and their children, Redondo now about ten, and John, who was born after I left for California, still live up the canyon where they've stayed since returning from Mexico the year before I left for medical school. I find their tipi just about dusk and feel my heart warm with delight upon seeing the glow of a suppertime fire shining like a Chinese lantern in the falling twilight. It's a scene I recalled often in California when I thought of Yellow Boy, his family, and the land high in the mountain pines. A wave of thanks to the great creator god of the Apaches, Ussen, fills my soul.

Through the dusk I make out the dark outlines of horses in the corral where the creek runs back into the big pines close to a nearly vertical canyon wall. There is enough white on Yellow Boy's paint that he's easy to see. I chew my lip, looking for my big, black Satanas until I see him wander out from under the pines and look in my direction, his ears up. Tying my horse to some bushes, I walk over to the corral to renew acquaintances with the stallion I named after the lord of the underworld.

Satanas pushes his nose out to me and we exchange breaths. Shaking his head, he snorts and sniffs again before lowering his head for me to scratch behind his ears and forelock. I hold out an apple for him and he takes it, making it snap in its juice as he crunches down on it, nodding and snorting.

"So, Hombrecito, you speak with your great horse before you speak with your father? It is good for my eyes to find you. You have been gone many seasons my son."

I turn slowly to look into the strong, peaceful face of Yellow Boy, who stands smiling at me, his arms crossed. "The sweetest fruit comes last in the meal, Uncle. My eyes longed to see your face and those of your family many times but saw only good memories. I left a boy, but return a White Eye di-yin, a medicine man. My heart fills with pleasure now that I see you."

We take right forearms and squeeze the other's shoulder in the pleasure of the moment. At medical school I often thought of the Apache father I called Uncle, who helped raise me after my father was murdered and who set the standards by which I take the measure of all other men.

"Come, unload your horse. Juanita and Moon-On-The-Water have made a feast for you, and my sons are anxious to see their brother, the di-yin." I know better than to ask how Yellow Boy's wives knew I was coming. They always seem to know when I'm headed their way and are ready with their best meals.

Yellow Boy's sons appear out of the gloom from the far side of the corral. Redondo, four or five when I left, rushes silently at us like a warrior on the attack, followed by his little brother, John, barely off the cradle board, his pudgy legs churning to keep up with his brother, but fast losing ground to the older boy. Yellow Boy holds up his hand to stop them and to make proper introductions.

"Ho, Redondo and John, come meet your brother, Hombrecito, who returns after many seasons learning to be a White Eye di-yin. He is a great warrior. Welcome him with respect."

The boys stop in midstride and are suddenly shy. Redondo leads the way, and standing straight and tall before me, says, "My father has spoken around our fire many times of my brother the great warrior, Hombrecito. Welcome to the lodge of our father."

Redondo speaks exactly as Yellow Boy trained him and

shows all the proper respect and courtesy a boy gives a man. I see Yellow Boy's barely concealed smile. I speak to my little brothers as though they are men.

"It is good to return to the lodge of my father and to see my brothers grow tall." Redondo's smile shows clear and bright even in the deepening twilight. "I will come to the lodge of our father when I have cared for my horse."

Yellow Boy says, "Redondo, you and John go to Moon and Juanita and tell them Hombrecito sits at our fire this night. I will help him with his horse."

Without a word they run for the tipi. Yellow Boy and I care for my horse and gear while he speaks of friends we knew on the reservation and how things have changed some for the better there since I've been gone.

Juanita and Moon-On-The-Water are delighted to see me, and, with Yellow Boy's assent, speak with respect and smiles, treating me like a son returned from a long, successful raid. The memory of their meal of venison, sweet acorn bread, chilies, beans, and dried berries still makes my mouth water.

As we sit around the fire drinking cups of hot coffee, Yellow Boy tells me of the years on the reservation while I was gone. Two years earlier, the Mescalero agreed to share their reservation with the Chiricahuas, who were about to be freed at Fort Sill, Oklahoma after being held as prisoners of war.

Asa Daklugie, the nephew of Geronimo and Chief Naiche's power, his primary advisor and shaman, as Geronimo had been before he died of pneumonia, was fourteen or fifteen when the Chiricahuas were put on a train for a Florida POW camp nearly thirty years earlier. He was sent to the Carlisle

Indian School in Pennsylvania and learned well the lessons of cattle husbandry. Now he's a leader on the reservation and a driving force to establish a cattle herd for the Apaches that is to become the envy of ranchers everywhere in the Tularosa Basin and beyond. Daklugie has little use for tribal policemen but he and Yellow Boy appear to get along well. Around the Chiricahua's fires Yellow Boy listened to stories of their years in the POW camps of Florida, Alabama and finally Fort Sill, and how they had been kept prisoners for twenty-seven years after they got on the train to Florida when the liar, General Miles, told them it would bring them back in two years.

Yellow Boy stares in the flames and says, "The Chiricahuas were in a bad place for a long time. I am glad Ussen, the great god who gives us our power, never used me to send them there and that I was lucky enough not to go myself."

I stay five days with Yellow Boy. I want to stay longer, but know my mother grows more anxious each day I'm gone. When I leave, we make plans for him to visit me at the ranch Rufus Pike left me in the Organ Mountains. I expect to have a very busy time getting my practice started and Rufus's ranch back in shape to raise a few cattle, and I need Yellow Boy's help.

Returning from Mescalero, I begin setting up my practice and dropping by to see my mother every day for lunch and two or three times a week for supper. She is a quiet matriarch who listens and never gives advice unless she's asked. We have long talks about my days in medical school and the personalities in the family I've not known since I was eight years old. She doesn't push me to reveal my true identity, saying only that it should be done when I'm ready.

My brothers and sisters, learning I've returned, and convinced I'm just a con artist trying to scam her out of money or land, bark at me and whine at her, but the M.D. after my name holds them at bay, and they even stop by my little office to get my opinion on how she's doing. I tell them the unvarnished truth: her health is rapidly disappearing.

It's hard to see her decline so fast now that I'm able to spend time with her. Within a couple of months she's bedridden and passes away in early September. Holding my hand, her last words to me are, "Henrique, live with honor and be strong like your father."

Suffering from the grief of her death alone, I refuse to deal with my brothers and sisters who don't know me and won't believe that I somehow managed to survive Father's murder and stay in the land of the living.

I know only one way to take the ache out of my soul from her passing, and literally run the grief out of my system. I run hard and long everyday like I did when Yellow Boy trained me to be a warrior and a survivor, and like a hot poker on a flesh wound, the running burns away the grief and anger at God gnawing on my soul for taking her so soon.

Late one afternoon a few weeks after my mother passed away, I'm in my office reading, the windows open, enjoying that smooth, after-harvest breeze drifting in the desert as the sun disappears. A gauzy orange, after-sunset glow fills the streets as the streetlights flicker to life. Stores are closed. The only sounds on the street come from an occasional Model-T burbling by, the creaks and jingle of chains from a team pulling a wagon, or the clop of horses ridden by cowboys heading for a saloon.

The steady thump of boots and the jangle of spurs appear in my consciousness. They grow louder as they approach my office from down the boardwalk and stop just before a loud, demanding knock on my door. *It never fails, people always need a doctor just before suppertime.* I swing my feet off the desk, turn up the lamp, and open the door.

A Mexican in a tan campaign jacket and pants, and a bright red shirt stands in the doorway staring at me. Although it's against the law in Las Cruces, he's armed. Bandoliers filled with cartridges hang across his wide shoulders and he wears a gun belt stuffed with cartridges and carrying a holster filled with a Model 3 Smith and Wesson revolver. A Winchester rifle rests in the crook of his arm. A big black mustache turned light gray from trail dust hides his lips. Although I guess he isn't much more than thirty, his skin has the bronze patina of a man spending his life in the desert. His face is lined with hard creases between his mouth and his cheeks, thin slashes streak across his brow, and the corners of his wide, intelligent eyes frame myriad wrinkles grown from constantly squinting against bright sunlight. He looks vaguely familiar, but I can't place him.

"*Sí?*"

He makes a little bow from the waist and speaks in a smooth, tenor voice.

"*Buenos noches, señor. Henrique Grace? Doctor Grace?*"

"*Sí, sí. Por favor, entra.*"

"*Muchas gracias, Doctor Grace.*"

He looks up and down the street and over his shoulder across the street before stepping inside and closing the door behind him.

Leaning his rifle against the doorframe, he removes and deferentially holds his sweat-stained, dirty gray Stetson with both hands in front of him, but tilts his chin up and looks me in the eye with obvious pride. He speaks educated Spanish mixed with understandable English, common for Mexicans living close to the border. I don't have any trouble understanding him or replying to his questions.

"*Señor Grace*, I bring you a message from *mi Jefe*."

"And, who is your *Jefe*?"

"*Mi Jefe es General Francisco Villa*. He says to tell you he remembers, with much pleasure, his days with Hombrecito and *Señor* Yellow Boy, Muchacho Amarillo."

Fond memories from eight years and more ago of adventures with my friend Doroteo Arango, now known as Pancho Villa or General Francisco Villa, great generalissimo of the *Revolución* in Mexico, fill my mind and warm my heart.

"General Villa! He is an old *amigo* I've not seen in many years. The message, *señor?*"

"*Mi Jefe*, he asks you to come and speak with him on a matter of great importance. He is in the mountains three days ride to the west. He sends me to find and guide you to him. Will you come, Doctor Grace?"

A week earlier, the *El Paso Times* carried an interview with Villa in Ciudad Juárez, just across the Rio Grande from El Paso. In the interview, Villa promised never to stop fighting for Mexico even though he was completely exhausted. After reading the interview, I tried to find my old friend, but no one seemed to know where he disappeared. All kinds of rumors were flying. One said he was negotiating for political asylum in the United States, although the *Times* interview suggested that would never happen; another said he planned to fight Carranza, who claimed to be first *presidente,* in Sonora west of the Sierra Madre; another that he was preparing to drive the Mormons out of the *colonias* around Casas Grandes and fight Carranza there.

"*Sí, señor,* I will meet with General Villa. The Apache, Muchacho Amarillo, he is to come also?"

Red shirt sighs and nods, his bronze skin turning a little pale. "The general, he asks me to also find and bring the great warrior, Muchacho Amarillo. Where is his camp? Will his people give me safe passage to speak with him? I have fought Apaches for many years in Mexico. They can make a man scream, begging for death a long time before he dies."

"I'll send word to him. Meet us here in two days from this hour. We'll ride then."

He smiles, obviously relieved.

"*Muchas, muchas gracias, señor.* I do not like being around Apaches alone." He holds up two fingers. "In two days, we ride in the night. I sleep at the livery stable with my horse. Send for me if you need my services. *Señor, adiós.*"

As he steps out the door and looks up and down the dark street, a dawning realization from far back in my mind prompts me to ask, "A moment please. Your name*, señor?*"

Looking back at me, he rolls his eyes toward the ceiling. "My Name? *Ay, yi, yi!* I am sorry, Doctor Grace. I have been at war so long I forget all my manners. My father named me Guillermo Camerena. *Mi amigos,* they call me Camisa Roja."

I wave him on out the door, cursing fortune under my breath. I knew I had seen that red shirt before. I drop into my desk chair, seeing the same scene haunting my memory for so many years, feeling the bile in the back of my throat, tasting again the bitterness of Rafaela's death, and wanting the satisfaction of killing the man who murdered her.

My fist hammers the desktop. Camisa Roja. Over and over I've remembered how he shot Rafaela; over and over I've seen her staggering toward me, blood spreading over the front of her shirt. Over and over I've yearned to avenge her. Now fate tricks me again. The man who killed her, the man I swore to kill, I don't even recognize when he's standing within two feet of me. I stare at the doorway and long for a swallow of mescal.

Pulling open my desk's middle drawer, I stare at the loaded revolver. I want to pick it up, walk down the street, and blow Camisa Roja to hell and gone. It's infuriating to feel the past drawing me back into the darkness of my teenaged years, darkness that, with the help of Yellow Boy, I left, and fought my way back to the light and a new life. Now the past and its debts return to call me to account. They're coming to cut me again and leave me bleeding, and I know I can't stop them.

I slam the drawer and curse God. Darkness settles on the land.

After a while I leave my office and send a telegram to the Mescalero reservation agent, C.R. Jefferis. I tell him I need Yellow Boy with me for an important trip into Mexico and that it will be a great favor if he lets him come with me. I ask him, if he agrees, to contact Yellow Boy with my request as soon as possible. Jefferis is a good, honest man and Yellow Boy is a tribal policeman. I don't doubt I'll soon see the man I call Uncle.

I have a late supper in a saloon down the street and return to my office to sleep on a cot. It's nearing nine o'clock, and even though my practice is very small, there are patients for me to see and tests and research on cases to do before I can leave. I doubt I'll sleep much. I'm full of adrenaline from thoughts of riding the big lonesome with Yellow Boy and seeing Villa for the first time in over eight years.

I sit by my door on the planked sidewalk and smoke my pipe for a while before locking up and stretching out on the cot to watch moonlight shadows creep down the sides of my office walls. It's a little chilly, but a thick Navajo blanket brings immediate, comforting warmth and overpowering drowsiness.

The dream, vaporous and wispy, doesn't wait long to appear.

I stand in the middle of a wide, shallow creek waving at Rafaela behind piñons on a canyon wall ledge. Turning from where she sits, I wade toward the cave on the opposite side. Horses we're keeping inside are nervous, snorting and stamping around. Something scratches against rock, like the point of a knife, like big claws digging in for leverage. Pulling back its hammer and shouldering my rifle at the same time, I hear Rafaela scream, *Hombrecito!* On a boulder above me, a huge jaguar in flames appears. He sails off the top of the boulder snarling in rage, front legs spread wide, claws extended, ready to rip me to pieces.

A steady click of frozen images measure time fluttering away; I pull the trigger, see the hammer slowly fall, a bullet streak for the jaguar's chest. The rifle's booming thunder echoes down the canyon as the twisting, tumbling jaguar sails past me, a flaming meteor falling to earth. Darkness. I'm on my back in the creek and opening my eyes I see bloody water all around me. Consuming flames around the jaguar, brilliant reds, yellows, and oranges roast my face. It roars its outrage as it struggles to stand, and failing that, digs its claws into the creek's flat limestone bottom, its mighty muscles dragging its paralyzed hindquarters forward so it can reach to hook me with its huge saber-like claws and drag me into its roaring fire. I'm paralyzed, I can't move as death, burning death, crawls to take me in its claws.

I jerk awake, sweat covers my face, and my shirt clings to my heaving chest, my heart pounding, and my breathing as though I've been running in the desert. I get up and move around to drive away the nightmare's last memories.

Drying my face with a towel, I check my watch and see it's only a little past midnight. I lay back down, reluctant to sleep, wondering if the jaguar will return.

The next evening, I sit outside on a straight-back chair tilted back against the wall of my office, watching the sun cast brilliant oranges, reds, and purples against high clouds. Twilight fades into the cottonwoods and willows along the

Rio Grande and stars begin to faintly twinkle overhead. After soft darkness settles and the streetlights spread their yellow glow, I go inside to wash up before I go for supper.

As I turn up my desk lamp, I see the dark outline of a figure standing in a corner. I jump back, almost falling over a chair, my mind racing to think what I might use for a weapon, and then I realize the man in the shadows is Yellow Boy.

I don't know how he does it. I learned some of his art when we lived with the Apaches in Mexico. I even got as good as some of the young warriors, but I was never as good as Yellow Boy or most of the other warriors. Never seeing or hearing Yellow Boy until it's too late, the man is a ghost, a classic Apache.

He wears his ancient sergeant's coat, blue with faded yellow stripes on the sleeves, and his flat-brimmed scout's hat, his long black hair, streaked with gray, falling past his shoulders. He's ready to travel. His straight-slash mouth curves up a little as he steps out of the shadows with his equally ancient Yellow Boy Henry rifle, his namesake, cradled in his left arm.

"Hombrecito. When Coyote finds Snake ready to strike, like you he jumps."

I laugh. "You walk as the spirits, Uncle. When I first see you, you are a spirit. Seeing you makes my eyes glad. I didn't expect you until tomorrow evening. Come. We eat."

The little restaurant and bar I frequent is five or six doors down the street from my office. The owner with piggy eyes, broad snout, and frizzy red hair that sits atop his head like a flaming brush pile, smiles and nods when I walk in the door, but grimaces when he sees Yellow Boy behind me. His piggy eyes also see Yellow Boy's Henry. I don't doubt he's heard stories about Yellow Boy and how deadly he is with the old Henry. Deciding discretion is the better part of business, he keeps his mouth shut as he shows us to a table covered with a red-and-white-checkered tablecloth.

Respect and manners dictate we eat first and I wait until he asks for my plans. After bowls of chili verde seasoned with the fires of Hell and wiped clean with blue corn *tortillas*, Yellow Boy belches his appreciation, leans back in his chair, and crossing his arms, studies me. After a while, he says in Apache, making me the only one in the restaurant who understands him, "So, Hombrecito, Arango sends for us." Although, Doroteo Arango has called himself Pancho Villa for years, Yellow Boy originally knew him as Doroteo Arango, and sees no reason for changing his name. "This is a debt we wait a long time to pay. We owe him much. Now he calls us."

"How do you know this, Uncle?"

"Five suns ago from the camp of the Apache, Pelo Rojo, an uncle of my wives comes to Mescalero. He says Arango's army crosses the Sierra Madre through El Paso Púlpito. Arango camps in a side canyon on the sunrise side of the mountains, less than a day's ride north of where his army now moves. He buys weapons, supplies, and bullets from the White Eyes across the border."

I nod. "That matches what I've been told. Villa sent Camisa Roja to find and guide us back to his camp. Villa says it's important that he speak to us. Can you believe it? Of all the people he might have picked, he sends the man I once swore to kill."

"Yes, I believe it. Ussen laughs many times at men, makes many jokes."

From inside his sergeant's coat, Yellow Boy pulls out one of his short black, baseball bat-shaped cigars and moistens the tobacco by pulling it past his lips before lighting it.

"The war between the Mexicans has lasted many seasons, Hombrecito. Many die, but much blood is yet to be spilled."

"You speak true, Uncle. Villa asks our help. He calls in our debt for saving our lives. We must help him with open eyes. How much blood must we shed for him until our debt is paid?"

Yellow Boy puts a fist over his heart. "When it is enough, here you will know."

I know he's right, but I want to say to Villa, *We go this far and no further because you saved us from that bear.*

"We'll meet Camisa Roja tomorrow night and ride for Mexico. I'll get Satanas from the ranch tomorrow."

Yellow Boy shakes his head. "Better we ride when no other man knows. I bring Satanas from your rancho. Your big rifle, Shoots-Today-Kills-Tomorrow, your medicines, blankets, and supplies, you make ready, then we go tonight."

"All right, before the moon clears the Organs I'll be ready to ride."

4. CHALLENGES

Camisa Roja sits cleaning his weapons in a kerosene lantern's flickering, smoky yellow light outside the livery stable door. He discusses the *Revolución* with Old Man Parsons, the liveryman, who leans against the doorframe with his arms crossed, the frown lines on his face, covered by week-old gray stubble, deepened by the shadows. Roja shows no surprise when Yellow Boy and I step into the circle of light. Parsons, seeing Yellow Boy, says nothing and doesn't waste any time heading down the stable aisle for his office in the back of the barn.

Roja salutes us with his hand up and palm out. "*Buenos noches, señores.*" He nods toward Yellow Boy. "You are Muchacho Amarillo, the great warrior General Villa says I must bring with Doctor Grace when I return. *Mi amigos* call me Camisa Roja."

Yellow Boy, his hand up, palm out, returns Roja's salute.

"*Buenos noches,* Camisa Roja. Many seasons pass since the *Hacienda* Comacho raid. You fight well there. The Apaches say you kill Elias and Apache Kid. If this is true, you are a great warrior also."

The furrows in Roja's brown face grow deep, hard, and pronounced. His eyes darken, angry thunderclouds never leaving Yellow Boy's eyes. He stands with a smooth fluid motion, kicking his stool out of the way with the back of his boot, right hand sliding toward his holstered revolver. "*Señor*, you were part of the raid on the *Hacienda* Comacho? I swore to kill every man I ever find in that raid."

Yellow Boy, relaxed, unassuming, stares back at Roja with narrowed eyes of his own and leans forward a little on the balls of his feet. I hear the hammer on the Henry nestled in the crook of his left arm click twice, loud and precise, as his thumb pushes it back to full cock. Roja hears the warning.

"*Sí, señor*, I was at the Comacho raid. Elias and the crazy *hombre* who shoots Comacho, they steal my daughter. She is Hombrecito's woman, Rafaela. Muchacho Amarillo and Hombrecito find Elias and take my daughter back. I send the crazy man to the land of the grandfathers."

Camisa Roja puffs his cheeks and blows. His shoulders relax and he crosses his arms, keeping his hands far away from his pistol as he stares at us.

"You are the one who shoots out Billy Creek's eyes? You are this *hombre? Muchas, muchas, gracias, señor.* The Comacho family and their *vaqueros*, we are all in your debt."

Yellow Boy slowly shakes his head. "No. I do not send this *hombre* to the grandfathers for the Comachos. Comacho deserved to die, deserved to suffer. He tortured Rafaela. I vowed one day to kill him myself.

"The crazy man challenges my word, challenges my power. He speaks to my daughter after I say he must not. He steals my daughter, steals Hombrecito's woman. Hombrecito and Muchacho Amarillo say this *hombre* must die. I have first right to kill him. I shoot out his eyes. He will never see me in the land of the grandfathers.

"Camisa Roja draws near to the grandfathers when he shoots Hombrecito's woman. Hombrecito and Muchacho Amarillo return to *Hacienda* Comacho the day after the Elias raid. Hombrecito burns hot with anger, burns to send you to the grandfathers. The Shoots-Today-Kills-Tomorrow of Hombrecito reaches far. You are gone. No *hombres* in the *hacienda*. Ussen smiles on you. Ussen lets you live that day. You still live. You have much good luck."

Camisa Roja bites his lower lip as he stares at the memory, shaking his head.

"I…I don't kill women…except in the *Revolución*. I killed no woman at *Hacienda* Comacho."

I step into the lantern's light so he can clearly see my face. I want him to understand the fire burning in my belly as long as he lives and that I haven't forgotten how my woman died. I speak through clenched teeth, "Oh yes there was. When you rode up with the *vaqueros* from El Paso Carretas, you swung off your horse, kneeled and shot at her running for the big piñons across the *arroyo*. She was wearing pants and a shirt, and I watched you take careful aim. It was a very long shot and you made it, goddamn you!"

He stares at me and then looks at the ground thinking. "Sí…I shot at a man running from the attack on my *patrón*. I did not know I shot a woman. Of this I have *mucho* regret, *señores*. I did not kill women then, but now I kill anyone my general says must die. It is war. *Comprende?* Doctor Grace, if you still want revenge, let us settle it now and be done with it one way or the other."

Yellow Boy shakes his head.

"No more of this. Hombrecito knows you did not deliberately kill his woman. If he wanted you dead, you would not be here now. His wisdom grows. Too many wander in the land of the grandfathers because they lived with their eyes open but did not see. This night we ride. Take us to Villa."

Roja relaxes, relief spreading over his face. "*Bueno.* Tonight, we ride."

I turn away saying nothing. *Someday, someday man in the red shirt, murderer of my wife, my life, my first and only lover, I...will...have...satisfaction.*

Camisa Roja wastes no time packing and saddling his sturdy little pony, loading his pack mule, and paying Parsons, who still sits in his office at the back of the stable keeping a close eye on the stable door for any appearance by Yellow Boy.

I say to Yellow Boy, "I can pay for the train to ship us and our animals over to Hachita or Animas to save us time and keep the animals fresh."

He shakes his head.

"I no ride iron wagon. You ride iron wagon. I ride the land alone."

He had seen Apaches who scouted for the Army against Geronimo shipped off to a POW camp in Florida thirty years earlier. He knew many of those men when they came back to

Mescalero in 1913 and heard their tales about life as a POW. He never rode a train in all the years I knew him.

We mount and ride out of Las Cruces at a fast canter, passing Mesilla, following the dusty road toward El Paso. It's an easy ride past big irrigated fields, the full moon rising over the Organs giving us plenty of light. Ten or twelve miles south of Mesilla, Roja turns toward the Rio Grande and uses a cattle crossing to its western side.

Yellow Boy and I look at each other, grinning. We're following nearly the same trail we used to the camp of Pelo Rojo, Red Hair, and his Sierra Madre Apaches thirteen years earlier. It was nearly the same time of year, peaceful, withered leaves floating in the Rio Grande current, frogs croaking, the moon reflecting from the water.

On the other side of the river, the trail leads up switchbacks to the plateau above the valley. On top of the plateau, we point toward Hachita, but bear south past the Hatchet Mountains on the eastern side of the New Mexico boot heel. Passing the Hatchets, the trails lead across gra'ma grass ranches down into Mexico. These are the trails Apaches, smugglers, and cattle thieves have followed since the time of the conquistadores. As before, Yellow Boy keeps us in the shadows of the mountains and hills and often pauses to check our back trail. Across the border, Camisa Roja leads us straight as a bow shot toward the eastern edge of the Sierra Luis, the low mountains near the border filled with a maze of canyons guarding the eastern front of the high sierras.

To reach Villa's camp we ride for two nights and sleep

during the day, each one taking a turn as sentry. When I stand guard, my mind returns to my days in Mexico. I remember the days and nights I had with Rafaela, the raids on the *hacendado* herds with Villa, and the life and death challenges I had from Apaches and a jaguar. It is the same jaguar invading my dreams not two days before; the same jaguar I dream is on fire. What can such a dream can possibly mean? I'm stumped, but believe mystical dreams have purposes and that eventually I'll understand what it's trying to tell me.

Deep in the third night, near dawn, we ride up a big, gravely wash leading into a wide canyon. We see tracks from a small herd of horses, a few cattle, and five or six wagons. As the eastern sky turns red, we can see firelight twinkling through dark tree silhouettes and smell smoke. Camisa Roja tells us to wait for him by the canyon's south wall while he alerts the sentries it's safe for us to come in.

5. NEW CAMP, OLD AMIGOS

I know the canyon. When I lived with the Apaches in Pelo Rojo's camp in the Sierra Espuelas, I rode through it all the way over its high pass and down into the San Bernardino Valley. Villa camps in a side canyon where spring water collects at the bottom of high red and beige cliffs on the eastern wall. The water fills a large natural tank to form a blue-green pool that overflows to make a small stream trickling a couple hundred yards further into the canyon before it disappears in a jumble of rocks. The steep walls of the canyon manage to support a few piñons taking root on ledges or lower in the talus, lying at shallow angles near the bottom. On the canyon floor junipers, cottonwoods, and sycamores provide shade and firewood.

Six wagons are parked under the tall trees. One, a chuck wagon, serves one of two fires. Several middle-aged women and young girls in threadbare, faded skirts and dresses work around it. One stirs a big, crusty black iron pot of bubbling stew; another stretches over a cast iron skillet, frying *empañadas* and then tossing them into a big cloth-lined basket; another turns sizzling meat on a rough iron grill. After three nights in the saddle, the smell of their simply prepared food makes my belly rumble.

Roja raises his rifle with his left arm and waves it back and forth. I see motion in several places high up on the cliffs from lookouts waving back. Roja motions for us to come on in.

Passing a makeshift corral, using the western wall of the canyon as one side while the other sides are made from ropes and brush, we see a fine palomino, an appaloosa, a brown-and-white paint, and a big black stud haltered and tied to trees. The stud snorts a challenge at Satanas, but it's ignored. Currying and brushing them until they are fit for a king, or a general, four men dressed in light canvas shirts and vests, khaki pants, and high boots banter among themselves while drinking coffee and smoking little cigarillos made from wrapping tobacco in corn shucks. Another brush corral further down the canyon, near where the spring overflow disappears, holds a few thin horses, mules, and gaunt steers.

Near the cooking fire, stacked like tipi poles for quick access, Mauser bolt-action rifles, their well-oiled barrels gleaming, stand ready for action. Six or seven men wearing campaign hats with a bronze medallion pinned on the front of the crown, lounge by the second fire, drinking coffee from heavy crockery cups. Their eyes never leave us, but they say nothing as we ride up.

Dismounting slowly, stiff from the long ride in the cold night air, we look around for a place to unsaddle and take care of our horses. A young woman runs up, eyes flashing, teeth brilliant white against her chocolate brown skin, her long black hair in a loose plait down her back. The curves of her supple, fecund body show through her shift, but her face shows years of hard times. Giving Roja a knowing smile, she takes our reins and leads the horses and pack mule off toward the big corral. The other women around the cooking fire crane their necks to get a look at us, and then go back to work.

Camisa Roja nods toward the young woman who took our horses.

"Magritte is a *soldadera*, a woman who travels with the army and helps with the cooking and supplies. She knows how to use a rifle too, and, if I mind my manners, sometimes keeps my bed warm."

He smiles, shrugs his shoulders and spread his hands.

"The general does not like it when his *dorados* sleep with the *soldaderas*, so most times my bed is cold. Your gear is safe with her and she will take good care of your horses. The men here are all *Dorados*, Golden Ones, the best of the best, the general's bodyguard. They are completely dedicated to him. All will gladly die before the general or his guests are harmed. You are safe here, *señores*. Come, fill your bellies with the morning meal while I tell the general I have returned with you."

The women around the cooking fire fill big pie tins with *tortillas*, beans, chili verde, and *empañadas*, and then hand us big crockery mugs of their hot, black syrupy coffee that has a kind of chocolaty taste I learn later comes from mixing coffee with ground roasted piñon seeds. The men sitting on big rocks around the second fire wave us over and make room for us to sit. They are friendly enough but give us only a little nod and say nothing more than a casual, *"Buenos días, señores."* They keep a close eye on Yellow Boy, no doubt wondering why an Apache, an enemy their fathers and grandfathers killed on sight for more than ten generations, passes freely into the general's camp.

The canyon fills with golden streamers of soft light pouring through the trees, highlighting little puffs of morning mist. Our simple breakfast more than lives up to the smells that made my stomach rumble. No more than five minutes after we begin eating, we hear a booming, *"Bueno!"* from the wagon farthermost down the canyon.

A door on the back of the wagon flies open. Out steps the man behind the memories I've carried for more than eight years. Long-waisted, thick in the middle, wearing knee-high riding boots, his big, black mustache still well-trimmed, its bottom edge hiding part of a broad grin, he wears nearly the same outfit as his men. Dark circles of fatigue surround his charismatic eyes no longer sparkling with the good humor I remember, his face aged far beyond the one from the times when we lived with the Apaches.

He throws up his arms and shouts. *"Buenos días, amigos! Muchacho* Amarillo! Hombrecito! After many years, I see you again."

Roja, grinning, follows him down the steps of the wagon, but respectfully hangs back as Villa, with short steps demanded from legs spending years in the saddle, shuffles toward us. Curiosity written on his face, Roja crosses his arms and tilts his head to one side as he watches the reunion of old friends.

We put down our pans and coffee and stand as Villa catches each of us in a bear hug, slapping our backs like prodigal brothers returning home. "*Por favor, amigos*, finish your *tortillas* and beans, it is a long ride from *Americano* Las Cruces."

Yellow Boy, a man of few words, seems unusually affable when he speaks for both of us. "It is good for the eyes of Muchacho Amarillo and Hombrecito to see our *amigo*, from many seasons past, now a mighty war chief."

Villa grins and continues to wave us back down to continue eating. Yellow Boy, an old-time warrior who learned to ride the desert and mountains not knowing from where his next meal was coming, is already done. One of the women brings Villa a cup of coffee. He groans with arthritis and fatigue as he sits down in front of us.

Taking a loud slurp of coffee and grinning, he glances around the circle of men before focusing on me. "Hombrecito, you stay in the school for doctors six years, *sí*?"

Smiling and a little proud of myself, I say, "*Sí*, general. I study medicine for six years in California."

Villa, his mouth hanging open, studies me a moment.

"It is hard to believe that an *hombre* so deadly with the rifle is now a *medico*."

He looks around at his dorados watching us, and back to us saying, "*Americano medicos* rode my hospital train and saved the lives of *mucho soldados* and *soldaderas* wounded in the battles with the armies of Díaz, but none could shoot like Hombrecito. I tell you, Hombrecito, to be deadly with your rifle is a good thing, to be a healer of broken men is better."

His brown eyes flashing with good humor, he looks at Yellow Boy. "And you, Muchacho Amarillo, both your wives still care for you on the reservation? Your sons, they grow strong before your eyes?"

Yellow Boy nods. "*Sí, Jefe.* The Mescaleros live in the mountains. My people no longer roam and raid as they did in the time of my father, but the little ones live well and grow strong. Maybe the White Eyes will not steal our land. Moon-On-The-Water and her sister Juanita work together well in my tipi. I have no need for two tipis as some men do with two wives.

"Word comes that your *soldados* move to cross the mountains to the Bavispe and San Bernardino Valleys. You fight your enemies again soon, *sí?*"

Villa nods with a smile. "*Sí.* Since no trains run east and west in Mexico, *mi soldados* march toward the sierras from Chihuahua to Sonora through El Paso Púlpito even as we speak. Once in Sonora, we will take Agua Prieta and then march south toward Hermosillo. I expect many men to join us on the way. Soon we will be rid of this dictator Carranza, but I speak more of this later. *Por favor*, eat and rest. We speak in private before the moon rises above the mountains tonight. *Viva Mexico!*" The men around us have been listening and respond by shaking their fists and yelling, "*Viva Villa!*" Villa grins and shakes his fist with them.

As we eat, Villa laughs and jokes with us, recalling the old days and telling his men stories of my shooting skill with the 1874 Sharps buffalo rifle Yellow Boy calls Shoots-Today-Kills-Tomorrow, but I named Little David, Yellow Boy's tactical savvy against Díaz's troops, Apache renegades Kid, Elias, and Juan, and Yellow Boy's deadly accuracy with his Henry rifle.

When we finish eating, Villa returns to work in his wagon and Magritte shows us a comfortable spot in the shade of some cottonwoods near the blue-green water tank where she's put our saddles and gear. We spread out our bedrolls and spend most of the day sleeping undisturbed. When I get up to answer a nature call in the middle of the afternoon, I see three of Villa's general officers coming into camp and five leaving.

6. THE REQUEST

Yellow Boy and I awake late in the afternoon. Shadows in the canyon merge into soft twilight, and tree frog peepers and crickets are beginning their songs. Magritte, still bubbling with energy after working all day around the cooking fires and taking care of our animals, tells us our suppers are ready and that the general wants us to join him. We bathe in the overflow from the tank and go to his wagon.

A man with black wavy hair combed to one side, bearing a striking resemblance to Villa, nearly as tall but not as thick in the chest and mid-section and holding a big accounting ledger, stands at the foot of the steps to Villa's command wagon. Villa is on the steps above him, gesturing with the palm of his right hand in a chopping motion for emphasis, giving orders.

"…And Hipólito, you be damned sure we get what we pay for, eh?"

Villa looking even more haggard than he did this morning, sees us and brightens. He waves his hand for us to come forward. "*Muchachos. Perfecto* timing. Meet Hipólito, my brother. He is also my cashier and purchasing agent. Now he heads for the border to buy more supplies for our long march."

We shake hands with Hipólito and exchange a few pleasantries before he says, "The wagon drivers, guards, and I have a long trip ahead of us. I will return soon and we can have a more convivial *conversación. Adiós, amigos.*"

Villa walks a few steps with him, still streaming instructions and warnings before slapping him on his back with a hearty, "*Adiós,*" to send him on his way. Villa turns to us and says, "Magritte and the other girls soon come with our suppers. We eat by my little fire here, eh?" He brings out a folding camp stool for himself and motions us to sit on logs around a small fire near the side of his wagon, facing away from the rest of the camp.

For a long while, he talks, making frequent hand gestures and laughing often about battles he fought in the *Revolución*. There is a pause in our chat. He frowns. Anger appears in his face and voice as he talks about driving out Huerta who murdered Madero, first *Presidente* after the *Revolución*. The frown becomes a thundercloud when he describes the civil war between him and want-to-be-*Presidente* Carranza and Carranza's leading general, Obregón.

"In my battles with Obregón he fights like a coward. He hides his men in trenches and behind the barbed wire like the Germans tell him. I almost had *El Perfumado*, The Dandy, at León. One of my cannons blew off his right arm, but he is one lucky son-of-a-bitch and lived when he should have died.

"Obregón and me, we have fought all over Chihuahua. That bastard…he executed a hundred and twenty of my officers at Celaya after they surrendered. Later he caught and hung my musicians, my great *música* band, and an inspiration for the army. More than eighty of them, he hung in the trees on the plaza at Aguacalientes. I nearly had him again at Aguacalientes. He let his supply lines get too long, but before I could cut them and chop his army to pieces, he turned and attacked my men at their supper. My men… they ran. They ran, Hombrecito. With victory nearly in their hands, they ran."

Yellow Boy frowns in disbelief.

"So, you build a new army with men that run? This not wise, *Jefe*. You never know if they run again when bullets fly."

Villa, resting his head against his hand with his elbow propped against his knee, sighs like he's admitting something hard to swallow.

"*Sí,* Muchacho Amarillo, you are right. But I must use everyone I can, from the old ones who ran to new ones I say must fight, and there are still many *hombres* with me who are of great courage who will help give the others the steel they need in battle."

I'm puzzled. "What do you mean by, 'New ones I say must fight'?"

He shrugs. "*Hombres* I did not call during the *Revolución*. They were needed with their families in the villages. I let them stay when I was fighting Díaz, but I need them now."

I see a sarcastic grin under the big mustache.

"Some come willingly, others I have to prod a little bit."

"Prod a little bit?"

His jaw muscles ripple and brown eyes flash, hard and cruel.

"Oh, you know how it is done. I tell them if they do not want to come with me, they can watch me shoot their wives and children, and then they can come with me. They never put me to the test when I tell them this, and I have never done such a thing. But I tell you, Hombrecito, even this terrible thing I can do for the cause of liberty, the cause of human freedom, the cause of justice long-delayed and long-denied to my suffering countrymen. *Sí*, I can and will sacrifice a few of the most innocent if it means justice for all."

I swallow the hard words I want to say to my old friend, to the man who saved my life and Yellow Boy's. This *hombre* is not the charismatic Villa I knew in the camps of the Apaches. He doesn't even sound like the man of military genius in newspaper stories about the *Revolución* battles, but a ruthless *bandito*. Before Madera came to power and the *Revolución* was against Díaz in 1910, recruits begged to join his army. Now, as Villa speaks to us in the fall of 1915, it's clear the *peons* don't want to fight in his civil war with Carranza, who was also part of the *Revolución* to overthrow Díaz.

While we eat he tells us about rebuilding his army and the trips he's made all over Mexico to firm up his support. The night chill draws us closer to the fire. Villa loves sweets and Magritte brings us a basket of freshly baked *empañadas* with a small honey pot, painted in bright red and blue geometric designs. We eat all the *empañadas* and half the honey, smacking our lips and licking our fingers in delight. After we finish, looking like swollen toads, we sit back from the fire. Right on time, Magritte magically reappears as if Villa had pulled some servant's bell in a *hacienda*. She retrieves the empty basket and honey, and brings us more coffee.

The taste of honey still on his tongue, Villa sighs, and grins. "*Amigos*, I have a favor I must ask of you."

I think *Here it comes*, a*lways a little foreplay first, and then brace yourself, señorita.*

Yellow Boy crosses his arms and cocks his head to one side to get an ear closer, and says, "We owe you much, *Jefe*. Tell us how we can begin to pay our great debt to you. This debt walks in my head many winters."

Villa shakes his head. "Muchacho Amarillo and Hombrecito, you owe me nothing, nothing." He stares in the fire thinking before roaring a big belly laugh, his eyes sparkling again.

"That bear cornered you and caught me with my pants down! I was lucky to get there in time. Any *hombre* can fight a bear."

He sighs. "Muchacho Amarillo, it is only you and Hombrecito that I can ask to do me this favor. Your help I ask only because you are my *amigos*, not because you owe me anything.

"Across the border in Columbus, lives a storekeeper, Sam Ravel, a Jew. No matter, that he is a Jew, I do business with whoever gives me the best deal, Jew, Catholic, or the devil himself. They say *Señor* Ravel comes from Europe far to the east. This *hombre* you know?"

We shake our heads. I've never heard of Sam Ravel or even been in Columbus, a little ranching town and train stop close to the border and about seventy miles due west of El Paso.

Villa, disgust written in his scowl, says "I give *mucho*

dinero to *Señor* Sam Ravel for bullets and rifles. He promises to deliver these things during my last trip to Ciudad Juárez when I speak with the *reportero*. I understand *Señor* Ravel must cross the border with great care when the army is not looking, and that maybe he cannot come to Juarez when we agreed. But the guns and bullets, I must have them now so my men are armed when we leave the Sierra Madre and march up San Bernardino Valley to take Agua Prieta. Who knows what we will find when we come out of the sierras? Maybe a big army already waits for us. I must have the bullets, if not the rifles. My army does not have many bullets. An army cannot fight without bullets.

"I send Camisa Roja, one of my most trusted men, to ask Ravel for my guns and bullets. Before he goes, I say to Roja, 'If Ravel does not have the guns, do not stir up trouble.' When Roja sees *Señor* Ravel, Ravel he says he does not know if Camisa Roja truly speaks for me. Ravel tells Roja *nada*, nothing, and sends him away."

Villa taps his temple with his right index finger. "I think this man Ravel plays a game with me and I do not like it. *Por favor, amigos*, ride to Columbus, see *Señor* Sam Ravel, and tell him I want my guns and bullets *pronto*. These things I have already paid for. If he cannot get them, then my *dinero* must be returned *rápido. Comprende?*"

Yellow Boy nods and I grin. I know exactly what Villa is asking us to do and I'm glad to do it. Sam Ravel sounds like a swindler taking advantage of our *amigo*. It's time to convince Mr. Ravel where his best interests lie.

Yellow Boy knows there has to be more and squints at Villa. "There are other matters we can help you with, *Jefe*?"

Villa's forefinger goes up. "There is one other thing, *señores*. Your *Presidente* Wilson, I'm told thinks maybe

Carranza ought to be Mexico's true *Presidente* and that I am nothing more than a *bandito* Obregón chases. I must convince *Presidente* Wilson this is not true.

"*Presidente* Wilson needs to understand that Carranza is not for the United States or Mexico. Carranza is for Carranza. He does not even like the United States. Even now he talks with the Germans about invading the United States if the *Americanos* go to war against Germany. I tell you, it is me," he slaps his chest for emphasis, "Francisco Villa, *Presidente* Wilson must recognize for the good of Mexico and the United States.

"A victory over Carranza at Agua Prieta will open *Presidente* Wilson's eyes to this if the *Americano* newspapers tell him it is so. In El Paso there is a *reportero*. I know him well from when he rides on my trains during the *Revolución* and writes *magnifico* stories of my battles, and we are *amigos* in El Paso after I escape from Huerta's prison. If he is at Agua Prieta, this *reportero* will see how I crush Carranza's army and can write a great, impressive story on the battle. *Presidente* Wilson will at last understand I am not a *bandito*, but first *Jefe*, a capable general who pounded Carranza's army to dust. After you see *Señor* Sam Ravel in Columbus, *por favor*, go to El Paso, find the *reportero*, and bring him back to me so I can look him in the eye and convince him to come with me to Agua Prieta for a great story. I can stay here another six days, waiting for my bullets and guns and other supplies from storekeepers across the border before I must join *División del Norte* in El Paso Púlpito. Can you bring this *reportero* to me before I leave this place? It is *muy importante* that he come with me to Agua Prieta."

"*Sí,* general, we can do this. What is the name of this reporter we must bring back to you?"

A big smile spreads over his face. "*Gracias, muchas gracias, mi amigos.* The *reportero* is *Señor* Queentin Peach."

7. SAM RAVEL

Riding to Columbus and catching a train to El Paso, finding Queentin Peach, and returning in less than six days means we have to leave that night and travel hard and fast. Magritte, pouring Yellow Boy and me a final cup of hot coffee before we head east and giving us a sack of *empañadas*, promises to take good care of our pack mule and supplies.

I guess Columbus to be eighty or ninety miles a little north of east from Villa's canyon, and that Hachita is maybe sixty miles a little east of north. Our options are to ride north and catch a train in Hachita or head directly for Columbus. I talk it over with Yellow Boy. The train might save us thirty miles of riding, but knowing his aversion to trains, and that we might have to wait a day for a train east from Hachita, we decide the fastest way to Columbus is to ride due east. If we're careful pushing the horses, we might make Columbus by noon the next day. Riding a little north of east I figure we'll hit the east-west rail line, which we can follow straight into Columbus, or the north-south road from Demining through Columbus into Palomas, just south of the border. In either case, it'll be easy to find Columbus.

Galloping into the star-filled, cold desert night, Satanas wants to run. Yellow Boy, who has the best night vision of any human I've ever known, leads the way in the bright moonlight using an alternating pace of fast walk, canter and brisk gallop that eats up the miles and keeps the horses strong and steady.

We water and rest the horses shortly after midnight. After an hour we're back in the saddle in mighty rough country. Everything from the chunks of black basalt rocks to cactus is sharper and bigger than anything I've seen in the country around Las Cruces or the Tularosa Basin. We stop again at dawn near a dilapidated windmill still pumping water in a tank made with rocks and cement.

I'm in good physical condition, but I'm not used to riding long uninterrupted distances. Muscles ache all over my body. Yellow Boy grins when he sees me hobbling around, teeth clenched.

"Hombrecito grows soft learning the ways of White Eye medicine. Be strong again, ride Satanas more."

He's right. I have to start riding again, and riding often.

We ride into the rising sun past randomly scattered thin creosotes, mesquite, cactus, and yuccas as if the hand of God broadcast the seeds. At midmorning, we see a long gray smudge low on the horizon, probably a rising smoke plume. Only big mines or some kind of town make plumes that big. We ride directly for it.

In an hour, the single big smoke plume becomes several thin plumes rising straight up and then folding over in the upper air. Their sources are tiny black specks of buildings far in the distance. Striking and following a road north toward the buildings, we soon pass a border marker shaped like an Egyptian obelisk next to a fence formed with many strands of barbed wire. The obelisk has US/Mexico Border chiseled into its sides. I guess the town in front of us, not more than three or four miles away, must be Columbus. My pocket watch reads 9:50. We've made great time.

Further up and on the east side of the road, we pass eight or nine long, weathered wood buildings with adobe mess shacks in the rear. They must be army barracks. Beyond the barracks are several stables nothing more than open sheds providing shade for the horses and some protection for saddles and other gear from the sun. Just north of the barracks and closer to the road are a couple of gray, weathered shacks, which I learn later, are the command headquarters for the officer of the day and the surgeon's quarters.

Paralleling the other side of the road is a deep *arroyo*, and just to the west of the *arroyo* is an adobe house where a clothesline strung between two twisted piñon posts holds pieces of uniforms hung out to dry. A hundred yards from the road, beyond the house, Cootes Hill rises small and barren, rough rocks and prickly pear the only growth covering its sides. Just before we cross the railroad tracks running east and west, we come to a small train station on the east side of the road, and the customs house on the west side of the road, opposite the train station.

Running seven or eight blocks parallel to and three or four blocks north of the train tracks, its streets dusty, deep in sand, and surrounded by the mesquite chaparral, sunbaked Columbus, a typical little southwest rail town, sits quiet and still in the desert. Dominating the other buildings, the wooden, two-story Commercial Hotel stands a block north of the train station and the two-story adobe Hoover Hotel sits directly next to the tracks and about three blocks east of the Commercial. A bank's windows across the street from the Hoover already reflect the glare of the morning sun. Near the station, a rooming house waits for the next load of passengers with overnight business in Columbus. I catch a glimpse of a church steeple sticking up above the rooflines on the north side of town. We later pass a post office and seven or eight stores, including a drug store. Scattered among the commercial buildings are several homes that fit right in with the mercantile stores.

Yellow Boy lets the horses drink at the train station trough while I go inside where it's cool and dark, welcome relief from the sun's bright glare. The white-haired clerk behind the ticket window, a pencil stuck behind his ear and several in his vest pockets, grins and nods like I'm not the first to ask him about Sam Ravel and the next train.

"Sam Ravel? Why, yes, sir, Sam's store is right on the corner, just a block up the street there by the side of the Commercial Hotel. Can't miss it. Yes, sir, lots of comin' and goin' at Sam Ravel's. Train east is due in about one o'clock this afternoon if you want to go to El Paso."

I buy a ticket for the next train. We lead the horses, still cooling down from the long ride, up the street to Sam Ravel's store. The store dominates the block. Through the vertical bars protecting merchandise behind big glass windows, we can see several customers inside. The laughing and talking we hear outside stops when we walk through the door. Two men play checkers at a table by the black coal stove and three or four women are browsing through and feeling several rolls of cloth. Seeing Yellow Boy, they freeze, their eyes growing wide, notice me beside him, and then relax. Nearly thirty years have passed since Geronimo, his warriors, and their families were shipped off to a Florida POW camp, yet ranchers who survived the Geronimo wars are still nervous around Apaches.

A thick, muscular blond man stands behind a counter watching his customers. His features bespeak someone from Eastern Europe, maybe even Russia. His hands are big and the scars on his face around his eyes and crooked nose say he isn't reluctant to fight with his fists. He has a strong accent, but his English is good. When I step up to his counter, he smiles and seems affable.

"Mr. Sam Ravel?"

"Dat is my name. Yah?"

"My name is Henry Grace. I wonder if there's somewhere we can speak privately?"

"Oh, shu. Der is my office. Come, Mr. Grace."

I turn to tell Yellow Boy I'll be back shortly but he's already drifted outside to stand with the horses. Ravel leads me through a curtained door into a supply room filled with sacks of grain and flour, rolls of barbed wire, harness, ranching tools, and myriad supplies for every imaginable farm or ranch need. We make our way to a walled-off corner next to a wide loading-dock door. A big roll-top desk is inside the makeshift office along with three chairs and a couple of shelves holding ledgers. A small window near the top of the outside wall gives the room plenty of light.

Ravel sits down behind the desk and motions me toward

a chair in front. He pushes aside a stack of papers and flips open a box of cigars. He offers me one, but I shake my head. He bites off the plug, spits it on the floor, lights up, clamps it in his yellow teeth, and grins.

"So, how can I help yah, Mr. Grace? Moving to Columbus? Maybe yah buy de Berman ranch for sale outside uf town? I can extend credit on any supplies yah need."

I smile and shake my head. "No, sir, nothing like that. I've just come from the camp of General Francisco Villa."

Ravel frowns and, taking a deep draw on the cigar, blows the smoke toward me. Leaning toward me, the cigar clamped in his teeth, his hands curling into fists, he says, "Yah? And what says General Pancho Villa dat yah come to me?"

"The general is camped near the border and buying supplies for his army. He says he ordered some rifles and ammunition from you. He expected you to deliver them when he was last in Ciudad Juarez. It's been over a week and he still hasn't taken delivery on his purchases. He has to have them soon and asked me to stop by to ask when you can deliver and where."

Ravel's fists are on his knees as he leans closer, scowling. The cigar still clamped in his teeth, he snarls, "Tell dat bandito dere is no ammunition and no rifles. Dere is United States embargo. No sale! If dey is supplied to Villa, I go to the jail. Nyet. Nyet guns for Villa."

I nod and smile. "The general thought there might be that kind of problem and therefore wants his money back."

Ravel shakes his head. "Nyet. No money back. Tell Villa I place his money against what he owes me after that bastard captain of his, Figueroa, who never paid $771.25 for the, uh…merchandise… took from me in Palomas last year after holding me prisoner for four days. You tell him dat, heh?"

I'm quick. I'm angry. I'm a pawn between a shyster storekeeper and a friend I no longer know, and I don't like it one bit. Before he blinks, I have him by his tie and my old long-barreled Colt cocked and stuck under his nose.

I say in a low whisper, "Now you listen to me, Mr. Ravel, I'm just the messenger. I'll give General Villa your reply. You know the general. He won't be happy you kept his money. He might want to give you a ride by the neck through the cactus. I'm not anxious to come back as a bill collector. If I do, you'll never know where the bullet comes from that kills or hobbles you for the rest of your miserable life. I know you'll figure out what to do. I'll be back in a day or two. You be ready to talk business. If you try to pull anything the next time I see you, that Apache who came in with me will roast you over a hot fire for days and you'll beg to die."

Not intimidated in the least, he relaxes and even grins.

"Gud! You tell General Villa I'm not happy dat he still owes me for dat Figueroa's merchandise. Dere is nothing I can do anyway because of de embargo. As yah must have seen, de army is in my backyard. I ain't afraid of yah."

I stand and he does too, fists clenched. "I'll be on my way. Think about what I said. I'll see you in a day or two."

His fists on his hips, he nods. "Yah, I be here. Tell Villa we settle accounts when I get my *dinero*."

8. SWEENY JONES

Leaving Sam Ravel's store, we find a cantina in the block by the train tracks, and, looking through its windows, see cavalry troopers, *vaqueros* from across the border, cowboys, and traveling salesmen crowded around its tables. The crowd becomes very quiet when we walk in. For a moment, all eyes are on Yellow Boy. In the silence I hear the hammer on the Henry click back to safety as Yellow Boy, his flint black eyes flat and menacing and merciless, return their stares.

The owner of the cantina, a short, thin man with a long drooping mustache, and greasy black hair combed straight back, steps forward with a disingenuous smile and makes a little bow-like nod with his head.

"*Buenos tardes, señores.*"

He motions us toward an empty table next to one used by a couple of troopers.

"*Por favor*, the table here."

I think *Henry, what in Hell are you doing in here?* And nodding, I say, "*Gracias, señor.*"

The customers begin to relax, minding their own business; all, that is, except the grizzled sergeant at the table next to ours who watches our every move. Gray hair, thin, burr length retreating across his high bald forehead, his face craggy and weather-worn shows scars from old battles and years of rough frontier living. I keep my hand close to my pistol. *Best watch him. If he starts making insulting remarks, Yellow Boy will blow his brains out.*

The waitress brings us coffee without being asked. The cantina owner isn't about to get in a row over selling whisky or beer to an Indian. We order enchiladas.

When the waitress leaves the table, the sergeant says, "Been a long time Yellow Boy. 'Member me?"

Keeping my hands below the table, I slide my thumb over the hammer of my pistol. Yellow Boy studies the sergeant for a few seconds, his narrow eye slits widen in recognition and he nods. "'Member you, Sweeny Jones. Many winters pass since we trail Geronimo."

Sweeny Jones breaks into a big grin and, nodding toward Yellow Boy, shakes the shoulder of the young man sitting with him. "Marv, this here gentleman is Yellow Boy. Best damn shot in the country. He'n pick the balls off a gnat at two hundert yards with that there old Henry. He scouted with me fer a while when Crook was a chasin' Geronimo. It's been years since I last seen him." He nods toward me. "Mister, how do you know this ol' hard-nut devil?"

Smiling, I relax and lean back in my chair. "He found me in the desert when I was a kid. Saved my life from some bad *hombres*. I'm a doctor now but we still ride together once in a while." I wave my hand toward our table. "Come on over and join us. You two can catch up on old times."

Plate and beer mug in hand, Sweeny Jones is in motion before I finish the invitation. His mouth filled with questions and enchiladas, he sits down next to Yellow Boy and sticks out his hand to shake mine.

"Sergeant Sweeny Jones, US Army, 13th Cavalry, and this here is Private Marvin Johnson." His scarred, rough hand with stubby short fingers has a good strong grip and I like him right away. "Henry Grace. It's my pleasure, Sergeant." Marv has another-world look in his blank eyes. He doesn't say anything, but shyly sticks out his hand and grips mine with the power of a vice.

Sweeny Jones asks all the usual catching-up questions. Yellow Boy tells him about his wives, sons, and his work as a tribal policeman. Sweeny shows him his sergeant's stripes and tells us about his life on the border. Our enchiladas come. We eat as Sweeny rambles on about life in Columbus at Camp Furlong, the army camp we'd passed on the other side of the tracks.

He concludes, "It ain't bad duty here in Columbus. Colonel Slocum, the camp commander, is easy goin' and the trains give us easy access to El Paso for blowin' our pay on hooch and whores."

I'm curious about why there's an army camp in Columbus. Sweeny Jones frowns and stares at me like I'm crazy. I shrug. "I've been in medical school in California for the past six years and haven't read the New Mexico papers much."

Sweeny's brows go up in surprise. "Why, no offense, it's

just that I figured a well-educated man like yourself knowed why we're here. It's the damned Mexican Revolution. They done tore hell outta the country in the fightin'. *Peons* looking to find a better life, gettin' outta the way of the army or trying to avoid bein' forced to join one side or the other, been comin' across that border wire like a brown river. On top of bein' overrun by the illegals, that there bastard Carranza has let the Carrancistas raid towns across the river in Texas all the way to Brownsville. Wilson said it had to stop and told the Army to make it happen. So here we are."

Nodding, I say, "I remember reading about that in the California papers. It just didn't sink in that there would be that many troops on the border. I guess you've been busy."

Jones shrugs and grimaces.

"After we come, it was quiet for a while until ol' Carranza and Villa got into it. After Obregón kicked Villa's tail, we hear Villa's been movin' his army north and edgin' west. Ain't nobody knows 'xactly where he's a goin'. My money says Agua Prieta if he's a goin' to Sonora. I s'pect purty soon he's gonna hafta cross the Sierra Madre. That'll be a hell of a job if he'n do 'er at all and still keep his army together. Ol' Yellow Boy and me was with Crook in the Sierra Madre. Yellow Boy knows how damned rough the country is. Hell, he's lived down there."

Yellow Boy leaned back in his chair, crossed his arms, and nodded.

"Villa ain't gonna come too close to the border with that army 'o his 'cause half of 'em'll desert into the states. I ain't heard yet which one of 'em, Carranza or Villa, ol' Wilson's said the US is gonna support, so the Army ain't havin' nothin' to do with either one. Me? I believe we oughta support Villa but ol' Wilson's gonna pick Carranza. He's already put an embargo on guns and bullets for Villa."

We talk for another half an hour while Yellow Boy and I finish our dinners. The windup clock hanging above the cash register tells me the eastbound train is due soon. I push back from the table.

"Gentlemen, it's been a pleasure, but we have to get going."

Sweeny and Marv shake our hands, Sweeny saying, "You boys come visit us over to Camp Furlong when your business is done." We promise we'll see them again soon.

Stepping out of the cantina's cool interior into the sun's fiery glare is like walking into a wall. Squinting at me, Yellow Boy nods toward the train station. "You ride the iron wagon to El Paso, Hombrecito?"

I look west down the tracks. There's no sign of the train in the distance.

"*Si*. I'm going to find Villa's *reportero*, Queentin Peach, and get him to come visit. I'll put Satanas in the livery stable here while I'm gone. I figure it may take me a couple of suns to find Peach and get back here. I doubt Peach will be use to long, hard rides, so it'll probably take us two nights to get back to Villa's canyon."

Yellow Boy glances off to the east.

"I go also to El Paso?"

I shake my head.

"Given the way you feel about riding the iron wagons and how the locals eye you when we walk down the street, it's best I go alone. I'll meet you in Villa's canyon in four or five suns."

Yellow Boy stares east down the tracks toward El Paso.

"Four or five suns at Villa's camp? *Bueno.* I tell Villa you come soon with *Señor* Peach. I say nothing of Ravel until you come. Villa maybe drags Ravel through the cactus if Ravel no find guns, bullets or *dinero.*

"Hombrecito, hear me. Stay out of his way when you tell Villa. Villa grows *mucho* angry *pronto*, no think, forgets his *amigos*, goes maybe a little *loco.*"

"I hear you, Uncle."

Yellow Boy nods. "*Bueno.*" Grabbing his saddle horn with his left hand, holding the Henry with his right, he swings into the saddle with a smooth, graceful leap.

"Train comes."

He points toward his eyes with his index and middle finders.

"Four, maybe five, suns at camp of Villa, I see you. *Adiós.*"

He heads south down the road past Camp Furlong and I lead Satanas up the street to the livery stable. In case I'm longer than a couple of days returning from El Paso, I pay the liveryman for five days worth of grain and grooming. Walking back to the station I hear a train whistle and see black smoke in the distance. On the train station platform, a small crowd of cowboys, salesmen, and soldiers gather, laughing and joking, looking forward to good times in El Paso.

9. 'QUEENTIN' PEACH

Watching from the window of an El Paso and Southwestern passenger car, I watch the tops of the mesquites and creosotes skim by, and think riding the train must be like flying in those machines I've read about in the papers. Looking away from the tracks and out across the rolling vastness of the Chihuahua Desert, the plains of creosotes look like a dark, forest-green ocean frozen in time. Liberally sprinkled with dried stalks of yuccas and century plants thrusting their stems above the surface and islands of light, delicate green mesquite, the land, bathed in the mellow afternoon glare of the western sun, pulls at my soul. I wish a good horse carried me and that I was not just something flying across it at unbelievable speed to save a little time.

I doze off and immediately see the burning jaguar coming for me. I'm frozen in fear but dodge its attack just in time to jerk awake as the train pulls into the El Paso Union Depot late that afternoon. I'm glad it's hot so the troopers and salesmen won't think it's odd that I'm sweating, sweating from the images in that hard, mysterious dream stalking me. Walking through the big, brick station filled with echoes of pounding feet and squealing children following their mothers, I stop at a ticket counter manned by a clerk barely old enough to shave.

"Pardon me, can you tell me where to find the *El Paso Herald*?"

He studies me for moment, eyeing my sweat-stained, dusty desert clothes, no doubt wondering who I am. I wear enough silver trim on my leather to be a Mexican, my long Apache style moccasins and canvas pants suggest I might be an Indian, but, like a cowboy, I shade my head with a big, dusty flat-brimmed Stetson and wear a blue bandanna around the neck of a white shirt covered with alkali dust.

"Yes, sir, I can do that. When you go out that door yonder, you'll be on San Francisco Street. Look to your right and you'll see the Mills Building. You can't miss it. It's the tallest building in El Paso. It sits on one side of Pioneer Plaza. Next to it on the same side of the plaza is a big white building. Bottom floor's a department store; the McCoy Hotel is on the upper floors. The *Herald* is right next to the McCoy. There's a big vertical sign on the roof that says *Herald* and there's a giant pocket watch showing the time on a post right outside the front doors. Must be ten or twelve blocks from here."

He points toward the doors.

"Out front there's real comfortable automobiles with drivers that'll take you anywhere in town you want to go.

They charge four bits or you'n take a trolley that runs down the middle of San Francisco Street ever half an hour that'll give you a ride for a nickel."

"Thanks. Think I'll walk." The kid stares at me like I'm crazy. I smile at how soft folks get living in town.

San Francisco Street reclines in the shadows of buildings on its southwest side; the buildings on the northeast side are bright in the soft glare of the setting sun. Automobiles and wagons in nearly equal measure roll down the street or are parked up and down the sidewalks. The kid is right, I can see the tall Mills Building standing out from the others maybe ten blocks down the street. By my watch it's 4:30, but the street is crowded with people flitting in and out of the stores, and the saloons and restaurants are becoming lively. In addition to the crowd of businessmen and women with long fancy dresses and hats, cowboys and Mexicans stroll both sides of the street. I jump in surprise the first time I hear the dinging bell and whine and grind of a street trolley whirring past, but the crowd ignores it like it isn't there. El Paso is far more energetic, far more pounding with the rhythms of life than dusty Las Cruces or the drowsy university campus where I've spent nearly all my time for the past six years.

I turn the corner at the Mills Building. Sure enough there's a little plaza. On one side is a big white building, the McCoy Hotel. It's maybe three quarters the height of the Mills Building, and next to it is a three-story building that reminds me of the Victorian houses covering the hills in San Francisco. A tall vertical sign on the roof says *Herald*. Three or four Model-T Fords are parked out front in the middle of the plaza.

A green and white-stripped awning shades the *Herald's* big double doors. As I cross the plaza, the doors fly open. A couple of men, waving their arms and jabbering a mile-a-minute, rush by before I can stop and ask them how to find Queentin Peach.

A man wearing a Panama boater straw hat tilted back on his head follows not far behind them, a lady holding his arm. He's a head taller than me, square-jawed and clean-shaven, in his mid-to-late thirties, and well dressed. He carries a suit coat folded over his left arm, wears a loosened necktie around an open-collar white shirt, and his dressy pin-stripped pants are held up with red suspenders. His lady is a fine-looking woman with jet-black hair under a big, blue velvet hat trimmed with ostrich feathers. Her dark almond eyes, heart-shaped lips, and a figure motherhood hasn't wrecked makes her stand out in any crowd. She wears a large emerald ring next to a gold wedding band, and from the way the man struts with her and the way she smiles and talks with him, it's obvious they are much in love.

The thought that Rafaela and I might have been like that couple if not for Camisa Roja flashes across my mind, leaving me to taste drops of bitter regret and frustrated rage. I hold up my hand, signaling them to stop as I approach. The man frowns when he sees me, his eyes taking in my grimy face and the dust-covered, eclectic clothes. He stops, stepping between the lady and me. Raising her eyes just over his shoulder, she studies me from her safe place behind him, a smile playing on her lips.

"Yes, sir? What can I do for you?"

I smile, trying to appear amiable. "Sorry to disturb you and your lady. I'm looking for a *Herald* reporter named Queentin Peach. I was hoping you might be able to tell me where to find him?"

He frowns. "And, you are…?"

I wince. "Sorry. Forgot my manners." I hold out my right hand. "My name is Doctor Henry Grace. I opened a medical practice in Las Cruces about two months ago and I have a message for Mr. Peach, with whom I need to speak right away."

The woman steps out from behind his back and crosses her arms as she stares at me. The man's eyes narrow, as he shakes my hand and looks me in the eye.

"You don't look like any doctor I've ever seen. I'm Quentin Peach. Friends call me Quent. This is my wife, Persia. Persia, Doctor Henry Grace." She gives me a coquettish nod and smile as he continues. "The only one I know who calls me *Queentin* is General Francisco Villa. What's his message?"

"Sir, with all due respect to Mrs. Peach, this is something I need to tell you in private."

Persia frowns and shakes her head. Quent glances at her, thinks for an instant, and waves his arm for one of the taxis parked on the plaza. The driver jumps out to crank it as Persia turns to Quentin.

"Lupe will have supper on the table in an hour. Please try to be on time. If you can't make it, call me. Doctor Grace is more than welcome to come with you."

I make a little bow. "Thank you very much, Mrs. Peach. I'm so sorry to interrupt you on your way home to supper, and I'll not keep your husband long. Have a good evening."

Persia smiles and makes a little curtsy. "It's a pleasure meeting you, Doctor Grace."

Peach kisses her on the cheek. "Thanks, sweetie, I'll be home as soon as I can."

The plaza taxi starts with a cough, a rumbling chug, and

a cloud of blue smoke. The driver jumps in and wheels it over to us. Quentin helps Persia climb into the back seat and gives the driver, a Mexican boy not a day over sixteen, a dollar with directions on where to take her. He grins and nods, showing two front teeth missing. Persia holds on to her hat as the taxi whizzes off down the street. They disappear after making a left turn on two wheels at the next intersection.

Peach points down the street. "There's a little bar down yonder where we can talk."

We walk down El Paso Street less than a block before he turns into a place next to a grocery store. A Mexican, the whites of his eyes yellow from dust and smoke, and wearing a white storekeeper's apron that gives contrast to his dark complexion, leans in the doorway, watching the bar's customers come and go, no doubt wishing they were more interested in groceries than whiskey. The saloon, overhead fans turning, is cool inside, its well-dressed customers bellied up to a mahogany bar sipping little shot glasses of whiskey and big mugs of beer. Peach slides into a booth by the window and motions me to sit opposite him. "Beer?"

I nod.

He calls across the room, "Hey, Max. Bring us a couple of cold ones, will ya?" The bartender gives him a thumbs-up acknowledgement.

The beers are cold and yeasty. The first swallow is mighty good after the hot train ride from Columbus.

Peach pulls a little notebook from his coat and takes a pen out of his pocket. "Now, Doctor Grace, what's so important that makes me late for dinner? This is about Villa, isn't it? I never hear from him unless he needs something."

I sit the beer mug down and lean into him, saying in

a low voice, "Yes, I have a message for you from General Villa."

"Where is he? Hiding out? I know a reporter who's talking to the State Department about letting him live on this side of the border. Is that what this is about?"

I smile.

"One question at a time, please, sir. I was with him in Mexico just south of the border less than twenty-four hours ago. He's buying supplies for *División del Norte* and planning to cross the Sierra Madre before turning north for Agua Prieta across the border from Douglas. He's asked me to guide you to a meeting with him. He's anxious to get his side of what's happened in the war with Carranza in the papers, and hopes to change Wilson's mind before he recognizes Carranza as *El Presidente* of Mexico. Villa believes you'll give an honest, accurate report on his taking Agua Prieta."

Peach nods.

"Yeah, old Poncho's smart when it comes to using the press. I believe he has the *peons'* best interests at heart, but he's lost too much power since the slaughters at Celaya, León, and Aguacalientes. I don't think he has a prayer of ousting Carranza as long as Obregón is in charge of the army.

"My sources tell me Wilson's already decided to recognize Carranza as *El Presidente*. He just hasn't done it yet. Besides, the *peons* are sick of war. Most refuse to willingly join Villa's army. He's surrounded himself with some real hard cases, and they can be damned mean. I hear they're tellin' Villa exactly what he wants to hear. It's likely most of the men he has in *División del Norte* now are kids who don't know any better or his *jefes* have bullied them into fighting for him. You're not telling me that he's planning to attack Agua Prieta are you?"

I'm surprised at how much Peach knows and his view of Villa's chances at overthrowing Carranza.

"Villa says he's going to attack Agua Prieta and wants you to do the story. Will you come back with me to talk with Villa? At least give him an interview?"

Peach takes a swallow of beer and stares at the table while his fingers drum a slow tattoo. His eyes drift back to mine. "Yeah. I want to go, but first I'll have to clear it with Hughs Slater, the *Herald's* owner and editor-in-chief, but I don't doubt he'll approve my going. When do we leave?"

10. REVELATIONS

The next morning, Quent and I leave for Columbus on the 5:30 train. He no longer looks like a townie businessman. He wears a white shirt with a red bandanna, canvas pants, mule-ear boots, a wide-brimmed Panama, and a vest holding a watch and a pen or two. He carries a shoulder holster with an old Wells Fargo Schofield Model 3 Smith and Wesson in an ancient leather satchel along with his notebooks and personal gear. And he has an 1894 Winchester in a horse scabbard, bulging saddlebags, a canteen, and a bedroll. I relax, thinking that maybe I won't have to nursemaid him across the desert after all.

The train pulls into Columbus about 8:00. The air is still cool but the sun's heat is coming on fast. We leave the station and walk up the street to the livery. Compared to El Paso, the little village seems like a ghost town. Doors to the stores are open, but there's little or no traffic on the dusty streets. At the livery stable, Satanas looks rested, ready for our return to the wild country. The liveryman sells Peach a roan gelding and says he'll buy it back when we return. I tell him we'll be leaving about sundown and want to rest there in the shade until we are ready to go. He still owes me for four days of livery time and grain on the money I'd given him for Satanas the day before, so he shows us a stall filled with fresh straw where we can stow our gear and spread our bedrolls for a nap. I tell him we'll be back after breakfast.

We walk down the street and stop at Sam Ravel's store. In addition to getting Ravel's answer on the arms delivery for Villa, I need to buy a coffee pot, coffee, and a slab of bacon. Ravel waits on me like I'm a stranger. We're about to leave when he jerks his head toward the supply room. "Can we have a word, Mr. Grace?"

I look at Peach. He grins. "I'll meet you outside."

Ravel motions me to a chair in his office. When I shake my head, he sits down and, groaning, joints still stiff early in the day, throws his feet up on his desk. He grins, showing his big tobacco-stained teeth. "Dah, yesterday after we talk, I ask, How I can help my *amigo*, General Villa? Here is deal I have. Yah tell him, dah? I can get him de bullets and rifles and I can dodge de embargo. He includes de $771.25 he owes me for de udder deal, he give me an extra $1000 against de embargo, an' he pays all wid gold, not dat wort'less script he uses. Den we do business, dah?"

I shrug my shoulders. "I'll tell the generalissimo whatever you want. You want me to say that?"

He grins, nodding. "Dah. Yah tell de generalissimo dat. Den maybe we do business."

Peach and I have a big breakfast at the John Dalton Restaurant. He hasn't said much about the trip since we made travel plans at the little bar in El Paso. He seems to have a mighty short supply of curiosity for a reporter. As we finish eating, he leans back in his chair and studies me, idly tapping his fingers against his coffee cup. "Doctor Grace why are we waiting until sundown to leave town for Villa's camp? Are you trying to keep me in the dark, literally, about Villa's location?"

I grin and shake my head. "Sorry if I've given you the wrong idea about who I am and my friendship with Villa. Maybe we can start over? How about callin' me Henry?"

"Okay… Henry. How about calling me Quentin, not 'Queentin' like our friend pronounces it. All my friends call me Quent and I'd be proud to call you a friend."

"Quent it is. It wouldn't make any difference if you knew exactly where Villa is now, he'll be gone in two or three days anyway. As for me personally, a little on my background will go a long way toward explaining the way I do things.

"When I was growing up, a Mescalero Apache cavalry scout, Yellow Boy, taught me how to survive in this country. When he has a choice, he always travels at night and holes up during the day. Says he can go farther and faster at night than during the day because the night air is so much cooler and you don't have to spend a lot of time looking over your shoulder for enemies. The horses don't work as hard and it's near impossible for enemies to find you unless they're mighty lucky. There're Indians, bandits, renegade soldiers, you name them, all bad *hombres*, drifting around out there in the big lonesome on both sides of the border. Blood's likely to flow if you run into them and they don't know you. I'm just being extra careful like Yellow Boy taught me."

"Got it. Mind if I ask you a personal question?"

"Depends. What do you want to know?"

"Well, I'm just curious why you're running errands for Villa when you have a medical practice in Las Cruces."

I shrug my shoulders. "I don't think of it that way. I know what I'm doing must look strange to someone who doesn't know my history. Villa, Yellow Boy, and I go all the way back to before the *Revolución* when Villa was Doroteo Arango and rustled cattle from the *hacendado ranchos* in Chihuahua."

Quent scratches his chin. "I haven't heard much about Villa's early life. I want to hear more about that later, but that still doesn't tell me why you're doing this."

Memories, some I haven't seen in seven or eight years, flood my mind. "In the days before the *Revolución*, Yellow Boy and I lived in a Sierra Madre Apache camp. It was led by a redheaded Apache named Pelo Rojo."

Quent's jaw drops. "A redheaded Apache? Since when is an Apache's hair any color but coal black?"

"If Apaches kidnap a child who is strong enough to survive, they'll adopt it. Rojo was taken as a child when Geronimo was murdering any and everybody up around Lordsburg in the early seventies. A great warrior named Juh, respected throughout the Apacheria and the Sierra Madre and who was a friend of Geronimo, raised Rojo. When I lived with the Apaches, Villa visited Rojo's camp two or three times a year to make deals for stealing *hacendado* cattle and selling the herd or butchered meat across the border. Yellow Boy and I had a score to settle with a couple of Apaches from another camp, a father and son the *peons* called Apache Elias and Apache Juan.

"Yellow Boy and I decided to ambush Elias and Juan at a place on the San Bernardino River and Villa went with us. We camped on a butte next to the river and planned to ambush Elias and Juan when they came to raid a supply train out of Douglas. A Mexican Army patrol stopped for the evening below the butte where we waited. We stayed quiet, waiting for the patrol to move on, but the biggest grizzly I've ever seen showed up. Shooting it meant giving ourselves away and the patrol coming up that butte faster than flies to a fresh cow patty, our chance of wiping out Elias and Juan gone. The bear mauled Yellow Boy when he tried to draw it off me. I put several arrows in it trying to get it off Yellow Boy but they didn't seem to make any difference. It had me and was about to crush my head when Villa landed on its back with a Bowie knife, and with unbelievable strength, drove the blade through the top of its skull.

"Yellow Boy and I feel like we owe Villa our lives for saving us from that bear. So here I am and Yellow Boy waits for us in Villa's camp."

Quent looks in my eyes and shakes his head. "That's quite a tale." He taps his cup with his thumb, thinking. "How long will it take us to get to Villa's camp?"

I shrug. "Yellow Boy and I left the camp early in the evening and got to Columbus by about ten the next morning. We were riding hard and Yellow Boy has the best night vision of any man I know. I don't see as well at night and you're not used to long rides. So lets say two nights of riding and a day holing up to rest the horses and for us to get a little sleep."

He frowns. "I don't ride much now, that's true, but I've been on long rides across the desert before. I don't think I'll slow you down. Ever hear of a deputy sheriff named Tom Tucker?"

The name flickers in the recesses of my memory. "Sounds familiar. Why?"

"Tucker took me on a long ride across the desert to help save Persia from her kidnappers." He shakes his head. "That was fifteen years ago. Time sure blows by, doesn't it? Anyway, we took down the kidnappers and set the man who sent them straight."

"Why did they kidnap Persia? Were you married then?"

"No, we weren't. I hadn't known her then more than a couple of weeks, but I was already smitten. On our first outing the men, who later kidnapped her, surprised and beat me senseless. They were trying to make me quit a story I was doing for the *San Francisco Examiner.* When I continued pursuing the story, they kidnapped her to lure me in the Jornada del Muerto where they planned to make sure we never came back. Fortunately for me, Tom Tucker went with me and they were the ones who disappeared"

"And what story was so sensitive that it nearly got you killed?"

"I was at the trial of Oliver Lee and James Gililland for the murder of Henry Fountain. I'd come to the conclusion that Persia's uncle, Ed Brown, was the killer of Albert and Henry Fountain and I was asking questions and uncovering evidence for a story that said so. I didn't believe Lee was guilty then, and I still don't."

My jaw drops. Quent had covered the trial for my murder. I would have given a fortune to be able to tell him who I really was and watch his face. I knew what really happened to my father and that I had survived. Of course

I wasn't about to tell him that, but I had to know why he thought he knew who did it.

"That case is famous in Las Cruces. Most people still think Lee is guilty. What made you think Brown did it?"

He holds up a fist and raises a finger every time he makes a point. "First, Brown lied about where he was when the Fountains disappeared, and then tried to cover it up. Second, he was with a Socorro bunch that conspired to murder Fountain two years before it happened. One of two places they picked out for an ambush was exactly where the Fountains disappeared. Third, Brown was known to pay assassins to murder people he wanted gone. Fourth, I had the hell beat out of me and was told to leave town when word got around that I was asking questions about Brown's involvement. Fifth, when I didn't leave and kept pursuing the story, Persia was kidnapped and I was told to leave the trial or she'd die."

"What happened when you and Tucker caught up with the kidnappers?"

Quent looks me straight in the eye and doesn't blink. "Tucker and I ambushed and killed all three. Persia got out of it without a scratch. Then Tucker rode up to San Marcial and set Brown on the straight road. Persia and I were there when he did it. Tucker told Brown that if there was ever a hint of harm to Persia or me, he'd better give his soul to God because his tail belonged to Tucker. Brown never bothered us after that."

I want to meet Brown and make my own estimate of his guilt or innocence. Maybe he had been the one who paid the killers I'd seen. Even I didn't believe Oliver Lee did it. "Where's Brown now?"

Quent smiles and shakes his head. "I suspect he's in

Hell. About five years ago he was sitting on a horse in one of his pastures when he was struck dead by lightning. I hear there wasn't a cloud in the sky when it happened."

I feel prickles crawl up my spine as I shake my head in wonder. I pay the waitress. We leave John Dalton's Restaurant and walk over to the livery to get some rest before heading for the Sierra Madre.

11. THE RETURN

By early dusk we're on the south road to Palomas. I find the spot where Yellow Boy and I rode up on the road two days earlier and follow our back trail toward the orange glow above the thin line of mountains on the horizon off to the west. I try the pace Yellow Boy and I used to Columbus. Quent's horse holds up better than I expected, but when we stop around midnight for rest and water, he's tiring so I shorten the distance for the fast gallop and he holds up without much strain the rest of the night. An hour or two before dawn I swing south to skirt the edges of the Hatchet Mountains along the eastern edge of the boot heel and then turn back west.

Quent rides well. He doesn't complain but it's obvious from the way he sits high in the saddle he's getting sore and his thigh muscles are cramping. Dawn begins to break, the eastern sky blood red, when I find a place to rest for the day near a pool of water in a nearly dry riverbed.

We rub down the horses and hobble them to graze on the grass and weeds along the banks. I dig a shallow hole and make a small fire. Quent makes coffee and we roast pieces of bacon on mesquite sticks for our breakfast. I take the first watch while Quent naps. It's early October and just enough shade from the surrounding bushes to scatter the mellow sunlight for a comfortable nap. Quent is up at mid-day to relieve me on watch without my waking him. It's deathly quiet all morning; not even quail calls or roadrunner clicks break the solitude.

I spread my bedroll in some shade and lay back with my hat pulled forward over the bridge of my nose. Dreamless sleep falls on me in an instant.

My eyes flutter open. I whisk my hat off my face only to see the sky a dark purple and darkness fast approaching. Quent sits cross-legged by the fire, writing in his notebook and paying no attention to the countryside. I'm tempted to give him a hard time about lowering our guard, but let it pass. After we eat, I listen to the dusk and watch for signs of dust from riders in the distance, but don't hear or see anything.

When the moon floats up off the eastern horizon, casting the creosotes, mesquites, and cactus in stark white light and inky black shadows, we ride southwest down the riverbed until I get my bearings from the dark mountain outlines against the rising stars and last glimmers of dusk. Before long we turn out of the riverbed and head due west. We tack around low-lying mountains sticking up to the north like black clouds blotting out the stars. Finding good water a couple of times, we stop to water and rest the horses.

The rising sun fills the mountain canyon mists with soft, gauzy light when I find the wash leading up the canyon toward Villa's camp. Quent studies the trail in the wash. "It looks like Cox's Army rode through here. I thought you said Villa was off from the main body of his troops."

"He was when I left. The trail coming in here from the Animas Valley shows signs of heavy pack-train traffic. Maybe they're bringing Villa supplies from across the border and he's either offloading them in this camp or routing them further south to *División del Norte* after checking the loads."

At the sound of wagon wheels grinding against the sand and gravel, the clink of harness chains, and the occasional snuffle of mules or horses, we ride off the wash into the junipers to stay out of sight and watch a short wagon train roll by. The wagon drivers are teenaged Mexican boys in rags and beat-up straw hats, their eyes squinting against the rising sun. Following the wagons, an escort of eight or nine older men, armed with ancient, lever-action rifles, stock butts held against their thighs, ride on sturdy little horses. The guard's faces are dark and hard, ready to give no quarter or to ask none.

The wagons and their escorts pass out of sight and we return to the trail. Quent says, "I guess most *Americanos* don't know and don't care that a large part of Villa's army is made up of teenaged boys. Two or three of those drivers had to be twelve or thirteen. During the *Revolución* Villa tried to recruit unattached men who weren't reluctant to leave home. That meant boys in their teens. They weren't married and they were easy to lure away from their villages because they were on fire to get out from under the thumb of the *patróns*. Their spirits hadn't been broken, they were strong, and it was easy for Villa to mold them into an imposing army. I wonder where he's getting his men now that most of the *peons*, even the young ones, don't want to fight anymore?" He pauses and looks at me with a grin and a wink. "Mister Winchester probably does his recruiting for him now."

I say nothing, but marvel at Quent's insight and understanding of what's happening with Pancho Villa.

A mile further and we see smoke drifting out of the tall cottonwood trees rising up in front of us. When we're in sight of the camp, Camisa Roja rides out to meet us.

He salutes us off the edge of his hat, his quick, brown eyes giving Quent the once-over. "*Buenos días,* Hombrecito. *El General*, he is anxious for your return. He sends me out every morning to look for you."

I give him a little salute in return. "*Buenos días, Capitán!* This is my *amigo, Señor* Quentin Peach*, the *reportero* General Villa asked me to bring. Quent, meet *Capitán* Camisa Roja, a *dorado* for the *generalissimo.*"

Roja, a grin hidden under his mustache, shakes the hand Quent offers him. "*Amigos,* beans, *tortillas,* and coffee are hot and waiting*. Vamos.*"

We ride into camp and give our horses to a man who offers to take the reins.

Magritte, busy at the cooking fire, sees me. She waves and calls in a throaty, lilting voice, "*Hola,* Hombrecito. Sit down, I bring something to eat for you and your *amigo.*"

It warms my heart to see her happy face again.

Roja motions toward Magritte. "*Señores,* eat your fill, I will tell the general you are here." He disappears among Villa's growing collection of wagons. The six wagons here four days earlier have grown to at least twenty, and there are maybe fifty men in the little camp fast becoming large.

Magritte brings us pans of beans, spicy sausage, *tortillas,* and coffee. After the long ride with nothing to eat but coffee and bacon, her breakfast is magnificent. Taking the pan and cup from her, I motion toward Quent. "*Gracias,* Magritte, *muchas gracias.* This is my *amigo, Señor* Quentin Peach."

Quent gives her an easy smile and nods toward her. "With much pleasure, *Señorita* Magritte."

Her eyes shining, she makes a little bow in his direction and turns to me. "Muchacho Amarillo speaks with *El General.* Eat, *señores.* Soon you see them."

Camisa Roja returns. His eyes are hard and narrow and anger is written in the scowl across his brow. "The general speaks with you soon, *amigos.* He has business that cannot wait. *Por favor,* eat!"

I nod and put the heavy crockery cup to my lips. A pistol shot booms, echoing against the canyon walls. Only years of discipline and training to be steady against the unexpected keep me from sloshing coffee all over my face and shirt. Quent jerks like he's just been snake bit but manages not to spill his breakfast, lucky his cup is sitting on the ground. No one else in camp, even the animals, pays any attention to the shot.

Camisa Roja looks over his shoulder, then back at us, and shrugs. "The general does not tolerate cowards and liars or *hombres* who try to cheat the *Revolución, señores.* He will see you now, after you finish your beans."

12. THE INTERVIEW

I hurry to finish my breakfast. Quent takes his time. Camisa Roja crosses his arms and stands with his back to the fire, warming against the morning chill. He keeps shifting his eyes toward Quent and frowning as if to hurry him along, anxious to take the guests to the general. I'm ashamed to admit, as childish as it sounds, I enjoy watching Quent make Roja squirm. Past wanting to kill Roja, thoughts of poetic revenge still cross my mind. I finish eating and give my pan and cup to Magritte. Quent leisurely finishes, stands and stretches, and motions with a flick of his hand for Camisa Roja to lead on.

Villa sits by a fire in a simple straight-backed chair, the back of his open hand beating the air as he emphasizes his points. He's speaking to Yellow Boy, who sits on the ground, leaning against a log and smoking one of his black cigars. About seventy-five yards further down the canyon are several mounds of fresh dirt. An old man, dirty, in sweat-soaked rags, is busy with a shovel digging a grave. A body, a man in a suit, is stretched out just beyond it.

Villa looks up when he hears our footsteps, his big black mustache curving into a smile under dancing eyes. "*Buenos días, señores! Muchas gracias,* Hombrecito, for bringing *mi amigo,* Queentin Peach, to my camp. *Muchas, muchas gracias* for coming, Queentin."

Quent, perfectly at ease like a stretching cat, shakes hands with Villa and Yellow Boy. "Quentin Peach, señor, my friends call me Quent. Doctor Grace has told me much about Muchacho Amarillo. It's a great pleasure to meet you."

Yellow Boy nods acknowledging first Quent and then me saying only, "Hombrecito." I learned long ago his squint warns me to be careful as he puffs his cigar.

Villa plays the gracious host for a few minutes, making small talk about our trip, describing how well he thought the trains ran in the United States, and how much he enjoys ice cream and peanut brittle at the Elite Confectionary when he goes to El Paso.

I occasionally glance past Villa's shoulder to watch the old man. He finishes digging, undresses the corpse, and rolls it naked into the shallow grave. Neatly folding the clothes, he sets them and the high-top shoes aside before covering the body. Although Quent pays strict attention to Villa, I'm certain he's noted the old man.

A heavyset woman from the cooking fires appears with a fire-blackened pot of coffee and mugs. Villa motions her to pour us all a cup and waves her away. He takes a slurp, smacks his lips, and leans back in his chair.

"Now, *mi amigos,* let us turn to business very important.

Queentin, we speak many times together during the *Revolución*. The stories you write in *los periódicos* speak true of what I say and do. Unlike most *reporteros*, you tell no lies. You do not...how you say...embellish the truth. You are a *hombre de honor*. I ask you to hear me once more and write in *los periódicos* only what you see with your own eyes and hear with your own ears. I ask also that you tell me with direct words what *Presidente* Wilson thinks of Carranza and of me. Will you do this, *mi amigo?*"

Quent stares at Villa a moment. "*Sí*, of course, general, we will speak the truth, when I return to El Paso, I will write the truth, and *Señor* Slater will print the truth in his *periódico*, the *El Paso Daily Herald*."

He opens the leather satchel he carries by a strap slung over his shoulder, pulls out a notebook, and uncaps the lacquered, forest-green-and-black marbled fountain pen he carries in his shirt pocket.

Villa, staring into Quent's eyes like he's looking right through him, takes another slurp of coffee. Quent doesn't blink returning the stare. Villa nods. "*Bueno*. Ask your questions, for what you will say in *los periódicos*, and then I will ask you mine about *Presidente* Wilson."

Quent rests his notebook on his knee and zips out a short line of characters across the top of the page in an unreadable, at least to me, shorthand.

"General Villa, you, General Zapata, and others are in a civil war with *Señor* Carranza. It's tearing Mexico apart. Tell my readers why you continue to fight this terrible war with such slaughter of your army?"

Villa's face darkens, a black cloud passing across the sun. His brown eyes flashing thunderbolts, he speaks through clenched teeth, his words angry, hitting our ears like hail rattling against a tin bucket. "Carranza is a rich son of a bitch robbing Mexico blind. He and his *hombres* have always slept in warm beds with clean sheets and soft women."

He stabs the air with his index finger to emphasize his point. "They can never be friends of the people who have spent their lives with nothing but suffering! Any chance these *hombres* have to gain an advantage, they will line their pockets and rob the people."

Pounding his fist on his chest, he says, "Against this greed and lies, Zapata, me, Francisco Villa, and others will die and spill rivers of blood rather than give any of Mexico to these vultures who tear at our people's guts."

The thundering, angry storm passing as quickly as it forms, he pauses for a moment, shakes his head, and looks at us with sad eyes. "After the *Revolución*, I was the one who brought the order and made the government work again for the people."

He slaps his chest with an open palm. "It was I, not Carranza, who did this, even though he says differently. *Mi* soldiers, *mi hombres*, they won the big battles of the *Revolución*, they suffered the most, these men and women, from Chihuahua and Durango, they made the greatest sacrifices. They spilled the most blood for the *Revolución*. Carranza he steals the *Revolución* from them and gives them nothing; only to his army from the other states does he give anything. In secret, he gives our lands back to the *hacendados*, the stinking, wealthy families we threw off their stolen ranchos during the *Revolución*. This is not right, *señores*. It is not justice. It cannot be allowed to stand. We will fight until Carranza and Obregón are no more and the suffering of the people ends."

Quent writes faster than anyone I've ever seen and finishes within a minute after Villa stops to take a swallow of his coffee. He reads back what he has recorded to Villa and asks him if it is an accurate record of what he had said. Villa nods. "*Sí*, Queentin, it is so."

Quent writes another line, beginning a second page in his notes, saying, "General, it appeared to the world that you were winning your war with Carranza until the battles in *Celaya, León,* and *Aguascalientes*. Your army, *División del Norte*, suffered huge losses in those battles. You never lost during the *Revolución*. What happened?"

Villa sits back in his chair, crossing his arms. His teeth are clenched, the muscles in his jaws flexing, his eyes flamed with grief and outrage. He shakes his head as he stares above our heads at the light blue sky turning mid-morning bright. When he faces us again, his is the saddest face I can remember.

"Queentin, in early April, I gather *División del Norte* at Salamancha. I speak to them before we march. I say, '*Muchachos!* Before it gets dark…we will burst into Celaya in blood and fire!'"

Villa clinches his fists and shakes them just above his chest. "In the *Revolución*, my army was invincible! My cavalry was bold, ferocious. Our enemies were wiped out or ran for their lives when they felt the ground tremble from the thunder of our horses' hooves, heard the whistles of my trains, felt death, sent from my cannons, fall from the sky, or died from bullets shot from tens of thousands of rifles and *pistolas*. I, their commander, never picked places to do battle. I always knew how to use my *muchachos* to the best advantage anytime, anywhere. I had only one strategy:

attack, attack, attack, enclose and overwhelm the enemy, never look back, never hold anything back during the attack. Across Mexico, I was everywhere and nowhere. My trains carrying our horses and artillery, my *muchachos* and *muchachas* riding on the top of the cars, appeared in battles where Díaz's generals thought we could never be. As you say, we never lost. I loved my *muchachos* and *muchachas* and they loved me. I was never wounded. I was invincible.

"Angeles told me we ought to take Veracruz after the *Americanos* left. He says we must wipe out Obregón, Carranza's little general, while I have the chance." He taps his temple with a forefinger. "Angeles, he has *mucho* light in his head. He is right, I know. But I have the understanding with Zapata. He fights in the south, I fight in the north. Veracruz belongs to Zapata. He does not take Veracruz and Obregón escapes with weapons Huerta, who you know Carranza murdered, bought and the *Americanos* held when they took Veracruz. Bullets, rifles, machine guns, trucks, uniforms, artillery and, and…miles of the damned barbed wire. *El Perfumado*, the perfumed one, the dandy, Obregón, he got all the equipment because Zapata did not take Veracruz."

Quent stares at him. "General, the reports are that Obregón effectively used that equipment and the land around Celaya to slaughter your army. Didn't you know he had it?"

"*Sí*, I knew." He says grinning with pride, "*Mi* spies, they tell me this."

Quent frowns, the crow's feet around his eyes deep. "Then why didn't you wait until you had an advantage rather than ordering your cavalry and infantry to charge men in trenches protected with barbed wire, and using machine guns, rifles, and artillery pieces? Why did you waste your army like that? With all due respect, sir, I don't understand."

Villa, again clenching his teeth, his jaw muscles rippling, stares at Quent for a long moment before sitting back with a sigh, shaking his head.

"I didn't care that Obregón had the weapons. *Mi muchachos*, they face bigger Díaz armies with the same weapons. We never lose. We are invincible. I always attacked. I always won. *Hombres* joined *División del Norte* because we always won. In Celaya Obregón squatted in the dirt like a whore waiting for business, like a spider for my heel to crush. I had to... how you say, *'pergarle al perfumado'*... whack the perfumed one. I had to kick the whore out of the way, crush the spider, or soon my *División del Norte* is no more, the *muchachos* they leave if they think I fear Obregón."

Yellow Boy's jaws clamp down on his disappearing cigar as he studies Villa through narrow, discriminating eyes. I know what he thinks. Villa played the fool at Celaya. Pride mixed with narrow military vision is a lethal cocktail. One good swallow and it can wipe out an army. The man before our eyes is no longer the smart, pragmatic bandit with whom we rode before the *Revolución*. I feel disappointment's nausea creeping into my soul.

Nodding as he writes, Quent completes his notes and sits back in his chair. "General, I've talked to some of my reporter friends who saw the two battles at Celaya and the ones after at León and Aguascalientes. They say you lost between a third and a half of *División del Norte* in the fighting. Will you be able to face Obregón in Sonora now with an army much smaller than you had in Celaya and León, an army that can't have much spirit left after losing so badly so often? My American Army friends in El Paso say the border is filled with deserters from your army."

Villa squints at Quent, his eyes narrow slashes. He slowly nods. "*Sí*, Queentin, *División del Norte* sank very low. Those *hombres* were not what they used to be. They ran then if you shook a bell. They ran for Chihuahua, up the train tracks on anything that moved – their feet, horses, mules – all of them, *hombres,* women, boys, girls, all running. It made me sick. I wanted to puke. All those I took care of and loved, they ran. It was a bitter, bitter brew I swallowed then, Queentin."

Quent scratches at his three-day beard and then crosses his arms. "So, what is your strategy now, general?"

Villa smiles and swings his arm toward the west in an expansive gesture. "We go over the Sierra Madre to Sonora. Carranza has no armies there, just a few undermanned outposts. There we rest and rebuild *División del Norte*. Agua Prieta is across the border from Douglas, Arizona. Not many Carrancistas are there. No trenches, no machineguns, no barbed wire. We run them out with one good charge by my cavalry. We rest. We rearm using guns and bullets we take from those who oppose us and with the good weapons we buy across the border from the *Americanos*. We move south, a gathering storm of fire and blood all the way to Mexico City that overcomes Carranza and *El Perfumado*. Now I have the questions I must ask you Queentin."

Holding up his left hand, palm out, Quent asks for a pause while he finishes his notes. He again reads them back to Villa for accuracy and says, "Just one more question, general?"

"*Sí?*"

"Who are in those graves down the canyon there?"

Holding up his hands, Villa shrugs.

"Disloyal cowards. Generals who did not want to go to Sonora. They say there must be an end to this war with

Carranza, and they want the lands promised them. Before they have the land, they must obey their general. They swear they will follow my orders when they become generals. They cannot leave their suffering men now. Cowards! I shoot them myself. The last *hombre*, I am sorry you see his burial, *mi amigos*. He has a store in Douglas. He tries to cheat me. He takes my *dinero* for two times what the *Americanos* pay for guns and brings me only half of what he says are there. Does he think I am a fool? Does he think I cannot count? He is the fool. He found the wrong end of my *pistola*, not the *dinero* he tried to steal from me. Now I have his rifles and his *dinero*."

I know Villa will not tolerate cheats and fools or the appearance of disloyalty from his men, even if obeying his orders means they are committing suicide. Still, I'm stunned. He is so casual about executing those close to him. I know discipline has to be maintained, but at what cost? Had I been in his boots, might I have executed those men? Or if I were one of his generals and saw that he was senselessly slaughtering my men would I keep my oath? God help the man who crosses him. God help Sam Ravel. Quent puts away his pen. Yellow Boy, his teeth still clamped on his cigar, glances at me.

I think *Maybe Villa is a little crazy. Maybe you have to be a little crazy to fight on when the odds are stacked against you. But as a doctor I know lots of lives are saved against the odds. We all tell ourselves little lies to get through the day because sometimes we get lucky, and sometimes fortune turns. Life is filled with tosses of the dice. Villa just wants another throw, another chance to make things right in Mexico. I can understand that even if Yellow Boy and Quent don't.*

13. JUST CAUSE

Closing his notebook and crossing his arms, Quent says, "Your questions, general?"

Villa leans back in his chair, and stares off down the canyon. "Queentin, since the *Revolución* started, I have been a friend of the *Americanos*. After my army took *ranchos,* mines, and factories from the wealthy *Americanos* in Mexico, *ranchos,* mines, and factories Díaz gave them, *ranchos,* mines, and factories rightfully belonging to the people. General Scott, he asks me to be a friend to the *Americanos* and give these things back. It cost me millions of pesos to give them back. It is *dinero* I can use to buy weapons and bullets, but I want the friendship of the *Americanos* more than the *dinero.* I gave the *ranchos,* mines, and factories back to the *Americanos* and other foreigners. When General Funston takes Veracruz, the *Americanos* ask if I will fight them over this. I say, *No, Americanos are my amigos. Take Veracruz, it is nothing to me.*

"Carranza, he lets his army raid *Americano ranchos* and towns across the *Rio Grande* from Brownsville to El Paso. It is so bad, the *Americano* Army puts *hombres* in *mucho* places along the border to stop this. Carranza he takes prisoner *Americano* Navy officers and then releases them. He opens fire on the *Americano* ship, *Annapolis*. He declares war on the *Americanos*, and then says there is no war, claiming it is all just a big misunderstanding. Carranza, he does not reply to *Americano* diplomats who represent *Presidente* Wilson. Without cause, this *hombre* Carranza, he takes from the people and foreigners their property. He takes their *haciendas*, their horses, their money, and their crops, even their furniture. Anything of value, he takes. He tries to make the people in Mexico City leave. He withholds food and water from them to make them go. He sends defenseless women to Veracruz locked in cattle cars. He closes courts and schools. He sacks churches and holds priests for ransom. He kills men and violates women for no cause. He tortures and rapes Mexico and he shows to the *Americanos nada, nada* but bad faith, insincerity, and hostility. I, Francisco Villa, *amigo* to the *Americanos*, I never do these things."

As Villa speaks, I feel the justice of his cause, feel his outrage and my own at Carranza, and hear a voice in my head say: *This is not right. This cannot be allowed to stand. Carranza must be stopped. Wilson has to recognize Villa as the President of Mexico.*

Villa leans forward and rests his elbow on a knee. He looks first at Yellow Boy, then me, and then holds his gaze on Quent. He speaks again, his eyes flashing fire. "Now, I learn from my *amigos* across the border that *Presidente* Wilson will say Carranza is the true *Presidente* of Mexico, and not Francisco Villa, Zapata, or some other true hero of the *Revolución*. I learn *Presidente* Wilson says no more guns and bullets for Villa. Is this so, Queentin?"

Quent, pursing his lips, slowly nods. "*Sí*, general, it is so. General Scott, your *amigo*, the Commander of the Army in the United States, told me he heard rumors President Wilson planned to do these things and begged him to reconsider. He said diplomats in Washington only last month advised the President not to do this thing. A day or two before Doctor Grace found me in El Paso I learned from a source who has never been wrong that Wilson will recognize Carranza as the true President of Mexico."

Villa stares at Quent and says nothing. His big right hand curls into a fist that he slams into his thigh several times while staring at the cliffs behind us. His words come with no emotion, a cold monotone. "So… this is how *Presidente* Wilson repays me for doing what the *Americanos* ask of me? This is *Americano* friendship? You tell him, Queentin, you tell him that now I don't give a damn what happens to foreigners in Mexico or my territory. I can whip Carranza and Obregón and all their armies. It is asking much to whip the United States also, but maybe I will have to do that too!"

Quent opens his notebook and begins writing. Villa, his face in a hard, determined squint, watches the smooth, elegant script fill a page. Yellow Boy and I look at each other. Yellow Boy looks at the cliffs and almost imperceptibly shakes his head. My heart is in free fall. Villa is losing his mind when he most needs to think clearly. He's no match for the United States Army. He has no chance to win his war with Carranza backed by the United States. The best thing is for him to disappear into the Sierra Madre. From far away

I hear a voice, "Hombrecito... Hombrecito?" Villa calls me back to the moment.

"*Sí*, general?"

He studies me for a moment to be certain of my attention. "Did you find *Señor* Sam Ravel in Columbus? What does he say?"

After seeing a dishonest Douglas merchant's body rolled into a grave not seventy-five yards from where we sit, I hesitate, but the die is cast. Ravel gave me his message and Villa wants to hear it.

"General, I spoke with Sam Ravel twice in two days. At first he said no deal and that he was keeping your money for a past debt, one owed him by General Figuroa. The second time I saw him, he says he can get the rifles and bullets past the embargo and delivered wherever you say, but you must pay him General Figuroa's previous debt of $771.25, you must give him an extra $1000 for him to get past the embargo, and you must pay in gold, not in the script you print."

Villa, his mouth open, stares at me as though he doesn't understand. When I start to repeat myself, he holds up a hand and shakes his head, his voice a whisper, his brown eyes filled with fire and lightning.

"*Señor* Sam Ravel will cheat Francisco Villa no more. I will drag that son-of-a-bitch screaming through the cactus and mesquite. Like the Apaches I will put fire on his cajones. *Mi dorados* will ride their horses over him until there is nothing left in the sand but blood and bone. This thing I swear."

He stares off down the canyon, saying no more. I see an artery pulsing near the hairline at his temple, his fingers curling again into fists before relaxing. No one says anything. I look at Yellow Boy. He sits with his arms crossed, the Henry rifle across his knees, eyes glittering, hearing the silent call to war, the call to avenge a wronged friend. Quent slowly shakes his head. He knows Villa means every word and expects him to do exactly what he says. I hope Villa catches Ravel when no innocent bystanders are around. If the *dorados* are filled with blood lust, innocent lives won't be worth a whorehouse penny in church.

We sit there, saying nothing, making few moves for maybe ten minutes, waiting for Villa to bank the fires of his rage. When he returns he's like a man coming out of a trance. He looks at Quent and says in a mellow tone. "Queentin, I ask another favor of you."

"*Sí*, general?"

"In maybe three weeks the *División del Norte* will be ready to sweep the Carrancistas out of Agua Prieta." He chops the air for emphasis. "*El Presidente Wilson* needs to understand that Carranza has not finished me and that I will rid Mexico of this tyrant. A great victory in Agua Prieta for *Presidente* Wilson, this will help open his eyes. I ask that he see this victory through your eyes, Queentin. Come with *División del Norte* and write what you see at the battle at Agua Prieta."

Quent doesn't hesitate. He looks him straight in the eye and shakes his head. "No, general, I can't come with you to Agua Prieta."

Villa's relaxed fingers slowly curl into a fist. "Why not? You—"

Quent holds up his hand, fingers spread to stop Villa's retort. "General, I have a loving wife and two young sons in

El Paso who depend on me. I can't risk their lives by risking mine for this adventure as much as I'd like to travel with you. However, in a day's time, I can take a train from El Paso to Douglas. Have someone send me a telegram when the *División del Norte* is two days away from Agua Prieta and I'll come. When I see your army, I'll cross the border and interview you and write what happens as seen from your side during your attack. You'll have your story and my wife and sons won't have to risk losing me in the wilds of the Sierra Madre. Can you accept that?"

A grin spreads into his cheeks. "*Sí*, Queentin, you and Angeles have the light of the sun in your heads. *Muy bien.* You will have your telegram at the proper time. You will hear my testimony and you will see *División del Norte* in battle. I ask only you write the truth of what you see."

"*Sí*, general, you know I write the truth."

Villa is still smiling when they shake hands.

I look in Yellow Boy's eyes. He gives me a quick little head bob, saying *yes* to what he knows I'm thinking. I turn to Villa.

"General, Muchacho Amarillo and I will follow you to Agua Prieta and do everything we can to help your cause, I as a doctor with a rifle, and Muchacho Amarillo as a warrior."

With great gravitas, Villa stares at us.

"*Muchachos*, there is much you will suffer if you ride with me. I can not ask you to make this great gesture, but I am very honored that you offer to fight the dictator with me."

I look directly into Villa's brown eyes.

"General, you once knew us as Apaches. We know what it is to sleep on the cold ground, suffer hunger, thirst, ice-filled winds, and the sun's fire in the desert and snow in the mountains. We know what it is to suffer the wounds of battle, but we have never feared our enemies or the coming day, no matter where we were. Your enemy is our enemy. Your cause is our cause. Your war is our war. We'll fight beside you until your enemy is no more."

Villa's face is solemn and earnest as he straightens himself to his full height, salutes us smartly, and shakes our hands. "*Gracious, muchachos.* I am proud to be your general. With men such as you, we will win a new *Revolución* against Carranza and Obregón."

14. A MATTER OF SURVIVAL

Magritte brings the fire-blackened pot and pours another round of coffee. Still grinning after Yellow Boy and I offer to join him in the fight for Agua Prieta, Villa raises his mug and says, "*Amigos*, I salute you. Mexico thanks you and in the years to come will remember your great contribution to the *Revolución*."

We raise our mugs to his, and clinking them together, take a long swallow of the strong, bitter but flavorful coffee, which somehow seems appropriate to the occasion. We talk for a while about the old days, of battles won and friends lost until Magritte appears and whispers in Villa's ear. He frowns and nods, waves her away. "Forgive me, *amigos*, but there is business that requires my attention. Get some rest, Queentin. I ask that Yellow Boy and Hombrecito ride with you back to Columbus."

Quent nods. "We know you're very busy, general.

There's no need for these friends to waste their time with me. I'll ride north to Hachita and catch the train there. It's closer than Columbus and even I can find my way north."

Villa shakes his head. "*Sí*, Queentin, Hachita you can find easy. But think, *hombre*. What will *Indios*, *banditos*, or a patrol from Carranza's army do if they find you?" He answers by drawing his finger in a slashing motion across his windpipe. "I cannot afford to lose you now that we are within a month of taking Agua Prieta and you writing about it. Who will tell *Presidente* Wilson of the thunder from *División del Norte* against Carranza's army? Our *amigos*, they will see you safe on the train in Hachita so you return in safety to your wife and *niños*. I trust these *hombres* with my life. You can too. It is much too dangerous to go by yourself. Eh?"

Quent snorts and grins. He knows it's useless to argue.

"*Sí*, general, Hombrecito and Yellow Boy will be good company to Hachita."

Villa nods, "*Bueno,* Queentin."

He turns to Yellow Boy and me. "*Amigos*, tomorrow I leave to catch up with *División del Norte* crossing El Paso Púlpito. You will find me there when you return from escorting Queentin to Hachita. Now, *mi amigos*, I must settle other business before I leave this place." He holds up three fingers. "Muchacho Amarillo and Hombrecito, three or four days at El Paso Púlpito?"

Yellow Boy nods. "*Sí, jefe,* three or four days."

The sun pours its fiery light from straight overhead when we return to the cook fire. Men loading the wagons with new supplies, their ragged shirts soaked in salty sweat, now sit eating in the cottonwood shade with their pans piled over with beans, beef stew, and *tortillas*. We join them, our mouths watering at the warm, savory smells coming from the cook pots, and we all go back for refills.

Maybe military life won't be so bad after all.

Yellow Boy claims our gear and horses from Magritte, planning to leave late in the afternoon. Quent and I need some naptime before the long night ride. We find a shady spot near the big tank, spread our blankets, and are soon snoring in the warm, clear mountain air.

Shadows are long on the western face of the canyon, the last of the day's light just on the tops of the mountains around the canyon, when Yellow Boy taps our feet with the barrel of his Henry to awaken us. We use the tank overflow to splash water on our faces and wash up to eat.

Magritte again brings us platefuls of fiery beef stew for our supper. While I finish, she sits down next to me, her large, doe-like eyes serious. "Hombrecito, you and Muchacho Amarillo join us?"

"*Sí*, Magritte."

A small coarse woman, her smile always ready to bloom, her spirit joyous, and insanely filled with life in a time and place where disaster is a heartbeat away, I feel drawn to her sweet, feminine earthiness. A smile, like a sunrise in a midsummer dawn, spreads across her face.

"*Magnifico*. After so many dark days the general still finds *amigos* who will fight Carranza with him."

I smile at her exuberance. Yellow Boy and I, only two men, won't make any difference in the fighting strength of the *División del Norte*. She glances around at the shadows falling into the canyon and then speaks in a low whisper meant only for my ears. "Do you need a woman, Hombrecito?"

I nearly drop my plate. She must be psychic. I haven't been with a woman since Rafaela was killed over six years ago. It isn't that I don't desire a woman's company and intimacy, but when other women remind me of Rafaela, the pain I feel drains the life out of me. Since her death I've come to believe I'm cursed. Those I love, die. They always die, violently and before their time.

I know my fumbling with my plate and my face must show my interest and curiosity. Where did she get the idea I wanted a woman? I feel my heart skip a beat. Maybe she wants me before I leave. *Maybe*, I think, *if I just make love to her and leave she won't be threatened by my curse.* Besides, taking Camisa's woman after he's killed mine, that'd be sweet justice. He'd never suffer like I have, but at least he'd taste a tiny bit of the bitterness I've felt.

"Why do you ask? I thought you were Camisa Roja's woman?"

She giggles, her sparkling eyes teasing mine before looking away.

"Hombrecito, I am Camisa Roja's woman. I won't dishonor him. There are many women who have no man, but they help *División del Norte*. Some fight with the guns; some make the camp and cook; some help the doctors. *División del Norte* has *muchas soldaderas* because the *hombres* are here. Some take nearly any man who asks them, others, like me, take only one."

I feel a momentary flash of disappointment as my admiration for her increases.

Oh well, I think, *this dance isn't over*. "How did you know I wasn't married?"

She shrugs and waves her hands.

"It makes a difference? The general, he has more than fifteen wives and he loves them all dearly. You decide if you want a woman, Hombrecito. If you do, I find you one. The general does not let us go to Agua Prieta with the men. The men, they do not like this. The women, they do not like this. But still we do as the general commands. He says the trail is too hard for us; we will die before the fight. He sends us to Casas Grandes to wait until Agua Prieta is taken. Then we come." She smiles and winks. "Maybe a little sooner than later, *sí*?"

I laugh. "*Sí*, maybe a little sooner than later. When I tell you I want a woman, you will find me a good one?"

"Oh, *sí*, a very good woman. You just tell me, I find you one." She gives my forearm a little squeeze, and then leaves us to return to the cooking fire now bright against the warm, golden dusk fading into cold black.

I look over my shoulder at Yellow Boy and Quent. Quent grins.

"It appears to me, you've made a mighty useful and good friend."

Yellow Boy shakes his head as he wipes his pan clean with a *tortilla*.

"Like traders of horses, women know when they find a good one, and they always know a buyer who will pay their price."

We leave before the moon is fully up, the trail toward the border, clear and distinct even in the weak nightglow.

Yellow Boy, his sense of direction gyroscopically perfect, heads northeast, the black outline of the sierras against stars rising to our left, the glow of the moon rising behind the eastern mountains on our right, to our backs the freezing black night of Chihuahua. We ride the horses at about the same mile-eating pace we used coming from Columbus. As I watch the backs of my friends fading into the darkness, I remember what Villa said about Carranza during Quent's interview: "…They can never be friends of the people who have spent their lives with nothing but suffering! … Any chance these *hombres* have to gain an advantage, they will line their pockets and rob the people. This is not right, *señores*. It is not justice. It cannot be allowed to stand. We will fight until Carranza and Obregón are no *mas* and the suffering of the people ends."

I believe I'm lucky to pay Villa my debt and at the same time make righteous war against Carranza, a man the United States ought to fight rather than embrace as an ally.

A half moon, providing enough light to easily avoid cactus and mesquite thorns, floats up above the mountains. We stop for water and to rest the horses at North Tank, a natural depression filled by a seep and rain a few miles north of the border.

Quent groans as he swings down from his roan. "My legs are killing me, not to speak of my crotch. Just not used to such long rides or riding at the clip you boys set."

Yellow Boy raises the edge of his hand to his mouth, signaling for quiet. His Henry rifle in the crook of his left arm, he disappears into the mesquites further up the wash that feeds the tank.

Quent and I loosen saddle and pack cinches and give the

horses a little grain. Hilo Peak, standing tall a couple miles to the southeast, casts long, moonlight black shadows off to our right. The tank water is good and cold, making us shiver and snap our teeth after a drink.

Quent pulls up his jacket collar to brave the chill. I sit next to him wrapped in a blanket, our breath forming little clouds that only partially evaporate before floating way into the darkness. Memories of Quent's interview with Villa swirl back into my consciousness.

"Villa's not winning like he did during the *Revolución* against Díaz, is he?"

Quent crosses his arms and shakes his head. "No, I'm afraid not. He doesn't understand that Obregón has him figured out and has sucker punched him three straight times in big battles. Villa fighting Obregón is like watching Picket's Gettysburg charge over and over by the survivors of the slaughter. Obregón will burn him again if Villa doesn't change his tactics. Another battle or two like the ones they had this summer and no more *División del Norte*, no more army in Chihuahua, no more opposition to Carranza. A tragedy waiting to happen, Villa just can't or refuses to see it. I hate to think what he'll be like after his army is destroyed and who he'll blame. I can tell you for sure, it won't be General Villa."

I feel a chill run up my spine, and it isn't from the cold. "Tell me what actually happened in Celaya. I've heard you mention the slaughter, and Villa talks about Obregón executing his officers and band. Why was Obregón suddenly able to do so much damage to an experienced army led by what the papers called a brilliant general?"

He scratches his chin, shrugs his shoulders and shivers. "Let me get my blanket first, it's cold."

He unrolls his blanket and wraps its over his shoulders before sitting down cross-legged next to me.

"Where's Yellow Boy?"

"He's right up the wash. You can bet anyone stalking us won't see or hear him until it's too late. Come on, tell me what happened at Celaya."

Quent wrinkles his nose and shrugs. "According to reporters I trust who were there, it was awful. When the Americans left Veracruz last year they left a storehouse of supplies that Huerta bought for a big army before he was forced to resign. Villa wouldn't listen to Angeles' advice and he let Obregón get his hands on the equipment, recruit troops from the unions in Veracruz, and get out of a deadly trap. Had he surrounded Obregón's army in Veracruz, their backs to the sea, the only way out past his guns, Villa, not Carranza becomes *Presidente*. But Villa let Obregón take all the equipment and men and get out of Veracruz without a scratch.

"Before Celaya, Obregón took time to train his men and study tactics used in the war overseas. I understand he even had some German advisors who taught him how to fight from trenches, and more importantly, he studied Villa's tactics. Obregón understands Villa's tactics and bullheadedness and can predict with almost mathematical precision what he'll do in a battle.

"As you might guess from listening to the interview, Villa has little respect, even now, for Obregón, a man Villa considers way out of his league as a warrior. Obregón knew what Villa thought of him and that Villa was an impulsive hothead. At Celaya Obregón set his own trap and just sat back waiting, allowing Villa's spies to find him. Obregón knew Villa couldn't resist attacking him, if for no other reason than to show all Mexico and the world who was the clearly superior general."

"Why Celaya? Why did Obregón choose to fight Villa there?"

"It doesn't take a genius to figure that out. Big farming fields with networks of irrigation ditches surround Celaya. It's down in a bowl; mountains surround it on three sides, but are too far away for Villa to pull cannon up their sides and shoot down on men in the trenches. Obregón saw the irrigation trenches as the perfect opportunity to use the same tactics on Villa as those being used in the war in Europe. He built machinegun nests for covering fire up and down the trenches, laid down barbed wire in front of the trenches, and positioned his artillery for maximum slaughter when Villa made one of his famous cavalry charges."

I shudder as I imagine that deadly field of fire. "How many soldiers did Obregón have?"

"Ummm, maybe six thousand cavalry and five thousand infantry. Villa probably had twice that many in *División del Norte*. On the sixth of April, Obregón sent out an advance guard of about 1200 men down the train tracks out of Celaya to look for Villa. Villa's troops caught them out in the open and began cutting them to pieces as they tried to retreat back to Celaya. Realizing his error, one of very few in the summer battles, Obregón jumped on an armored train, drove it out and saved most of them.

"After that first little encounter, Villa didn't doubt he'd crush Obregón at Celaya. Angeles still tried to talk Villa out of attacking Obregón hunkered down in those trenches with machine guns behind barbed wire, but the general wouldn't have any of it. It was a matter of pride. You heard him in the interview. He had to 'whack the dandy' to keep the recruits coming and to hell with the cost.

"The morning of the seventh of April, Villa had his first wave of cavalry make a line three miles long, facing Obregón's trenches. All day long, again and again, forty times, they charged those machine guns and artillery and were slaughtered. They were being told to ride into a rain of lead and steel. It was suicide. They knew it was suicide, but they went anyway, over and over again.

"Villa had his artillery pounding away at the trenches and they were pretty accurate. The problem was his shells, made in Chihuahua, weren't worth a damn. A lot of them didn't explode. He might as well have been throwing big rocks for all the good his artillery did.

"As the sun went down Villa stopped the charges and pulled his men back to rest and recover. Obregón kept his artillery pounding them all night. The next day was even bloodier. Obregón hid Yaqui sharpshooters in dugouts all around the trenches and flooded the fields with drainage ditch water where Villa's cavalry charged. The Yaquis picked off cavalry and infantry while the horses floundered in the mud and water. Obregón's own cavalry charged Villa's from both ends of their line just when it looked like they might actually break through the center of Obregón's lines. Devastating. Villa's right side broke, then the center, and finally the left. He rode into the middle of it with his *dorados* and drove Obregón's cavalry back so his men could retreat and save their artillery pieces."

My mind's eye picture of the slaughter makes me nauseous. "Then, did he retreat and pull back from Celaya?"

Quent shivers and says through clenched his teeth, "Nope. There was a week's standoff while Villa and Carranza waged a little propaganda war in the Mexican newspapers. Retired soldiers and new recruits for both sides started pouring in. By the thirteenth of April, Obregón had about fifteen thousand men, and Villa maybe twenty thousand. The second battle started on the morning of the thirteenth and went into the night, when there was heavy rain. This battle was a lot like the first one, except this time, on the second day, Obregón's cavalry caught Villa's infantry on both sides of a charge that was about to break through his lines. When Obregón's cavalry hit Villa's infantry, they threw down their weapons and ran, leaving artillery pieces, comrades, everything. Villa had to retreat.

"Villa had about three thousand killed and six thousand taken prisoner at Celaya, and God only knows how many wounded. In addition to the *soldados*, he lost about a thousand horses, five thousand rifles, and thirty-two artillery pieces. On top of that, Obregón executed a hundred and twenty of Villa's captured officers. It was an unmitigated disaster."

I try to whistle, but can't pucker. "You said Angeles advised him not to attack Obregón like that. Why? Why didn't he listen?"

"I don't know, except to say that maybe the old Bible proverb, *Pride goes before a fall*, has it about right. Now I want to ask you a question, if it's not too personal."

"I'll tell you if it's too personal. What's on your mind?"

"Today I heard you attach yourself and Yellow Boy to a man who, because of his pride, led thousands of his men to slaughter in horse charges against trenches, barbed wire, machine guns, and artillery. I was shocked to hear you say you and Yellow Boy wanted to join *División del Norte* and so was Villa. He doesn't expect you to come back after you take me to Hachita. Are you and Yellow Boy going to just keep riding when you reach Hachita? You surely don't want to waste your life for a mad man crazy with pride…do you?"

I stare at Quent and slowly shake my head. "You don't understand how I was raised. To answer your question, in a word, yes. I'd waste my life, and know I was wasting it, because I gave Villa my word that I'd fight for him. Maybe I'm a fool, an ignorant fool, for offering to fight with him, but when I… we, Yellow Boy and me, give our word, we stick by it come the fires of Hell or sinking sand. If a man doesn't keep his word, no one or group can depend on him."

"So you'd die for a fool's pride just because you gave him your word?"

"Yes."

"You're right I don't understand how you were raised, but I do understand the importance of keeping your word. Out here it's a matter of survival."

15. PANCHO VILLA RETURNS TO MEXICO

Yellow Boy emerges from the shadows, and jerks his head toward the wash. Time to go. We tighten cinches, let the horses drink once more, and then ride up the wash toward the top of a low pass where we can see, maybe twenty miles away, the Hatchet Mountains wrapped in moonlight shadows their dark outline framed by the stars on the distance horizon.

Down in the flats, tall gra'ma grass and water still stand in a few pools along the major washes. Yellow Boy heads straight for Big Hatchet Peak. An easy ride, dry summer grass and a few desert bushes cover the land, flat in all directions except for an occasional dip into a brush-lined *arroyo*.

A faint smudge of gray brightens the eastern sky as Yellow Boy leads us toward a wash at the entrance to a canyon in the shadows of Zellar Peak on the northern end of the Big Hatchets. We initially stop at a water tank made from galvanized sheets of iron and filled by a dilapidated, creaking windmill out in the flats not more than a mile away from the canyon entrance. Fresh tracks mixed in with those several days old show riders use the tank often. After watering the horses and filling our canteens, we disappear into the canyon and make a dry camp. After rubbing down the animals with handfuls of grass, Quent and I build a small fire, boil coffee, and heat the pot of stew and *tortillas* Magritte sent with us. I take the first watch.

Early morning shadows are growing short when a cavalry patrol comes down the trail around the mountains at a fast trot with scouts out a quarter mile on either side of the column. The lead scout reminds me of a bloodhound sniffing a trail, sauntering back and forth looking for fresh signs. He leads the column to the tank where the troopers water their animals, smoke, rest a while and then reset their cinches before riding for the gray, hazy mountains to the southwest. I breathe a sigh of relief as the dust from their column fades into the bright morning air.

The trooper's dust barely settles before a short string of pack mules, led by a couple of women, come down the trail from the north. Their timing says they must have waited for the patrol to pass. I study them with my old field glasses while their animals drink and they take turns finding a relief bush. Their faces brown as the country through which they ride, they wear simple shirts, skirts, and big brimmed hats; they carry lever action rifles. *Soldaderas*. I make out the shapes of small covered boxes on the mule pack frames just the right size for carrying ammunition, a most valuable cargo for General Villa.

The rest of the day passes with no signs of anyone else.

Back on the trail at dusk, Yellow Boy leads us around the northern end of the Big Hatchet Mountains. Most of the night's ride, we stay near a dry river where small pools of water still linger, and occasionally, see lights twinkling on the northern black horizon. Hachita.

We ride up to the Hachita train station a little after the moon begins its downward arc, probably an hour or so after midnight. Not a soul stirs. Quent dismounts. Stepping up on the platform, he takes the chalkboard schedule hanging beside the ticket window to a bright patch of moonlight and reads it before returning it to its place in the shadows. He returns to us grinning.

"We're lucky on our timing, boys. There's a train due in here about 2:45. I ought to be in El Paso by 6:00. I thank you for accompanying me this far. Rest a little while, and then take off. I'll be fine."

Yellow Boy stares at him and I shake my head.

"No, I don't think so, Quent. We promised the general we'd see you on the train and that's what we'll do."

He shrugs his shoulders.

"Okay. Suit yourselves."

Dismounting, we lead the horses to a nearby water trough, and loosen their cinches. While the animals drink, I say to Quent, "I'll keep the roan for you and use it as a pack animal until you need it in Douglas."

"Thanks, Henry. That'll save the paper a little money."

Yellow Boy leads the horses away from the station to a mesquite thicket down the tracks from the platform and, out of sight, gives them some grain.

Dangling our legs off the platform edge, Quent and I wait for the train. The story he told me at North Tank about the battles in Celaya generates all kinds of questions that buzz in my mind like angry bees.

"Quent, how did you come to know Villa?"

Scratching his scruffy beard, he smiles.

"I was covering the *Revolución* for the *Herald* and briefly met him while I was with a group of reporters riding around the countryside on his trains carrying his army to battles. I wanted to learn how a bandit managed to become a charismatic general who was pounding the stuffing out of a professionally trained federal army. When I became vaguely familiar to him, he gave me permission to interview several of his generals and I wrote stories describing some of their most successful battles. Several pieces were picked up and carried in the big national papers. After Díaz took off, I figured the war was over and didn't waste any time returning to El Paso to reclaim my wife and two little boys, who I hadn't seen in months."

I shake my head.

"You and Villa seem a lot more friendly than just casual war acquaintances."

Quent grins and nods and crosses his arms against the cold night.

"Oh, as you correctly guess, there's a lot more to it. I guess you want it all."

I grin and Quent grimaces.

"It's a long story…"

"We've got plenty of time."

"Yeah, I guess we do if you're staying until the train comes. It was like this. After Madero came to power, Villa settled in Chihuahua City, owning, if my memory serves me right, four or five butcher shops. Madero's government was slow and inept, and pretty soon the *peons* began local revolts against the government they'd fought to install. Madero asked Villa to help his government's commanding general, Huerta, put down the revolts. Villa recalled his troops and put himself and men under Huerta's command. Problem was, Huerta was contemptuous of Villa as a general, and Villa claimed Huerta was just a little drunkard.

"One morning Villa was having one of his bouts of raging fever, I believe he has malaria, when a messenger showed up and said he was needed at Huerta's headquarters. He gets off his sick bed and goes. When he shows up, he's arrested, accused of stealing a horse, and marched out to be shot. Men in the firing squad are loading their rifles when a messenger appears with a firing squad cancelation order from Madero and orders that Villa be sent to prison.

"Villa was in prison for months, and that's when he learned to read well and passably write. He began writing long letters to Madero begging him for help. Six weeks before Madero was assassinated, Villa escaped."

"How did he do that? Somebody slip him a gun?"

Quent, shaking his head, leans back on his hands and grins.

"No, it's better than that. He told me he walked out through the front gate disguised as a lawyer. He had on a long black coat, dark glasses, and held a handkerchief in front of his face like the smell of the place was bad. He got through to Juarez, crossed the border into El Paso, and stayed under the name Doroteo Arango at a seedy place exiles used called the Hotel Roma.

"I ran into him one day in 1913 at the Elite Confectionary. Sitting there big as you please in a bowler hat, eating ice cream and drinking a strawberry soda pop, I didn't recognize him at first, but, of all people, he remembered me. He jumps up out of the chair and shakes my hand, grinning and talking like I was a long lost brother. We must have talked for a couple of hours.

"I visited him at the Hotel Roma a couple of times and interviewed him once at the Emporium, a Greek bar popular for men who left Mexico to escape one firing squad or the other. Even then, he kept his ear to the ground on what was going on in Mexico. In his hotel room, he kept a cage full of pigeons that maintained his connection with someone in Ciudad Chihuahua. He never did tell me who sent the birds. I had to laugh when he told nosey neighbors he had a very delicate stomach condition and had to eat squab.

"When he learned Huerta had assassinated Madero, he sent word and asked me to meet him at the Elite Confectionary for a bowl of ice cream. He roared up on his motorcycle just before I arrived and he waited for me at the door. His face looked like thunderclouds rolling off the Franklins and there was lightning in his eyes like you saw yesterday. He shook my hand, but said nothing. We went inside and he bought us each a bowl of ice cream. We sat in a corner and ate a few spoonsful before he spoke.

'Queentin, you hear that no-good, murdering bastard Huerta has killed Madero?'

'*Sí*, Pancho, I've heard that assassins killed Madero and that Huerta has taken power. I didn't know he was behind Madero's murder, but suspected as much.'

'Oh yes, Queentin, Huerta ordered this disgusting thing, this a little bird told me, I do not doubt it is true. When I return to Mexico, I castrate Huerta myself before I order him dragged to death. He is not worthy of a firing squad. This I promise you, I will bring down Huerta!'

"I nodded. 'I don't doubt that you will.'

"He put down his spoon and looked me in the eye. 'Queentin, will you lend me three hundred *Americano* dollars?'

"Three hundred dollars! That's a lot of money in any man's bank account, but I had it and wanted to give it to him even though I didn't think I'd ever see it again.

"I shook my head. 'No, *señor,* I won't lend you three hundred dollars.'

"He bowed his head and nodded. '*Si, comprendo, amigo.* It is *mucho dinero* I ask, I know.'

"I didn't have the heart to tease him and said, 'Pancho, I won't lend you three hundred dollars, I'll give it to you.'

"His head jerked up, his eyes wide and smile big. '*Hombre! Muchas gracias, muchas, muchas gracias.* I thank you and the *Revolución* thanks you!'

'I suspect I know, but why do you need the *dinero*?'

'With the *dinero* I have already and this *dinero* from you, I will be able to buy horses, rifles, and bullets for me and my *amigos* before we return to Mexico to end the reign of Madero's murderer.'

'Three hundred dollars won't buy many horses and rifles. How many of you are returning to Mexico?'

"He looked at me with somber eyes above a smile fixed in place as though it had been chiseled out of granite. 'There are eight *amigos* and myself. Nine *hombres*. Nine is enough to bring down the murderer, eh?'

"I smiled and shook my head while we finished our ice cream. On 6 March 1913, I waved good-by as I watched him and eight men ride their horses across the river and disappear in the dust on the other side. By September, he had an army of six to eight thousand men and was kicking hell out Huerta's army. By November of that year, in less than eight months, a man who had never been to school and who learned to read in prison, controlled the state of Chihuahua and was rebuilding it. I figured the dollars I gave him were well spent."

Sitting there in the cold night air, I marvel at Quent's story, but I understand full well how Villa had gathered a big army so fast. He recruited Yellow Boy and me, and he never asked us to join the fight.

16. RUNS FAR AND HIS WOMEN

We don't sit on the platform long before an old gentleman wearing an engineer's hat and jacket, and carrying a lighted coal oil lamp, comes ambling down the street. When he sees us, he pauses for a heart beat as if slapped by the cold hand of suspicion that men who unexpectedly appear late in the night are up to no good. Giving us the once-over and looking around to see if there are others with Quent and me, he continues on down the dusty road toward us. Off in the distance, we hear a train's faint rumble and see a flickering light far out in the mesquite.

Raising his lantern to get a good look at our faces, the old man says, "Howdy, boys! Yuh expectin' somebody on the train? Kinda early fer travelin' ain't it?"

Quent nods to him and says in his best reassuring southern drawl, "Mornin'. Yes, sir, it's early, and I need a ticket to El Paso."

Up close, the old boy looks kind of comical, white hair sticking out from under his hat like straw under a barn door, missing a couple of front teeth, and air from his big bulbous nose whistles through a bushy mustache that looks tilted because the left side is longer than the other. "Well, son, you come to the right place. Come on inside, and I'll fix you up."

Quent and I shake hands on the platform and look each other in the eye in the light from the passenger car windows before he steps aboard.

He looks tired and sad when he says, "Henry thanks for all your help. Be careful in those mountains. I just hope Villa doesn't get you killed or kills you. Send a telegram to the *Herald* a couple of days before you want me at Agua Prieta. I'll be there before you."

"Thanks, Quent. I appreciate you coming so far to see Villa and all the background you've given me. Give my best to your beautiful bride and those two fine boys, and call me any time I can help you. *Adiós.*"

Quent's smile says it all. "*Adiós, amigo.*"

In five minutes the light on the train's caboose is disappearing into the night and the old man with the lantern is smartly stepping back to his house in Hachita. Yellow Boy and I tighten cinches and head back toward the Big Hatchet Mountains. Taking a little different route than the one we'd used to approach Hachita, and stopping to rest the horses only once, we're back at the previous day's camping spot as the sun drives away the dawn.

My mind, in turmoil, flickers from one thought to the next. I'm not sleepy and tell Yellow Boy that I'll take the first watch. He finds a shady place under a rock shelf, and after sweeping a yucca stalk under it to ensure no rattlesnakes have already claimed it, is soon in a deep sleep. I find the sentry spot he used the night before and settle down to think through all the things I've heard in the last three or four days.

Nothing moves all morning except for coveys of Gambrel's quail scratching around in the dust and a coyote that slinks out of the bushes along a wash as he heads for a long drink at the water tank. The day's shadows have nearly disappeared, the sun directly overhead, when I glance over to the shelf where Yellow Boy naps. He's gone. I'm surprised and laugh when he appears out of thin air and squeezes my shoulder.

"Uncle. You're quieter than Coyote. No one comes."

He sits down beside me and purses his lips. "Uhmmph. This I know. Get some rest my, son."

I give him my canteen and crawl up under his shelf for my nap.

It's late in the afternoon when he taps my foot with the barrel of his Henry. Seeing my eyes pop open, he puts his fingers edge-wise in front of his mouth to signal for quiet. I nod. He holds his hand to his ear and jerks his head toward the tank. The sounds of horses moving and men's voices are in the distance. I crab over to my gear and pull Little David out of its saddle scabbard. Edging down the wash, we crawl up on some boulders and peep over the edge to see the *llano* spread out below us.

A cavalry patrol, making camp at the tank, gathers brush for a fire, erects several small tents, and works on their horses and mules tied to a picket line. Seeing a patrol at the tank on two consecutive days says the Army must be keeping a close eye on things up and down the border. I wonder how many of Villa's rifle and ammunition deliveries they've intercepted or *peons* they've turned back.

Studying the men with my field glasses, I recognize Sergeant Sweeny Jones giving orders to Private Marvin Johnson and five or six of his army brothers while a lieutenant strolls around with a big pair of field glasses, scanning the country toward the border before turning north toward Hachita.

Yellow Boy uses his telescope to study the soldiers. "Sweeny Jones and Johnson set up camp. New lieutenant leads."

"I saw Jones and Johnson. How do you know the lieutenant is new?"

"Hat new. Face burned red from sun. Wait until dark. Before moon, we go."

When we camp in a canyon, Yellow Boy always picks a place with a second way out, the proverbial *rabbit hole* for escape. In this canyon all we have to do is to lead our horses up the wash, over a little pass, and then down another wash behind the ridge above us on our left side which will block the soldiers' lines of sight toward us until we're well clear of the Big Hatchets.

I'm a little nervous going up the wash. It's hard to see loose rocks and there are big boulders scattered about that make us wander back and forth across the trail. I needn't worry. Yellow Boy's cat eyes bring us through. We top the wash; carefully find our way in the loose talus down the backside of the ridge, and in less than an hour are long gone. Swinging south of the trail we used riding for Hachita, it's past midnight when we reach the border. Stars in the dawn above the sierras are fading by the time we ride into Villa's canyon.

Tracks show numerous wagons, supplies for *División del Norte,* and a small herd of horses, have recently come down the canyon wash. We ride on to the remains of Villa's camp, find a shady spot by the big tank, take care of the horses, and make a small fire for coffee and the remains of Magritte's victuals.

Yellow Boy makes signs for me to stay quiet and not change what I'm doing. Glancing down the canyon, I see nothing; when I look back he's already disappeared into the shadows. Wearing my old pistol butt backward on my left hip, I casually ease its retaining loop off the hammer.

I twist the stick holding the *tortillas* into the ground between two rocks next to the fire, put on the coffee pot to boil and the beans on to heat, before sitting back from the fire and relaxing. Wrens stop their chatter. The only sounds are from the greasewood fire crackling and popping.

I'm ready to take the *tortillas*, warm and toasty, off the fire and glance down the canyon. Three Apaches, a warrior and two women, sit on their horses, watching me. The warrior cradles a Winchester in the crook of his left arm. I try to appear relaxed, but I'm lucky I don't drop the *tortillas* in the fire.

Waving for them to come on to the fire and speaking my pidgin Apache, I say, "Friends. Come. Share this food with me. There is enough." They slide off their ponies. The warrior leaves his horse with the women who watch his every move and so do I. He looks familiar, but I don't recognize the rough, hard-looking women. I wonder if they might be from Pelo Rojo's camp about a day's ride southwest across the mountains. Middle-aged and bow-legged, the warrior walks toward me with an easy, self-assured stride. Hair long and shiny, black with streaks of gray, face flat with high cheekbones, eyes not much more than narrow slashes under a high forehead, he's fearless and powerful enough to make war alone. Wearing a bandolier across his chest, he carries a Mauser bolt-action rifle he probably took from a Mexican soldier, and a revolver handle protrudes from his canvas pants pocket.

Nearing the fire, he waves his hand about waist high in an arc parallel to the ground.

"Hombrecito! Many seasons, no see. You grow. Still carry Shoot-Today-Kills-Tomorrow? Still with Yellow Boy?"

He's Runs Far, a scout from Pelo Rojo's camp. From my days at the council fires of Rojo, I remember Runs Far when he often appeared with information none of the other men knew, but he had little else to say. He was always respectful of me because of my marksmanship skills even though, by rights, I was just a novice warrior.

Smiling, I salute him. "Runs Far! Many seasons pass. My eyes are glad to see you. Bring your women to the fire. There is enough for all of us. Yellow Boy rides with me."

Runs Far smiles and turns long enough to motion in the women as Yellow Boy appears beside me. Runs Far and Yellow Boy laugh, make jokes about being old men no good for riding the raiding path, and sit down in the shade back from the fire to catch up on news from across the seasons, to share information about the fighting in Mexico, and movements of American cavalry patrols just across the border.

Before coming to the fire, the women turn their horses loose in Villa's brush corral. Tough, mean looking characters, their faces betray nothing of their femininity. They wear calf-length moccasins beaded in decorative designs and cloth shifts gathered at the waist by wide leather belts in which sheathed knives are stuck. They're short, the tops of their heads not reaching my chin, their hair is tied back with blue and white patterned bandannas. One of them carries a flour sack over her shoulder, and as they approach the fire, they wave me off toward Yellow Boy and Runs Far. I'm glad for them to take over cooking and I watch their work with interest as I listen to Yellow Boy and Runs Far swap news and lies.

Out of the sack comes an ancient black, dented and scratched cooking pot, a sack of corn meal, and a collection of dried roots, piñon nuts, and a piece of smoked meat in a parfleche. They rig up a tripod to support the pot over the fire. They add water to the pot along with a few pieces of meat and some of the roots they've chopped up, and put the *tortillas* on a flat rock near the fire to stay warm.

Fast, efficient, they never say a word. seeming—as if by telepathy—to anticipate what the other will do and when. With the stew over the fire, they produce a couple of blue enamel cups, pour themselves coffee from our pot, and sit back to wait while their stew simmers and the men talk.

Runs Far tells Yellow Boy what's happening to the People in Pelo Rojo's camp and other villages. I hear Runs

Far say, "...the Mexican war on the east side of Sierras makes life hard for the People. Little remains. Cattle, gone. Horses, gone. Corn, gone. *Grandes haciendas* empty or only starving *peons* left. Bad, very bad. More better on the west side, but still bad. Few mines we raid; few supply trains but not much on them to take. Warriors range far, many killed in foolish raids."

He waves a hand toward the women. "Some women with no child and their man killed, they ride with warriors. Those who can fight and hunt, shoot straight, shoot long, we use. Your woman, a strong warrior, Hombrecito, they remember."

Yellow Boy studies the women. "Shoot straight? Shoot long?"

Runs Far nods. "Yes, those with rifles shoot straight, shoot long. Many have no rifle, they use knives and bows well, but they have no rifles."

"Women warriors? What does Rojo say?"

Shrugging his shoulders, Runs Far says, "Once many warriors in camp of Pelo Rojo, now not so many. Rojo says people need more children. From Mexicans and Yaquis, warriors find, take. Women also take new children. Rojo says good!"

Runs Far nods toward the women. "We see many young boys travel with Arango's army. Some fight with army, brave like Hombrecito when he avenges father and comes to the camp of Pelo Rojo. If we take boys, beans, and meat from Arango's army, Rojo's camp grows strong again."

So, Runs Far and the women had seen the young boys, some not more than eleven or twelve, in the *División del Norte* approaching El Paso Púlpito.

Runs Far asks if we know where Arango is, and frowns in surprise when we tell him with the army at El Paso Púlpito. "*Banditos* in Rojo's camp say Arango is finished. This is not true?"

Yellow Boy shakes his head. "Arango is with his army. Listen to me. Arango has few supplies and many men. He needs food, bullets, and warriors who know how to fight. The children you see are his warriors. They are too old and they have been trained in Arango's army. They will never become Apaches. Those you take, you will have to let go or kill. Their fathers fight Apaches all their lives. They hate Apaches. Arango knows where Rojo camps. You know he is there many times before the Mexicans try to wipe out each other. Arango even knows where the camp hides if raiders come.

"Hear me, Runs Far. You take Arango's children, his soldiers? You take his meat, his beans, his mules? You take his bullets? No. You will not do this. You do this and Arango wipes out Rojo's camp to the last warrior, woman, and child. There is no escape. Stay away from Arango. I, Yellow Boy, tell you this as a brother, warn you as a friend, and I will kill you as an enemy of the People if you do not listen."

A cloud of anger drifts across the face of Runs Far and disappears and his rippling jaw muscles relax. Leaning back, crossing his arms, and staring at the women who are preparing to take the stew off the fire, Runs Far slowly nods. "Yellow Boy speaks wise words."

The women wave for us to come eat. Between the five of us, it doesn't take long for the stew to disappear. The women remember Yellow Boy and me very well, and especially Rafaela, who, fearful of her ghost, they won't mention her name, but are clear to whom they refer.

Runs Far tells us to take a siesta and that he will take the first watch. The women scout around the camp, but find little left they can use. I find a place to sleep under a cottonwood and Yellow Boy under a willow not far away.

Coals from the little fire cast an orange glow against the darkness when Yellow Boy taps my foot. I blink awake, stretch and look around the camp in the cold canyon air. Runs Far and his warrior women are gone.

17. FINDING VILLA

Light from a fingernail moon is enough to find our way when we leave the canyon. The land south is flat and dry with broad stretches of mesquite and creosote and short stretches of grass sufficient to support a few cattle. There are *arroyos* to cross and patches of cactus and mesquite and sharp rocks to navigate but we still make good time.

Riding at a steady trot, I begin to think about Villa and his war. I wonder where my impulsiveness in volunteering to fight with Villa will lead. Of course, we don't have to return to *División del Norte*. As Quent said, even Villa doesn't expect us to return to his war. He expects us to hop on the train with Quent or just keep riding back home, never to see him again. But, believing in the justice of Villa's cause, we gave our word to fight with him. For us it's better to die than to lie, never giving our word unless we were willing to keep it to the bitter end.

I smile at the memory of Magritte, a plain, coarse woman

with a good heart. I like her, even to the point of fantasizing about taking her as a lover, in part to denigrate the man who killed my woman, but much more to satisfy my need for intimacy. How ironic that Camisa Roja, always one step ahead of me, is her man. Still, with my mind winding down away from years of day-to-day academic work, constant study, and helping patients, I remember more and more often the intimacy Rafaela and I shared, and how much I miss and need her.

Maybe, I fantasize, I'll ask Magritte to find me a good woman after all. I remember she said Villa ordered that no women come on the march through the mountains to Agua Prieta. My despair at that thought tells me I really do want and need a woman to help me through the cold and lonely nights, and it makes me ashamed of my profligate desires. Who am I anyway, but a twenty-seven year old doctor, barely out of medical school, fanaticizing about sleeping with the first woman who shows me any kindness? Disgusting. Still…

So absorbed by my thoughts in the dark shadows of the night, I nearly ride Satanas into the rear of Yellow Boy's horse. Yellow Boy sits staring a little east of south. Rather than coal mine darkness, the horizon south has a low, golden glow.

"What is that?" I whisper.

"Hmmph. *División del Norte* fires."

I stare at the glow and think we're like men sitting in a small rowboat, listening to the roar of a big waterfall as the current, too strong to escape, pulls us forward faster and faster, straight to the long fall over the edge of the precipice. We ride on. The glow grows brighter. By the time we stop to rest, water, and give the horses grain, we can even see flickering firelight scattered off clouds sailing out of the west. The night air is freezing cold, and, as we've done many times before, Yellow Boy and I sit back-to-back wrapped in blankets to share body warmth and to keep watch in every direction. Now that I've seen the sky glow from all those fires, the size of Villa's army starts taking form in my mind as a real thing, and my curiosity beings to work overtime.

"Uncle?"

"Hombrecito?"

"How many *hombres* do you think there are with Villa in *División del Norte?*"

He thinks for a moment. "*Muchos hombres.* Maybe more than one hundred one hundreds."

"You really think Villa has ten thousand men out there? He can't have collected enough supplies to support that many men."

He shrugs. "Maybe so. Fires burn far down the trail. *Muchos hombres.*"

"But, Uncle, where will he get water and feed for his animals and food for his men? There is only Colonia Oaxaca next to the river on the other side of the pass. It was flooded out ten years ago. Ranches around there can't possibly provide enough to supply that many *hombres* and that much livestock even for a day. His army will die of starvation before he even gets close to Agua Prieta."

"Maybe so. Many wagons come with army. Maybe carry food, water, grain for animals. Maybe it is enough until Arango takes Agua Prieta. *Quién sabe?* Who knows?"

It's beginning to sink into my brain how complicated it is just to move an army, never mind keeping weapons ready to fire or tactics and strategies. That idea increases my respect and admiration for our old friend's capabilities. My pride grows at knowing him well.

After an hour's rest, we ride on toward the steadily increasing glow. A few hours later we're close enough to distinguish individual fires, and see the tiny dark outlines of wagons and shadowy forms of horses or mules, and perhaps a few cattle. As far as we can see with our binoculars and telescope, the fires stretch from behind hills to the east and into El Paso Púlpito. We move forward slowly, picking our way, watching the line of fires, ready to run if necessary.

Near a dark, shadowy smudge of a mesquite thicket close by the entrance to El Paso Púlpito stands a barely discernable horse. Silently, Yellow Boy swings toward it. He motions me to ride wide and come up on the horse from behind. Yellow Boy ties off his pony and approaches the horse on foot while I wait, revolver in hand, several yards away hidden in the shadows of the thicket.

The horse, his ears pointing up, looks at Yellow Boy with curiosity. We hear the double click of a pistol pulled to full cock and a familiar growl from off to one side: "*Quién es*? Who comes to my bed?"

I speak better Spanish than Yellow Boy and don't hesitate to answer.

"Muchacho Amarillo and Hombrecito come to join General Villa. There's no need for weapons. Who are you?"

There is a deep belly laugh. A thumbnail snaps against a match and, in a near blinding flash of light, we see Villa on his knees, a blanket over his shoulders. He's not twenty feet from the horse. "*Muchachos,* welcome to my *hacienda*. Be careful. You'll get shot wandering around outside a military camp like this. I thought you might change your minds about offering me your help. It is all right if you do."

Yellow Boy walks over to him and kneels down on one knee as they shake hands. "We give our word, we keep it. You want, we leave."

Villa laughs again, shaking his head. 'No, no *amigos*, this I do not want. *Por favor*, forgive me, I mean no insult. Wait! I saddle my horse. We go to my fire in the camp and have some coffee and *frijoles*."

He saddles his horse and we ride toward the pass entrance using the same path we had been following. As we near the trail into El Paso Púlpito, sentries rise out of the mesquite, guns at the ready, see it is Villa with two *compadres*, and smiling, wave us along.

It must be an hour before dawn and already the camp is stirring. When we reach the fire in front of Villa's command wagon, a man, ancient of days, a blanket across his shoulders, hobbles out of the shadows and holds out a hand, offering to take our horses. Villa swings down from his saddle and hands the reins to him, saying, "*Gracias*, Juan. *Amigos*, give Juan your horses and packhorse. He will take good care of them. He loves the horses and helps me *mucho* with mine, is this not true Juan?"

The old man grins. I don't think he had more than three or four teeth in his head and his words come in a hard-to-understand croak. "*Sí*, general, I do what I can for you and the *Revolución*. Your horses, *señores*?"

We give him our bridles and the lead rope for Quent's roan. Juan leads our mounts and the roan toward a picket line near the wagon.

Sombrero tilted back on his head, Villa steps in the wagon, returns with three cups, and pours coffee, strong, bitter, thick, and the caffeine concentrated enough to wake the dead. A couple of swallows of the syrupy brew make my heart race.

Yellow Boy, who hasn't said anything since leaving Villa's sleeping place, takes a long slurp, smacks his lips, cocks his head to one side, and says, "Arango, why you sleeping in the mesquite far from your fire?"

Villa raises his brows and shrugs. "Some *soldados* think they know better than the general. They think the only way to take command is to kill me. They are right. I sleep away from the camp, in a different place every night, so they cannot creep up and murder me in my blankets. Also I never take the first bite of my food, this the cooks do in front of me. I learn the hard way I must do all this or be killed by *mi amigos. Comprende, muchachos?*"

Yellow Boy glances my way, and nods.

The stars begin to fade and the sky toward the east glows with a tinge of red. The entire camp begins to stir; fires grow brighter and the sounds of occasional loud voices and banging pots float toward us from up and down the trail as the tide of darkness recedes.

18. EL PASO PÚLPITO

Off on the low ragged edge of the eastern mountains, the cold black horizon begins turning crimson orange and other fall-yellow colors. Villa looks down the trail of fires, studies the golden glow in the east and nodding says, "*Amigos*, you do a fine thing for me. I am very grateful." He waves his arm in a vertical motion toward the campfires stretching back down the road, their glow slowly dimming in the gray distance.

"Already a week on the road and this is only the beginning of a very hard march. Between here and the river at Colonia Oaxaca there is not much *agua* and few supplies. We have to fill our bellies with what we find. At Oaxaca we will take grain and meat from the *ranchos* on the *rio*."

I wonder, after hearing Quent, whether Villa plans to buy it or commandeer it.

"I ask you, Muchacho Amarillo, to hunt game for the

dorados and show my scouts where they can find water, and you, Hombrecito, to work with *mi medicos*. The trail down to the floor of El Paso Púlpito Canyon is very steep, deadly and narrow, and requires very skillful wagon and caisson drivers. *División del Norte* has some of the best wagon drivers in Mexico, but the trail down …"

He shrugs and waves his hands.

"…We may lose a wagon or two."

Yellow Boy stares at Villa, not a sign on his face of what he's thinking. I nod and say, "*Sí,* general, we understand."

Villa grins. "*Bueno! Amigos* spread your sleeping blankets by *mi* fire and eat out of the same pot Juan fixes for *mi* and *mi* generals. *Mi* generals and I value your company and advice and we all have *mucho* to do, eh?"

As we sit drinking our coffee by the fire, Villa explains why *División del Norte* must use the very dangerous El Paso Púlpito to accomplish what the Carrancistas think impossible. He takes a yucca stalk and draws a winding line in the dust and puts a cross at each end.

"*Señores*, this is the trail through El Paso Púlpito, the east end where we sit is here and Colonia Oaxaca there. A few well-placed men at either pass entrance can stop practically any army except fast cavalry who can ride through in the night and return their fire from inside the canyon. If *Carrancistas* block El Paso Púlpito on the east side they force me to lead *División del Norte* across the northern sierras, much closer to the American border. That close to the border, many *soldados* will risk running across the border. If we go further south we come closer to Obregón's big army and risk a battle very dangerous to us both. To get over the mountains and succeed at Agua Prieta, *División del Norte* must cross here at El Paso Púlpito.

"I send my cavalry here a week earlier than the wagons and infantry to fight through and retake the eastern entrance if Obregón tries to hold it. But the pass stands empty, silent, waiting to swallow us like a big snake. Now we must get out through the west side entrance where Obregón can place a small force to try and bottle us up in the canyon. Again, a fast cavalry solves the problem.

"Now, most of the cavalry and pack mules march ahead of the wagons and infantry. They ride on ahead down Púlpito Canyon to fight through any Carrancistas that might try to trap us in the canyon at Colonia Oaxaca."

Seeing me grimace when he mentions fighting Carrancistas at Colonia Oaxaca, Villa grins. "Oh, I hope *El Perfumado* has an army at Oaxaca. Dead men don't need bullets and guns. My men can have them."

I nod, grimly remembering the pass and canyon when I was trying to find a place to hide from Díaz's soldiers thirteen years before. The steep, narrow trail drops nearly twelve hundred feet over a distance of about three miles as it snakes along the edges of steep drop-offs, and makes switchback turns so tight I doubt a team and wagon can squeeze around them. The last half-mile to the canyon floor drops a gut-wrenching 600 feet, and begins with a view of nearly the entire length of El Paso Púlpito Canyon named after towering Pulpit Rock, a huge volcanic monolith nearly ten miles away.

Make the least mistake on the narrow trail down to the canyon bottom, and wagons, animals, and men will fall to be smashed to pieces in end-over-end crashes down the nearly vertical sides of the ridges to the bottom of the canyon. The bottom of the canyon falls another thousand feet in nearly fourteen miles, only about a one and a half percent grade, to Colonia Oaxaca, a small Mormon farming village, badly damaged, but rebuilt after flooding on the Rio Bavispe ten years earlier.

The greatest danger for an army marching down Púlpito Canyon to the Rio Bavispe comes from rain. Runoff from the mountains can turn the canyon floor's dry wash into a roaring flood, wiping out everything before it. Villa knows he gambles with the very existence of his army in betting it won't rain until the *División del Norte* reaches Colonia Oaxaca, and orders the infantry to march to the top of pass and camp the morning we arrive.

Cold and windy with little water or grass for the animals, the camp offers little comfort to men already tired and hungry, but the infantry can help get the wagons and cannon caissons down the last half-mile of steep grades and switchbacks. Forty-two artillery caissons and well over a hundred wagons must move down the steep grades and switchbacks of the pass. Not having been around teamsters much, I can't imagine how to get those heavy guns and big baggage wagons down the first two and a half miles of steep trail, never mind the last half-mile of canyon trail which looks vertical by comparison. No other army has marched over the Sierra Madre like this before. The Carrancistas don't believe *División del Norte* will survive to reach Colonia Oaxaca; Villa doesn't doubt *División del Norte* will make it.

Taking a final swallow of coffee, Villa says, "*Mi amigos*, I have much to do this day. Take some rest, and then find us some fresh meat, eh?"

Yellow Boy and I raise our cups in salute as Juan brings a big, black stallion, the one we saw being curried in the canyon close to the border, the one that reminds me of Satanas. Villa gracefully swings into the big silver-trimmed saddle with the oversized saddle horn, large enough for a small writing desk, and tipping his little flat-brimmed Stetson to us, rides off to see and be seen by his men.

Not having been back to her grave since I buried her, I want to visit Rafaela's cairn and pay my respects. Yellow Boy, worried that her ghost might be there, nevertheless thinks the spring and piñons nearby make a good place to nap and goes with me even though he usually avoids burial places.

At the spring, I don't have any problem finding her cairn; it's like I'd built it the day before. Staring at it, what might have been comes to mind, and how her killer and I were now shoulder-to-shoulder fighting a common enemy. I shake my head in awe at life's strange twists and turns and remember what Yellow Boy said about Ussen enjoying playing Coyote tricks on the people.

Yellow Boy walks a big semicircle around the water tank, looking for fresh tracks around the spring, but finds none. He makes a nest out of pine straw for a nap in the junipers and tells me to call him at mid-morning so that I can nap while he keeps lookout.

I find a spot so I can see up and down the canyon all the way to the south end of the wash where I occasionally glimpse the infantry and supply wagons pulled by horses and mules and somehow hear, from even a half mile away, harnesses creaking, singletree chains making random bell-like clinking, and men calling to their teams and friends in the cold, still air. Creeping along, they look like a gigantic centipede moving inexorably forward up the trail toward the top of the pass. Unable to sleep, I lie there and stare blindly at the endless line of men and wagons rattling by as memories my days with Rafaela drift, soft floating clouds, across my mind.

The sun is a little past its zenith when Yellow Boy and I ride to the top of the pass. The line of men, horses, mules and donkeys, cattle, wagons, and artillery caissons we pass reminds me of a river flowing with a current too powerful to resist, flowing up the mountain, flowing against gravity.

At the top of the pass, the trail turns to the southwest, its ruts running down a long medium grade, crossing a wash, then suddenly swinging along the side of, and about half way up a long juniper-covered ridge, before gently descending toward the edge of the steep, last half-mile grade that twists back and forth, north and south, between sharp switchbacks. From where I sit on Satanas, I can see Pulpit Rock Canyon stretching south between high cliffs and ridges. At the place in the trail where the last of the cavalry horses and pack train mules begin the descent to the bottom, it looks as if they are pouring over the edge of a cliff and disappearing into oblivion.

Yellow Boy studies the slow moving horses and marching men for a few moments and shakes his head.

"So many, Hombrecito, so many, they look like warrior ants on the move."

From a distance, the long, slow-moving column does look like ants on the march.

"Sí, Uncle, they march like ants. I hope they find supplies

along the Rio Bavispe like lucky ants. Their animals already look worn out."

He points to the ridges off to the north on our right.

"I hunt the mountains there. You take the ones south."

"*Bueno*. Good hunting, Uncle. *Adiós*."

He nods, and without a word, turns his paint toward a big canyon filled with junipers a couple of miles away. I ride up and around a ridge toward the south, toward mountains standing tall and green with high cliffs forming splashes of white on their sides. I cross the trail, a steep animal trail with no switchbacks used by deer and the Apaches, I used for hiding from Díaz's army when I rode down to Oaxaca ten years earlier.

I find a buck resting in the junipers over the next ridge and take him with an easy shot from Little David. I start to field dress him, but decide Juan probably can use every piece of him except his snort. I let him bleed out, tie him across my saddle, and return to the top of the pass a couple of hours before the sun disappears behind the mountains.

División del Norte soldiers and equipment waiting to go down the cliffs spread out on a small plateau about a half-mile wide and a mile long at the top of the pass. Wagons and caissons waiting to descend are end-to-end on the trail all the way back past the entrance to the pass. Myriad small fires begin to appear all over the plateau and down the pass trail. They help take the edge off an icy wind that started blowing in mid-afternoon, making the men and animals even more miserable.

I drop the deer off with Juan and explore down the trail to the canyon floor. The steep grade faces west, and while the western sides of the mountains are already in dark shadows, the eastern sides still have good light. I wait until a break opens between those that stay at the top and those nearing the bottom and then ride down the trail to the bottom, thinking that if nightfall catches me, I'll dismount and lead Satanas back to the top of the pass.

In several places the trail bed is barely wide enough for a wagon to get through, and in a few others, boulders have to be moved. Satanas makes it to the bottom while the light is still good. The last of the cavalry that started early this morning has pushed on toward Oaxaca, probably intending to ride using torches until they reach the Rio Bavispe and water and grain for their horses and mules.

At the end of the trail down from the top of the pass, a large water tank gives men and animals a cool drink of water. I swing down out of the saddle and let Satanas drink. From what I've seen, the trail looks impossible for wagons much less the heavy cannon caissons to make it to the bottom without running away or sliding off the trail's edge.

In the fast vanishing light, Satanas works hard to climb back to the top of the pass, and there are places where I have to lean far forward in the saddle to avoid falling off backwards. When we reach the top edge of the steepest descent, I dismount and trudge to the top, giving him some rest. Walking up the trail I meet Sinolo Gutierrez, a *División del Norte* captain of engineers, leading a couple of hundred men carrying torches, picks, shovels, ropes, and leading mules in harness. Sinolo salutes me and stops to talk. Somehow every officer knows Yellow Boy and me.

"You have been all the way to the bottom, Doctor Grace?"

"*Sí, capitán*, all the way to the water tank. It is a hard

ride, even with a strong horse such as this one. In some places the way is just barely wide enough to get a wagon through, and in others it is partially blocked by boulders that have rolled down from the ridge cliffs. I don't see how you will be able move the cannon caissons down that trail to get through, or, for that matter, the wagons."

In the falling light, he stares off down the canyon toward Oaxaca and shrugs. "We will find a way. The general says it must be done, so we do it. We will work through the night to make the trail ready for the wagons when the sun comes. Gracias, Doctor Grace. *Adiós.*" He salutes me and rides forward to the front of his men.

I mount Satanas, and ride on up to the plateau at the top of the pass. Makeshift tents, most no more than tiny lean-tos have sprung up like toadstools after a spring rain all over the plateau and back down the trail east.

Villa's wagon is parked a little off the trail near the drop-off from the down side of the pass. Juan cooks a venison stew and gives me a welcome nod as I ride up. Unsaddling Satanas, I rub him down and give him a little extra grain in his ration. Yellow Boy hasn't returned. Ordinarily I wouldn't give his absence a second's thought, but these are extraordinary times. Who knows what kind of dangers he might be facing? Especially for an Apache warrior, I'm not about to raise the alarm like a worried kid. If he isn't back by morning, I'll quietly look for him.

A meeting of Villa and his generals held next to his wagon breaks up. The generals smile and nod at me as they walk by the fire to mount their horses tied off on a picket rope. All seem friendly except Rodolfo Fierro, one of Villa's closest confidants. Tall and thick-bodied, he has a round

Mongolian face with a long, pointed mustache and black predator eyes that look you over like a butcher eyeing a piece of meat. I soon learn the men call him The Butcher because he loves executing prisoners or killing anyone who crosses Villa. He studies me a moment, his hands resting on the pistols hanging at his sides. I stare back, resting a hand on my pistol.

Villa appears from his meeting and plops down with a groan on the steps of his wagon. "Ah, Hombrecito, it is good to see you, *mi amigo*. Where is Muchacho Amarillo?" Fierro sticks out his lip, gives a little shrug, and moves on. I know one day Fierro will test my mettle. Let him. I was raised to be ready for men such as Fierro.

Nodding toward Juan, I say, "I brought a buck in earlier in the afternoon and just returned from looking at the trail as far as the water tank at the bottom. Muchacho Amarillo left to hunt in that canyon there to the north and hasn't returned yet."

Sighing, Villa nods. "Hmmph. What do you think of the trail?"

"The last half mile is very steep and has tight switchbacks. I'm not a teamster or an engineer, but it'll be very hard to get the wagons down to the water tank, much less heavy cannon caissons. I'm not sure it can be done."

He laughs a big hardy belly laugh.

"Of course it can be done. If Sinolo cannot do it, I will find someone who can."

Waving his right arm in a wide expansive gesture toward the trail, he says, "This trail, it is nothing compared to problems a general faces when men fight in big numbers. We will get down this sorry little trail, I promise you, one way or the other."

I smile. "I'm sure you will, general."

We sit and talk while Juan cooks our supper. As Juan begins spooning stew in our plates, Yellow Boy rides into the firelight circle, a doe thrown over his saddle.

Delighted to see Yellow Boy Villa says in a pleased, jolly voice, "Fresh meat! *Muchas gracias* Muchacho Amarillo! Come, fill your belly from Juan's pot."

Yellow Boy hands the deer over to a grinning Juan and slides off his paint pony. "*Buenos noches*, general. I smell your cooking pot a long way off. My belly is empty. I feed my pony and join you."

I'm relieved to see him, but there is a look in his eyes that says something isn't right.

Villa gestures toward the stew pot. "Juan makes a pot of very good venison stew. Hurry back, *amigo*."

Returning from the picket line, Yellow Boy takes the pan and spoon Juan hands him, fills his plate and shovels in the chilies and venison like he's famished. Finishing supper, we sit around drinking coffee, using the hot cups to warm our hands against the night's chill, and reminiscing about the old days in Pelo Rojo's Apache camp ten years before.

Villa turns up his cup for the last drops of coffee and stands.

"*Muchachos*, I see you *mañana*. I must see to *División del Norte. Hasta luego.*"

We wave him off as he disappears into the night. Yellow Boy lights one of his cigars and stares off down the trail to the canyon bottom where we can see faint flickers from the torches of men working. I wait for him to tell me his news as he blows blue-gray smoke into the night.

"Apaches watch the camp."

I was taken aback. "Did you see them?"

"Only their tracks. There were three riders, Runs Far and his two women."

I didn't need to ask him how he knew it was Runs Far and his two warrior women. Yellow Boy read and recognized tracks like they were sets of fingerprints under a detective's magnifying glass.

"What do you think they're after? Supplies? Boys?"

He sticks out his lower lip and nods. "Runs Far is a fool. He thinks only of today like Elias and Juan raiding across the border. Runs Far and those two women must stay away from Arango's boy soldiers. If they do not, Arango will kill all the People he can find. *Mañana*, tell Arango I hunt and scout the canyons and valleys for enemies. You speak true, but he will think I look for Carrancistas, not Apaches."

"*Sí*, Uncle. I will speak so. I expect we will be here a few days while the engineers get the wagons and caissons down to the wash in Púlpito Canyon. You know where we go?"

"*Sí*, I know."

19. JESÚS, JOSE, AND MARCO

Yellow Boy and I saddle our horses before dawn. During the night a brutal, freezing wind comes. Water stands in buckets under a filmy layer of ice, so cold it makes our teeth ache to drink it, and the horses take only a swallow or two after their grain. Yellow Boy speaks in Apache, his voice low, intended only for my ears. "After I find Runs Far and his women, I return."

"Do you think Runs Far will listen to your words?"

"Runs Far listens or Runs Far dies. He has no other choice." Before mounting, he rests his ancient Henry rifle in the crook of his arm, grimaces against the cold and stares into my eyes. "Hombrecito, hear me. If I am slow to return, do not let Arango stand between you and the trail home. He is roaring *tigre* trying to kill the wolves who shame him. Arango no longer thinks like a chief. His anger makes him do foolish things. He does not choose his fights. His pride chooses for him. Arango wins no land, wins no treasure, wins no honor, and spills much blood. He blames others for fights he loses and does not learn from his losses. His pride makes him blind. You must watch Arango. Maybe he blames you for his bad choices. You leave before this happens."

"This I will do, Uncle. Ride well. *Adiós*."

One hand gripping the saddle horn for balance, he springs up on the paint, nudges him forward with his knees, waves good-by with a little shake of his Henry and disappears into the cold, black dawn, heading north into the cutting wind whistling through the canyons.

The eastern horizon burns with a brilliant orange glow and fires matching it are springing back to life all over the camp as I remember Yellow Boy calling Villa a raging tiger. I tremble inside thinking that Yellow Boy's choice of metaphor for Villa speaks of my dream.

I mount and walk Satanas east, back along the trail where the men make wagons and caissons ready for the drive to the bottom of the canyon. Unlike the *dorados* and officers who look in pretty good shape, the enlisted men look haggard and cold wrapped in their thin blankets trying to capture some warmth by their little fires. Stopping to talk with them, I learn that all they have to eat is a little thin corn gruel flavored with a few chilies or maybe a couple of *tortillas* and a cup of rationed water until they reach the Bavispe.

Near the pass entrance, at the end of the line, I find a few wagons driven by young boys hauling medical supplies. Since Villa didn't allow *soldaderas* on this march, the boys also serve as medical assistants. I'm the first American doctor to join them, but Villa expects *medicos* from both sides of the border to join him after he overruns Agua Prieta and begins his march to Mexico City.

Doctor Miguel Oñate, in charge of the medical assistants, looking distinguished and commanding, has a shock of thick white hair and a well-trimmed beard reaching to the edge of his collar. His dark, weather-bronzed face, wrinkled like a contour map of the mountains, and large blue eyes peering through silver-framed glasses, show kindness and demand respect.

After we shake hands, he offers me coffee and asks in fluent English about my background. He seems impressed that I'm not long out of medical school and knew the general before the beginning of the *Revolución*. He adds he went to the medical school in Mexico City, and that he had a practice in Chihuahua when Madero asked him to support Villa at the beginning of the *Revolución*.

Oñate pats the breast pocket of his long coat and finds a cigar, lights it, and with a ten-mile stare and faint smile, crosses his arms, leans against the wagon, and nodding looks toward shadows fading away on the ridges, recalls good times, even those occurring during war.

"Those were good days, a righteous cause, Doctor Grace. One night after a battle, when there were many wounded, the general comes to me and says, 'Miguel, there has to be a better way to help the wounded besides carrying them off the battlefield on a stretcher to die.' The other *medicos* and I consider the problem and tell him we ought to make the train cars so we can first operate at the battle and treat the wounded like they are in the hospital and then carry them to a real hospital for recovery. The general, he doesn't hesitate to have them made. He gave our doctors about forty *Servicio Sanitario* boxcars, enameled inside so they were easy to keep sanitary and wash down after operations, and they carried the most up-to-date medical instruments and medicines. Using those boxcars, the care our wounded soldiers received near the front and their speed in reaching hospitals stood above even European standards, and outclassed the United States Army. No longer needed after the fighting stopped, the medical staff working on the train just *phsssst.* They evaporated like drops of water on a hot skillet. I believe most of them went back to the United States or stayed in Chihuahua to help the *peons.*

"Now, Doctor Grace, we have far too few *medicos,* the *soldaderas* who help us with the wounded stay behind, replaced only by a few young, untrained assistants, and we have few *medico* supplies, most of these going to the officers. We march for about a week and already the *soldados,* they suffer."

I shake my head against the anticipation of men being maimed and killed. "I've seen the men this morning. Their suffering will grow much worse. Some will die in this pass, smashed to pieces on runaway wagons and caissons that slip off the very steep and narrow trail on the way down to the bottom of Púlpito Canyon."

Doctor Oñate grimaces, eyes narrowing. "I have not yet seen the trail to the bottom. There are always injuries when an army this size moves. Already a wagon backs over a man, one is badly burned by a grease fire, another has broken ribs from a mule kick, and one has a bullet wound in his thigh when his rifle accidently discharged. Don't ask me how that happened. Yes, the *medicos* have been busy already on this march and if we find the trail forward as bad as you say, then we will have our hands full."

Three teen-aged boys, maybe fourteen or fifteen, appear from behind the wagon. Doctor Oñate waves them over to meet me. Handsome young men, eyes full of mischief, they carry old Winchesters and wear bandoliers filled with ammunition.

"Doctor Grace, these young men and a few others will assist us with the medical work."

I shake hands with Jose Soto, the oldest. He has a thin smudge of a mustache, thick black hair that sticks out around the edge of his infantry cap, and a perpetual squint like he's staring at the sun. Marco Guionne, the youngest, short and very dark-skinned, has a grip like iron. *Probably*, I think, *an Indian from the south*. His smile is quick, and he laughs often.

Jesús Avella the middle one, tall and serious, an inch or two taller than Jose and Marco, makes the strongest impression as he grips my hand in a firm shake and looks me steadily in the eye. He wears an infantry cap like Jose's except the bill is shiny and the rest of the cap perfectly maintained. With brilliant white teeth and striking, brown eyes he reminds me of the Villa I knew ten years earlier. I learn over the weeks we're together that Jesús is fearless but even-tempered. He wears a holster carrying an old revolver in addition to his bandoliers and, in the days to come, earns the respect of old, battle-hardened *soldados*.

The boys are all friendly and eager to shake my hand, but their eyes look past me to Satanas and *Little David* in its saddle scabbard. Jesús nods toward Satanas. "Your stallion is magnificent, Doctor Grace. I have never seen such a rifle like the one he carries in the gun scabbard."

Marco grins, his eyes full of good humor and mischief as he says, "It looks very old. Does it shoot cartridges? Does it—"

I hold up my hand to stop the questions and move to pull *Little David* out of its scabbard. They frown in surprise when they see the big bore, long barrel and offset hammer, and grunt when I let them heft its ten pounds. I pull a .45-70 cartridge out of my vest pocket and hold its length between my thumb and forefinger for them to see. "This cartridge fits that 1874 Sharps Rifle used years ago for hunting buffalo. The cartridge has been standard US Army issue for a long time. It's not used much anymore."

Jose asks, "How many times can you shoot before you have to reload?"

"Once. It's a single-shot breech loader."

They smile at my apparent naïveté and shake their heads. Marco says what they're all thinking.

"A gun that shoots only once before reloading will get you killed in a war, señor. A soldier has to shoot many times before reloading. Ask the general to give you a Winchester. You will not live long if you use this old single-shot rifle."

"You don't need a repeating rifle if you're a sniper, *muchachos*."

Frowning, disbelief in his voice, Jesús says, "You, a long-range marksman, Doctor Grace? I mean no disrespect, but will you show us your skill?"

The medical wagons are far down the trail from the camp at the top of the pass, and from where we stand there's over a half-mile clear line of sight to the next ridge. I point toward a lone juniper about 300 yards away. "Who wants to risk their hat as a target on that juniper yonder, the one that stands out from the others on the ridge there?"

Jose's squint tightens as he stares at the juniper and pulls off his hat. I doubt he can even see the juniper. Marco and Jesús laugh as they too pull off their caps. Jesús says, "We all offer our hats, Doctor Grace. If you can hit just one at that distance, it will be an honor to wear the mark of such a shot. Wait while I get a mule and I will take them to the bush."

Disappearing behind the wagon, walking among the horses and mules tied to the wagon waiting to be harnessed, he returns riding bareback on a tall, red mule. He takes the caps from Jose and Marco, and looks to me for instructions.

"Put the caps about head high on the bush so the bills point toward the ground and leave them an arm's length apart."

As Jesús rides out to the bush, Doctor Oñate takes a puff from his long gambler's cigar blowing it out of the side of his mouth into the suddenly still air. "Where did you learn to shoot, Doctor Grace? This is a very rare talent for a doctor who spends most of his life with the books."

"I lost my father at an early age. The old rancher who raised me taught me to shoot and gave me the rifle."

"Ah, *comprendo*. I shoot also, but never at a distance such as this one. I can barely tell there is anything there. How do you hit anything you cannot see?"

My eyes are good enough that I can tell where the hats are, but the design of the caps and the way I had Jesús hang them helps me too. Their bills are made of shiny acetate and the way the sun strikes them gives each a weak glint that's easy to pick out. Every good marksman has his secrets and I have mine.

"I have very good eyesight, Doctor Oñate. Perhaps I will be lucky."

He shrugs and takes another puff from the cigar. "Perhaps, Doctor Grace. We wait to see."

A horse snorts behind us and we turn to see Camisa Roja sitting in his saddle, grinning.

"So, Dr. Grace, you give us a *demonstración* of your shooting skill, eh? *Bueno.* I have wanted to see you shoot for a long time. May I watch before I leave on an errand for *El General*?"

I don't like the smirk on his face and wish he stood by the hats. I'd change his smirk soon enough.

"*Si, señor*, I am happy for you to know my skill, such as it is. I want these *muchachos* to understand the measure of a rifle is not just how many bullets it holds."

Roja nods as he cups a match to light a corn shuck cigarette against the wind. "*Bueno*, Doctor Grace. You do these *muchachos un servicio*. Don't mind me. I must ride on soon."

His heels thumping the sides of his mule to make it trot faster, Jesús returns to the wagon. Looking back at the juniper, he shakes his head. "I can barely tell the caps are there. They look like little black dots, Doctor Grace. Let me find some sticks and I'll bring them in closer where you can at least see them from here."

"No, let me try them at this range. If I miss, then you can bring them closer, eh?"

He shrugs and grins at Jose and Marco, who stand with crossed arms, waiting for me to make a fool of myself, and nods deferentially at Roja.

I step away from the wagon to get a true sense of the

wind. Blowing again out of the west, cold and steady, I'm in luck. I toss some dust in the wind to get a sense of the wind's speed, counting 'thousand-one, thousand-two' to see how far it drifts in a couple of seconds.

Little David's vernier sight and three cartridges are still in my vest pocket from yesterday's hunt. I attach the sight to the stock with thumbscrews and adjust the vernier screws for 300 yards, a ten-mile per hour crosswind, and thumb the smallest aperture sight into place for highest resolution.

Roja continues to sit his horse, watching my every move. The boys and Doctor Oñate come to stand behind me as I spread a blanket, sit down, rest my elbows on my knees, and sight down the long barrel to aim just above each glint. The caps all have good sight pictures. I drop the breech, load a cartridge, and hold the other two cartridges between my palm and fingers of my right hand.

I'm ready. I sight on the first hat; pull the hammer and set trigger back and take a deep breath. The sight picture wobbles a little above the first glint, but becomes rock solid when I slowly exhale to half and hold. The trigger takes practically no pressure to make the hammer fall. The Sharps booms and kicks back in a hard thump against my shoulder to jar lose pleasant memories of Rufus Pike teaching me to shoot. Thousand-one, thousand...the first cap sails into the wind and I hear gasps of disbelief behind me as I cycle through the next two rounds dropping the breech to eject the shell, reloading, sighting, and firing in the smooth, continuous motions Rufus Pike taught me.

A second passes after the last shot. All three hats sail high in the air: two land behind the bush, the third tumbles in the wind and glides down to land in front. The men and boys behind me give a collective sigh and Jesús runs to mount the mule in a flying leap. I collect my brass, and stand to see Oñate, Jose, and Marco still staring at the juniper with their mouths open.

Roja, somber, says nothing as he nods, salutes, and rides on up the trail. Jose speaks for the rest of them. "*Madre de Dios*. Never have I seen such shooting."

I smile, slide *Little David* back in its saddle scabbard, and walk back to the *medico* wagon to await Jesús's return. In a few minutes the mule trots up. Jesús, smiling from ear-to-ear, slides off her back waving the caps. The first one, belonging to Jesús, I hit in the middle of the acetate bill, the second, belonging to Marco, has a nick on the back edge, and Jose's has a hole in the top within an inch of dead center. Lucky shots, but I'll never say so. The boys proudly put on their mutilated caps, salute me, and run off to show their friends evidence of the *Americano* doctor's marksmanship.

Doctor Oñate raises his brow, makes a little click, and extends his hand. "Doctor Grace, the general will want you at the front, not back with the *ambulancias*. We welcome you whenever you can help us."

I shake his hand. "*Gracias*, Doctor Oñate. I'll help as much as I can, anywhere I can. I go to watch and maybe help on the trail to the bottom of the canyon. I'll see you when your wagons roll."

Grinning, the cigar clamped in his jaw, he waves his arm up the trail. "*Bueno! Adiós*, Doctor Grace, see you soon."

20. OVER THE EDGE

Men and animals suffer while waiting their turn to clear Púlpito pass. Each day colder and dustier than the one before, icy wind slashes through the men's thin clothes and blankets, carrying the dust churned up by thousands of feet and wheels creeping down the west side of the pass. Grit settles into cooking pots, turns eyes red and watery, and makes bandannas over mouths and noses a basic necessity.

Natural water tanks disappear as buckets, thousands of cups, and finally pieces of cloth soak up the last few drops of water. The few known springs, most not much more than slow seeps, take a long time to refill barrels. Only miserly water rationing keeps back raging thirst and once a day allows the making of thin meat stews, *tortillas*, and coffee, with just enough water left over to keep the animals alive. Fires for warmth and cooking burn all the wood, brush, and dry weeds around the camp; each day the men scavenge further up the ridges to find more. Land around the camp and back down the road east appears decimated as if by swarms of locusts consuming everything in their path.

Dark cumulus clouds slow the coming of morning light. Wagons wait in a long line east down the El Paso Púlpito road, ready to take their turn going down the steep, pack-mule trail, now a wagon road.

As each wagon's turn in line finally comes, the men driving start down the backside of the pass in fear and trembling, and if they successfully reach the canyon bottom, drink with their horses and mules long, gulping swallows of good cold water at the big, spring-fed tank and wearily cross themselves, giving thanks to God for surviving the descent. They watch their animals, careful not to let them drink too much and founder, and find it hard to believe they're somehow more blessed or lucky than their friends who slipped off the trail edge and fell to their deaths, or lie in agony, waiting to die in the *medico* wagons.

The first wagons in line carry the medical supplies and baggage. Our plan is to park these near the water tank to make a temporary hospital for survivors from wagon crashes. Villa asks me to ride Satanas down the trail in front of the first *medico* wagons to help guide the drivers away from dangerous spots. Jesús drives the first *medico* wagon, followed by José and Marco driving the second and third wagons. At a signal from Villa, I lead the wagons forward. The drivers have been told to stop at a wide shelf-like place less than half a mile from the canyon floor, reconnoiter the rest of the trail down, and decide at that point whether to chain their rear wheels to help with braking.

Jesús and the others easily guide their wagons down the two and half miles of moderately steep grade from the top of the pass to the appointed stopping point. Soldiers, acting like traffic cops, signal the wagons behind to stop or go. From the stopping point, we can see miles of Púlpito Canyon, majestic in the gray morning light, ridges rising out of the mists, daring us to take the plunge over the edge to the rough trail below, already ground to fine powder from the cavalry and pack-train columns staggering toward Colonia Oaxaca.

I hand Jesús my field glasses. He studies the trail noting every narrow stage, every tight turn, and places where there might be soft spots. A wagon stuck in a soft spot with little or no maneuvering room can only be freed using the iron nerves and muscles of men waiting in the pass to come free it. Jesús raises his brows and motions toward Marco with my glasses. I nod and he hands them to Marco and José to use.

While Marco and José study the trail, Jesús pulls out a couple of short chains from the back of his wagon. On each rear wheel, he passes a chain between the spokes, pulls the chain back around the iron wheel rims, and bolts the chain ends together after wrapping them around an iron bar bolted to the side of the wagon bed. This keeps the back wheels from turning and takes the load off the driver's foot brake.

Marco finishes with my binoculars and passes them to José, who uses them to stare longer than the others at each dangerous point on the trail. Returning my glasses, Jose's hands tremble, and color has left his face.

I have a bad feeling. "Are you all right? You don't look so good."

He shrugs his shoulders and manages a weak grin. "*Sí*, Doctor Grace, I am all right. It's just that high places, they… worry me." He licks his lips, dry with fear, but holds his hands up, palms out toward me. "But I can do this."

"I know you can, but if you drive your wagon now, you might make a bad mistake. I'll find another driver to take your wagon down."

Eyes wide, he shakes his head, and pleads, "Oh no, Doctor Grace, I can drive this trail. I'll be fine. *Por favor*, do not shame me in front of *mi amigos*."

I know better. A voice in the back of my mind says not to let Jose drive, but the thought of his wounded pride outweighs my better judgment. "Are you sure you can do it? Make a mistake and we might have to bury you."

"*Sí, señor*, I can drive the wagon. I will make no mistake."

I nod. "Okay, my fine young *amigo*. Do you want to put chains on your rear wheels?"

"*Sí*, Doctor Grace. Jesús and Marco use their chains and I do also."

"Good! Get 'em on and let's go."

He grins and returns to his wagon. In ten minutes Jesús, Jose, Marco, and the other *medico* drivers follow me down the steep descent.

Jesús, his face a study in concentration, clucks and whistles to his mules, encouraging them to pull hard against the balky resistance from sliding, chained wheels. The mules strain for a few yards until the trail's steep incline and thick, lubricating layer of dust take over, make the locked wheels slide with not much more resistance to the downward slope than a turning wheel on flat ground.

He guides the mules down the middle of the ruts. Stopping Satanas, I stand in the stirrups and look back toward the wagon, and watch for and point out soft places to avoid and places where the trail edge comes especially close to the ruts. Jesús maneuvers his team perfectly, laying a clear set of tracks for José to follow. Dust fills the air as the locked wheels cut the ruts wider and deeper, and a raw, cold wind blows across the canyon, the sun flashing in and out from behind dark billowing clouds and short, swirling snow showers, the falling snow literally becoming brown with the dust in the air.

The first switchback, within a quarter mile of the shelf where the wagons stopped, has the tightest, steepest turn on the way down, but the turn banks up slope, allowing the drivers to have more speed in the turn without rolling over. From down the trail, I stop again and watch them advance, my heart pounding. Jesús clears the switchback faster than I'd like but he doesn't seem to have any problems. José's team follows Jesús's team tracks well, creeping along slowly and carefully. Marco, careful to keep plenty of distance between his wagon and José's, appears perfectly in control of his team.

With my field glasses I see José's face frozen in fear, his foot on the front wheel brakes so hard the wheels barely turn, making the wagon fishtail from one soft spot to the next. Marco minimizes his front brake use by first letting the harness gently push against the mules' back legs before he applies pressure to the front brakes.

The second switchback, less than a tenth of a mile farther on, swings wider than the first turn, the trail swinging back toward the south from almost due north. Much trickier than the first turn, the curve slopes away from rather than into the ridge, and the approach into this turn falls much faster than that of the first switchback. Jesús, rolling too fast into the turn, his face twisted in a frown, eyes concentrating on every foot of trail forward, shows he knows what to do, riding his front brake and nearly locking his wheels before he releases them at the last moment so the team doesn't drag the wagon round and roll it over the edge. I breathe a sigh of relief as he straightens out, the wagon rocking back and forth a little but quickly steadying as he heads down the long steep grade to the bottom, slowly gliding into the last switchbacks.

José stays on the front brake, and locking his front wheels slides into the second turn, going much slower than Jesús. He lets off the front brakes in time to make the turn, but reflexively hits them hard again before his wagon is fully through the turn. The wagon top tilts towards the drop-off. José, seeing his mistake, takes his foot off the brake. His wagon balances on the right side wheels for maybe thirty or forty feet, as if suspended in time and trying to make up its mind whether to right itself or tip over the trail edge.

My heart beats like a trip hammer for a few seconds, and then I begin to believe he might actually make it. José sits on the driver's bench, his eyes wide, staring across his right shoulder, staring at the rocks far below waiting to catch him. I frantically wave for him to move up to his seat's left side, hoping his weight is enough to tip the wagon back to all four wheels. José won't move.

Hitting a large rock in the ruts, the right front wheel twists to the left and suddenly the wagon flips over the edge, throwing José in mute silence off the bench, cartwheeling to the rocks below. In slow motion the dead weight of the wagon suspended over the edge slowly drags the pitifully braying mules, straining to hold it, over the edge. The wagon and mules fall, twisting and turning into the boulders, where José already lies broken and bleeding.

Smashing into boulders hugging the side of the ridge, the falling wagon seems to explode sending surgical sheets fluttering down on junipers like big white birds, rolled bandages unwinding in long white streamers, and brown bottles of carbolic acid sailing through the air in long arcing trajectories ending with a *whoosh* and the sound of exploding glass that leaves the dry rocks looking like they've suddenly sprung leaks. The rear axle, with the wheels still attached, breaks free of the splintered wagon bed and bounces down the steep slope gaining speed until it hits a boulder and flies apart sending the wheels twisting and flipping crazily across the ridge like silver dollars tossed on a gambling table.

I feel helpless and guilty knowing this is my fault, knowing I might have prevented José from dying this way. I clench my teeth and motion Jesús, Marco, and the other drivers to continue down the trail, while I stare for a moment at the bright red spot where José's bloody, crushed body lies. We can't reach him until the other wagons are past and at the bottom of the canyon. It makes little difference. José has gone to the grandfathers, and the greatest sadness I've felt since Rufus Pike died covers me like black smoke, thick and suffocating.

At the bottom, Jesús and Marco roar down the trail in a cloud of dust to the place where we intended to park the *medico* wagons. Jerking reins back for the mules to stop, yelling, "Whoa! Whoa!" riding the front wheel brakes, and scrambling off the driver's seat, Jesús brings his wagon to an abrupt stop. He runs to the back of his wagon, drops the tailgate, and yanks out a stretcher. Marco, stopped behind Jesús, rummages in his wagon, grabs bandages, splints, and a sheet. They scramble for the steep slopes to gather up their friend and ease his suffering.

I gallop Satanas around in front of them, and put up my hands, yelling, "Stop! Stop!"

They look at me like I'm crazy. Marco's eyes narrow into a threatening squint as he shouts, "*Señor*, we must go to Jose! You saw what happened! He lies on those rocks bleeding and needs our help. He might die. We have to hurry. We cannot let him just lie there and die alone." Jesús nods and turns to run on leaving Marco to argue with me.

I put up my hand again.

"Stop! Listen! Listen! Look up there on the trail above where Jose lies."

Brakes squeal and grind, desperate men call to their teams in attempts to steady wobbly wagons, and rocks roll off the trail edge to bound down the ridge, sounding like pistol shots as they smash into or ricochet off boulders far below.

"*Muchachos*, you know in your hearts that José is no more. There is nothing we can do except bury him. I let him drive when I should have made him walk and now he's dead. I cannot, will not, let this happen to you. Do you think José will be the only driver off the edge today? You saw what happened. You risk your lives going to Jose when, at any time, a wagon might fly off the trail with you below it. When there are no more wagons or rocks to fall on us, we will gather all the bodies and give them, every one, a respectful funeral, a funeral for brave men who have died with as much honor as any who fall in battle. Now, go on. Tend to your teams and prepare to help Doctor Oñate and me when we need you. *Vamos.*"

Jesús and Marco study the trail down the ridge slopes. Slowly, the truth of my words sinks in, and staring at the ground between their shoes, they return to their wagons.

As dusk falls, men from the top of the pass walk down to help us retrieve bodies scattered like seeds down the slopes. High on the rocks, torchlight reflecting in their tears, Jesús and Marco lift José's broken body on to their stretcher and begin the slow hike back down the trail with me leading the way. It is the longest walk of my life, tears welling out of my gut, throat filled with a ball of fishhooks. Villa's war has already taught me an immensely hard, valuable lesson and a shot is yet to be fired.

The little cemetery we begin that night grows as the rest of the wagons and cannon caissons roll off the top of the pass. A few men survive their wagon or cannon caisson crashing off the trail edge. Suffering massive injuries, there is little we can do for them except ease their pain. Like all our other supplies, there isn't much morphine, and Villa orders that it be used only for those wounded in battle.

I remember the herbal medicine I learned while living with the Apaches and send several men to collect little buttons of peyote cactus while Jesús and I collect other plants like yerba mansa and Syrian rue. The fusions I make with the peyote and other plants can deaden pain, but most of the survivors don't live long enough to know their benefits.

Butchered for meat, the mules killed in the wreckages replace food supplies running low or already gone. A fire built at the bottom of the canyon roasts meat for the men arriving from the top of the pass.

Yellow Boy thinks of mule meat as one of the basic food groups and I ate my share during the years I lived with the Apaches. It's not something I'd go out of my way to eat, but there in the cold and back-breaking labor, its fat dripping in the fire smells as good as the best cut of sirloin steak. My mouth waters to eat some, but my share, as does that of all the *medicos*, goes to starving, thirsty soldiers.

Knowing the snow and rains will come no later than the first of November Villa and his commanders work day and night to hurry things along and beat the floods sure to come roaring down the washes. Villa spends hours riding his big battle horses up and down the Púlpito pass and canyon trails to Oaxaca, encouraging the men with his charismatic presence, telling them vulgar stories, and haranguing them to move faster. Villa's commanders use hundreds of men with picks and shovels and teams of mules to pull boulders and junipers out of the way to smooth and widen the trail along the bottom of the canyon, turning what was once only a pack-mule trail into a passable wagon road.

The wind is not nearly as cold and raw at the bottom of the canyon as at the top of the pass. Afraid that if they stop for rest they won't get up, Villa keeps the men moving once they are on the canyon floor, promising them a day to rest and forage for supplies when they reach Colonia Oaxaca, and telling them the quickest way to unlimited water is the thirteen-mile trek down the canyon to the river. The men keep walking, some holding on to the wagons to help them along, others, torches to light the way.

The trail down the canyon also takes its toll of men, mules, and wagons. Although the wagon drivers don't have to worry about rolling off a narrow road and bouncing hundreds of feet down the canyon's side, some get stuck with their heavy loads and have to be pushed and pulled out of soft places, and some slide off the narrow trail and turn over. At first, the men try to push or pull the wagons back upright and salvage supplies, but soon learn there is most often few supplies left to save. They begin cutting the mules loose and leaving the wagon for the rains to sweep away.

21. COLONIA OAXACA

Looking over my shoulder back up Canyon Púlpito, its long hall of mountains filling with ink-black shadows in the falling light, a strong sense of pride for the men who make this hard march fills me. Years before, Rufus Pike had me read to him in the evenings as we sat on his shack porch high in the Organs. Now I recall reading him a translation of *The War With Hannibal* by a Roman historian named Livy. Some university professor gave it to Rufus after he guided an archeological expedition to cliff dwellings in the Gila wilderness. The book told the story of the Punic Wars and how Hannibal crossed the Alps to attack Rome. Livy wrote that Hannibal's army crossing the Alps, an unbelievable achievement, caused panic throughout the empire. I smile when I remember that story. Hannibal and General Francisco Villa must have been cut from the same cloth.

As we approach Pulpit Rock, the huge monolith gleaming in the last light from the sun, men and animals catch the musky, wet scent of the river coming up the canyon on an evening breeze. They want to run, to stampede for the water but they're too weak, and can only walk a little faster. Satanas, smelling the water, jerks at his bridle, wanting to run straight for the river. I hold him back, wanting the men to know that their suffering and courage gives them first place at the water.

I'm the last man in Villa's long, serpentine column of men, horses, mule-pack trains, wagons, and cannon caissons that, by sheer force of will make it across the Sierra Madre and march out the west side of El Paso Púlpito. The sun disappearing into the night, floating below orange, purple, and vermillion clouds on the far horizon, signals the end of a very long march down the canyon.

Passing Pulpit Rock, I see the glow from fires up and down the river. The cavalry and mule train packers already here for several days, having scavenged for supplies up and down the Rio Bavispe, now cook meals to fill our starving bellies.

We follow the deep dusty ruts of freshly churned sand, pointing straight for the big, fallow fields next to the river and cross a rough caliche road running north-south, paralleling the river. All the way to the river I looked for lights from Colonia Oaxaca, but see none except for maybe one or two in the dark outline of a distant house up the road. I wonder if *Revolución* fighting drove away the Mormons who built the place or if they decided to move on after the 1905 flood.

Wagons park in random groups all over the big fields next to the river. We rush past them, only stopping when the mules stand in the river up to their bellies, drinking their fill, and their drivers have jumped down from their wagon benches in whoops of joy to bury their faces in the cold clear water. I let Satanas drink while I drink a few double handfuls before I begin filling my canteen to give the patients in the wagons a drink. Doctor Oñate, Marco, and Jesús and other *medico* wagon drivers are doing the same thing.

In a field just above the river, Villa's wagon stands apart from the others, his big warhorses tied to a nearby picket line as they eat their grain. Juan, working at his cooking fire, ignores Villa and his commanders meeting under a large, tattered piece of canvas tied to one side of his wagon. I hear anger and frustration in their raised voices.

Myriad stars glitter in a velvet-black sky as I unsaddle Satanas, brush him down with handfuls of grass, and hobble him so he's free to graze. Juan, with a big toothless smile, waves his stewpot spoon at me to come eat. I don't give him any argument. For the past five or six days, I've been living off what I can make the land give me and the smells from Juan's stewpot twist my stomach with a ravenous need to eat.

Juan ladles steaming beef stew into a big tin pie pan and tosses me *tortillas* from a flat piece of iron next to the pot. I remember the women in Villa's camp close to the border using the same fire-blackened cooking iron to fry meat and bake *tortillas*. Out of the big, fire blackened coffee pot, Juan pours a tin cup full of strong, soothing tea made from desert willow and hands it to me, nodding and mumbling *de nada* when I thank him. Men all over the camp will make and drink the tea and use it to wash the sores on their bodies. I expect to do the same.

Looking around for a place to sit, I hear from across the fire, "*Buenos noches*, Doctor Grace. The ground next to the wagon wheel makes a good easy chair. Come keep me company while you eat."

It doesn't take long to see the flash of the bright red shirt in the flickering firelight. Sipping from his tin cup, Roja sits relaxed, leaning against a wagon wheel.

Sitting down beside him, I wiggle the bottom of my cup into the dirt to hold it stable. "*Buenos noches, señor*. I haven't seen you since you watched me shoot for the *medico* boys. Where've you been hiding?"

He shrugs while he rolls tobacco in a corn-shuck cigarette.

"I hide nowhere. *El General* he sends me and other riders across Sonora to scout the land and learn the news. It is a big country, Doctor Grace, many miles to ride, much to learn. I am the last one back to camp just this afternoon. It takes a long time to tell *El General* what I learn."

My mouth stuffed, I just raise an eyebrow to raise a question. Roja shakes his head.

"No, *señor*, I speak only to *El General*. You will know what I tell him when he decides to tell you."

I nod and swallow.

"This I understand, *amigo*. Never betray your *jefe's* confidence. I respect you for this."

He smiles and takes a deep draw off his cigarette.

"*Gracias, señor*. I know you understand. Tell me of the trip across the pass and down the canyon. No one tells me anything about the march over the pass and down the canyon since I speak with *El General*."

He waves his arm in a sweep covering the camp.

"The men, they look in very bad shape. They say days pass since they drank more than just a little water and ate a few *tortilla* crumbs."

"Unfortunately, they all speak the truth. Everything went wrong that could go wrong. We ran out of supplies a day or two after the wagons parked at the top of the pass and it didn't take long for the men and animals to drink the springs and tanks scattered around the pass dry. Getting all the wagons and caissons down that steep trail to the canyon's bottom took longer than *El General* expected because the men had to make a wagon road out of that narrow pack-train trail down the canyon. The trail down the western side of the pass was cut to ribbons and ground to deep powder by the sliding wheels and men and mules marching on it, making it very slippery and dangerous. The freezing wind, sometimes mixed with snow and dust, sometimes so thick from trail dust you couldn't see your hand in front of your face, made every living thing in the pass miserable, almost ready to lie down and die, but Villa didn't let us lie down, made us keep marching, and so we made it to the Rio Bavispe."

Roja smokes slowly as I speak, taking an occasional long drag on his cigarette and nodding he understands, but keeping his eyes focused on the ground between his boots

"Coming off the top of the pass, twenty men died in wagon crashes before they reached the bottom, fifty so badly hurt that half of them died before we made the river, another three or four died on the canyon trail, and we lost ten wagons and three caissons. The country between Púlpito Rock and the bottom of the pass is lined with the graves of many brave men, *señor.*

"Men with smashed hands, broken arms and legs, and

torn up internal organs doctors can feel through their skin, fill the *medico* wagons. On three or four of the men we amputated a leg or an arm because they were so badly crushed gangrene was inevitable. Those men suffered in terrific pain until I remembered plants the Apaches use. My fusions eased their pain a little, but nearly all of them have died."

Camisa squints at me and shakes his head. "It sounds more like a bloody battle than a long march across the mountains."

"A battle? *Si*, a battle every step of the way, and our *compañeros* won it!"

As I speak, the meeting between Villa and his generals breaks up. Villa shuffles over to the fire to take the plate and cup Juan holds out for him. He joins us, sitting down with his legs crossed, and looks at us from across the little fire. "So, at last, we cross the mountains, eh, Hombrecito?"

"*Sí,* general. A march to remember, a hard march with courage, one deserving of old men's toasts to battles won."

He nods towards Roja. "Has this *hombre* told you his news?"

"No, general. He says I will know when you decide to tell me."

A grin forms under his mustache.

"Ha! Camisa Roja is my most trusted man. I can trust him to guard my bed when I am with the *señoritas* and not speak a word about it. But you, *amigo*, the *División del Norte* owes you much for all the hard work you do with the broken men and the way you ease their pain. My other *medicos* do not know the desert plants as you do. This they tell me. *Muchas, muchas gracias,* Hombrecito."

"It is nothing, general. I am a doctor. I do what I can, when I can, for anyone who needs my help. This I have sworn to do."

"*Sí, sí*, this I know. Camisa Roja, tell Hombrecito, Doctor Grace, the news you bring us while I eat my stew and *tortillas*. A long day and I am starving."

Roja takes a final draw on his cigarette and blowing the smoke toward the brilliant stars, crushes the butt in the dirt.

"The *Revolución* fighting along the Bavispe drives off most of the *patróns* of the great *haciendas* leaving the *ranchos* with little or nothing. Most of the villages have so little food the *peons* are close to starving. We will find little in the way of supplies from the *haciendas* and villages between Colonia Morelos and Agua Prieta.

"The Carrancistas have come to Sonora, an army marches up from the south through Sinaloa and another lands from the sea in Guaymas. Maytorena, our commander in Sonora, has deserted and is in the land of the *Americanos*. The men he left behind will not fight without him, and when Carranza's troops came to Hermosillo the cowards practically gave it to them. Agua Prieta now has three thousand men and they furiously dig a trench around it to stand against us. The situation becomes worse by the day, Doctor Grace, much worse than when *División del Norte* left Casas Grandes."

I watch Villa eating and listening as Roja tells me the bad news. That he might have to fight two Carranza armies and that food supplies for *División del Norte* are scarce to nonexistent doesn't seem to bother him.

"General, what will we do?"

He wipes his mouth with the back of his hand, sucks a piece of food out of his teeth, and shrugs and smiles.

"We do as we planned, Hombrecito. I discuss this with my generals. They fully agree with me.

"What can we do? If we return to Chihuahua, the men will starve and die of thirst after having suffered so much coming across El Paso Púlpito. If we retreat, most will never leave El Paso Púlpito alive and *División del Norte* disappears with them. These men do not know what the word retreat means. If we retreat now, they will never fight tyranny again for as long as they live. The Carrancistas in Agua Prieta cannot stand against me. *El Perfumado*, Obregón, he must try to hold Hermosillo, the capital of Sonora. My spies tell me Diéguez commands them. I beat this man before. He runs in the heat of battle.

"As we planned, our blood and thunder can still take Agua Prieta. We will resupply from the guns and bullets the Carrancistas surrender, use their *dinero* to buy food supplies and bullets, and rest the men and animals. Then we go to Hermosillo and whip Diéguez again. When we do this, men will come to the *División del Norte* again and no longer run away. Mark my words. By this time next year, we eat steak and *frijoles* in Mexico City and Carranza and Obregón will be dead or hiding with the *Americanos* who love them. You wait. You will see this happen. I, General Francisco Villa, Commander of the *División del Norte,* say it will be so."

I believe him.

22. YELLOW BOY RETURNS

As the fire burns low and the night grows old, Villa and I discuss the patients in the *medico* wagons. Camisa Roja rolls and smokes another cigarette, listening, saying nothing. Doctor Oñate suggested to Villa that he leave the wagon-crash survivors in Colonia Morelos and send them back to their families when they are strong enough to be driven north to a train.

"So Hombrecito, what do you say about Oñate's idea for leaving the men in the *medico* wagons at Colonia Morelos?"

"If they are looked after at Morelos, it's the right thing to do, and knowing the Mormons, they wouldn't hesitate to help them all they can. We're going to need all the wagons and supplies we can find for Agua Prieta."

Villa nods, scratching his chin in thought. "*Sí*, I agree. We will leave the men in the *medico* wagons at Morelos even if we have to leave *medico* assistants to look after them."

He stares out into the dark toward the black, jagged eastern horizon outlined against the stars and changes the subject. "Do you remember when Muchacho Amarillo and I found you and Rafaela in the canyon where you killed *el tigre* and she taught you the true pleasures of being a *hombre?*"

Roja studies me and I wonder where the question will lead. Villa enjoys women and likes to talk about the ones he remembers best. I tell him, "*Sí*, general, I still have dreams about *el tigre*, and I'll never forget that time with Rafaela." I don't tell him I've thought about those times nearly every day since Camisa Roja killed her.

We talk for a while about the old days before he gets around to the question for which he's been making longer than normal conversation, "Hombrecito, where is our *compadre*, Muchacho Amarillo? He is not with us on the hard march over El Paso Púlpito. He brings no meat. None of the scouts see any sign of him. You think he is hurt, maybe killed or wounded by the Apaches that live in those mountains yonder?"

I, too, am concerned about Yellow Boy. The scouts not seeing any signs of him doesn't bother me. I'd be more worried if they had. If I had to guess, Yellow Boy and Runs Far have been playing cat and mouse in the mountains northeast of us and we'll probably see him again down river as we approach Colonia Morelos. "He probably went north to Rojo's camp. His wives still have relatives there and he needs to learn how they're surviving the *Revolución*. We ought to see him soon, maybe before Colonia Morelos."

Camisa Roja frowns. Villa laughs and slaps his knee. "Ha! Camisa Roja does not know he has a brother who leads an Apache camp in the sierras?"

"No, general, I know of this camp and have looked for it, but never found it. But I never learned why this Apache *jefe* is called Pelo Rojo. There are no Apaches with red hair."

I smile.

"The Apache is called Rojo because his hair is red. When he was a small child the Apaches stole him from the *Americanos*. Juh, a great warrior, raised him as a son. Rojo has never led his people on raids north of the border."

Camisa Roja blows a long stream of smoke into the cold night air. "Wise Apaches will stay away from this army. If they come sniffing around for plunder we will kill them all, *sí,* general?"

Villa stands as he nods. "*Sí,* but, the Apaches will mind their own business with my army. I know their camps, their *hombres*, and their women. I know where they live, and they know I know, eh Hombrecito? Now, *muchachos*, I visit with the men of *División del Norte* and give them strength to march day after tomorrow. *Buenos noches.*"

We salute him as he shuffles off into the darkness to mount the magnificent appaloosa Juan has saddled for him. Camisa Roja says he needs sleep and heads for his blankets somewhere just outside the circle of light from Juan's fire. I find the sack of plants I've been using to make teas for the men in the *medico* wagons and start brewing a pain killing tea for the night. While the tea brews, the other *medicos* and I visit our patients and tell them that General Villa plans to leave them in Colonia Morelos, a two or three-day march down river, and then send them on to their families and villages when they're strong enough. To a man, they all manage to smile when they hear the news. I doubt if more than a handful will make it to Morelos. There are just too many with bleeding internal injuries, too many we can't save with our feeble, healing power.

I spend a while at Doctor Oñate's fire, discussing the patients and what can be done for the men throughout the camp who suffer from skin sores and a host of other ailments that come from exposure to the desert with little food and water. Given our supplies, our only options for treating most of the men come from herbal concoctions like the willow tea. The potions offer some relief, but most can expect a long, painful march to Agua Prieta.

It grows late. Exhausted, I slide under my blankets next to the coals of Juan's fire. I'm fast falling into a dreamless sleep when I feel a hand squeeze my shoulder. My fingers instantly curl around my revolver's handle, my heart galloping. In the low glow of the few coals left in the fire, I stare into the black eyes and slash-like wrinkles of the man who found me hiding under tumbleweed caught in mesquite nearly twenty years earlier. Yellow Boy. Instantly awake, I'm relieved and filled with gratitude to Ussen that he's returned.

I grin and start to speak but he holds up the edge of his hand to his mouth for silence and points up river. Easy to slip past without being seen, most of the fires have burned down to nothing but beds of gray ash on top of orange coals that give little light. At the river we turn south, upstream, careful to step on rocks so even the most experienced tracker can't follow our path unless he's an Apache.

A couple of hundred yards from the last fire, Yellow Boy turns up a deep, dry *arroyo*. We wind past so many bushes and trees that before long we can't see or hear the river and come to Yellow Boy's pinto and another horse that looks familiar, hobbled and nibbling brush. A pot of coffee bubbles on the coals of a small, hot fire and he motions me to take one of the tin cups on his blanket. I pour myself a cup and then fill his as he sits down by the fire.

He nods his thanks and leans back on an elbow, studying me, and says in that mixture of Spanish and English he likes to use, "Hombrecito, you make it through El Paso Púlpito with Arango. *Bueno.* My eyes are glad to see you, my son."

"It pleases my heart to see you, Uncle. You've been gone a long time. Even Arango asks about you. I told him we'd probably see you by the time we reached Colonia Morelos. Why didn't you stay with us in the camp?"

He takes a long slurp of his steaming coffee and lights a cigar. "Better for me to stay out of sight. Yaquis watch Villa for the *Carrancistas.* I watch Yaquis. Army of *Carrancistas* in Sonora. Some go to Agua Prieta, some to Hermosillo. A hard fight in Agua Prieta comes for Villa and his men. Even now the *Carrancista jefe* digs a ditch around Agua Prieta. His men dig faster than a rat trying to hide from a rattlesnake.

"I come to Arango's fire at Morelos. Tell Arango you speak to me this night. Give him my words."

"He already knows about the *Carrancistas.* His scouts told him."

"*Sí,* it is true, but they not know about the Yaquis. You tell him I watch. He will think it is a good thing."

The coffee, still scalding hot, burns my gullet all the way down. It feels good to know Yellow Boy covers our backs. "Where'd you get the horse? I've seen him before."

"Horse of Runs Far."

"Did you kill Runs Far?"

He looks in his coffee as if embarrassed and shakes his head. "No. Only take horse. I tell Runs Far again to stay away from Arango's army. No take *muchachos*. Runs Far, he listens? Maybe so, he has ears. He comes back, I kill him."

"You know he'll come back, and he'll be on the lookout for you, making it ten times harder to catch him."

Yellow Boy nods.

"Hombrecito speaks true, but I will stop Runs Far. Arango must have no reason for war on Rojo's camp. You see."

We talk through a second cup of coffee. Yellow Boy tells me what he's seen as he covered the mountains and Rio Bavispe and San Bernardino valleys trailing Runs Far and his two women.

"Mormon tribe gone. Houses, pueblos empty. Fields have nothing. No horses. No cattle. No sheep. All gone. Even Apache no come now. Bellies of Arango army stay empty long time."

"Arango knows this. His scouts have told him already. What do you think he'll do?"

Yellow Boy shrugs.

"In war, weak always die. Many die on trail to Agua Prieta. Starve or by bullets, all the same, *hombres* die. Bullet easier. Quick. To die without food, takes long time and much courage. Arango knows this. Do not forget what I tell you before, Hombrecito. Arango never blames self for army defeat. Leave before he says you are the reason he loses."

"*Si*, Uncle. I will do this."

I understand Yellow Boy doesn't want me to wind up inside the tiger he thinks we're riding. Yet, I can't imagine being blamed for the defeat of *División del Norte.*

Finishing another cup of coffee, Yellow Boy promises to meet us in Colonia Morelos in three days. I leave him and creep back to my blankets. Even with a belly full of strong coffee, I don't have any trouble finding sleep.

23. COLONIA MORELOS

Thousands of human and animal feet and wagon wheels soon turn the road to Colonia Morelos, once hard-packed caliche, into a fine, white powder the lightest breeze lifts and flings on the men and animals. The road stays within sight of the Rio Bavispe most of the way. At least we no longer suffer from thirst, but day-by-day hunger gnaws at empty bellies.

Villa sends sorties off along the river, gathering what they can to feed the men – fish, frogs, turtles, cattails, anything that fills starving bellies. He sends hunting parties into the foothills of the eastern side of the Sierra Madre and into the Tigre Mountains on the western side of the Bavispe. He takes corn from two or three tiny Mexican villages and a couple of big *ranchos* along the way, leaving enough for the villagers to get through the winter but leaves nothing at the *ranchos*. Most of the men make it through the worst of the march, food supplies from the land barely enough to keep them staggering forward. Still, many die. Many rough, quickly dug graves mark the roadside with those who collapse in their tracks and have no strength to stand again.

Late in the afternoon of the third day out of Colonia Oaxaca, the dark outlines of houses and stores emerge in the dusty light. We've reached Colonia Morelos, where the Bavispe joins the Rio San Bernardino and makes a long, sweeping turn to run south on the western side of the Tigre Mountains.

Two small boys, one maybe five or six, and the other about twelve play outside around the open door of a small adobe house well back from the rivers. Scouts who've been sent ahead of the column ride up to meet Villa. I'm too far away to hear what's said, but I see him pointing at the adobe and nodding at their answers to his questions before he waves the column forward to camping places north of Morelos, up the Rio San Bernardino.

After tending the survivors, I leave the *medico* wagons and ride over to Villa's command wagon. I don't see Villa in his usual daily meeting with his generals.

"Where's the *jefe?*"

Juan, with a conspiratorial grin, nods back down the river toward the adobe. A Mexican widow and two little boys live there. She told the scouts that the Mormons leaving Morelos have not returned. Without her husband, killed under Villa's command fighting at Parral three years earlier, she went to Morelos seeking her sister's Mormon family and work. The Mormons, including her sister's family, just leaving when she arrived, gave her a little money to look after the village until they returned. Juan tells me that Villa's visiting her because he remembers her husband, and that he's spent several hours consoling her inside the adobe, with the door barred to keep the boys out.

The boys take their supper at Juan's wagon with Jesús, Marco, and me. The oldest son of the widow isn't much younger than Jesús. He wants Villa to take him with us. I suspect that if things had been different between Villa and his mother, Villa would have conscripted him. As it is, next morning Villa tells the boy he needs to stay and help his mother and brother and that perhaps he can join the *División del Norte* in another year or two. Villa leaves them a little food, and promises more, like he promises the entire army, after they take Agua Prieta.

Later that evening Villa returns from the widow's house, and, with a big grin, slowly folds into a chair Juan sits out for him. Juan hands him a cup of the pungent, slightly bitter chocolate-tasting piñon-nut coffee. As long as Juan adds sugar to it, Villa doesn't care if it comes out the wrong end of a cow. He takes a few slurps and stares a long time at the *División del Norte* fires stretching far up the San Bernardino River.

Many more of our patients in the *medico* wagons have survived than I expected. When we learn the Mormons are no longer in Colonia Morelos, Doctor Oñate, the other *medicos*, and I decide to make our patients comfortable in the back storeroom of a large mercantile building and to leave several *medico* assistants to change bandages and give them my pain-killing concoctions until they all can be taken to a train home. Villa approves our plan but worries about having enough *medicos* at Agua Prieta if so many have to stay at Colonia Morelos. We're discussing what else might be done when I glance across the fire and see Yellow Boy standing there with his arms crossed.

I grin and shake my head. Villa sees me and looks over his shoulder in the direction I'm staring. He whoops, "*Madre a Dios!* There you stand! We have missed you many days, *amigo*. All is well?"

Yellow Boy walks around the fire, gives each of us a hard one-two handshake and sits down between Villa and me. Juan's hands tremble when he hands Yellow Boy a cup of coffee. He knows Yellow Boy and doesn't fear him; still, the shock of seeing him seemingly appear out of thin air brings back hard memories that stretch across decades of Apache outrages in Mexico.

Yellow Boy takes a long slurp from the steaming cup, and nods speaking in Spanish that is better than his English. "*Si, Jefe*, all is well. Yaqui scouts, they leave. Watch *División del Norte* no more."

Villa grins. "Ha. Probably stayed long enough to count us and then take the numbers to *El Perfumado*, who will tell Calles, digging the trench at Agua Prieta, to save his men and leave. The *División* will massacre them in one charge. Any sign of the Carrancista Army?"

"No sign, *Jefe*. I search mountains on both sides of *rio*."

"Do you bring us meat, *amigo*? My *hombres* are near to starving. Now they live only on what we can find on the land. We are not Apache. They don't find much."

"*Si, Jefe*. I bring a deer. Mañana I find more."

"Ah. *Bueno. Bueno*. The wild game saves our lives."

"*Sí, Jefe*. But taking the animals leaves Apaches hungry in the season of the Ghost Dance. They will raid the line-of-march for food, guns, maybe even captives."

Villa squints at Yellow Boy and slowly nods his head. "Let them come. I know where they live. If they touch my men or supplies, I will send my *dorados* after them and they will be no more. This I swear."

Yellow Boy looks Villa in the eye. "*Sí, Jefe, comprendo.* This I say to Rojo when I see him. Rojo understands."

Villa grins and relaxes. "*Bueno.* Apaches are our *amigos.* I have no desire to strike them. When Agua Prieta is taken, I will help *mi amigos.* How fares *mi amigo* Rojo?'

"Days are hard. Too many warriors die in raids. Boys have no uncles or brothers, no teachers. Most warriors have two maybe three wives now. Food and supplies run low. The *ranchos* on the east side of the *sierras* have only a few cattle." He nods his head, "*Sí, Jefe.* The days are hard."

Villa nods. "*Sí, mi amigo.* Days are hard. They will be better when I whip the Carrancistas and *El Perfumado.*"

We speak of many things until Juan leads Villa's palomino around for him to mount and ride up the line of campfires to speak with and encourage his men. I watch his back disappear into the darkness and marvel at how the *bandito* I once knew and considered a friend has become the *generalissimo* I now serve.

24. UP THE SAN BERNARDINO

Yellow Boy leaves before dawn leading our pack mule to look for game. He says he plans to range the hills back toward the village of Bavispe because there are too many sorties ranging the mountains north of Morelos. Every available officer hunts. Even the Butcher, Rodolfo Fierro, leads five men into the Tigre Mountains off to the southwest looking for mines to raid, deer to hunt, or deserters to execute.

I've come to hate the sight of Fierro. I've never known anyone who enjoys killing more. His black eyes bore in on you, imagining, I'm sure, he's slitting your throat or putting a bullet in your brain, taking pleasure in watching the light go out of your eyes. Most of the men in *División del Norte* hate and fear him. Knowing he's the one who'll probably come after them, they'd rather starve than desert.

I spend most of the day helping Doctor Oñate and six

assistants set up a little hospital in Colonia Morelos for the men left behind. We do all we can to make the hospital's patients comfortable, and before leaving a couple of hours before sundown, I brew up a fresh batch of painkiller, showing the assistants how to make it.

The infantry and wagons won't make more than five or six miles on the soft sandy road before stopping for the day. Riding Satanas, it'll be easy enough for me to catch up with them before dark.

A couple of miles up river from Colonia Morelos, I see four or five riders sitting on their horses, casually smoking and watching something thrash around in the river. As I draw closer I can see a horse floundering in soupy sand and a man trapped on it, bellowing in rage at the men watching him. Galloping up to the little group, I hear, "… You sorry sons-of-whores get me out of here…throw me a rope. Goddamn you…I'll march you against the wall and have you all shot… I'll cut off your cajones and strangle you with your own *mierda*…I'll…get me out of here! Hurry up, Goddamn it…"

The men sit unmoving as Rodolfo Fierro sinks deeper and deeper into the muck. The horse's strength is gone and its struggles grow weaker. The deeper the man sinks the more he screams orders and threats. Water is filling the impression in the sand made by the sinking man and horse. By the time I ride up to the men watching him, Fierro is up to his chest in the thick soup and his horse snorts to keep water out of her nostrils, straining to keep above the water line, its grunts pitiful. Fierro's screams and orders croak into a pleading tone that sounds even more obnoxious than his original outraged orders and curses.

I peel off several coils of my *reata*, a rawhide rope *vaqueros* use, to make a big loop as Fierro screams, "You sorry bastards pull me out of here, I can not die like this. *Dios* will punish you. General Villa will punish you! Help me, in the name of *Dios*, help me!"

The mare struggles, and in a last burst of strength thrashes to pull herself out before her nose slides under the soupy, sandy water.

A *dorado* who outranks the others shakes his head.

"No *reata*, doctor. General Fierro stands many of our men against a wall, orders them shot to pieces and then burns them in a pile after he personally puts a bullet in their heads. He did this even to the *generalissimo's* most loyal soldiers because he thought they looked at him wrong. He has cursed God and has threatened to kill us all, at one time or another. Now let him pull his own way out. If he does, he will most certainly kill us. I'm tired of waiting for it to happen. This is justice from God, do not interfere."

By now, Fierro has his head tilted back to keep the water at his chin and he's begging as he puffs and gasps for breaths, "*Por favor… por favor…* please… please *señores* I forget all this… just pull me out."

I stare at the *dorados* for a moment and shake my head. I save lives, not take them. The water comes up to Fierro's nose. I whirl the reata loop and throw, but from my unpracticed hands, it falls short. In a gurgling, thrashing scream Fierro's face slides under the water and he's gone.

The *dorado* nods.

"There is justice in this world, Doctor. You see it here. It is too bad about the mare. *Adiós*."

The horsemen ride up to the road, never look back, and disappear. I coil up the rope wondering if I've really just seen God's justice.

A couple of days later I speak to the *dorado* and ask what happened. He looks me in the eye and, I believe, speaks the truth.

"Doctor Grace, we hunted all day and found nothing, no miners, no deserters, no game, nothing. On the way back to the column, we stop to fill a water cask. The mare sees a coiled rattlesnake and crow hops out of the way just as Fierro is dismounting. Fierro falls backwards, his boot hanging in the stirrup. In a panic, the mare runs, dragging Fierro into the wet sand there by the river."

I understand his story perfectly. The place is one of several major pools of quicksand along the San Bernardino. Neither Fierro nor the mare have a chance once they are in it unless someone throws them a *reata* and pulls them out.

I say, "*Señor*, I won't say anything to General Villa unless he asks me directly."

A smile flashes on the *dorado's* face. "Ah, *muchas gracias*, Doctor Grace, that is all we ask."

In his grief over losing Fierro, Villa never asks, and I never tell.

On the sixth day out of Colonia Morelos, we camp about six miles down the San Bernardino River from John Slaughter's Rancho San Bernardino, which spreads out across both sides of the border. After supper, Villa asks Yellow Boy and me to join him in his wagon for coffee. Villa sits in his chair behind his battered field desk, I on a stool across from him, and Yellow Boy, as usual, on the floor, leaning his back against the wagon box with the butt of his Henry rifle on the floor between his moccasins, its barrel resting against his shoulder. The air cool and pleasant, dusk not quite gone, a coal-oil lantern spreads golden light and dark shadows in his office while we relax with our scalding-hot coffee.

Staring out the door, Villa thoughtfully scratches the stubble on his chin, and clears his throat. "*Amigos*, we are within three days march of the border and the road west from the San Bernardino Rancho is another three days march to Agua Prieta. Hombrecito, *mañana* mount your great black horse, and ride north to the Rancho San Bernardino. The *rancho hacienda* has a *teléfono*. Tell the rancher you ride with Francisco Villa and ask him to let you call *Señor* Peach in El Paso. You know how to find Queentin using the *teléfono*?"

I nod. I know Quent's house address and I saw a telephone there when I had supper with Persia and him during my trip to El Paso. I don't doubt the *Herald* has several *teléfonos*. It'll just be a matter of catching Quent at the right time and place.

Yellow Boy looks from me to Villa and back again. He knows what the *teléfono* is but doesn't understand how the spirits guide your voice to just the right person on the other end, and if the truth be known, neither do I.

Villa says, "Ask Queentin to take the early morning train from El Paso and get off at the San Bernardino cattle pens. They're far from anyone else and right at the tracks. The railroad calls the place San Bernardino Crossing. The train from El Paso should be there by the middle of the afternoon, day after tomorrow. San Bernardino Crossing is about a two-hour ride from the San Bernardino *rancho casa*. I ask that you and Muchacho Amarillo meet him there with the horse you saved for him and bring him back to the *rancho hacienda*. I will meet you there and we will talk of my plans for the attack on Agua Prieta and learn what he knows about Wilson and Carranza."

Puzzled, I ask, "Why use Rancho San Bernardino? Why not pick Quent up in Douglas and bring him back to you on the trail? Are you friends with the owner of the *rancho*?"

Villa grins. "*Sí*, Texas John Slaughter is *un amigo bueno*. In fact he is my banker."

My eyes widen. "Your banker? Texas John Slaughter holds your money? I remember Rufus Pike telling me stories about Texas John Slaughter and how he was sheriff in Cochise County back in the days when the Earps and Clantons were going at it. Rufus said Slaughter had a *rancho*. I guess it must be the San Bernardino. How did he ever get to be a banker? How'd he get to be your banker?"

Villa laughs and slaps his knee. "It is a good story Hombrecito. I first met *Señor* Slaughter when he caught me taking some of his cattle for my army when we were fighting Díaz in the *Revolución*. I tell you Hombrecito, Slaughter is fearless. There I was with his cows and twenty men, but he had a big shotgun and would have fought us all until we were dead or gone if I did not pay him for the cows I was taking. I give him a few gold Reals for the cattle. He tested every one with his teeth before he let us have the cattle. He says to me, 'Pancho, when the fighting is over, come back and see me. I'll tell you how to make gold honestly with cattle.'

"After Madero came to power, there was no more fighting. I go back to Rancho San Bernardino and speak with

Señor Slaughter. He tells me he owns two butcher shops in Bisbee and had a meat market in Charleston before the great earthquake destroyed the town. I had *mucho dinero* I saved from the *ranchos* the *hacendado* families left during the *Revolución*. I ask him to keep *mi dinero* safe and invest it for me. I went back to Chihuahua and started four butcher shops myself. As he told me they would, the butcher shops made *mucho dinero* and the *dinero* I give him, he has multiplied many times over in other businesses. Huerta, that old son-of-a-bitch, took all my property in Chihuahua. My only *pesos* are in the care of *Señor* Texas John Slaughter and now I need them. The *hombres* of *División del Norte* have much hunger. Perhaps he will lend me more. He is very honest. He will give me my *dinero*. Soon we have a good visit at the *rancho* San Bernardino, eh, Hombrecito?"

"*Si, jefe*, and we will bring Quent."

25. SAN BERNARDINO CROSSING

A large, one-story ranch house with a big front porch glows white in the afternoon sun. I tie Satanas to the white rail fence around an emerald green yard and walk up a hard caliche path to the porch in front of a fancy, carved dark wood Mexican-style door. I knock and hear the creak of a chair and the shuffle of feet. John Slaughter, wearing his famous pearl-handled .44 and looking out of place in his slippers, opens the door. He's short, with fearless eyes that directly challenge mine, a fine white beard covering his chin, and thinning gray hair wrinkled by a distinct hat line.

"Mr. Slaughter?"

"They call me Texas John Slaughter. Yes, sir, that'd be me. What can I do for yuh? We ain't hirin' right now." He looks over my shoulder at Yellow Boy, who stands behind me, "Especially Apaches, we ain't hirin'. They's supposed to be on the reservation. Where'd he git that ratty old cavalry jacket any ways?"

"Sir, I'm Doctor Henry Grace. Pancho Villa sent me ahead of the *División del Norte* to ask if I may use your telephone to call a gentleman in El Paso? The gentleman here with me is *Señor* Muchacho Amarillo. He's a member of the tribal police on the Mescalero Reservation over in New Mexico."

Mentioning Pancho Villa brings a smile to Texas John, and he opens the door wide for us to come in.

"All right. Just don't want my throat cut by no Apache desperado. Come on in. Why shore, be glad to lend 'er to yuh. It's a right handy gadjit. Why I use 'er ever two or three days myself. It's a hangin' on the wall right over there. Come on in the kitchen when yore finished. I'll get Maria to make us some coffee. She's a damn good Mex cook."

Yellow Boy finds a place to sit on the floor and keep an eye on Texas John and his .44.

Calling the *Herald* first, I reach Quent on the first try. The operator knows how to connect to a telephone close to his desk, and he answers on the third ring. Quent promises he'll be on the train out of El Paso early the next morning and will meet us at San Bernardino Crossing that afternoon. I ring off, relieved that the telephone connection was so easily made.

Yellow Boy and I have a cup of coffee with Texas John who takes a long slurp and smacks his lips while sitting at his long, kitchen table.

"Damn good coffee. Ain't had to drink none mixed with piñon seeds since I started making money on this here ranch. Viola, my ol' lady, is over to Douglas doing some shopping. S'pect she'll be back in a few days. So, ol' Pancho is movin' that army of his west?"

He's right about the coffee, although I've developed a taste for the piñon flavor. "Yes, sir, General Villa marched the *División del Norte* across the Sierra Madre via El Paso Púlpito and then from Colonia Oaxaca to Colonia Morelos and up the Rio San Bernardino."

Texas John frowns. "Great day in the mornin'. You mean he actually got his army cross El Paso Púlpito without losin' ever one of 'em? Most generals I know on both sides of the border say it ain't possible, but if you say so, I guess he done it. I read all sorts of speculatin' in the papers about what he'd do if he made it across the mountains. What's he plannin'?"

"I understand that when he gets to your ranch he'll turn west and take Agua Prieta."

"That there might be harder than he thinks. I hear General Calles has his men diggin' night and day puttin' a trench and barbed wire around Agua Prieta. But I ain't one to underestimate ol' Pancho. He'n get er' done. So you said he sent you over here to call somebody in El Paso?"

I take another swallow of Texas John's coffee, feeling my body start to fill with nervous energy. "Yes, sir. Yellow Boy and I plan to meet the gentleman I just called, a reporter for the *El Paso Herald*, Quentin Peach, at San Bernardino Ranch crossing tomorrow afternoon."

Texas John grins. "Quentin Peach? You just called Quentin Peach? Ain't it a small world? Why I read his column in the *Herald* all the time. Be interestin' to meet Mr. Peach. When's Pancho comin'?

"I understand General Villa plans to visit you in the afternoon and discuss some banking business before leaving for Agua Prieta."

"That'll be fine. I'll make us up some ice cream. I know he'd crawl across Chihuahua for a bowl."

I see Yellow Boy, who listens carefully to every word in our conversation, frown at the mention of ice cream. He doesn't know what it is.

I say, "Yes, sir, I know he's partial to ice cream. How do you make it way out here in the desert without ice?"

He grins, "Aw, ain't nothin' to it. Got me a good ice house, and bring it over by the wagonload from Douglas. If yuh got ice, all yuh got to do is keep stirrin' the recipe until she freezes and eat 'er while she's still froze."

Yellow Boy still looks confused. I decide I'll explain ice cream to him later and ask Texas John, "Mr. Slaughter, it's getting late in the afternoon. I wonder if you'd mind if we make camp outside your yard fence before it gets dark?"

"Why, hell yes, I mind. Ain't no need for you boys to camp outside. Maria's a good cook and I want you to have supper with me. I got a spare bedroom or two. Come on and sleep inside. Be my guests."

He's right. Maria is a very good cook and supper is fine, but Yellow Boy decides he'll sleep on the porch.

We reach Slaughter's cattle pens next to the train tracks around mid-day. A tin-roofed lean-to provides shade and the air is cool and comfortable in the bright sunshine. We relax in the shade and wait for Quent.

While we wait, Yellow Boy smokes and I walk around the mesquite looking for peyote buttons and other plants I can use for medicines. No more than an hour passes when Yellow Boy stands up and stares off down the tracks. There's a black smudge in the sky just about where the tracks ought to be. He walks over to the rails and puts his ear against one. In a few seconds he nods and says, "Iron wagon come." I check my watch. The train is about two hours early. *Strange. Trains run late, never early.*

We wait. Before long, we hear the distant rumble and rattle of the train and its cars in the distance and see the engine's black smoke plume standing out clearly against the iridescent blue sky. The engine comes in sight followed by a long string of cars, maybe sixty or more, far more than normal for a daily passenger run that very rarely has more than three or four passenger cars.

The engine shows no signs of slowing down and sweeps by us like a big black bullet. Amazed, I stare at the passenger cars. They're packed with soldiers wearing Mexican Army uniforms. Between the passenger cars are several flat cars loaded with machine guns, several large artillery pieces, barbed wire and boxes of ammunition and artillery shells. Three flatbed cars follow, each carrying a gigantic searchlight that must be at least five feet in diameter. Some of the soldiers in the last cars even grin and wave out the window as they sweep by.

Yellow Boy and I look at each other and frown. "Weren't those Carrancistas?"

Yellow Boy nods. "Si, Hombrecito. Carrancistas."

"What are they doing on a train north of the border? Have we been invaded by Mexico? Where do you think they're going?"

Yellow Boy shrugs his shoulders and returns to the lean-to shade. I follow him. *Surely that wasn't Quent's train. If we're lucky he'll be along later like he said. Maybe he'll know what's going on.*

I finish gathering medicinal plants and Yellow Boy naps. I try to make sense of why Carrancistas are on a train in the United States, but draw nothing but blanks. It just doesn't make sense. When I'm ready to stretch out on my blanket, Yellow Boy says he'll keep watch.

A distant train whistle jars me awake. Yellow Boy stares down the tracks at a black smoke plume advancing through the mesquites. My watch shows a little after 3:00. Far down the tracks a big smoking engine rolls towards us on the shiny steel rails. It whistles a mournful long and a short hoot, indicating it's coming to a crossing and begins slowing down. It grinds to a clanking halt at the stock pens. I see the engineer wave at us from his perch inside the engine and I wave back. From the passenger car next to the caboose, a man, carrying saddlebags and portfolio case over his shoulder, his pants stuffed in high riding boots, dressed like a cowboy, and a Winchester in the crook of his arm, steps off the train. Quent. The conductor leans off the back of the caboose, waves the roll signal to the conductor and yells, "Board!" The engineer waves back to him, moves some levers inside the engine cab and the train begins to roll.

Yellow Boy and I lead the horses toward Quent. Grinning under a big, flat-brimmed sweat-stained Stetson, he meets us halfway to the lean-to and sticks out his hand. "Howdy, boys. You look like hell. Haven't you had anything to eat in the last three weeks?"

It does my soul good to see him again. After three weeks with Villa in the Mexican wilderness it seems like a lifetime since he boarded the train in Hachita. We shake hands all around and mount.

We don't ride more than thirty yards before questions begin flying out of my mouth. "Quent, a couple of hours ago a long train came by here and it looked like it was filled with Carrancista soldiers and equipment. The Carrancista Army on American soil? What's going on?"

Quent shakes his head, his face grim, eyes angry. "An outrage. That's what's going on. Wilson recognized Carranza as the official President of Mexico ten days ago and to be sure he stays that way, he let Obregón send General Calles three infantry brigades up from Piedras Negras, through El Paso, and then across the US over to Douglas and back across the border to Agua Prieta. On top of that, General Calles has been able to pull troops in from other defenses. Instead of twelve hundred soldiers, Villa will be facing about seven thousand men in trenches with machine guns behind barbed wire and minefields. The slaughter will be worse than it was at Celaya."

Speechless, I stare at him. Yellow Boy stares straight ahead, muttering, "No damn good. No damn good."

I say, "But...but Villa's men are starving. He thinks he'll have a resupply point on the border after he takes Agua Prieta and the battle won't take more than a couple of hours. He has to take it or he's finished."

Quent shrugs. "He doesn't know that Wilson's officially recognized Carranza or even that Wilson has let Carranza ship troops to Agua Prieta. If he tries to take it, he'll certainly be finished. I shouldn't even have come. I'll never be able to write what Villa wants, but I gave my word. Here I am. Where's Villa now?"

"He's with his banker getting money to buy supplies after he takes Agua Prieta."

Quent's jaw dropped. "Banker? What banker? What banker is fool enough to do business with the *generalissimo*?"

"Texas John Slaughter."

Quent looks at me from under his raised brows. "The old fire-breathing sheriff from Cochise County? The one who owns San Bernardino Ranch? That John Slaughter is a banker?"

"Yep, he's a banker. Not an official one, you understand, but friends and neighbors give him their money for safekeeping and to invest it when he thinks it's a safe bet. Evidently, the *generalissimo* has a good-sized stash with the sheriff too."

"Damn! Who'd have thought, or hearing about it, believed it's true. Is that where we're going now? To Slaughter's place?'

"That's where we're going."

"Well, when I give Villa the news, just be sure you're not in the line of fire. He'll be blind with rage."

Yellow Boy nods and mutters, "*Sí,* very blind."

26. BAD NEWS

S wishing its tail at flies and nibbling at gra'ma grass, the general's palomino stands hobbled next to Texas John's white rail fence when Quent, Yellow Boy, and I return. As we tie our horses near the general's, the ranch house front door opens and Texas John shuffles out followed by Villa. They laugh and joke about Pancho coming back to steal more of Slaughter's cattle and eating up all his ice cream. Villa's vest pocket holds a folded sheaf of white paper and he's motioning us to hurry inside. We leave our gear on the porch and sit around Slaughter's kitchen table, a stack of bank papers and a fat, fancy fountain pen on the end where he and the general have been drinking coffee.

Maria sets out three more cups and pours us coffee before disappearing into the other side of the house, saying to Texas John as she trundles out the door, "Call if you need me, *Patrón.*"

We're all barely seated before Villa says, "So, Queentin, what says *El Presidente* Wilson?"

Quent has already opened a notebook. There's a pregnant pause as he finishes a sentence he scribbles in that unreadable shorthand script of his. He lays his green lacquered pen in the seam of his notebook and looks into Villa's anxious brown eyes. "It's not good, *mi amigo*. Wilson recognized Carranza as First President ten days ago and made permanent the temporary embargo on arms to you."

Villa stares at the tabletop in front of him, slowly shaking his head, and mutters, "Betrayed." Red in the face, he smacks the table so hard coffee nearly sloshes out of our cups and shouts, "The Goddamned *gringos* have betrayed me after all I do for them!" He beats his chest with a hand trembling in fury and roars in a voice sounding like a wounded bear, "They have betrayed me!"

Quent continues.

"It gets worse. Wilson cannot let you win in Agua Prieta. He is afraid a Carranza defeat will embarrass the United States and give the Germans too much influence on Carranza. The Germans want Mexico to attack the United States in order to keep it out of the war in Europe. He's let Carranza send three brigades of infantry and their equipment from Piedras Negras into Laredo, then ship them north up across Texas to El Paso and across the United States border to Douglas and into Agua Prieta. Hombrecito and Yellow Boy saw one of the trains filled with soldiers pass while they were waiting for my train. They can tell you what I say is true. Instead of having twelve hundred men for a fight, General Calles now has seven thousand. General Funston has been ordered to Douglas with soldiers and has been ordered to attack you if your bullets and shells land in Douglas or if you cross the border during the fight for Agua Prieta."

Villa, the fury of thunder and lightning in his eyes, stares at Quent. His hands resting flat on the table ball tightly into fists. Texas John, scowling, shakes his head. "That ain't right. Hell, it ain't even legal. Why that fool Wilson is transporting an army across the territory of a country that claims it don't favor either side."

The room grows still except for the bubbling coffee pot. Villa's hands slowly relax, and blowing like he's coming up for air, he slumps back in his chair.

"Traitors. The *gringos* are traitors. After all I did for them, after all Carranza did to them and they choose Carranza? Those *gringos* now in Mexico had better pray to God that they do not cross my trail. I am through protecting the *gringos*. Any *gringo* I see in Mexico will die."

Quent picks up his pen, ready to write. "What will you do now, general? I understand a trench behind barbed wire now goes all the way around Agua Prieta. Calles has in place many machine guns and artillery to fire on your men. General Funston prepares to attack if he thinks you threaten Douglas. Wilson will not let you take Agua Prieta, even if he has to use *Americano* soldiers to stop you."

Villa stares at a Winchester hanging above the door lintel. The house is quiet except for the *tick-tock* of the pendulum of a grandfather clock in the hall next to the kitchen.

Slowly, Villa's eyes lock on Quent. "I...will...attack... Agua Prieta. Yes, I will attack Agua Prieta and the entire United States if I need to. I have cannons my men died getting through El Paso Púlpito. I have twice the men as Calles. My army is hungry, even starving. My army does not fear this fight. They want it. They show great courage to march all this way. I will take Agua Prieta, a little anthill I step on and smash in two hours on the way to Hermosillo. Wilson will regret the day he did this thing to Francisco Villa, to Mexico, to its people. Funston better stay on his side of the border. I will attack Douglas and burn it to the ground if I have to."

Villa's fist slams the table in frustration. "All those years I guaranteed *Americanos* and other foreigners protection in my terrains. All those years and this is how I'm repaid? Many *gringos* will die because of this, Queentin. Put that in big black letters in your *periodico*."

He smiles at Texas John Slaughter. "*Señor* Slaughter, *muchas gracias* for your help with *mi* banking, the *magnificó* ice cream, and the use of your *teléfono*. You are an honest *hombre*, not like our *presidentes*. *My* friends and I, we must leave now for there is much to do. *Adiós*."

Slaughter shakes hands with Villa and then us. "*Adiós*, Gen'ral. I understand you need to go. Good luck against Carranza. It's a pleasure meetin' yuh boys. *Adiós, hombres*."

We ride southeast toward the river. Over the border and within a couple of miles of Slaughter's place we cross a dusty road. Villa stops at the road and points into the dark orange sunset and scattered purple clouds.

"*Muchachos*, Agua Prieta and Douglas are thirty kilometers west. Take the road and scout out the way. Make sure Calles has no men in El Paso Gallardo to ambush me. If he's there, Yellow Boy brings me this news. Queentin, you go to Douglas and do your interviews. Find out what goes on there."

He pulls a paper from the sheaf of papers in his vest pocket and hands it to me. "Hombrecito, take this paper from Slaughter, go to Douglas. It is a line of credit, as good as *dinero*, the storekeepers there will accept it. Send to El Paso for shirts and underwear for the *muchachos*, the sores on their bodies will not go away unless the rags go. Order also four wagonloads of hay for the *División animales,* and, find out where *medico* supplies in Douglas can be bought. I see you in *tres días* on the *llano* before Agua Prieta. Be careful, *mis amigos. Adiós*."

27. DOUGLAS

We ride into Douglas about midnight, American soldiers everywhere. A couple of miles outside of town we pass several artillery pieces being set up to point south, and, a little further on hundreds, maybe thousands, of four-man military tents, the straight lines of their pyramid tops disappearing into the northeast darkness out over the *llano*. Camp Jones.

Torches line a couple of dusty roads running parallel to the border. High ridges of dirt appear to zigzag between them, thrown there by hundreds of men digging a trench or filling and stacking sacks of dirt along the trench's edge facing the border. A half-mile south, torches light up the border at Agua Prieta. It's impossible to see much there except the turmoil of men moving around in the flickering lights swinging picks and shovels.

Quent looks for a building with a high roof for a better

view. Near the center of town we find the five-story Gadsden Hotel, its mansard roof cut off flat in a widow's peak and trimmed in fancy scrollwork. Quent grabs my arm. "The top of that roof is perfect. It's at least sixty feet off the ground and can't be more than three-quarters of a mile from the border. We'll be able to see everything with our glasses come daylight. Come on. Let's see if we can get us a room and if they'll let us get up on the roof."

Yellow Boy doesn't say anything but I know he doesn't like the idea of staying inside the big White-Eye house. The clerk, an old man, glasses at the end of his bulbous nose resting above a great white mustache, needs a shave but otherwise looks presentable. His eyes study Yellow Boy while he talks to Quent or me.

"Howdy, gents. What can I do for yuh?"

Quent says, "We need a room for the night." He pauses for a heartbeat watching the old man's face. "I'm Quentin Peach, maybe you've read some of my articles in the *El Paso Herald*? Allow me to introduce Doctor Henry Grace and his associate *Señor* Muchacho Amarillo, Mescalero tribal policeman."

The clerk frowns. "Tribal policeman, huh? Reckon I have a room for you two fellers but the 'Pache has to sleep on the roof. Everbody in the place'll leave if they find out they's under the same roof with a 'Pache."

I want to laugh out loud and strangle the miserable old coot at the same time. I glance at Yellow Boy whose expression hasn't changed since we walked through the door. He understands everything the clerk says, but I turn to him and say in Apache, "Uncle, this is too good to be true." He nods but says nothing, his eyes sparkling, Coyote the Trickster, always thinking it's fun to fool the White-Eye.

I say, "*Sí, Señor* Muchacho Amarillo sleeps on the roof."

Quent keeps a straight face as he asks, "Well, can we sit with him a while up there?"

The clerk smiles in relief. "Don't see why not." He pushes the register toward Quent. "Sign right there for me please, sir. It's gonna be fifty dollars a night for the three of yuhs."

Quent raises his brows and shakes his head: highway robbery for a hotel room in a dusty smelter and railroad town, but he lets it go.

The clerk rambles on, "Tell the 'Pache to keep his head down up 'ere. It might get kinda dangerous. Everbody says Pancho Villa's comin' and they's gonna be a big battle with Carranza's boys down yonder 'cross the border in Agua Prieta. General Calles has got them Mexicans digging a ditch all the way around the village, stringin' barbed wire, and plantin' minefields. Ought to be one hell of a turkey shoot. I don't care if them Mexicans kill each other off as long as they stay on their side of the border and don't shoot in this direction.

"Army's afraid old Villa might raid Douglas too. I hear they got three thousand men down there in Camp Jones, and a bunch of artillery pieces scattered around ready to blow him to Hell and gone if he tries crossin' the border."

The clerk gives us a room on the fifth floor and explains how the door at the end of the hall leads to stairs going up to the roof. We thank him, take the horses to a nearby livery stable, and then return to head upstairs for the widow's peak.

There are so many torches all over town that even without a moon we get a clear picture of the defenses against *División del Norte*. About three-quarters of a mile south is the border fence and just beyond is the large rectangular outline of torches around Agua Prieta that General Calles defends. East of the hotel and running parallel to the border are the lines of torches where soldiers dig. Scattered around town are bonfires where men take a break to eat and drink coffee. Adding to the strings of torch fires are clusters of torches used by crews setting up artillery to point south on the other side of Agua Prieta.

Yellow Boy shakes his head. "Many Villistas die here, Hombrecito. No place to fight. There are better places, better times. Not here, not now."

Leaning out over the edge of the widow's peak rail, using his field glasses to study the frantic activity below us, Quent looks over his shoulder and nods. "Yellow Boy is exactly right, Henry. If Villa's pride and anger get the better of him he'll lose half his men again and still not take Agua Prieta."

Looking down the street running in front of the Gadsden, I see a woman carrying a basket filled with loaves of fresh, hot bread, and behind her a boy about twelve carrying a coffee pot and five or six cups. They're heading for crews eating by bonfires further down the street. I'm so hungry, the whiffs of her fresh-baked bread drifting up to us in the cold night air nearly drive me insane. I have to have that bread.

I run down the stairs, taking them two at a time, and out into the street. My hands are shaking and I'm near to fainting when I give her twenty dollars, four or five times what she planned to make selling her bread and coffee a slice and a cup at time.

I tell her if she'll come by the hotel at mid-day she can have her basket, pot, and cups back. Up on the roof we each eat a whole loaf and fight the urge to devour the last two loaves and drink all the coffee. Our bellies full, we block the door with a chair from the hall leading to the stairs, and soon fall asleep listening to the clanks and scrapes of men grunting to swing picks and lift shovels as they heave dirt out of their ever deepening trenches growing under a million points of light in a coal-black sky.

The creek, cold on my feet and ankles is soothing, but a feeling of dread fills me and I don't know why. Rafaela is there on the ledge and waves at me and I to her. I hear the horses and mules snorting and stamping around; they're afraid of what they smell or hear, or maybe what they don't hear, for the birds are silent. Rafaela screams my name and I turn toward a roaring ball of fire surrounding the outraged jaguar soaring toward me. Swinging the heavy rifle up to defend myself is like lifting it out of viscous, sticky molasses, there's no time, no time before the thing will be on me...

Suddenly I'm bathed in cold air, holding Little David, confused, disoriented, my heart pounds, and I'm out of breath, wildly looking around for the ball of fire about to fall on me. But there is only the velvet-black night sky filled with millions of twinkling stars and the fluttering orange and golden glow from the fires in the streets below and Quent snoring. Shivering, I lay Little David back down beside my bedroll, wrap my blanket around me, and only half-heartedly try to find sleep again.

* * *

We awaken as the sun burns the edge of the sky leaving the color of blood, dawn brightening into day. Still wrapped in our blankets, we use our binoculars and Yellow Boy's telescope to view the frantic ground activity. To the south, General Calles' men have finished digging a trench all the way around a rectangular area that sits right up against the border. Over two miles of trench, about 1000 yards long on the sides parallel to the border, and about 800 yards long on the sides running north to south have been built to stop *División del Norte*. Up and down the trench, bags filled with dirt surround machine guns. Inside the rectangle are connecting trenches that lead to cover or to hard-to-see artillery pieces.

It takes me a little while to figure out that the shiny streaks we see near the outside edges of the trench are reflections off coils of barbed wire, a barrier, I learn later, more than twelve yards wide. Beyond the barbed wire the desert bushes have vanished and the ground is literally bare for several hundred yards in all directions around the perimeter of the rectangle. Wagons parked all over bare ground provide men with shovels digging small, shallow holes. A second crew unloads thick flat pots and carefully places them in the holes. A third crew does something to the pots, and a forth crew covers them up again. Hundreds, maybe thousands of the pots are buried and no one goes among them after the last crew leaves.

I point toward the wagons.

"What are those things they're burying in the ground?"

Quent stares at them a moment and grunts, "Uhmm,

uhmm. Land mines. Step on one or trip a wire to the trigger and boom, you're dead."

A little to the west of the Agua Prieta trench stands the guarded gate in the wire fence serving as the border crossing at Douglas. Mexicans, mostly women, children, and old people carrying blankets, pots and pans, and other essentials, or staggering under huge bundles on their shoulders form a steady, brightly colored river flowing north through the gate. Across the border, Army troops guide them toward the stockyards where tents wait.

The zigzag trench the Army digs runs between Fifth and Sixth Streets. Every two or three blocks they put up a machine gun or mortar station about two hundred yards forward of the main trench line and run trenches from these points back to the main trench. For stability and protection, soldiers fill the trench dirt into burlap bags placed on top of the loose dirt and sand running in front of the trenches. At the rate the Army has its men digging their trench, I figure they'll reach John Slaughter's ranch before Villa leaves.

The town folk, even at this early hour, stand around in groups or move from one hotel or store to the next as if getting ready for a big sporting contest. They don't seem at all concerned that Villa might roar across the border and slaughter them all. No doubt they think the Army will protect them. Didn't General Funston tell the Mexicans there'd be hell to pay if bullets or shells from south of the border fell on Douglas?

We warm up the rest of our coffee and bread downstairs on the hotel's kitchen stove and finish the syrupy coffee and toasted bread before taking our gear and leaving the roof. Quent plans to do some interviews for the *Herald*. Yellow

Boy wants to scout the defenses. Having to call El Paso and make some orders for Villa, I discover the Gadsden has telephones you can pay to use. Trying for about an hour, I finally make connections in El Paso using the name and number Villa gave me. I ask for five thousand shirts, undershirts, and underpants and four wagonloads of hay shipped to Douglas as fast as they can be loaded on a train. The voice on the other end of the line assures me the order will leave for Douglas that day.

Leaving the Gadsden, I see a sign down the street that reads *R.H. Thigpen, M.D.* I go in Doctor Thigpen's office, but there are no patients in the seats and no nurse. The office appears empty. I call out, "Hello?" and hear a chair scrape the floor in a back room. A middle-aged man in his shirtsleeves appears in a doorway. He smiles and sticks out his hand as he comes to meet me.

"Sorry, my receptionist had to run an errand. I'm Doctor Thigpen. How can I help you, sir?"

I smile and we shake hands.

"Good morning. I'm Doctor Henry Grace from Las Cruces over in New Mexico. Pleasure to meet you, Doctor Thigpen. I'm a Villa *medico* and I'm trying to find where to buy medical supplies. I was hoping you might tell me."

The thick bushy brows rise on Thigpen's high forehead fronting graceful valleys of wrinkles. "Doctor Grace, it's a pleasure. You look very young to be a doctor. I wish my associate from down the street, Doctor Miller, were here to meet you too. If I might ask, how did you come to help General Villa?"

"I knew him from before the *Revolución* and owe him a debt of honor. I hate to be rude, but I'm in a bit of a hurry. If you can you tell me where to go for supplies?"

"Oh yes, sorry to be so nosy. We actually have a very good pharmacy here in Douglas, what with the smelter being here and all. It's about three blocks west of here and is very well-stocked. There are several others about as good, but more expensive. If you need anything just let me know and I'll be glad to help you."

"Thanks, you're very kind. I hope we can visit again when I'm not quite so rushed. Good luck, and *adiós.*"

I find the pharmacy Doctor Thigpen describes, and learn the pharmacist has the medical supplies and in the quantities we need.

The sun is more than half way to the western horizon when we finally head north out of town and swing southeast toward Gallardo Pass. There is only a golden glow in the western sky when we see distant points of light: *División del Norte* cooking fires, stretching into the distance up and down the road near Gallardo Rancho. We find Villa's wagon and Juan busy at his fire. He runs up to take our horses and says the *jefe* is talking with his generals but will be along soon for supper.

Juan returns to his stew. We're afraid to ask what's in it. He pours us a cup of coffee while we wait. Being reminded the night before of how real coffee tastes, we grimace at the first bitter swallow of his piñon nut brew. In an hour or so, Juan starts ladling stew into pie pans and Villa walks into the circle of firelight. He takes off his hat and sweeps it before him in a grand bow. "*Buenos noches, señores.* Are you back to tell me what I already know?"

Yellow Boy's face remains mask-like, but Quent and I frown, unsure what Villa means. Quent says, "*General?*"

Villa smiles as if he knows all the great secrets of the

universe and isn't telling. "*Sí*, Queentin, *mi* scouts tell me Calles makes good use of the extra men sent him, men sent from Texas and across *Nuevo* Mexico and Arizona to get there. A great trench surrounds Agua Prieta and is filled with men and machine guns. Barbed wire is rolled out around it, and for hundreds of yards in all directions the brush cut and land mines planted to blow us all up. Oh, *sí*, General Calles tries to make Agua Prieta impregnable with his guns and mines, but my *hombres* have not come empty-handed. All that work and broken men it took to get my big guns across El Paso Púlpito, now it will pay off, eh, Hombrecito?"

I smile and nod. "I hope so General. We paid a very high price to get them here. I know your wagons are loaded with many shells."

Quent says, "General, I hope these shells explode better than the ones at Celaya and León."

Villa's smile grows.

"*Sí*, Queentin, these shells have *mucho* power. They are shells made in Europe we captured and saved during our fight against Huerta. We will pound Calles so hard in Agua Prieta, he will either explode in the dust or disappear across the border to his *Gringo* protectors. Then we will walk into Agua Prieta without firing a shot. My men will die of hunger before they die from a Calles bullet. They fight for food and new guns and bullets in Agua Prieta. Ready and desperate to fight Calles, they want to fill their bellies and their rifles."

Quent says, "From what I've seen of Calles' defenses, your artillery must shoot with great accuracy to accomplish what you want. It's too bad Angeles is no longer in charge of your artillery. He'd know exactly how to do it."

Villa shakes his head and stares at the ground. "It is my

fault he left, Queentin. He never returned from a mission to the United States after someone convinced him I believed he was a traitor and wanted to execute him. I have one angry moment and a skilled commander leaves. I do not blame him. I am too quick to judge him, for, as usual, his advice logically fit exactly what I needed to do. But he trained many skilled artillerymen. We'll be OK."

He's quiet, staring at the fire a while. "Hombrecito, you find the places of the *medico* supplies and order the clothes and hay from El Paso? The *Americano* soldiers let you cross the border without holding you up?"

"Sí, General, I found the *medico* supplies. They are there if we need them, and the clothes and hay will be on the next train from El Paso. The *Americano* soldiers let us pass as long as we carry no guns or bullets for the battle."

"*Bueno. Mañana* we begin the work of the people against Carranza."

28. AGUA PRIETA

We follow the dusty road out the mountains and see Douglas, a patch of scattered blacks, browns, and gleaming whites shimmering far in the distance against splotchy greens and desert tans stretching off to the blue-gray horizon. A barren strip of creosote bushes and mesquite on its south side separates Douglas from Agua Prieta, a small white patch inside a black rectangular outline, a literal death trap, General Calles's trench. Outside the trench, the bare ground stands out in sharp contrast to the *llano* surrounding it. The bare earth looks mottled, the dirt churned up by crews chopping away the brush to leave sharp white and tan spikes waiting for a running horse or man to impale a foot, and hidden just below the surface of the churned earth, those exploding pots of death we saw men burying a couple of days earlier.

Taking Agua Prieta is impossible now, and if he tries, many men will die, Ussen help us all.

Quent, Yellow Boy, and I ride in the group of *dorados* following Villa in front of the cavalry. The air crackles and pops with excitement. At last we can see the place for which we've marched so far and suffered so much.

Villa waves us on while he stops off to one side of the cavalry column to talk with its commander. With broad arm-swinging gestures, Villa tells him to lead the column wide of the cleared area, go around Agua Prieta and camp on its western side. He plans for the infantry to camp on the eastern side and for both units to stay out of range of Calles' artillery.

After the commander salutes and says he understands, Villa resumes his position at the head of the column, occasionally stopping to study the defenses of Agua Prieta with his binoculars. About three miles east of Agua Prieta, he stops, calls his artillery commanders, and points toward a line of low depressions and swales just to the north of the road. They talk for a few minutes, Villa again waving his arms in great sweeping gestures and pointing to several places in the depressions before the commanders ride off toward the north to scout positions for artillery placement.

Quent sees my puzzled look.

"Villa will probably put his cannons in those low places. At this range the gun flashes will be hard to see from Agua Prieta and should reduce the accuracy of returned artillery fire. From those positions he can also shoot almost directly west and not worry about hitting Douglas, which will, no doubt, bring the American Army out against him. Smart move."

As we continue down the road, the buildings and defenses of Agua Prieta begin to assume individual outlines, men looking like ants scurrying about in the dirt in front of the trench, the barbed-wire barrier shining in the bright sunlight.

An American Army contingent chugs up to the border fence in staff cars, grinding gears, raising a dust cloud that slowly drifts in puffs south across the border fence. One of the cars has two gold stars painted on the doors. The officers climb out of their cars and study us with large-lens binoculars.

Villa turns his stallion, the big black one that thinks he's Satanas, off the road and heads for them at a gallop. Instinctively, they step back from the fence and closer to the safety of their cars. Pulling the stallion up in a cloud of dust, Villa dismounts, grinning. He walks to the wire fence and reaches across to shake hands with an officer.

"*Buenos días*, Major. I am General Francisco Villa come to relieve General Calles of his command at Agua Prieta."

He swings his arm to his officers who dismount, their faces masking boiling anger. Villa introduces each of his commanders, who step up to the fence and reach across to shake hands with the American officers.

Introductions complete, Villa points to the cars. "You know, *señores*, your *gringo* Army becomes too dependent on automobiles. The only reliable transportation in this country is a horse. Take care you treat your put-puts well or you might wind up walking in the heat of the day. Ha!"

One of the officers, a lanky, blond lieutenant with his campaign hat pulled down to his eyes says, "General, do you expect to take Agua Prieta today?"

Villa grins from ear to ear.

"Sure, Mike. Just as soon as the rest of my Army gets here." Then he says in Spanish, "Will the *Americano* Army help Calles?"

A short officer, not over five-four, two stars on his collar, in his late forties, jowly, a thick, trimmed gray mustache and goatee covering his face, his droopy, sleepy eyes missing nothing, walks up and says in Spanish, "Is this General Villa? "

The lieutenant nods. "General Funston, allow me to introduce you to General Francisco Villa."

Villa and Funston shake hands across the wire and Funston says, "Allow me, sir, to assure you that the United States intends to remain neutral in any coming battle between you and General Calles. However, I must warn you in the strongest possible terms, if you fire into the United States, the Army will not hesitate to retaliate. I hope we understand each other?"

Villa looks down at General Funston and grins.

"Oh, *sí*, General Funston we understand each other very well."

Then the smile disappears. The expression on his face becomes solemn, deadly serious.

"Hear me, *señor*. My cannons and rifles do not now, nor have they in the past pointed toward the United States. I give you a message for your *Presidente* Wilson. I know about this illegal and immoral thing he has done to Mexico. I will not tolerate the passage of more Carrancista soldiers through the United States. I am warning *Señor* Wilson that if such a thing happens again I, Francisco Villa, will not feel responsible for the lives of Americans in my territory."

He motions toward Quent, who has his notebook out, transcribing everything he hears in the conversation between Villa and Funston. "This is *Señor* Queentin Peach, a reporter for the *El Paso Daily Herald*. Queentin, I want you to publish what I have just told General Funston. I desire *los periódicos* tell the world what I have said."

Quent nods.

"It will be published, General."

Funston stares a moment, smiles, and says, "I will send Mr. Wilson your message, General Villa."

They shake hands again and Villa says, "I am in your debt General. *Adiós.*"

Villa grabs his saddle horn, swings into the saddle like a young man, and leads us back toward the road where *División del Norte* continues to march.

We ride wide of the minefields and Villa again stops about a mile due south of Agua Prieta where he and his commanders spend a long time studying the little village with their binoculars. They say little as the horses stamp and swish their tails at buzzing flies tormenting them in the warm sun.

Yellow Boy, Quent, and I study the defenses of Agua Prieta with our high-powered glasses. I see several artillery positions inside the village and along the trench. The barbed wire alone is a formidable barricade, and with rifles and machine guns firing from the trench, appears to me impossible to breach. The wire is too wide, the trench too well covered by rifles and machine guns, and the line of defense too short and solid for the cavalry to give the infantry, running across at least two hundred yards of cleared ground covered with buried mines and sharp stobs, any support through distracting charges or flanking attacks.

I finish my survey and look toward Yellow Boy. He continues to stare through his telescope, the Henry rifle balanced across his saddle. Quent looks for a few moments, stops to write, and looks again.

It seeps into my consciousness that the coming battle will be the first one I've ever witnessed involving more than about ten men. I have no military knowledge or skills, only the philosophy Yellow Boy and Rufus Pike taught me years ago about the need for being "cold and cakilatin" to survive in hard and dangerous country. Villa has to be "cold and cakilatin" as a military commander. But, he also has maybe ten thousand men who are fast running out of water and starving. They haven't eaten much of anything in the three days since their stop at the San Bernardino Ranch.

At last, Villa lowers his glasses, points first toward Aqua Prieta, then toward the west, and finally back to the east. I barely hear him rattling off his instructions before seeing the commanders salute and ride off toward the advancing troops. He turns to us. "What do you think, Queentin?"

Quent shakes his head. "I'm not an expert, General, but it looks like a mighty hard nut to crack, maybe even impossible. Your men will be cut to pieces by all those machine-gun positions and riflemen in the trenches, not to mention all the land mines scattered over that bare area the men have to cross. And there is the artillery if Calles decides to lower his guns. What's your strategy?"

Villa leans forward in his saddle, his eyes glittering. "Three words: Attack. Attack. Attack. That is my strategy and it always will be. First, use the cannons we worked so hard to get here. We will pound away on Agua Prieta and the minefield until it is gone. The men with machine-guns and rifles cannot shoot what they cannot see. The moon will not be up until an hour or two after midnight. By that time we will be across the barbed wire and fighting in the streets."

"That all sounds reasonable, General, but what about

the searchlights Hombrecito and Yellow Boy saw when the train from Texas passed carrying Carrancistas? They'll be a lot brighter than any moon."

"Queentin, where is the electricity in Agua Prieta to power these lights? They are useless without the electricity."

Quent nods. "You're right, General, there is no power in Agua Prieta. The Americans have electrical power in Douglas. Do you think they'll let Calles use it?"

Villa stares at Quent and shrugs. "General Funston says the *Americanos* will favor neither side. Does he lie?"

Quent stares back at Villa's narrow, questioning eyes. This time, Quent shrugs.

Villa rides to the west where the cavalry makes camp. We ride back to the eastern side, near the artillery, and make camp in a low area behind a slight rise that put us out of sight of Agua Prieta. We make a fire and brew coffee while we wait for the infantry, artillery, and *medico* wagons to arrive. Looking back toward the pass we still see the high dust clouds typical of cavalry and wagons, and then a few hours later the lower clouds from the shuffling feet of the infantry. It takes the cavalry a couple of hours to get past us before the artillery and supply wagons begin appearing. Soon we flag down Juan and show him where we're camped.

Agua Prieta sits on the only accessible water wells except for a sulfurous one several miles out on the plains. The water barrels on the supply wagons are nearly empty and after three days march from Slaughter's ranch, most canteens are dry. Villa sends wagons around Agua Prieta to get water from the smelter drainage ditches. That water is dark and has a hard, nasty taste, but the animals are thirsty enough to drink it and it keeps them from dying of thirst.

The infantry continues to march in behind us all afternoon, through the night, and into the morning of the next day to set up their camps and give the men a little rest. As twilight falls into full darkness, Villa stands at the top of the rise and studies the lights of Douglas and Agua Prieta. He checks his pocket watch often and looks back toward the northeastern sky where faint moon glow seeps over the black horizon.

The next morning Doctor Oñate sets up the *medico* wagons around a central supply wagon, and we make sure the medical assistants clearly understand what the items are when we ask for them. Jesús and Marco begged to come with us rather than stay in Colonia Morelos and will work with the *medico* wagons and drive ambulances. However, the long march up the San Bernardino Valley and across Gallardo pass has taken its toll. Like all the men and boys, volunteers or conscripts, they are gaunt and hollow-eyed, and no longer have the spring of youth in their step.

Jesús, as we work to get the *medico* wagons ready for business, asks, "Doctor Grace, when the battle comes will you be working here with the *medicos* or killing Carrancistas?"

I shake my head. I don't know.

"I'll be where the General wants me. Now I plan to work with the *medicos*. Why do you ask?"

"Both jobs are *importante* and you are very good at both. It must be hard to choose between them."

"I'm a doctor. I've sworn to save life, not take it. But I have also told the General that I am at his command. I will do what he commands me to do."

"*Bueno, Doctor Grace, muy bien.*"

As we work, the thrust of Jesús question begins to haunt my mind. *Am I a killer or a healer? Is it possible to be both?*

All morning of the second day, a steady stream of messengers comes to Villa's command wagon. They report on cannon locations, artillery shell counts, readiness to fire, status of cavalry and infantry units, all the myriad things that tell a general his army is ready to fight. Scouts, Yellow Boy among them, manage to creep up close to the edge of the clearing surrounding the Agua Prieta trench. They bring details of artillery positions and how soldiers stand shoulder to shoulder in the trench and how the village is filled with men in Carrancista uniforms.

When the sun is straight overhead, commanders gather around Villa's wagon to discuss strategy. He asks Quent, Yellow Boy, and me to listen in. He sounds angry as they talk, making frequent references to the many more soldiers and weapons in Agua Prieta than he anticipated because the Americans betrayed him. He plans to soften up the Agua Prieta defenses with artillery fire late in the afternoon, blow apart sections of barbed wire, explode the mines in the cleared area, and then punch through the barbed wire and east-side trench with a hard assault. If need be, they will attack a second time, still focused on the east but with assaults on the other sides, including the one next to the border, to keep Calles too busy to support the east with re-enforcements from those positions. If those attacks fail, the artillery will rain down death and destruction once more before another attack.

"No one," Villa says, pounding his thigh with his fist, "no matter how well-defended, can stand against such an attack. We will slaughter them all. Those that escape out of Agua Prieta, the cavalry will ride down. If they surrender and pledge to me, let them live. If they do not, execute them.

It will take time in the dark to cross the minefield and dodge a few bullets until we are on the wire. The cavalry must wait for the first breach or they will be riding over top of our own infantry."

Quent cuts his eyes to me and shakes his head. Yellow Boy, his face a mask of frozen concentration, listens. I don't know what to think.

The meeting soon breaks up, the commanders, heading back to their men, ready for the evening dance of death. We stand to leave too, but Villa waves us over to his table. "What do you think of the plan, Queentin?"

Quent grimaces and shrugs. "I don't know, General. Maybe it will work. I'm not a military man, but it seems to me that Agua Prieta is just too well-defended, has too many soldiers inside the trench. Yes, you probably outnumber them maybe two or three to one. But they are behind trenches and piles of dirt and your soldiers are exposed. Many will die. It's better to just bottle them up or pound them with artillery until they surrender."

Villa shakes his head, his eyes flashing, his hands clinched in fists, and in a moment of lucidity, says, "Those goddamned *gringos* have done this to me. I will fight them too if I must. I cannot stay here for long. Obregón will send armies from the south, from Guaymas and Hermosillo and corner me against the border. I am out of supplies. My men need good water, beans, and *tortillas*. Most of all they need bullets and my artillery needs shells. We can march around Agua Prieta and never fire a shot, but always Calles will be at my back as we go south. Unless he is stopped, I will always be worried about being trapped between two armies." His fist pounds his table. "We...must...take...Agua Prieta. Do you understand this, Queentin?"

"*Sí, Jefe,* I understand. I say only that it will be a very hard battle with many losses."

"Perhaps, Queentin, perhaps. We will see. Hombrecito, are the *medicos* ready?"

"*Sí,* General, we are ready and as I told you earlier I know where to buy more supplies in Douglas if we need them."

"*Bueno.* Keep your big rifle close by. You may need it. Let us hope there are not so many casualties that you need the extra supplies. Muchacho Amarillo, I ask that you stay with me to carry my directions to the commanders and tell me the truth of the battlefield."

Yellow Boy nods. "*Sí, Jefe.* I go where you tell me..."

A distant boom trailed by a low whistle. Villa is instantly up and moving toward the rise from where he studied Agua Prieta. To the north there is an explosion high in the air in the direction of Villa's artillery placements. Within seconds there is thunder from Villa's artillery and louder whistles. At the top of the rise we see flashes of fire over Agua Prieta followed by distant pops and little puffball clouds that drift back toward the east. Flashes and distant booms come from the artillery in Agua Prieta followed by brighter flashes, immediate booms, whistles ending in bright flashes, loud, drum-like thuds and gray puffball clouds. More of Villa's cannons return fire, their aerial explosions creeping closer to the western side of the Agua Prieta, several rounds fall in the cleared area outside the barbed wire and a few even trip mines setting off secondary explosions.

Villa, arms crossed, stares at the artillery exchanges, a sardonic smile under his mustache. I hear him mutter, "So, Calles, you think you find my guns and make me waste shells.

Do not worry *amigo*, I have plenty of both, and when I finish with you, the *gringos* in Douglas will know the power of my guns also."

Quent hears him, too. "General do you mean that? You'll turn your cannons on Douglas?"

Villa's smile turns to a big grin as he walks back to his wagon. "No Queentin. It is only a fantasy. I can and will fight Carranza and the *gringos* if I must, but only one major enemy at a time *por favor*."

Calles' fires his first shot around 2:00 P.M., and the duel between the big guns lasts a couple of hours. None of Villa's artillery is damaged, but the steady stream of people leaving Agua Prieta for the tents in the Douglas stockyards increases.

Yellow Boy watches the entire time as Calles and Villa hammer away at each other. When it stops, I ask him, "What did you think of all that artillery fire, Uncle?"

His arms crossed around his rifle, he looks over his shoulder at Villa, studying maps at his field desk. "Many seasons ago, I scout for *gringo* army. See little-big guns Crook use against Juh and Geronimo. These guns, they are big guns. Shoot plenty long. Kill many with one shot. Villa, he brings fire."

29. BATTLE OF AGUA PRIETA

Punctured by points of light from stars without number, the cold night sky lies blacker than Satan's soul. I stare into the abyss with Yellow Boy, Quent, and Villa, and tremble from a mixture of cold, excitement, and a growing sense of dread. Agua Prieta spreads out before us in the black notch outlined against the stars by the San Jose Mountains to the south and the Huachuca Mountains to the north. *División del Norte* infantry move toward the edge of the minefield for the 8:00 p.m. attack on the eastern side of Agua Prieta.

Torches on tall poles along the trench around Agua Prieta cast flickering yellows and oranges across the barren strip beyond the barbed wire. I listen with my head cocked to one side, trying to pick up any sounds from the squads of men crawling through the creosotes and around the mesquite, inching as close as possible to the barbed wire and trench before they run into the hail storm of bullets, waiting to fall. Only the wind gently sweeping through the mesquite and creosote makes any sound.

A shout, a muzzle flash, and the snapping crack of a rifle from near the northeast corner of the Agua Prieta east trench. There are a few scattered shots up and down the eastern trench line, but nothing from the surrounding desert. Yellow Boy smiles. "*Bueno.* Soldiers know to stay quiet, move closer."

A minute goes by. Two. Three. Another shout and a shot cracking from near the center of the trench. A cacophony of screams and yells fills the void as bright orange and yellow streaks of fire and sharp snapping thunder from hundreds of rifles and machine guns rolls like a wave across the barren space toward the barbed wire. The light under the torches grows soft and fuzzy as thousands of bullets strike the trench edge, throwing dust into the air.

The eastern trench sparkles with its own streaks of bright orange and yellow fire, points of almost continuous light that swing back and forth from swiveling machine guns up and down the length of the trench, and the air is filled with the mottled roar of thousands of rifles mixed with the sharp, staccato rumble of machine guns. The wave of brilliant orange and yellow fire washes on into the maelstrom. Squads advance on their bellies, hugging the ground under the fire from the trenches, two hundred yards, one-fifty. A flash of light and dull thudding explosion, a successful landmine, brings screams and bodies once hugging the ground twisting in agony and death.

A hundred yards from the barbed wire the wave of orange and yellow fire thins and slows. The smell of cordite mixed with the iron smell of blood and stench of death drifts back to us.

Seventy-five yards. Firing from the trench increases, a downpour of lead, death, and cries resulting from instant mutilation and shock.

Sixty yards. Growing thinner the wave of orange and yellow flames advancing toward the wire pauses, seems to gain strength, increases again, advances a few more yards, and pauses.

Fifty yards. The wave becomes a breaker, stationary, hung in time for seconds, ragged, the firing steady. Places in the line advance, some all the way into the torch light from the trenches, but none reaches the gleaming jagged edges of the barbed wire before falling back into the dark. The wave crest of fire thins and begins washing backwards into the desert weeds, creosotes, and mesquites.

Villa grinds his teeth and pounds his thigh with his fist. He bellows into the void, "It's all right *muchachos*, I'll send you some help. Goddamn you Calles. Goddamn the *gringos*. They are the reason these *muchachos* are being killed."

I start running down the rise toward the *medico* wagons, wave at the wagon Jesús drives, and jump in the back when he slows for me. The team plunges into the darkness down a trail cut through the brush to a place where the squads are to reform and bring the wounded.

It's so dark Jesús nearly drives into a large group of men staggering back from the bare ground where bullets still splatter, whine, and ricochet to kill or wound someone at the wrong place, at the wrong time. Seeing the wagon, the men run for it, croaking, "Water, water, for the mother of God, please, water."

Jesús roars past them, yelling back, "No water! Doctor wagon! Where are the wounded?"

They wearily thumb back over their shoulders and disappear into the dark. Jesús slaps the reins across the backs of the mules, and whistling and yelling at them, charges on toward the trench. We're nearly to the edge of the minefield when we find the wounded and dying scattered like cracked mesquite seed pods in the desert brush.

Jesús brings the mules to a sliding stop and I jump off the wagon. Other *medicos* are hopping out of wagons that follow ours. It's a descent into Hell. I see a dark lump stretched out by a yucca and run forward. It's a boy not more than fourteen or fifteen. The bottom of his shirt is shiny and black. I whisper, "Easy, *muchacho*," pull his trembling hands off his belly and see a wound leaking blood. His breathing gurgles in his throat. With his last bit of strength he grabs my arm and leaning toward my ear, whispers, "My mother, tell her I am no more..." His head drops to one side and he's gone. I stare at him in sorrow. He's died in my hands, I don't even know his name and I have to wrench his death grip off my wrist before I can crab over to an old man in shock, his leg nearly shot off a few inches below his knee. I tie it off with a tourniquet and yell for Jesús to help me get him to a wagon.

For a few minutes, we run hunched over through the brush, dodging stray bullets, picking up men smeared with blood who might live at least until our wagon, packed with the wounded, bloody and groaning in misery, returns to the *medico* wagon circle. We begin fast, deliberate work. Shivering from shock, begging for water, many of those we bring back die, shot to pieces, their blood loss unstoppable. But there are some we're able to save who were grazed or lucky enough to have a bullet pass through without hitting vital organs or blood vessels. We even manage to save some who have an arm or leg shot away, but for reasons I've never understood, don't bleed to death before we can help them. There are so many wounded that our supplies begin to run low with the first round of men treated at the *medico* wagons.

In the light from a coal-oil lamp, I'm extracting a bullet from a boy's calf muscles when Yellow Boy, grim, his eyes filled with fury, appears at my wagon and yells above the moans and screams of pain, "Hombrecito! To Villa! *Pronto!* Bring Shoots-Today-Kills-Tomorrow. *Pronto, pronto!*"

Doctor Oñate has just finished work on a patient next to mine. He washes his hands off in black smelter water and says, "Go, Doctor Grace. I'll finish for you. The general needs your rifle. *Vamos.*"

I rinse my hands, tear off my blood-smeared doctor's apron, and run to my saddle, and snatch up Little David and a bag of cartridges.

Running for the rise where Villa paces, I catch up with and ask Yellow Boy, "What's going on?"

He snorts and says through clenched teeth, "*Gringos!*"

I don't understand. It doesn't make any sense. The United States is neutral, or so said General Funston. Before I can ask Yellow Boy to explain we're on top of the rise and standing next to Villa. I look toward Agua Prieta and understand Yellow Boy's anger. Three long fingers of bright white light sweep over the minefield and dry plains beyond. It's the searchlights Yellow Boy and I saw with the troop train. Villa is practically screaming.

"Those bastard *gringos* have given Calles electricity for those damned lights. He'll slaughter *mi hombres* crossing that minefield."

Villa is right. The lights are bright enough to show the lumps of dozens of bodies scattered around the minefield on the east side of the trench. The infantry has already started a second attack across the minefield, the men hitting the dirt and playing dead as the fingers of light sweep by. Machine guns on the trench occasionally sputter slashing flame when the operators think they see movement, men crawling forward, in the penumbra of the beams. Villa growls, "Hombrecito, from the bushes at the edge of the minefield, can you kill those lights?"

It's an easy shot.

"Sí, general."

"*Bueno. Por favor*, stay low and don't get yourself killed, eh?'

"I'll be careful."

He pauses a moment, thinking, "You do that, *mi amigo*. Listen. Shoot the operators first, and then the lights. We attack from all sides this time, but mostly on the east side. *Comprende?*"

"*Sí*, general."

It appears Calles put the searchlights on the tops of specially built platforms. The next two are on a line north about two hundred yards apart from the first one and about a hundred yards inside the eastern trench. I catch another ride with Jesús driving his wagon back to pickup more wounded. When the wagon stops, I jump out and run toward a couple of big creosote bushes on the edge of the minefield past more dead and shot-to-pieces men. Limbs are snapping off the creosotes and mesquite as stray bullets whine through the brush. Instinctively I lower myself into a crouching run, holding Little David across my chest. In the glare of the searchlights, I can see the little plumes of dust sprouting from impacting bullets. The haze from the dust makes it hard to tell where anything is except when the searchlights sweep the nearby cleared area and surrounding bushes. Three men in front of me run with their rifles across their chests like me. The man ahead and to my right points toward the clearing and yells at the others. A long finger of light is sweeping for us. They dive for the ground. I'm right behind them as the finger of death sweeps over us.

Instantly, we're up again and running. The man to my left collapses, staggering forward as if he's tripped over something. He falls face down in the dirt, unmoving. When I reach him, I see a large dark spot in the middle of his back and turn him over. He's center shot straight through his heart. Not three feet from where I kneel, a passing bullet, sounding like an angry bee, whacks a limb from a creosote bush and it goes cartwheeling off into the darkness. We're not more than ten yards from the edge of the clearing. I crawl forward on my knees and elbows until I find a shallow depression between two big creosotes and have a clear view of the eastern trench and searchlights.

The closest searchlight is no more than three or four hundred yards away. It's easy to see the operator swinging the beam back and forth in the glare of the reflector. The near misses make me hug the ground, my heart pounding in my ears. I want to dig a hiding place with my bare hands in the blood-soaked sand.

I start to sit up and rest my elbows on my knees for the shots, but a round of machine-gun fire whines through the top of the creosotes, raining branches and leaves into my hair, leaving the same smell the creosotes make after a hard rain. I've enjoyed the smell of creosotes after a hard rain since I was a little boy sitting with Rufus Pike on his shack porch. The smell has a strong calming effect on me. The thunder from the guns at the trench dims to a distant rumble. I decide to shoot from a prone position even if the angle for Little David is awkward.

There's no wind. I roll on my side and flip up the adjustable sight on Little David. I set the vertical vernier sight to four hundred fifty yards and dial the smallest pinhole I have. I look through it trying to find the light operator. It's too small, not giving my eye enough light to see much of anything. I dial it open a click and retry it – still too small. One more click does it. I drop the breach, slide in a cartridge, and snap the breach closed while holding the four extra cartridges in my trigger hand with my last fingers.

Jesús's question drifts through my mind. *Are you a killer or a healer?*

I roll over on my belly and sight on the small black outline of the operator moving the first searchlight back and forth. I pull the set trigger and wait for maximum operator exposure as he swings the light to my left. Through the vernier pinhole, I watch him swing the light through a couple of cycles of back and forth across the eastern side minefield.

As I concentrate on the searchlight operator, the yells and gunfire around me fade into silence. I take a deep breath and let it half out on his third swing back across the minefield. His outline is clear and sharp when the hammer on Little David falls. The old buffalo gun roars and kicks against my shoulder. Its thunder, standing out clearly from the snap and crack of Mauser and Winchester rifles, makes my ears ring. I forgot the wax plugs for my ears. The operator disappears and the long finger of light stops its swing toward the south. I crab to a yucca, its stalk shot to pieces ten yards to my left.

I drop the breach and slide in another cartridge intended for the bright spot above the center of the reflector of the first light. The set trigger comes back and the old buffalo gun roars once more. The finger of light streaking across the eastern minefield in front of the trench disappears. Men all around me, ecstatic, bellow, "Viva Villa, viva Villa!" The general has turned out the light looking to kill them all.

The second searchlight suddenly swings in my direction and pauses in the puff of smoke from Little David. Shots from rifles pepper the ground around the creosote and then the light moves on. I crab another ten yards to the right from where I'd been, reload, wait until the operator outline is its maximum size, and, aiming a little high at the second light, I fire. That operator too disappears. Rifle shots churned up dust in the area where I'd been. It takes two quick shots to get the second light. I aim too high on the first shot to compensate for the range. The third light stops sweeping the minefield, its operator gone, its beam pointing straight up, like a silver saber stabbing the black sky. I guess again on the range and on how high to shoot above the center of the light for the bullet to drop in the right place to hit the arc lamp. It's on a very shallow slant and hard to hit. It takes me three tries. *Hombrecito, you need to do some serious target practice.*

The second attack, which excludes the border side of the trench, its main thrust again on the eastern side, starts at

10:00 P.M. After knocking out the searchlights fewer men die, but none make it across the barbed wire and into hand-to-hand combat with the Carrancistas. The men begin pulling back around midnight no more successful than before. A new wave of wounded and dying floods the *medico* circle of wagons. We do what we can for the men and boys but our supplies are nearly gone. The worst times in the *medico* wagons occur when the wounded beg for water and all we can give them is the stinking black stuff from the smelter drainage ditches.

Quent appears at the wagon where I work sewing up a grazing wound in a boy's scalp. "Are you all right, Henry?"

"Yeah. I'll be fine if I can get this kid's scalp sewn back together. They're not going to take Agua Prieta, are they?"

He puffs his cheeks and shakes his head. "Nope. It's not going to happen. Villa's in a rage saying it's all the *gringos'* fault. Too many troops, too many guns at Agua Prieta."

"What do you think he'll do now?"

"Pound the hell out of Agua Prieta with his big guns and then leave. What else can he do?"

I shrug, feeling empty, disoriented. Villa has mentioned nothing about what he'll do if we fail to take Agua Prieta.

"Has he said where he's going?"

Quent shakes his head. "He's mentioned trying to take Hermosillo several times, but nothing firm. I'm not sure if he knows."

There is a sound of sharp, hard thunder followed a few seconds later by another boom echoing across the hills, and then another, and another all followed by distant exploding pops in the distance. Quent smiles when he sees my frown.

"It's Villa's artillery. He's going to shoot the hell out of that little village, but he knows Calles will just hunker down, wait him out, and won't break. It's just a waste of shells."

The artillery pours it on. I'm told there were more than three thousand shells fired between one and two A.M., which tapers off to a few hundred in the next hour before finally stopping. The smell of cordite and smoke from the guns drifts into camp and lingers a while before it's gone. In the freezing night air, men huddle by fires, and try to drink the awful coffee made with smelter ditch water.

We're out of medical supplies and still there're men who desperately need attention. Early on we divide the wounded into three groups: those we know will die, those severely wounded who will live if we can stop the bleeding and prevent infection, and those who can wait until we can get more supplies. The second group receives the lion's share of the supplies and attention. The third group lies by fires, smoking, and drinking what tequila and whiskey can be found for them. As soon as it turns light, I'll take a wagon and cross the border for more supplies.

30. ON THE PRECIPICE

We wait until the golden edge on the mountains pours out the sun's fire to spread morning light across the dry, ragged plains. I lead *medico* supply wagons flying blue-and-white *medico* flags, racing down the dusty trail around Agua Prieta to the north-south road leading into Douglas. I hope the soldiers in Agua Prieta don't think my wagons and others flying the same flags driving into the minefield for the wounded make good targets. Bodies are scattered all over the cleared desert like seeds blown by the wind, but most lie concentrated against the impenetrable, invisible wall formed by the storm of bullets raining from behind the trench wire.

Calles's men have already crossed the trench and taken in men still alive near the wire. I learn later that Calles offered amnesty to any soldier who deserted and that at least forty-five were unaccounted for that day. Many men disappeared on the trek up the San Bernardino. No one, not even their immediate officers, reported them missing, and after Agua Prieta many more disappeared.

American soldiers at the border crossing wave us through. I direct the empty supply wagons to pickup the undershirts, underpants, shirts and hay order at the rail station while I head for the pharmacy Doctor Thigpen recommended.

The pharmacy owner is just raising his shades and opening his doors when I pull up. I'm through the pharmacy, moving faster than a magician hiding doves and rabbits, picking over the shelves to buy twenty pounds of cotton, twenty yards of gauze, peroxide, iodine, painkillers, quinine caps, carbolic soap, alcohol, chloroform, zinc oxide, and syringes. As I load the wagon, a mercantile store next door to the pharmacy opens and I buy forty quilts.

Doctor Thigpen and another man walk through the door as I pay the clerk, using the now dirty, creased letter of credit Texas John gave Villa. Thigpen smiles as he extends his hand.

"Doctor Grace, this is Doctor Miller, the other doctor I mentioned when you were here last."

I shake Doctor Thigpen's hand and Doctor Miller's.

"Gentlemen, it's always a pleasure to meet a colleague."

Doctor Miller says, "Last night, with several of our friends, we watched the bombardment and attack on the trenches from the roof of the Gadsden Hotel. The death and misery must have been horrific on both sides of the trenches."

Doctor Thigpen nods.

"Why, there were even casualties here in Douglas. We know stray bullets or shrapnel wounded several people, and I understand a soldier was killed when a stray bullet hit his exposed cartridge belt. I guess it's impossible for bullets and shrapnel not to come to this side with Agua Prieta so close to the border. The only way you might avoid it is if you stayed inside, and even then there are no guarantees."

I grimace.

"Yes sir, you're right, bullets and shrapnel know no border. I hate to hear folks on this side were hurt, but it's a risk they take and can't be helped if they have to watch."

Doctor Thigpen sighs. "Doctor Grace, from what we can see this morning, it appears General Villa's forces took very high losses. No doubt there are many wounded. If you need any help, we feel it's our Christian duty to offer our services as doctors, and we'll be happy to assist you."

His offer is like manna to a man starving in the desert.

"Doctors, you're a gift from heaven. We ran out of medical supplies last night. Some of our wounded haven't had any medical attention in six or seven hours. I'm sure General Villa will be very grateful if you can come."

Thigpen motions toward the door. "We anticipated that might be the case and have a buggy and our medical bags outside. We'll follow you."

On the way back, I see hundreds of men who, having reached the smelter ditches for water, are at the border fence holding their pails across the wire, begging for clean water, and the smelter workers are giving it to them. By the time I return to the *medico* circle, half the severely wounded have died. Doctor Oñate, frantic to help the wounded receiving little or no attention when they were brought in, rushes toward my wagon and the new supplies. Some of these men are going into shock and one or two have died. The *medicos* scramble to gather what they need to clean and bandage wounds from the supplies I've brought. Thigpen and Miller pull up behind me, jump out of their buggy, pull off their coats, roll up their sleeves, and go to work with the rest of us.

A few hours after we begin work, Villa appears and walks among the wounded, giving comfort and praise to the men for their courage and sacrifice. Headed in my direction, I see him look toward Thigpen and Miller, busy bandaging wounds. Frowning as he approaches, he says in a low monotone, "Hombrecito, why are these *gringos* here among our brave wounded?"

"They're from Douglas. Doctors Thigpen and Miller. I met Thigpen when I looked for supplies in Douglas three days ago. They volunteered to help us and I brought them with me when I came back with the supplies. I knew you'd be grateful for their help."

Villa's quirt dangles from his right wrist and he slaps his pants leg with it as I speak. "*Sí, gracias. Por favor*, bring them to my wagon when you finish here."

"*Sí*, General. We will come in an hour or two."

"*Muy bien.* See that you do." He gives his pants leg an extra hard swat with the quirt and walks off.

The sun is low in a blood red sky when Thigpen, Miller, and I walk to Villa's wagon. Four soldiers and Camisa Roja, his *dorado* jacket covering his scarlet shirt, sit off to one side smoking. I wave to him and he salutes me with a smile and a tip of his hat. Villa sees us and nods while he continues to listen to *dorados* gathered around his desk. I'm exhausted. I haven't slept in two days, and in that time have seen more death and destruction than I expected to see in a lifetime. The *dorado* meeting finishes and they salute and leave. Villa waves us toward chairs sitting at cockeyed angles in the sand by his desk.

I feel dread filling my guts when I see anger flashing in his brown eyes, and think, *What now?* He sits back in his chair, folds his hands over his belly. He cocks his head to one side and growls, "So, Hombrecito, you bring Doctor Thigpen and Doctor Miller to help us, eh? *Muchas gracias, señores...* Many thanks for nothing!"

I'm humiliated and disgusted. Thigpen and Miller had volunteered their services and had worked without rest since they arrived. Such kindness doesn't deserve his snarling anger.

Thigpen stands up, Miller an instant behind him, and says, "I'm sorry we've been of no help to your wounded, General. We'll leave now."

Villa's quirt whistles through the air and slaps the papers on his desk with a loud whack. He roars, "No! You will sit down *señores*. You will leave when I tell you to leave. Sit down!"

Thigpen's hands go up, palm-out in front of him. "*Sí*, certainly, General, we are sitting down." Miller doesn't say a word. He stares at Villa and sinks back down on the chair.

Villa leans forward, resting his elbows on his desk, looking at Thigpen, then Miller. "I have always extended guarantees to the persons and property of you *gringos*. With my own eyes, I have watched over fortunes of precious metals for *gringos*; with my own hands I buried your treasures safely out of the reach of enemies. Your families have enjoyed my protection."

He leans back and stares at them. They stare back. Thousands of men and animals move and work in front and behind us but I barely hear them. Villa clenches his teeth, and, with a thunderous frown quirts his desk papers again.

"Your *Presidente* Wilson has betrayed Mexico, betrayed Francisco Villa, and betrayed *División del Norte*. For four days not a single bite of food has passed the lips of my men and me. We are starving; we are here sacrificing our lives. For water we are drinking the discharge from your Douglas smelters. This, while you, whose families and treasure I have protected, sleep in the lap of luxury. Your government is playing a high hand in its attempt at scuttling the peace, prosperity, and freedom of Mexico."

Villa's roar grows louder as he speaks. Red in the face, he emphasizes each point by pounding his fist on the desk. He rises from his chair and leans forward to glare at Thigpen and Miller.

Quent, a frown across his brow and fire flashing in his eyes, walks around from behind the next wagon and stands watching Villa.

Villa points at a general watching from nearby, his smoke-yellowed eyes wide, his mouth open like a fish out of water, trying to gulp air. "My general, bring back the artillery!" He points toward a low point near the road. "Take it down there and turn it loose on those sons-of-bitches in Douglas." He looks around at other officers and then at me. "The Negros in Douglas are ready to all side with us. I did not want history to record our side as the offender, but the cowardly bastard Wilson has left us no other alternative."

He looks at Thigpen and Miller and snarls, "From this moment on, I will devote my life to the killing of every *gringo* I can get my hands on and the destruction of *gringo* property." He points at Camisa Roja watching with the enlisted men and points his quirt at Thigpen and Miller and says in a loud voice, "Execute them! *Señores Gringos* I give you one more hour of life. Make your peace with God."

Thigpen and Miller slump back in their chairs staring at Villa, their jaws dropped in disbelief. Quent and I stare in shock, shaking our heads, the "No!" on our lips unuttered. Camisa Roja, draws his revolver, points it at Thigpen and Miller and cocks it. He throws down his corn-shuck cigarillo and crushes it with this boot, looks around at the soldiers watching, and motions like he's tossing a ball toward them underhanded. Six of the men stand. They sling their rifles over their shoulders and come forward to pull Thigpen and Miller out of their chairs. They stand up dumb, shaken, as they are led away. I'll never forget Thigpen's eyes pleading for help. The general who Villa ordered to train the artillery on Douglas has disappeared. I know he obeys any Villa order without question, and so does Camisa Roja, who doesn't look at me as he marches the doctors away to their death.

Villa slumps in his chair and tosses the quirt on his desk. I stand and lean across the desk, looking him in the eye as he stares back at me with his angry brown eyes. "General, this is an outrage. You cannot…you must not do this. These men helped you. They volunteered to come help with your wounded. No one asked them to come. No one offered to pay them. The people in Douglas have done nothing to you. Some have even died because of stray bullets and shrapnel. If you do these things you are the worst criminal in Mexico."

His fist is a blur as he hits the left side of my face. It has the impact of a mule kick; I stagger back but don't fall. I hear his revolver clear his holster and make a loud double click as he cocks it. Yellow Boy's Henry clicks to full cock behind me followed by the sound of Mauser rifle bolts cycling cartridges into chambers. Villa keeps his eyes on me, the big Colt steady and leveled at the middle of my chest. "Hombrecito, you do not call your *jefe* names. It is disrespectful. You pledged your service to me. You work for me until I say you are done. *Comprende?*"

I see the anger in his eyes draining away. I'm so disgusted, I want to curse him and die. Rufus Pike's mantra to me when I was a child flashes in my mind, *Cold and cakilatin', Henry, cold and cakilatin'.* From the corner of my eye, I see Yellow Boy and Quent, and remember Quent's beautiful wife and two little boys in El Paso.

I bite the inside of my lip and take a deep breath. "*Sí,* I understand, but, *Jefe,* I will never respect you as General or *hombre* again if you do these terrible things."

The anger in his eyes evaporates. He looks down at his gun hand and runs his other hand through his hair, the look on his face dazed and confused like a fighter after a hard punch.

Quent, sensing that Villa is stepping back from the precipice, says in a calm voice, "General, there is not a man alive who could have taken Agua Prieta without destroying an Army ten times the size of yours or taking weeks or months to starve Calles into surrender. The Americans ensured that you would lose this battle. It is nothing to them that you lose. They think they will be safer and can fight the Germans if you lose. You will live to fight another day. But if you do these things, murder men who come to help you, fire your cannons against helpless women and children without warning, even your own countrymen will spit on the ground when they speak the name of Francisco Villa. You will never be able to raise another army. You will be despised more than any *bandito*. Hombrecito speaks the truth. Do not do these terrible things."

Villa lets the hammer down slowly and carefully, lays the revolver on his desk, and slumps into his chair. He rubs his temples with his strong, stubby fingers and stares at the ground. I hear the hammer on the Henry behind me return to safety. Gradually, the soldiers with the Mauser rifles relax and go about their business. I don't move and neither does Quent. I look along the road and see mule teams pulling cannons into place.

Villa looks up. There is a haunted, startled look in his eyes. "My God, Hombrecito, what am I doing? The treacherous Americans are making me lose my mind even to the point of executing friends and firing on women and children. This I cannot do no matter what the bastard Wilson does to me. *Sí*, Queentin, I will live to fight another day."

He takes a slip of paper, finds a pencil in his vest pocket and scribbles a note. He hands it to me and says, "Take this to Camisa Roja, *pronto*. I instruct him not to execute the *Americano medicos* and to escort them to the border. You tell him I said this, eh? He will be a few hundred yards south of this wagon. I always listen to execution shots to ensure that they are done and done on time."

I nod and walk almost run away from Villa's wagon to find Camisa Roja. Quent told me later that he then wrote a second note to the artillery general, telling him not to fire on Douglas, and he gave Yellow Boy that note to deliver.

It doesn't take long to find Camisa Roja, smoking a cigarillo off to one side of his firing squad. His men sit lounging, leaned back on their elbows, totally indifferent to the tragedy about to happen. Fifteen yards away Drs. Thigpen and Miller on their knees, eyes closed, and their hands clasped in front of them, pray. I can hear them mumbling as I hand Camisa Roja the note, and say, "The general says no execution. Escort them to the border and let them go."

Roja takes the note and reads it. "*Sí,* Doctor Grace, so the general orders. Tell this to our *medico* friends while I dismiss the firing squad."

I walk over to Thigpen and Miller. Hearing me, they open their eyes. I'm startled by the look of serenity on their faces.

"Gentlemen, the general sends you home and deeply regrets this ordeal he's put you through..."

They throw up their arms and yell, "Hallelujah!" so loud they startle me, and Thigpen saying, "Thank you, Jesus! Oh, thank you, dear God. Doctor Grace, we have been praying that God's will be done, and he sent us grace."

They laugh and slap each other on the back.

"Hallelujah!"

I don't know what to say about prayers being answered, so I just continue, "Capitán Roja will escort you back to the border, and I personally apologize for this treatment. You deserve so much better than this."

Thigpen smiles as he pushes himself up and dusts sand off his pants.

"Doctor Grace, it is I who thank you. We have our lives back. It is enough."

31. ADIÓS, AMIGOS

Yellow Boy, Quent and I sit on a Douglas Station platform bench looking like gaunt, hollow-eyed desperados waiting for a train. We say little, each lost in his thoughts about the talk we had with Villa a little more than an hour earlier....

Villa calls us to his wagon and we sit around his campaign desk, drinking coffee under the ragged old piece of canvas Juan tied to the edge of the campaign wagon to give us shade from the sun climbing out of the night. Saying nothing through one cup and into the next, he stares out across the plain at Agua Prieta, the hunkered down, ugly, and impregnable little village where so many of *División del Norte* died. In the middle of the second cup, he says in a low voice, "Queentin, you return to El Paso this day? What will you write of this disaster?"

Quent leans forward to rest his elbows against his knees and cradles the cup between his hands as he stares from under his brows, cool and unflinching, at Villa. "General, I will write of the great courage of your men. I will write of how they tried to take a fortified position that no army, north or south of the border, can take. I will write how the Americans betrayed a friend by recognizing Carranza, by shipping his army across the United States to Agua Prieta, and by providing electricity to their searchlights. I will say you disappeared into the desert with *División del Norte* and will reappear where and when the Carrancistas least expect you as you continue your battle against the despot. That is what I will write."

Smiling, Villa sighs and relaxes. "*Bueno*, Queentin. All you have said is the truth." I notice Quent says nothing of the aborted executions of Thigpen and Miller or of the recalled orders to shell Douglas.

"Just for my own curiosity, General, and off the record, what are your plans now?"

Villa points a finger pistol at him, the promise clear and certain what happens if his plan goes on the record. "I will leave five thousand cavalry here in the north. They go first to Cananea and demand of the no-good bastard, *gringo* mining company, supplies and $25,000 or I, Francisco Villa, will leave nothing they own standing. I will their drag their *jefes* by their necks across the desert and all will be afraid to work for them. Oh yes, *mi amigo*, the *gringo* business men will give *Señor* Bastard *Presidente* Wilson an earful of the anger they feel from the enemy he made for them.

"The cavalry will also keep Calles off my back while the rest of *División del Norte* goes to Naco. It is only a day's march to the west. In Naco we will rest a few days and I will resupply from the *gringos* in Bisbee, those greedy little bastard merchants there will ignore the embargo. I will tell my countrymen of the deal the traitor Carranza makes with the Goddamn, son-of-a-bitch *gringos*. I will take his army away from him with the truth of deals with the *gringos* he tries to hide and I will chase him like the rat he is into his hole.

"When my men are ready, we will take Hermosillo from Diéguez, I have fought that fraud in battle before, and after Hermosillo? Why, *Señor* Peach, we will celebrate the birth of *El Niño de Christo*, the Christ Child, in Mexico City. That is *mi* plan, Queentin, off the record, of course." As Villa speaks Quent puts down his cup and takes notes. He stares at Villa a moment and says, "General when you take Mexico City, call me. I'll come to do your story."

Grinning, Villa nods. "*Bueno*, Queentin, the story will be a good one." Scratching his beard's stubble, he turns to Yellow Boy and me. "*Muchachos*, you have more than paid any debt you thought you owed me. This is not your war. Go back to *Nuevo* Mexico."

My ears burn from all the cursing and swearing with which Villa wraps any reference to *gringos*, to Americans. It isn't that I feel swearing is particularly objectionable, I'd heard plenty of it in my time, but that Villa, who so rarely swears, is so vitriolic in his anger at the Americans. He's still not right in his mind, still crazed with anger only partially under control. I remember with photographic precision exactly what that black hole at the end of his pistol barrel looked like when he pointed it at me, and I wondered if that was the last thing I'd see on this earth. He needs help much more now than when he led his army to the eastern entrance of El Paso Púlpito. I can't leave. He's close to slipping into the abyss and taking huge numbers of men, men I know well, with him. I have to stay.

"General, I will stay as long as I am needed. Your wounded need all the doctors and medicine you can provide them."

He looks at me from under his brows and nods. "*Sí*, Hombrecito, we need you. You are a great *hombre* to stay with *División del Norte* in these dark hours. I will always, always remember what you do. *Muchas gracias*."

Villa's brown eyes look in Yellow Boy's flat, impassive eyes, black as obsidian, staring back at him. "And you Muchacho Amarillo, what will you do?"

"I go, *Jefe*. There is no honor riding against *hombres* hiding in holes with shoot-many-times guns. Better to wait until *los hombres* come out of their holes. Better to fight when they no expect you. Lose too many warriors when enemy fights from holes behind rope filled with thorns. I go."

He pauses a few seconds, continuing to stare hard at Villa, the cool morning still as the death all around us.

"I come back if you shoot my son, Hombrecito. It will take a long time for you to die. *Comprende*, Arango?"

Villa stares back unblinking, slowly nodding.

"*Sí*, I understand. You are a great friend, Muchacho Amarillo. *Muchas gracias* for all you have done for *División del Norte*."

We continue chatting as friends until Villa glances at the sun, takes out his watch, and looks at it.

"*Amigos* the train east comes in one hour and a half. I know Queentin is anxious to return to El Paso and his very beautiful wife, *Señora* Persia. *Por favor*, Hombrecito, escort him to the train. We will speak more when you return. *Adiós, amigos.*"

A long moaning call and distant black smoke plume rising above the creosotes, mesquite, and cactus to the west bring me out of my reverie. We watch the train approach and make no move until it stops at the station, then stagger up as passengers step off the platforms at the ends of their cars.

Quent and I shake hands.

"Good luck, Henry. Villa's on the edge of a high cliff with far to fall. You can bet he'll get his tail kicked in Hermosillo, and it'll probably be the end of *División del Norte*. Watch him close and stay out of his way. When you get back to Cruces or El Paso call me. We'll have supper and you can tell Persia and me about your adventures with Pancho Villa and *División del Norte*."

Quent is a keen observer of personalities and he's been amazingly accurate in predicting Villa's next moves, and I know he's exactly right.

"I'll be careful. Give my best to Persia and keep your sons close. *Adiós.*"

He and Yellow Boy grab the other's right forearm and slap each other on the back.

"*Señor* Yellow Boy, you are wise to leave. Villa would be a much better and more successful general if he used your tactics. Good luck on your ride to Mescalero. Watch your back."

Yellow Boy nods. "Go in peace, *amigo*. Make the tracks of straight words."

Quent picks up his gear and climbs up the steps of a passenger car. He salutes us as the train puffs out of the station, soon to disappear down the long, curving ribbons of shining steel.

Yellow Boy and I talk awhile in Douglas. I give him Satanas to keep safe as he mounts and rides toward the sun after saying, "Hombrecito, keep Arango to your front."

I return to my patients riding Quent's roan. Even though it's my choice to stay, I feel alone and abandoned, unprotected from the furies, but strongly feeling it's unethical to leave what's left of *División del Norte* now.

So many wounded, so few hands. I change bandages and clean wounds, treat skin sores, and administer painkillers. I remember Villa's near cold-blooded murder of two good men and his order to shell Douglas, and the memory drives my spirit low and into the shadows and darkness.

As I work, I also recall finding myself face-to-face with Camisa Roja a few hours after stopping the executions. Smiling, he says, "*Buenos tardes,* Doctor Grace. I come to tell you that I have seen your *Americano* friends safely across the border."

To his apparent surprise, I grab his hand and shake it.

"*Muchas, muchas gracias, señor*, you stopped a great tragedy and give my mind a little peace. I am very grateful."

He shrugs and looks a little embarrassed.

"I only do what I am told, *señor*. It was nothing."

I suddenly realize how quiet it is. Hundreds of small fires are scattered around the *medico* circle of wagons, but there is no distant laughter or sounds of men talking, no clink of harness chains, or an occasional guitar strumming to support a mournful song of love for a *señorita* far away. There is just the occasional stamp or snort from the mules. It's like the entire *División del Norte* died at Agua Prieta, and I guess, in a way, maybe it did.

I can't put off sleep any longer. Blankets on hard ground never felt so good. I pull the blankets over my shoulders and fall, exhausted, into a deep, dreamless sleep blotting out the horror and anger filling the last three days.

32. TRAIN TO HERMOSILLO

L eaving Agua Prieta in an early dawn fog, the wounded unable to walk or ride, crowd into wagons moving west toward Naco. Villa, with an escort of *dorados*, Camisa Roja among them, splits off from the main force in the turbulent, gray light to meet his Yaqui general, Urbalejo, ten miles south at Cabullona.

All day and well into the night, beaten, weary, thirsty and hungry but not ready to quit as long as the charismatic man who leads us refuses to accept defeat, we crawl toward Naco and reach it near midnight where Villa and General Urbalejo await us. A few make fires, but most of the men, after taking care of their animals, just wrap up in their blankets and collapse on the ground. It's nearing the last quarter of the night before the other *medicos* and I manage to ease the wounded out of the wagons and look after them before we too fall exhausted to the ground wrapped in our blankets.

Early in the morning, wagonloads of supplies Villa ordered from Bisbee, including flour and beans, of which the men have had very little since entering El Paso Púlpito, come across the border and are instantly surrounded in the starving camp. There is good water and enough from Naco's wells that men and animals can finally drink their fill. At first, I don't believe I can drink enough, but after a couple of canteens in less than an hour I want no more. I'm beginning to understand that the little things in life, like a swallow of cool, clean water and a crust of bread, are its true luxuries.

Rest, food, and enough water over the next five or six days bring a trembling flicker of life back to most of the men. It's like watching Lazarus covered with the pustules of decay, suddenly filled with the breath of life, rising from a dusty grave. From death-like silence, life around the cooking fires returns in a low rumble as men stagger up from their knees and begin looking after each other and their weapons.

Two or three days after we reach Naco, Villa calls me to his wagon, his eyes still blazing with self-righteous fury, a smile under his big, black mustache, he tosses me a sheaf of papers tied together with lose loops of string through punched holes to make a thin book. He expects this proclamation, his Naco Manifesto, will bring Carrancista generals to his side and win over the people who want an end to the war between him and Carranza.

"Read it, Hombrecito. Tell me what you think."

I sit down by his desk and carefully read every word. The proclamation claims that Carranza will use a Díaz style of government and return lands to the *hacendados* who will once more enslave the *peons* as they did before the *Revolución.* He claims that in exchange for five hundred million dollars in loans and allowing Carranza soldiers to cross into the United States, Carranza signed an eight-point pact with Wilson giving the United States unprecedented control of and access to Mexico's resources. Villa clearly states that, without question, he considers the United States the primary enemy of Mexico and, therefore, his archenemy.

Trying to absorb the angry words in one pass from his tight rolling script is like trying to drink from a fire hose, and it takes a while with my poor Spanish skills to finish and hand it back to him.

"General, this is a powerful condemnation of the United States for meddling in Mexico's affairs. I can't predict how much good it will do. What will you do with it?"

"I am publishing it in a *periódico, Vida Nueva.* I started it during the *Revolución.* We will see what happens then, eh? Maybe I send it to Queentin to publish also? The *gringos* must understand what an ass this *Señor* Wilson is. In any case it is done. Now I will plan for attacking Hermosillo, the capital of Sonora. General Urbalejo knows of two thousand Yaqui fighting men who will help us. They can make a difference, they are great fighters and sharpshooters, like you, *mi amigo. Sí,* Hombrecito, I will have my due with Diéguez at Hermosillo."

Over the next three or four days, Villa meets several times with his generals. Doctor Oñate, the *medico* assistants, and I set up a hospital for the wounded like we had in Colonia Morelos. There are over four hundred we will have to leave in Naco. When strong enough, they will be put on a train and sent back to Chihuahua and their homes.

* * *

Villa finds a freight train to carry us to Hermosillo. I don't know how he did it, but I suspect more threats to the mining company at Cananea helped. The veterans say it reminds them of the old *Revolución* days, and their spirits lift even more. The rumors claiming the general will attack Hermosillo and drive on to Mexico City spread through Naco like a whirlwind through the mesquite, filling the hearts of every man in the *División* with a desire to finish what he started.

Late in the afternoon of the sixth day in Naco, a long empty freight train puffs into the little station, and the *División* begins loading horses into boxcars and its meager supplies and artillery pieces on to flat cars. Most of the men ride on top of the boxcars.

Villa will ride with his generals in the caboose, study maps, and talk tactics. He offers me a place to sit, but I tell him I want to be near the men in case I'm needed. Frowning, he nods his assent.

"Very well, Hombrecito. A *medico* needs to be close to his patients, but on the train the only time the men need medical attention is when they fall off, and if they do, there is nothing you can do. We will not stop for them."

He grins, "Take care you do not fall off, eh? It can be a long way to water and Muchacho Amarillo will come after me if I lose you."

"No, General, I won't fall off," I say, thinking it's probably better to fall off the train than to be slaughtered during futile charges at the certain Hermosillo trenches and barb wire.

Near midnight the train engine groans against its load, puffing and creeping out of Naco, southwest toward Cananea. After it's up to speed, the old engine only makes fifteen or twenty miles an hour, but sitting in that little breeze is bad when your clothes are thin. It's freezing cold and the black, gritty smoke shades the face of every man, making his wrinkles and creases standout like shadowed canyons, and the whites of his eyes blood-shot yellow. Men sitting toward the front of the boxcars wrap up in their blankets, turn their backs to the wind and try to keep from freezing or drifting off to sleep and falling off. Still, riding the long, puffing dragon is far easier than a foot or horse march, and much faster. No one complains.

Wrapped in my blanket, I watch the stars and track our direction. In a couple of hours the train swings back toward the northwest, and then turns due west for a little while before turning due south. It stops for water and coal under the dim, coal-oil lantern lights of Santa Cruz, chugs off again, swinging back and forth around a series of tight curves against dark mountains, turns west at San Lázaro for a couple of miles, and begins a long northwest run again. Near Buena Vista the sky begins to turn gray against the outline of black mountains, and we turn roughly due west again before rolling southwest. The sun is glowing bright yellow against blood-red clouds when we stop in Nogales for an hour to take on more coal and water and the men make nature calls.

All through the night my mind burns with images and sounds that dart randomly in and out of my thoughts like squeaking bats in a dark cave, images of men being killed in the bright beams of searchlights or blown up by dynamite hidden in the ground; whistling inbound artillery shells and the thundering staccato *whump, whump, whump* of brilliant fireworks-like displays from shells exploding over and in Agua Prieta; ragged pops and roars of rifle fire and machine guns from long wavering lines of bright orange and yellow streaks approaching each other and then receding; a tide of death leaving bodies scattered in the cleared space around Agua Prieta looking like flies stuck to glue-covered paper; men with pails at the border fence begging for water; the snarling anger of Villa as he orders Thigpen and Miller executed and Douglas shelled.

As a teenager I lived for a while with the Apaches in the Sierra Madre and saw men tortured to death, heard their screams as they begged for mercy, begged to die. I learned to harden myself to the torture but never accept it. As a doctor in training, I'd seen many indignities done to the human body, much suffering and misery, and I learned, just as I had with Apache torture victims to lock my feelings, images, and the screams of pain away in my mind and never go there except when some demon unlocked them in very bad dreams. Now all the suffering I'd seen as a boy and young man floats free in my mind with interest compounded on an infinitely greater scale, and I wonder if I'll ever be or feel normal again.

The questions haunting me since Camisa Roja appeared at my door, keep asking: *How much is enough? How much is enough to repay Villa for saving my life and Yellow Boy's?* Wise Yellow Boy left when Villa said it was enough. I did not. I ignored the best advice Rufus Pike ever gave me when I was growing up: *Henry, to survive in this here land, you gotta be cold and cakilatin'.* I knew he was telling me not to think with my heart, to coldly decide the best thing to do, and then do it.

What had I been thinking? Why had I stayed? Deep in

my soul, I know the answer. I can't leave the men who've become part of my soul, men with whom I've suffered hunger and thirst, men of great courage marching across mountains and deserts, their bodies covered with sores, to face death from bullets and exploding shells, men who fought in the hope they might somehow, with the grace of God, get back to their families. No, I can't leave these men now, even if Villa goes completely crazy and destroys us all.

While we wait in Nogales, the sun floats higher, a brilliant yellow in blood-red morning clouds. *Perhaps*, I wonder, *a harbinger of things to come?* Men water their horses and give them hay off the flat cars. Street vendors appear out of nowhere, hawking hot burritos and baskets of fruits and vegetables from far to the south. Villa tells his commanders to feed the men and gives them money to buy what they need.

I haven't yet bought any fruit or burritos when Camisa Roja walks up and hands me a couple of burritos wrapped in corn shucks. "*Buenos días*, Doctor Grace, where are you riding?" I point to the top of the car next to me, my mouth too full to answer. He nods back toward the flat cars. "Come on back to the flat car where I ride. There is not so much a chance of falling off there and you can get some sleep. You won't get much when we reach Hermosillo."

"*Gracias, señor.* I'll get my rifle and gear off the top and be right along."

He rubs his sleeve over his face smudged with black grit, and grins. "*Bueno.*"

The train rumbles south, and the sun climbs slowly and steadily, its heat growing as it heads for the top of its arc. We doze in little catnaps never lasting more than five or ten minutes before the crawling dragon jerks us back to consciousness.

At last, Camisa's curiosity overcomes his manners.

"Doctor Grace, may I ask you a question? It is none of my business and please do not answer if it does not please you to do so."

I look him in the eye. "*Sí?*"

"Muchacho Amarillo is not on the train. He is on a mission for General Villa?"

"No. He returns to Mescalero, back to the Reservation. He leaves the *División del Norte.*"

Camisa frowns, "Why does he do this? There is much fighting left to do."

"General Villa said Muchacho Amarillo's debt to him for saving his life was paid many times over and he ought to go if he wanted. So, he left."

"But why? General Villa and Muchacho Amarillo are *amigos*, no?"

"*Amigos? Sí*, they are *amigos, amigos buenos*, good friends, but you know that Muchacho Amarillo is an Apache. He will die to keep his honor. He will never hesitate to go on revenge raids with his *amigos*. He has no reluctance to kill anyone or anything if that increases his power and keeps his honor. He rode with the general until the general said his debt was paid. He might have stayed longer except he thinks there is no honor in killing yourself by riding at the demand of a man gone loco against men in holes with many-quick-shots guns. It is more honorable to put a pistol to your eye and pull the trigger."

Camisa frowns and grunts in surprise. "Hmmph. So Muchacho Amarillo thinks General Francisco Villa is *loco*? It is a good thing he leaves. He might not live long around *División del Norte* if he thinks this."

"*Sí*, Muchacho Amarillo thinks this and sometimes so do I."

His brows shoot up. He opens his mouth to speak but I interrupt him. "Remember the two *Americanos* you nearly executed at Agua Prieta? I brought you a written reprieve from the General for them and you took them back to the border crossing at Douglas?"

"*Sí?*"

"They were American doctors who came only to help the wounded. Villa sees them in the *medico* wagons, suddenly decides he doesn't like Americans anymore and orders those doctors executed and Douglas shelled. That's crazy."

He sticks out his lower lip and shrugs. "He was just a little angry. He killed no doctors. He didn't shell Douglas. He just gets carried away in the moment, that's all. That doesn't make him *loco*, Doctor Grace."

"You could have fooled me. All right, then forget intending to execute the *Americanos* or shelling Douglas. I learned in medical school that doing the same thing over and over when you know it will fail is *loco*. How many times has Villa sent *División del Norte* charging machine guns, barbed wire, and trenches only to see thousands of men and horses die. He loses and loses and still does the same thing over and over again. How many times has he ordered men to charge the wire and machine guns, tell me, señor? How many times?"

Camisa Roja stares at his boots for a long time before looking me in the eye. "Too many."

"*Sí*, too many."

"So why do you stay, Doctor Grace?"

"I guess I'm a fool."

He smiles and shakes his head. "No, I understand. You have great loyalty to the men you have suffered with, as well as the general, but mostly the men, *sí*?"

I'm struck by his deep insight into the bonds between men who have suffered together. "*Sí*. Mostly the men."

"You are a good man, Doctor Grace. Be careful around the general. I might be ordered to shoot you too, and I wouldn't like it, but I'd do it."

We laugh, but I feel like a man holding a stick of dynamite with a lighted fuse. We ride for a while saying nothing, but neither of us can sleep. My curiosity, long sleeping about the man in the red shirt, awakes and stretches in my mind. "*Señor*, you awaken questions that have slept in my head a long time. May I ask them?"

He raises a brow and looks over at me. "You won't try to shoot me, *señor*?"

I laugh. "No, I understand now that killing you will bring me no honor, no power. But I'll confess that sometimes I want you to feel the pain I felt when my wife died in my arms from your bullet. I know life isn't fair. Life is a game of chance. I know all I can hope for is to break even before the game ends."

He stares at me, his black eyes searching mine. "What do you wish to know?"

"When I lived with the Apaches, word came that a man wearing a red shirt, a *camisa roja*, killed Apache Elias and then a little later Apache Kid. Were you the one who killed them?"

"*Sí,* I blew the sons-of-bitches straight to Hell, and I was glad when I did. Why do you ask?"

"You cost Muchacho Amarillo and me the pleasure of doing the same. We swore vengeance after Kid and Elias helped Billy Creek steal my wife just before their raid on the Comacho *hacienda*. Tell me what happened when you found them."

Camisa Roja holds his rifle like Yellow Boy holds his when he sits, butt firmly between his boots, the barrel resting on his shoulder. His hand strokes the barrel as he stares off in the distance, his eyes watching images in his mind.

"After the *hacienda* raid, men who knew them said Apache Elias, his son Juan, Kid and Billy Creek were part of the raid. I heard that some Apache had killed Creek and I hoped I heard the truth. And so it was as I learned when Muchacho Amarillo told me in Las Cruces. I swore that if I ever found those other bloodthirsty bastards I'd kill them. Kill them on the spot, no matter where.

"They disappeared in the Sierra Madre for a while, but I knew they'd come back and they did. Elias's band started raiding the villages up and down Rio Bavispe. Elias looked more like a Mexican than an *Indio*. He liked to dress like a *peon*, put on a big hat to help hide his face and walk around the village the day before his night raid so he knew the places of its treasures and defenses.

"The *patrón* had no work for the *vaqueros* after the raid so I drifted across the mountains and tried to find work at the mines in *El Tigre Sierras* on the west side of the Rio Bavispe. The Garcia Mine hired me as a guard, and I rode over to San Miguel every two or three weeks for supplies, a little tequila in the cantina, and maybe a little something else if the *señoritas* in the cantina were willing to take only a few pesos. One day I bought a sack of supplies and was tying them to my saddle when I happened to look down the street. Elias, in his hat and white pants, comes walking toward me. I did not believe it. I might search in the *sierras* a lifetime and never find him. Now he walks down the street practically begging me to kill him?

"I stay between the horses so he cannot see me when he passes. I pull my rifle from the scabbard, remembering the torture of *mi patrón, Señor* Comacho. With a horse between us, I shoot him in the knee, just like *Señor* Comacho was shot. Elias, he makes no sound as he falls in the street, but I see him pull a *pistola* from the waistband under his shirt. So I shoot him in his elbow just like *Señor* Comacho was shot. My anger, it takes me. I see everything in red. I shoot Elias in the other knee, the other elbow, and I shoot off both his ears. Still he says nothing. Only looks at me with his eyes glowing like hot pieces of burning coal. He can't move, helpless, bleeding on the caliche, when I walk up to him and I say, *Damn you, Elias* and I put a bullet right here."

He holds a finger on the spot between his eyes. "The *Rurales* were ready to shoot me for killing an innocent man until I told them he was Apache Elias and showed them his horse. Ha! Then they want to give me a medal."

His story, with the exception of a few minor details, matches what we heard in the Apache camp of Pelo Rojo. I regret I'm not the one to pull the trigger on Elias, but Camisa Roja took a full measure of vengeance and I'm glad to hear his story. He gazes west for a while, looking toward the low mountain ridgeline as the train rocks along through winding canyons and on to a scraggly *llano*. He looks over at me and says, "You wish also to know of Apache Kid, Doctor Grace?"

"*Sí*, many claim they kill Kid. The story told in the Apache camps says you killed him."

"*Sí*, I killed that *Indio*. I knew Kid was in the Comacho *hacienda* raid. About a month after I killed Elias, I received word at the mines that Comacho's elder son was returning to the *hacienda* to begin again and needed his *vaqueros* to help with the herds that were scattered all the way to Casas Grandes. I returned to the *hacienda*. Two weeks later I went hunting in the Sierra Las Espuelas on the western side of the *rancho*. I stopped to rest my horse on a ridge and was having a smoke when I saw three Apaches in a little camp far down the ridge below me. I took my rifle and eased down the ridge to get a better look at them and to be sure there were no others around before I killed them."

He thumps his fist against his chest. "I had already decided in my heart that I must kill them all. They must be treated like snakes too close to the *hacienda*, killed before they strike innocent ones. Close enough to see them clearly I realized there are two women and a man. One woman clearly younger than the other, I guess about fifteen or sixteen. She is a beautiful *señorita*, high cheekbones, and raven's wing hair. I didn't kill women in those days, but these are grown Apaches as deadly as men and I know I must kill them to protect the *hacienda*. Even so, I hate that I have to kill her. But the *hombre*! He wears a dress coat, vest, and pants. I know without a doubt he is Apache Kid. I cannot believe that in the space of six weeks I have found, purely by accident, two leaders of the Comacho raid.

"I wait until the man and women sit close by their fire.

Just as I sight on Kid, the girl stands and heads for the bushes and the older woman takes something from the fire and hands it to Kid. I shoot. The shot is long and hard to make, but I am lucky and the bullet goes through the middle of his back. He pitches forward into the fire and doesn't move. The woman recoils and falls on her back, rolls to her hands and knees and starts to run. I shoot again and drop her after a step or two. She screams something at the girl. A very long, hard shot with her on the ground I have to shoot two more times before I kill her. I wait and watch for the girl before I go down to the camp, but see her nowhere. I ease down to the camp, searching the brush in every direction. Still, I cannot find the girl. I never find her. Kid and the woman I put together under a pile of stones. I consider scalping Kid to prove I killed him, but take his watch instead, and return to the *hacienda* with the meat I take on my hunt. The other *vaqueros* say I did a good thing for them the day I killed Kid. That is my story, Doctor Grace."

"*Gracias,* Camisa Roja. Your story matches the one the Apaches heard. I beat Kid in a shooting match once and won his new Winchester on a bet. I gave it back to him, and then he betrayed Muchacho Amarillo and me at the Comacho raid. A thief and coward like him deserve to die the way you killed him."

A quizzical look filling his face, Camisa Roja stares at me. "We all deserve to die, Doctor Grace, but how and when, no one, no one knows except God."

33. AMBUSH AT SAN PEDRO DE LA CUEVA

Generals Diéguez and Flores defend Hermosillo against Villa's attacks using the same tactics as Obregón at Celaya, León, and Aguascalientes, and Calles at Agua Prieta. On the *llano* east of Hermosillo, thousands of *División del Norte* horses and men and boys lie slaughtered, stiff with death and decay, scattered like brown husks of winter wheat under a brilliant sun and a deep water blue sky black with buzzards. All the survivors of the last desperate charge, except my friend General Francisco Villa, know and feel the end of the war in their souls. Many deciding not to die, change their allegiance and desert to the Carranza side or begin the long walk home alone.

Villa curses the *gringos* and Woodrow Wilson and swears he will personally execute any man he catches deserting. He keeps his best, his *dorados*, in reserve and asks me to stay back from the fighting with Doctor Oñate and the medical assistants to bandage the wounded and give solace to the dying.

As his army evaporates, Villa writes a long letter to Generals Diéguez and Flores. He repeats the claims in his Naco Manifesto, which Carrancista generals ignored, and asks them to give their opinion to the charges. I believe he hopes they will enter into some kind of negotiation with him. General Flores sends him back a note. I'm at the command wagon when a pompous little Carrancista captain appears. He briskly salutes, hands a note to Villa and asks to return to his commander. Villa takes the note, waves him away, and sits down to read.

I hear him mutter, "My God, why are these bastards so blind? Traitors. All of them are traitors." Villa, his face red, curses and vituperations flying from his mouth like vomit, hands me the note. It says that Villa has no proof of his accusations. Carranza's side has won and is recognized as the lawfully recognized government by the major countries in the world. He, Villa, should join them in rebuilding Mexico, not destroying it. Diéguez doesn't bother to send a reply.

División del Norte, now probably not more than five hundred men, begin preparations for the long ride home over the mountains to their villages in Chihuahua and Durango. The survivors divide the rations left from the living and the dead. There should be enough to get us all home without starving because so few survived to share the once meager supplies.

Each man carries two full bandoliers, leaving a mule-pack train to carry supplies and extra rounds of ammunition.

A couple of miles outside of Hermosillo, Villa stations twenty men to cover our trail in case cavalry come out to harass us. One of the men guarding the trail told me later that they stayed at their station two days and never saw the first rider leave Hermosillo.

The road east out of Hermosillo runs straight for the distant mountains across a dry *llano* scattered with anemic creosotes, mesquite, cactus, and short dry grass. Macario Bracamontes leads Villa's troops toward the *sierras*. An older man with kind eyes and a big gray mustache to go with his big, busy eyebrows, Bracamontes knows and senses the trails and roads through the mountains like they are some long, unforgotten lover always fresh in his mind. He spreads the column out as we cross the *llano* to keep down dust and has the scouts stay far out on the wings to ensure Carrancistas do not catch us with a surprise attack. We make good time the first day and by late in the afternoon, the mountains, not much more than gray and brown lines on the horizon warped by trembling mirages earlier in the day, turn to high peaks covered in dark green and white snow.

On the second day, we leave the road east and turn north into canyons passing between green mountain ridges and along small, normally dry rivers, where water still flows. We mostly follow firm, sandy riverbeds, but sometimes cut across country when Bracamontes knows the river loops back on itself. The road along the rivers gains altitude but has no steep climbs all the way to San Pedro de la Cueva. For three days, on one of the most pleasant rides I've ever had, we follow the streams passing through high mountain canyons, the air cool and crisp, the sky a brilliant royal blue. With enough to eat and drink, the men begin to regain strength.

The morning of the fifth day I'm toward the front of the column with Bracamontes who expects to be in San Pedro de la Cuevas early that afternoon. Nearing the end of the last big canyon before the easy descent into San Pedro, shots pour down on us from the canyon sides killing men in front and on either side of us.

At the sound of the first shot, Bracamontes wheels his horse to face the column. Standing in the stirrups, bullets whistling and ricocheting around him, he shouts, "To the sides of the canyon! Take cover! No shooting until I give the orders! *Vamos! Vamos!*"

He wastes no time joining me behind a huge boulder as the sounds of rifle fire echo down the canyon and bullets thump into the moist sand or ricochet off boulders into the piñons around us. The shooting suddenly stops. Deathly quiet, the only sounds come from the men hit and still alive, moaning in pain, begging for help, and probably bleeding to death.

I say to Bracamontes, "Let me and a couple of others drag the wounded out of the line of fire so we can at least stop the bleeding. They don't deserve to die here after all they've been through." I start to plunge out to grab a man but he grabs my arm in an iron grip and won't let go. "Wait! *Un momento, por favor,* Doctor Grace. I will ask that they do not shoot while we recover our wounded."

He cups his hands to make a megaphone and yells, "*Señores, por favor*, do not shoot while we get our wounded."

A bellowed reply echoes down the canyon. "*Banditos!* Take your wounded and *vamos!* You die here if you try again to raid San Pedro de la Cueva!"

Bracamontes frowns at me. He calls out. "*Señores*, we

mean you no harm. These men fight in the *División del Norte* commanded by General Francisco Villa, not with *banditos*. We return to Chihuahua."

Silence, then a voice filled with wonder, "General Francisco Villa of the *Revolución*?"

"*Sí!*"

"Do not shoot, *señores*. We will show ourselves and come to you."

Bracamontes puffs his cheeks in a blow of relief. "*Sí*. Come forward while we gather our wounded. I will meet you in the canyon entrance."

Men and boys appear as if by magic out of the canyon walls. All live in San Pedro de la Cueva. The *alcalde*, the mayor of the village, leads them to meet Bracamontes at the entrance to the canyon. His eyes filled with sadness, the *alcalde*, holding his hat in both hands in front of him as though approaching a *patrón*, studies Bracamontes. I hear them speak as I try to stop the bleeding on two of the wounded men. Four others already stare at heaven with lifeless eyes.

Bracamontes, ram-rod straight and making eye contact with each one, steps up to the group and salutes their leader. "I am *Commandante* Macario Bracamontes of *División del Norte* under the command of General Francisco Villa."

The alcalde nods and looks at the ground. "*Commandante* Bracamontes, I am Maiseo Garcia, the *alcalde* de San Pedro de la Cueva and these *hombres* come with me from the village. We have made a terrible mistake, *Commandante*. Yesterday, we learned of armed *hombres* approaching our village. We believed they were *banditos* who have raided us many times: burning our homes, raping our women, and taking our grain and beans so we starve in the winter."

He lifts his head and sticks his chin up. "We suffer this no more. We come to ambush and kill these raiders. Now, after shooting some of your men in warning, we learn we have made a terrible mistake. We attack the soldiers of the hero of the *Revolución*. Maybe we even kill some of General Villa's soldiers. We humbly beg your pardon and ask you come to our village so we can give you a little food and rest, all we have left after many raids by the *banditos*. For any *hombre* we have killed, one of our village men will take his place, and any *hombre* we have wounded we will care for until he can rejoin you. We beg you not to attack us for this grievous mistake."

Bracamontes, eyeing the *alcalde* and saying nothing, pulls out his crook-stemmed pipe and tobacco tin. He takes his time to fill the bowl and light it with a big Red Head match. With a good red coal glowing in the bowl, he blows a puff or two of the fine tobacco smoke into the breeze and nods to the alcalde.

"*Señor*, your mountains are filled with many bad *hombres*. Men who are deserters, *banditos*, gunfighters, or *Indios*. I am *simpatico* with you protecting your women, your homes, and your properties. This, every *hombre* must do. But you shoot my soldiers? You must correct the terrible mistake you and the *hombres* of your village make. *Señor* Garcia, you act as a wise *hombre* acts. I accept your offer to restore my wounded to health and to replace the soldiers you have killed."

The *alcalde's* shoulders sag with relief. He sighs and says, "*Ah, muchas, muchas gracias Commandante. Por favor*, come to our village. Let us share our *tortillas* and *frijoles* with you and your *hombres*. Where is General Villa? When he comes, we will give him a feast."

Bracamontes shakes his head. "General Villa does not travel so fast. He comes in his *commandante* wagon. I warn you, *señor*. Today General Villa is not in a forgiving mood. He has been betrayed by the *Americanos*, by *División del Norte* deserters, and by Carranza *Commandantes* who will not listen to him. He has lost battles at Agua Prieta and Hermosillo and his anger knows no bounds against those disloyal to him. He will think those who shot his soldiers disloyal and will execute them, everyone. I advise you to take your men to the mountains until the *División del Norte* passes on."

Garcia frowns at Bracamontes. "But, *Commandante,* how can General Villa shoot anyone when he does not know those to blame for these accidental shootings? We do not know who shot the soldiers even if we wanted to tell. He will not do this terrible thing. He cannot do this terrible thing. We will not leave. We cannot leave our *casas* and hide like rats in a stable. We are *hombres*."

Bracamontes bites down hard on the stem of his pipe showing his teeth. He stares at Garcia saying nothing. They stand there seemingly suspended in time. At last Bracamontes says in a low voice filled with threat, "I have warned you, *señor*. If you stay, you play the fool. Now take my men to your village so Doctor Grace might have a chance to save them."

34. MASSACRE

Villa, his brown eyes flat and lifeless, stares at the *alcalde* like a rattlesnake contemplating a rat frozen in place, certain its brown fur will make it disappear against the sand. "So *Señor* Garcia," he growls and slaps his wagon desk with a loud whack from his quirt, "your village men think they can murder heroes of the *Revolución*?"

Garcia jerks his head to one side as if he's been slapped. "No, oh no, General. We are very sorry we have done this thing. We did not know…"

The fury in Villa's soul from the defeats at Agua Prieta and Hermosillo fill his voice, the quirt slaps the desk even harder than before, and he snarls, "You feel free to murder men who have faced death many times battling the dictator Carranza, the dictator Huerta, the dictator Díaz? You betray heroes who pass by this dung hill of a village?"

Holding his hat with both hands in front of him, Garcia

licks his lips and stammers, "No...no, General. Por...por favor, we did not kn...kn...know who your men were. We thought they—"

The quirt is faster than a striking snake and leaves a nasty cut across Garcia's face that stretches from just below his left eye across his nose to the far side of his right cheek. "Traitors! Traitors! That is what you are, *señor.*" Villa bellows from deep in his guts. He makes a fist with his right hand and holds it in front of the *alcalde's* face. He speaks through clenched teeth. "At last I hold some traitors in my hands. By God these traitors will not escape justice."

Blood splattered all over his clean white shirt, his left eye already swelling shut, Garcia seems to find iron in his core and stands straight, refusing to back up from Villa's bullying onslaught. His voice no longer sounds pleading, but coolly reasonable. "*Por favor*, General. We have offered to make amends by replacing men we killed and providing shelter and nursing for those we wounded. We are feeding your entire army and its animals even though it means we will starve this winter. *Por favor*, we..."

Villa spits on the ground, gently slapping the quirt across his palm leaving faint, dark red stripes of Garcia's blood.

"*Sí, Alcalde*, oh *sí*, you most certainly will pay, this I, General Francisco Villa, promise to the world you will pay."

He points toward a *dorado* just at the edge of the lantern's circle of light. "Search this privy of a village. Put every man over the age of twelve years in the corral. Do it now! If any escape I will hold you personally responsible. I will give these traitors their judgment *mañana* when the sun comes over the *sierras. Vamos!*"

Dorados, rifles ready, step out of the shadows to take

the *alcalde* and the men with him to the corral. The *alcalde* tries to reason with him once more. "General, we did not know, *por favor*, we…"

His eyes hooded, the anger pouring from his soul makes him deaf.

"Damn it! Take these traitors away. My ears are ready to puke from their whining. *Vamos*."

I watch the scene play out as if in a bad dream. The village men have refused to leave their homes. *Surely*, they think, *General Villa, such a great man, a champion of the poor, certainly he will understand our mistake, accept our apology and offer of just restitution for the men killed. Surely, he will do this. There is no need to hide in the mountains as Bracamontes warns us. He cannot be serious.*

But, when Villa learned what happened, he sank into a cold fury, swearing, slapping the quirt hard against anything in range. It makes me heartsick to see him that way and I wish I were somewhere else. I start to speak. I have to talk him out of abusing these people. He might even put Garcia in front of a firing squad. I see Bracamontes and then Camisa Roja standing back in the shadows give me tiny, covert shakes of their heads. Best to wait until he calms down before offering a contrary opinion. He always calms down. I wait and say nothing.

Villa plops down in his field chair, tossing the quirt on his desk. I wait a little while for him to relax, and then excuse myself to feed my horse and take care of the few wounded who lived to ride out of Hermosillo.

I find my doctor's bag, check bandages on the soldiers, and then go to the corral. There must be sixty or seventy men and boys in the cold night air sitting huddled together for warmth inside the corral. Captain Gomez, the *dorado* in charge, gives me hot water off his fire and lets me through the corral gate. I motion Garcia over to me.

Garcia is shivering from the cold, his face a bloody mess, the cut requiring stitches and disinfectant before it turns into something lethal. Still, he comes and stands straight, his chin stuck out in defiance, saying nothing.

I take his chin in my hand and look at the cut in the light of a lantern. "*Señor*, that quirt will leave you an evil scar. I am a doctor. I have medicine to make you feel better and to keep it from filling with pus. I stitch it together so it does not look quite so bad, eh?'

He nods. "*Muchas gracias, señor*, but you are wasting your time. The general will kill me tomorrow when the sun rises over the mountains."

"I don't think so, *señor*. He has always been a friend to the poor and treated them with great respect. He knows your hard life."

Garcia looks at me like I'm crazy. I shrug.

"He's just bitter and angry that the *gringos* have betrayed his trust and he has lost big battles with Carrancistas. He'll cool down tonight, and think more clearly by first light."

A dark figure rises out of the huddle of men and walks toward us. From his robes I see he is a priest, young, close to my age, and he reminds me of Father Braun in Mescalero.

The priest says, "I pray to the great, merciful Father that your words are true, *señor*. General Villa is a mighty warrior who can snuff us all out like a man pinching off a candle. We will pray long and hard tonight that the general's heart is filled with God's will and justice by the coming of the sun."

"I'm sure that it will be so, Father. *Por favor*, help me

with *Señor* Garcia. I want to get this cut cleaned and sewed together before it becomes infected."

"Certainly, *señor*. How can I help?"

I don't sleep well. I dream of the jaguar on fire and feel his claws hook into my pants, pulling me toward the flames, drawing me to his sabre-like teeth. I awake sweating in the freezing air. As I try to go back to sleep, I see again the look on Villa's face at Agua Prieta when he orders the execution of Doctors Thigpen and Miller and the shelling of Douglas. Now he's even more filled with hate. Surely he won't execute Garcia. The village people are the ones for whom he's fought all these years. I feel anxious, suspended in a purgatory of my own making, frozen into inaction as though reality has become a dream. My head thinks Villa is crazy and will murder Garcia. My heart feels it won't happen.

I hear Juan making a fresh pot of coffee. I stay in my blankets until the sound of him pouring a cup and then I stagger up wrapping my blanket around me. Juan hands me the scalding hot brew. "*Gracias, señor.* Is the general up yet?"

He shakes his head and says in his ancient, raspy voice, "He is not here all night, Doctor Grace."

I stand by the little fire, drinking my coffee and watching the mountain range outline turn from smoky gray to dim orange. When liquid gold pours across the edge of the sky, Villa still has not appeared. Birds begin welcoming the dawn and somewhere in the village, a rooster crows. I study the light filling the edge of the mountains outlined on the black mirror of the big, still lake at the edge of the village, and look around to see a couple of sleepy *dorados* and Juan near the cooking fire. Villa still has not appeared. By now, he's usually finishing his breakfast and talking to his generals.

The sun's brilliant, golden circle floats above the ridgeline, throwing shafts of light through the trees and village houses. The brilliant orb seems to stop and balance on the edge of the high mountains, casting a straight, golden road across the lake.

A cold realization settles in my mind: *He's going to shoot Garcia.* Somehow I have to stop him. I look toward the corral and see Villa leading a double column of *dorados*, Mausers on their shoulders, marching smartly behind him. I want to vomit. This can't be happening. I throw down the cup and blanket and run for the corral gate.

By the time I reach the gate, Villa and the *dorados* are inside the corral and I hear him say, "Captain Gomez, form the prisoners in straight columns of five each, and get that God-damned priest out here."

Gomez is reluctant to touch the priest, who is on his knees, hands clasped in entreaty, and saying, "*Por favor* General, *por favor* spare these *hombres*. In the names of God and the Holy Virgin do not take the lives of these innocent men."

Villa glares at him and snarls, "Get away from me, you sorry excuse for an *hombre*. God does not spare traitors and neither do I. They must die. They must all die!" He kicks the priest backwards and walks away from him.

I stride through the gate, puffing from my run and head

straight for Villa. A hand from a red sleeve grabs my arm in a vice-like grip and jerks me back.

Gomez's *dorados* begin forming the huddled bunch of men and boys into columns of five, lining them up by similar heights one behind the other, and making each row stand four or five feet apart.

The priest crawls on his hands and knees through the dust to face Villa again. "General, in the name of God, do not do this thing, I beg you from the dust. Do not do this. Mercy. In the name of God, Christos, and the Virgin show mercy."

Villa's hand drops to his pistol, his eyes boiling hatred, teeth clenched in anger. He glances up to see the eyes of every man in the corral on him. He looks at the first row of five, two stooped gray heads and three boys who couldn't have been more than fourteen.

"Very well, priest! I will show mercy. Take that first column of traitors and get the hell out of my sight. I warn you, *Padre*, never, ever let me see you again or I swear to the god you pray to, you will never see the light of another day."

The priest crawls erect and runs wide-eyed to the first row of old men and boys. He waves them out of the corral like they're chickens, running them through the crowd of *dorados* just inside the corral gate.

The *dorados* finish forming the columns of five. I make a quick count. There are thirteen columns of five and one of four. Villa paces back and forth in front of them, slapping his leg with quirt. I see the young men and boys looking at each other across the columns, the youngest have tears on their cheeks. The grown men stand tall and stare straight ahead.

Gomez steps up to Villa and salutes. "The columns are formed, General."

Villa nods, and with his fists against his pistol belt, he looks at the columns. "I, General Francisco Villa, *Commandante División del Norte*, have found the men in this village guilty of murdering heroes of the *Revolución*. You are all traitors to Mexico, to the *Revolución*, and to *División del Norte*. The penalty for such treason is death by firing squad. Colonel Soto, you know what to do."

The leader of the *dorado* column behind Villa steps forward and begins barking orders. A *dorado* with a Mauser steps to face the first man in each column ten feet away. I try to jerk away but the grip grows tighter, stronger. From behind me I hear running feet and a loud wailing plea, "Nooooo, General! For the love of God, no! Mercy I beg you!" The priest bursts through the *dorados* at the corral gate and stumbles to fall on his knees behind Villa.

It is as though, for a moment, time stops. No one breathes or blinks as they stare at the priest. Villa, his right hand reaching for his pistol, turns on his heel to face the priest.

"You stupid, stupid man, I told you to stay out of my sight."

The pistol seems to clear its holster in slow motion. I see Villa thumb its hammer back and it falling as he squeezes the trigger. It's like being shocked out of a dream when I hear the roar from the big .45 echoing across the mountains. Blood and brains spray out the back of the priest's head. He falls backward, flopping in the dust, his mouth and eyes still open in supplication, a bright red spot on his forehead between his eyes.

My arm is out of that steel grip and I'm on Villa in an instant, bellowing, "You bastard! You no good bastard..."

my fists pummeling his thick hard body, careless of how or where they land. I get in three or four wild solid punches before I'm stunned senseless from a blow from behind and see stars. I fall forward and to one side of Villa. A boot kicks my shoulder and rolls me over on my back. I have a hard time trying to focus my eyes until I and see a brilliant red shirt inside the *dorado* coat of the man standing over me with a Mauser.

Villa springs to his feet graceful as a big cat. "*Gracias, Camisa Roja.* We must talk with this half-breed Mexican who loses his mind. Take him to my wagon and wait for me. This will not take long, eh? *Vamos!*"

"As Roja and another *dorado* take me under the arms and drag me forward out the gate of the corral, I hear the metallic hiss of Colonel Soto's saber as he pulls it from its scabbard. He holds the shiny steel with his arm straight up and barks, "Ready..." Fourteen rifle bolts make a jangly metallic marching sound as they're pulled back and pushed forward to load shells. "Aim..." I'm stunned and semi-conscious but I distinctly hear the scream of an eagle and lifting my eyes to heaven see it floating high above us just before I hear, "Fire!"

The staccato roar from the rifles rolls across the big lake and echoes back. Fourteen bullets to kill sixty-nine men and boys, the life-blood and future of an entire village snuffed out in less than a second.

Why God? Why? sounds over and over in my pounding skull.

35. BETRAYAL

Camisa Roja and the other *dorado* drop me on my back by Juan's fire and disappear. I don't remember anything for a while after that. When I open my eyes, the sun is past the top of its arc and Villa and Camisa Roja sit drinking coffee while they watch me. I sit up and gingerly touch the big goose egg on the back of my head. Memory of the morning flashes back. I feel sick and hang my head between my knees to keep from vomiting. Off in the distance, I hear the steady toll of a church bell and mournful, eerie sound of women keening.

No one else, not even Juan, is near Villa's wagon. Villa, taking a big slurp of coffee, sits back in his field desk chair, his legs crossed at the ankles.

"So, Hombrecito, your head is no longer filled with the darkness? Maybe you want no more to help Francisco Villa fight dictators, eh?"

He cocks his head to one side to hear my answer, his eyes staring through me. I say nothing and stare back at him, forcing myself not to blink, a fire of rage beginning to burn in my guts.

"A general must always do what is best for his men, Hombrecito. You want to leave, and I demand it. Go! Camisa Roja," he nods toward Roja leaning against the wagon, a Winchester cradled in the crook of his arm, "will show you where the trail begins over the mountains. *División del Norte* will rest here another couple of days. You will leave and I will see you no more. That is a good thing for both of us. *Adiós, amigo.*" He looks away and stares toward the mountains across the lake.

I roll up my blankets, stagger up off my knees, saddle, and load my horse. Juan, appearing from behind the chuck wagon, comes forward, and with a toothless grin, gives me a sack. "Food for your journey, *amigo. Vaya con Dios.*"

"*Muchas gracias, señor,* you are a great friend."

When I'm ready, Camisa Roja, saying nothing, his face betraying nothing of what he might be thinking, leaves the wagon and mounts his horse. He lays his rifle across the pommel of his saddle and nods toward the northern end of the lake. I lead the way toward the far end of the lake and follow the trail north that runs beside Rio Moctezuma.

Fog still drifts in my brain as the horses, in a slow walk, pass down the trail and around a bend in the river. Soon the big trees by the river and a rough ridge on our right shutter the view back to San Pedro de la Cueva. Camisa Roja rides up beside me, sticks the muzzle in my ribs behind my right arm and pulls the hammer back on his Winchester. I curse myself for being a fool and not realizing this was coming.

After all the warnings from Yellow Boy, Quent, even Camisa Roja, after all the warnings, I'm caught unawares.

Roja says, "Hand me your *pistola* and continue to ride a little in front of me, *señor*. If you try to run, I will kill you where you sit. *Comprende?*"

I nod and sigh as I pull the old Colt from its holster and hand it to him. "*Sí, comprendo.*"

We follow the trail into the wide river canyon. I glanced over my shoulder at the rifle pointed at the middle of my back. Roja holds it steady, his eyes locked on me. "So, Camisa Roja, *el jefe* decides I'm a traitor too, eh?"

"*Sí, señor*. The general says that as half Mexican you are a traitor to Mexico, and as half *gringo*, a traitor to him and *División del Norte* like all other *gringos*. Even worse, you struck the general, a cowardly sign of disrespect punished by firing squad. It is only because you and the general are *amigos* from long ago that you are not standing in front of a firing squad now and making the general's heart very sad to watch you die."

"So you do the general's dirty work?"

"I always obey orders, *señor*."

Memories, perhaps my last ones, fill my mind. "*Sí*, I remember you told me that a lifetime ago. Is that the same rifle you used to murder my woman during the Comacho raid?"

He sighs. "*Sí*. It is the same. It has killed many men and a few women. Whoever, the general says to shoot, I shoot."

We ride on up the canyon, saying nothing and watching the shadows lengthen as the sun falls toward the mountains on our left. The wheels of my mind furiously turn, trying to think of a way to escape. After a while I remember the lessons Yellow Boy taught me and know I have to be patient and wait for my chance, or I'm dead for certain. The memory of Rufus Pike speaks to me, *Cold and cakilatin', Henry, cold and cakilatin'.* I'm determined that somehow I'll survive and I keep talking trying to lure Camisa Roja off-guard.

"Why are you taking me so far up river before you do your duty?"

"*El General* does not want to hear the shot that kills you, and he wants to speak truthfully to Muchacho Amarillo when he comes looking for you that the last time he saw you was on this trail. He does not want to execute both his friends from the old days. He did not want you executed, but you gave him no choice. Now I have no choice, Doctor Grace. Ride on and be silent. You will not distract me."

The coals of rage burning in my gut grow brighter. If I survive, Villa's days are numbered and few, and I will take great pleasure in closing his eyes forever.

Putting the horses into a trot, we ride up the canyon four or five miles, following the river's many twists and turns. We come to a long narrow meadow lined with trees, the water in the river a mirror in long shallow pools soon to be dry.

"Doctor Grace, turn your horse across the grass and into the trees next to the river."

I hope to make a break for it when we approach the brush by the creek, but he's careful, watching my every move, and I can't risk it. We stop in the green grass a few yards from a sandy spit on the river. He nudges his horse up close to mine so the barrel of his Winchester is teasingly close enough for me to grab, but not quite.

"Get off your horse, *señor*. Take off the saddle and your equipment. Leave it here, and lead your horse to that big cottonwood."

Putting my hands on the saddle horn, I lean forward across the pommel to dismount. As my right foot clears the stirrup and I swing my leg across the back of my horse, I begin falling to its left side while still holding on to the saddle horn and keeping my leg on the saddle like I'd seen Apache warriors do at full gallop, the horse's body to hide them, as they shoot at enemies from the underside of their mount's neck.

When I first begin the fall, I give the loudest, most unnerving scream my lungs and fear can give me and rake my horse's back with the crossing spur. It startles him so badly he crow-hops into Roja's horse, already starting to rear, and knocks it off its feet and over on top of Roja before he can clear his stirrups and bail out. His rifle makes a thunk sound as it hits the hard sand and discharges.

It seems to take a lifetime for me to bail off my bucking horse, and I hit the ground with a jarring thump. I roll to my feet, expecting to be shot. Roja's horse, still on its side, is kicking and struggling to roll up on its stomach so it can get its feet on the ground and stand. Roja has dropped the rifle so he can use both hands, one to handle the reins and the other to hold on to the saddle to stay with and control the horse.

He sees me coming and lets go of the saddle to grab my pistol stuck in his belt as I fly in a long, body-extended leap to land on top of him. The impact of our bodies colliding knocks the screaming horse back over on its side, again pinning Roja's leg against the ground. I swing wildly trying to hit him anywhere. He throws up his left arm to fend me off while he tries again for my revolver stuck in his belt.

Pumped with adrenaline, fighting for my life, I have strength I've never known. In my fury, I roundhouse a fist against the side of Roja's head, and hit him on the left temple. Stunned, he suddenly goes limp, unconscious.

I jerk my revolver out of his belt, thumb the hammer back and fire just as the horse gives a mighty heave, struggling to stand with the weight of us sprawled on him. The barrel of the pistol is just inches from Roja's temple, but with the horse struggling I miss when I pull the trigger. I think, *Oh to Hell with it*, and club him against the side of his head. As his horse, trembling in fear, begins to stand, my feet touch the ground giving me the leverage I need. I grab him by the collar of his red shirt and jerk his body out of the saddle and throw it to the ground.

I step back and cock the old Colt once more, not sure what I'm going to do. Gasping for breath, I feel the flood of adrenaline begin to recede. Memories of Rafaela swoop into my mind, her sweetness and devotion, how his bullet burst through her shirt, the anger and rage I've felt for so long and wanted to vent. Anger and rage that Yellow Boy's calm, reasonable words muzzled. Now! Now I hold his death in my hands and he's going to die!

My hands shaking, breath coming in gasps, memories of him aiming at her, and her blood, her blood all over the front of her shirt and covering me as I hold her, I cock the Colt, point it at his head and fire. Sand and gravel next to his ear erupt in a tiny geyser. I fire again, and again, and again missing each time. I can't make my hands stop shaking long enough to put a bullet in his brain.

Steady. Nice and steady.

With both hands I point the pistol at the center of his chest, *I'll be damned if I miss this time, you son of a bitch.* I pull the hammer back and sight at the middle of his chest.

The front sight is steady as a rock on his heart. I pull the trigger. The hammer falls with a hard metallic snap.

I stare at the old pistol in disbelief. Pulling the hammer to half cock and opening the loading gate, I push five empty cartridges out of the cylinder. I do a quick mental count. I always keep one cylinder empty under the hammer, there was one shot while we were on the horse, and four misses at his head. Six.

Camisa Roja, you are the luckiest man I've ever known.

Shadows grow long, the sun behind brilliant waves of orange and purple clouds sending twilight. My mind steadies. I bend over, my hands on my knees, wanting to vomit. I've never been so close to crazed, cold-blooded murder. I don't know what to think, but the sense of relief I feel not killing him lifts a ton of weight off my shoulders.

He moans and starts to stir. I feel his pulse and look at the place where I smashed him with the pistol. He should be all right, maybe a bad headache and sore head for a while.

His horse is standing, head down, pulling at spare clumps of grass a few feet away. I bring the horse over to him, pull the coiled reata off his saddle, tie his hands and feet, heave him across the saddle, and tie him in place. He's nearly conscious when I write Villa a little note on paper from my prescription pad and pin it to the back of Roja's *dorado* jacket.

The note says:

Ustedes me traiciona, señores.
Muchacho Amarillo es mi padre.
Compensaré.

Which translates,

You betrayed me, señores.
Yellow Boy is my father.
I will repay

I lead Camisa Roja's horse back to the trail for San Pedro de La Cueva, tie the reins behind the saddle horn, slap him on the rump, and watch him trot off down the trail as I gather Roja's weapons and ammunition while twilight turns to darkness.

I load my horse and head up river. I figure I'll have about a day's lead by the time Villa sends *dorados* after me. With a little luck, I'll beat them to the border before I have to kill them all.

36. LONG RIDE HIDING

As the crow flies, San Pedro de la Cueva lies about 140 miles from Agua Prieta. The actual distance I ride between the two villages probably covers more like 180 miles. I stay high on the ridges or off in the *llano* brush, always watching for the *dorados* I know Villa will send for my head. I've never made a harder trip, and I survive by being in great physical shape and by knowing how to live in the deserts and mountains like an Apache, like Yellow Boy taught me.

After tying Camisa Roja across the back of his horse and sending him back to Villa, I ride on up the river trail, intending to put as much distance as I can between me and Villa's *dorados*. Black, thick night comes quick in the river valley, but twilight lingers high on the mountains. I can see my breath like steam in the still, cold air, and my fingers grow numb holding the reins as I watch a waxing crescent moon float above the eastern mountains casting inky, black shadows and long white reflections off the still, black pools left in the nearly dry river. There's no sound anywhere, even from night animals or the river, except for the occasional snort of my horse, the creak of saddle leather, and the crunch of its hooves on sand or the clink of river pebbles.

Solitude holds me like a lover, close and gentle, leaving my mind free to roam. Mostly, my is filled with what happened today. The shadows in my mind creep from feelings of being very lucky that I'm alive: to the memory of anger burning so hot and bright that I tried five times to shoot a man and missed; to outrage, separating me from Villa forever, for murdering an innocent priest and sixty-nine men and boys; to my promise of vengeance that will send Villa and Camisa Roja or me to the grandfathers. My fists clench against the reins, my fury making me want to snarl and roar like an enraged grizzly or jaguar. It's startling to feel such primal emotions and to hunger for the pleasure of ripping the heart out of a man I once called friend, one to whom I swore allegiance, one for whom I would have died. My horse flicks his ears back thinking I'm speaking to him, but I'm just mumbling. "You're a mean, crazy bastard, a mad dog that has to be taken down. You…you're as bad as Wilson…worse…you've betrayed everyone who went to war with you, including me and all the *peons* you promised to defend but murdered for your pride…damn you."

As thoughts about Villa fade, new ones as stinging and as intense bring Camisa Roja. I marvel at how his life intertwines with mine. I remember the first time I saw his red shirt and how his shot hit Rafaela in her back and burst through the front of her shirt. I remember how empty, how dead I felt when I learned the same bullet that killed Rafaela also killed the baby, our child, she carried inside her. Yet, somehow, Roja managed to keep the scales from tipping too far toward revenge by killing two of my worst enemies, Apache Kid and Juan, before Yellow Boy and I risked going after them a second time.

Today providence favored us, both of us still alive after trying to kill each other. Again I mumble, "Why didn't I put a bullet in him? Why didn't I just reload and kill him? Why did I send him back to Villa alive? Now I'm running for my life. Now I have to hide every step of the way back to Las Cruces." My mind turns over and over our history, trying to look at it from different angles, trying to put its facets in perspective, each event illuminating the other like a diamond spreading bright sunlight in different directions with a rainbow of colors. I see much, but understand little. Camisa Roja: red rider of the Apocalypse? Some kind of power from Ussen? Will I ever to be free of him?

When the arc of the moon approaches midnight, and its brilliant rim shines bright white, a great weariness falls over me. My horse needs rest and grain if it is to carry me to the top of the mountain ridges, and I need to rest to stay alert when the sun comes. I begin looking for a place to stop where we'll be safe.

In a grove of cottonwoods growing in the brush back from the riverbank, I dig a hole and light a small fire. The spot, surrounded by big boulders, shields us from the icy wind flowing down the river canyon. I hobble my horse in a stand of dry grass, rub him down, and give him some grain.

Huddled over my little fire's coals with my blanket over my shoulders and warming my hands, I try to think through what I need to do and how to do it. I know it's close to the time of the Ghost Dance, maybe early December. It'll snow soon and that means slow, dangerous, energy draining rides to get through mountain snow and down to the river valley village of Moctezuma. I don't know the country. It might not snow at all this far south except near the tops of the mountains, or the valleys might fill with snow and stay that way all winter. I decide I have to ride during daylight up on the ridges like Apaches, stay out of sight, keep an eye on the main trails for an ambush, and cover ground as fast as possible to have the best chance of beating bad weather and staying out of the reach of Villa's assassins.

I awake sweating several times, dreams of the jaguar, dreams of being led to a rock wall, being blind-folded… waiting… hearing bolts on rifles click into place… waiting… hearing a sword clearing a scabbard… waiting… hearing the words, "Ready… Aim…" give me little rest.

Up before dawn, I shiver by the fire, eat more of the victuals Juan put in my sack, and drink the remains of the coffee I made the night before to warm my insides. As birds start twittering in the gray light filling the canyon, I hide the remains of my fire, brush away my tracks, and leave the big trees on a deer trail following a long wide draw running to the top of the mountain ridgeline.

It's a hard climb to the ridgeline, so steep I must dismount and hold on to my horse's tail to make it, and even then nearly slide off the trail on loose shale near the top. On the ridgeline by mid-morning, the view fills me with wonder. Far below I can see Rio Moctezuma and north, never-ending ranges of mountains. Taking out my field glasses, I study the trail along the river and see no signs of any rider forward of or on my back trail.

After three days, the mountain ridges along the Rio Moctezuma smooth into a high plateau that defines the east side of the river valley. Except for working my way across two or three gorges with creeks flowing to the river, I make good time on an easy ride along the edge of the plateau.

Watching the river trail with my glasses, I see only old men or boys with donkeys. I rest a day and do nothing but wait and watch. Still, I see no *dorados*. I know Villa is not going to let me get away after nearly killing and escaping from Camisa Roja.

"Why," he'd say, "you tried to murder a hero of the *Revolución*."

He believes I'm a traitor to him and to Mexico. He knows I believe he has betrayed the *Revolución* and he has betrayed me by massacring the men at San Pedro de la Cueva, by murdering the priest, and by ordering me discreetly executed. He knows Yellow Boy and I will be back to kill him if I can return to New Mexico. I said as much in the note I pinned to Camisa Roja's shirt.

Rufus Pike's words, "Ye gotta be cold and cakilatin', Henry," settle in the front of my mind and stay there. I try to think like Villa and recall what he's done in the past. For men he thought were traitors, he waited until they thought they were safe and then assassinated them in front of the world. He relishes any trick, any dramatic embellishment in front of an audience to make justice that much sweeter.

I have an epiphany. Villa will wait to kill me on the north side of the border surrounded by *gringos* he thinks betrayed him. My murder will leave a message: *You can run, but you can't hide from Pancho Villa.* I smile at my certainty of what he plans and remember the line I wrote on the note I pinned to Camisa Roja, "Muchacho Amarillo *es mi padre*." Villa's life will end long before mine after Yellow Boy learns what happened. Still, I resolve to take nothing for granted.

I follow the Rio Moctezuma Valley past Moctezuma, then to Cumpas and on to Los Hovos, where the trail passes through rough mountains to the mining town of Nacozari de Garcia. I sell Quent's good, steady roan that's carried me a long way, and buy a train ticket to Agua Prieta and Douglas. From Douglas I catch the eastbound train to El Paso. It's late in the day when the train stops in Columbus, New Mexico, to take on water and coal for the roll to El Paso. I look out the south side window across from me and see soldiers going about their business at Camp Furlong. It feels mighty good to be back in the United States, even dusty, little Columbus.

Soldiers and businessmen board the train. Two or three more hours and soldiers will enjoy their liquor in the company of El Paso prostitutes and businessmen will sip expensive whiskey in hotel bars. One or two soldiers frown when they see me but say nothing. I know I must look and smell like a tramp. I had no time to clean up before catching the train in Nacozari or in Douglas. I don't care. I'm headed home.

Part 2

When the stars threw down their spears,
And watered heaven with their tears,
Did He smile His work to see?
Did He who made the lamb make thee?

—William Blake

...Today he can discover his errors of yesterday and tomorrow he can obtain a new light on what he thinks himself sure of today...

—From *The Oath of Maimonides*

37. RETURN TO MESCALERO

After disappearing for three months, my return to Las Cruces produces a lot of speculation and rumors in the barbershops and ladies' clubs. The few patients I had before I left now see other doctors. I have to start from scratch rebuilding my practice. But, first I rent a mustang gelding, and head over San Agustin Pass for Mescalero.

Falling snow drifts back and forth in a slow, bitter wind at Yellow Boy's tipi, still deep in a box canyon a few miles from Mescalero. Nearby the pine trees in the brush corral by the cliff offer a good windbreak for the horses. In the gloomy twilight I can make out Yellow Boy's old paint, a couple of mules, and, to my relief, Satanas, all staring at me, their ears erect. I lead my gelding into the corral. Satanas trots up, and after sniffing and establishing his authority with the mustang, pays it little attention as he puts his nose up close to my face. I breathe in his breath and he takes in mine. I give him a quick little rub down before he returns to nibbling hay tossed out on the snow inside the corral. I take a handful of the hay and rub down the mustang before turning him lose to nose the hay with the other animals.

Taking my saddle, bedroll, rifle, and bulging saddlebags, I walk to the tipi and stop just outside the door flap. I can hear happy end-of-the-day sounds, children playing, an iron pot lid clanging, and women laughing.

I smile and call out, "Yah-ta-hey!"

A man's raspy voice replies, "Ah-ho!" In a moment the door flap raises, and from around the edge, I see the round, smiling face of Moon-On-The-Water as she motions me inside. I step into the cozy firelight. The air is filled with the belly-gnawing smells of venison stew and fry bread, the cedar smell of burning piñon, and cigar smoke.

Cleaning his Henry rifle, Yellow Boy sits on the far side of the fire grinning as he motions me to come in and sit down beside him. Juanita and Moon-on-the-Water clap their hands that I've returned safe, and taking my things, wait until Yellow Boy speaks before they say anything.

Yellow Boy says, "Welcome, my son. It is more than two moons since I see you. You are well? Arango still lives?"

I pull off my gloves and hold up my hands up to the fire letting, them soak in its warmth.

"Yes, Uncle, I am well. Arango still lives."

He lays the oiled rifle, its barrel and brass action gleaming in the firelight, across his knees and, pulling the stub of his black cigar from his mouth, blows a long stream of smoke up toward the smoke hole.

"You ride a long time in the cold wind from the town of the crosses. Sit by the fire and warm yourself. Juanita and

Moon will fill our bellies soon from their stew pot. Speak, women. My son returns from a long raid in Mexico."

Speak they do, chattering about their glad hearts now that I'm back safe after a long ride, how cold the winter feels that year, and the good time they all have at Father Braun's Christmas service. They say they don't fully understand this thing the *padre* calls Christmas, a happy time celebrating birth with much color and the giving of presents, but they believe they can learn the ceremony.

Moon begins filling heavy clay bowls from the big pot of stew, passing a bowl and cedar wood spoon first to me, their guest, then to their husband, smaller bowls to Redondo and John, who sit back in the flickering fire shadows quietly watching and listening to the adults, and finally Moon fills bowls for herself and Juanita. Juanita passes me a basket filled with hot fry bread she has just finished making and pours us coffee from an old blue speckled pot nearly black from years at the fire. They tell me of a rare scandal where a young wife has run off with an old Chiricahua man who returned to Mescalero from Fort Sill just the year before, a survivor of the Geronimo wars and prisoner-of-war camps in Florida, Alabama, and Fort Sill. Yellow Boy listens and shakes his head

After cleaning our bowls and belching our appreciation for the good meal, we sit around the fire recalling old times, good and bad, while the women clean up their cooking area. Yellow Boy tells his sons a Coyote story, one of many the Apaches tell about the trickster. Coyote always makes mistakes after being warned what will happen.

In Yellow Boy's story, Coyote defecates on Walking Rock after he's been warned to leave the rock alone. After

Coyote insults Walking Rock, it rolls after him, chasing him across deserts, over mountains, in caves and out, up and down rivers, through forests and down valleys until Coyote agrees to wash the feces off. Redondo the older son, laughs, which also makes, John, too young to really understand the story, laugh, and I laugh, too, even though I've heard it many times before.

The women put the boys under their blankets, and then bid us warm sleep, Juanita giving Yellow Boy a covert smile, and Moon giggling before sliding under their blankets, leaving Yellow Boy and me to speak in private.

We light our tobacco, he a new cigar and me a pipe. We smoke a while, relaxing in the slow, flickering light until we hear a gentle snore or two from the direction of the wives' blankets. Yellow Boy says, "Speak of your time with Arango."

I tell him about the march to Naco, the train ride west to Nogales, and then south to Hermosillo, where nearly all that's left of *División del Norte* die in terrible, blood-soaked charges against machine-gun nests and men in trenches behind coils of barbed wire, the destruction ten times worse than anything I witnessed in Agua Prieta. I speak of Villa growing crazier by the day, claiming the *gringos* have caused all his defeats. Yellow Boy listens carefully and watches my face, nodding occasionally, and grunting, "Uhmmph... ump."

I tell him what happened at San Pedro de la Cueva. He crosses his arms and slowly shakes his head as I describe how Villa executed the village's men and boys, murdered the priest who begged for their lives, and how I tried to stop the massacre and was knocked unconscious. I describe what happened between me and Camisa Roja and how I shot at him four times from not more than seven or eight feet and missed every shot, and how on the fifth try steadied my hands, pointed the weapon directly at his heart, and pulled the trigger, the hammer falling on an empty chamber. I told him about tying Camisa Roja across his saddle and the note I pinned on his shirt when I sent him back to Villa.

Yellow Boy, frowning, holds up a hand, palm out, to stop me. "Wait, Hombrecito. You shot and missed four times and after your hands were steady you pulled the trigger again but the cylinder was empty?"

"Yes, Uncle, that's the way it was."

He shakes his head, his jaw teeth clamped tight on the cigar. "Why didn't you reload and finish him?"

I've asked myself that question a thousand times on the way back home and never found a good answer. "I don't know, Uncle. I wanted him dead for killing my wife and child. He had just tried to kill me. I owed him his death. I know by letting him live he will be one of those Villa sends after me. Yet, somehow, I feel I did the right thing. I tried to kill him standing so close that it was impossible to miss, but I missed. I missed four times. I guess after the last try with an empty cylinder, I decided it just wasn't his time to die. Ussen was protecting him."

Yellow Boy blows his smoke toward the flap hole, stares at the fire a few moments and nods.

"A man must listen to the spirits when they speak to him. Perhaps you will die when Camisa Roja returns, perhaps not. You have left it for Ussen to decide, but the tracks you put on the paper speak true, Hombrecito. As my son, we will repay Arango for this betrayal. When do we leave?"

I shake my head. "I believe Arango will come after me north of the border, maybe in Las Cruces. He sent no one to try and catch me after I sent Camisa Roja back. He always executes anyone he thinks is a traitor. He will send *dorados* north to get me. Of this I have no doubt. Isn't it better to let him come after me where I know the ground, and end it where I have an advantage than to try and find him in Mexico?"

Yellow Boy stares at me for a few moments before his gaze returns to the black and red coals forming under the lowering orange flames. "Arango knows where you are, Hombrecito. Camisa Roja knows where you work. It is very dangerous to be the bait in a trap. A wrong move and you die. Ambush is best for vengeance. Mexico, we ought to go there. We kill Arango and Roja quick and be done with them before he sends assassins after you."

"You speak wise words, Uncle, but I believe I'm safe for a while. I'll speak with Quentin Peach about news from Mexico and learn what he thinks. Now, Villa licks his wounds in Chihuahua and needs every *dorado* to rebuild his army before he can move north to fight Carranza and punish the Americans for their betrayals. I must be on my guard when he comes north. Let us think on these things some more. Perhaps we will make a good plan for an ambush before he tries to kill me."

Yellow Boy tosses his cigar on the coals where it sizzles and flares before turning to gray ash. He sticks out his lower lip and shakes his head. "This is a very dangerous thing you do, Hombrecito. I do not like it, but I always stand with you. Juanita's body calls mine. I go to her blankets. We will speak more of this."

"Yes, Uncle, we will speak much more of this."

38. VILLA RIDES NORTH

The abrupt, growling ring of the new telephone, an alarm clock going off at odd times of day, consistently surprises me. I take the earpiece off the hook and speak into the horn.

"Doctor Grace here."

A distant, female voice that sounds like she's speaking while holding her nose says, "One moment, please, I'll connect you with Mr. Peach."

I hear the click and buzz of relays and switches down the wire, and then above the low static rumble, the tinny, but clear, unmistakable southern-smooth accent of Quentin Peach, as usual in a rush and avoiding any polite chitchat.

"Henry? Quent. Say, do you remember the talk we had back in January about your adventures with our friend and escape from the man in the red shirt?"

"You know I do. What's going on?"

"I just received a copy of a telegram Zack Cobb, the customs collector here in El Paso, sent the State Department about two o'clock. I can't say how I got it or the source of his information, but I'd bet money it's accurate. Wanna hear it?"

"Fire away."

Quent reads.

"Villa left Pacheco Point, near Madera, on Wednesday, March 1 with 300 men headed toward Columbus, New Mexico. He is reported west of Casas Grandes today. There is reason to believe that he intends to cross to the United States and hopes to proceed to Washington. Please consider this possibility and the necessity of instructions to us on the border.

"Henry, this is what you've been waiting for. If he gets up here close to the border, he can send a few *dorados* after you in addition to whatever else he's planning."

"Yeah… you're right." I study a calendar on my desk. "Let's see. Today is Friday, March third. Depending on how many men he has and where he started, he could be on the border in a week to ten days, so he might be in Columbus by the tenth. Hmmm. Thanks, Quent! If you hear anything else about this, will you let me know?"

"Absolutely. What are you thinking?"

"I'm thinking I'll wire Yellow Boy and get him down here by Monday afternoon and then decide what to do. My guess is we'll head for Columbus and then maybe south to meet our friend head-on. You want to come?"

"Yeah, but I need to talk to Persia and Hughs Slater here at the *Herald* before I make any commitments. Tell you what, I'll call Monday evening and we can go from there."

"Sounds like a plan. I'll be here. Talk to you then. Adiós."

"So long."

I hang up the earpiece, sit down at my desk, and scribble a telegram to the Indian agent in Mescalero asking that he release Yellow Boy immediately to help me again with another project in Mexico. Finishing, I'm out the door and down the street to the telegraph office, anxious for action, anxious to be rid of the ominous worry hanging like a dark cloud in the back of my mind that someone will try to assassinate me one bright morning right here in the middle of a Las Cruces street.

Yellow Boy, in his ancient, threadbare blue cavalry jacket, sitting on the floor with his back to the wall, the butt of his rifle stock jammed between his high, fringed boot-moccasins, its barrel resting against his shoulder, reminds me of the first time I saw him in daylight twenty years earlier, two days after he had saved my life.

The telephone rings, and, as usual, I grimace at the unexpected bell. Yellow Boy doesn't look too comfortable with its raucous sound either. As we expect, it's Quent.

"Henry? Quent. I was with reporters meeting with Commanding General Gavira in Juarez this morning, and I'm just back from confirming what he told us. He claimed Villa is still headed for the border. Gavira asked General Pershing to be on the lookout for him. Cobb says Villa will be here tonight or early tomorrow and told his contact in Columbus to let him know as soon as Villa shows up. What are you going to do? Persia says for me to do my job, just not to get shot. Hughs thinks there's a chance for a good story and says to do what's best. I want to go with you. It might be my last chance to see Villa alive."

"Thanks, Quent, you're a great help. Villa can move his cavalry fast, but he can't move as fast as Cobb says. It doesn't make any difference to us anyway. We're planning to find him before he finds us. We'll be in El Paso sometime tomorrow, depending on what Yellow Boy does, and we'll work out the travel details of our little hunt after we get there. I'll call when we get in. Give my best to Persia."

"I'll do it. See you tomorrow."

I turn to Yellow Boy who's lighting a cigar.

"Quent's source believes Villa could be in Columbus tonight or tomorrow. He's cautious and can't move as fast as they believe. If we're going after him from Columbus, then I figure we'll have to be there no later than three days from now. The only way we can get there in two days without wearing out our horses is to ride the iron wagon and take them with us. I know you don't want to ride the iron wagon, but can you change your mind in this case?"

He puffs his cigar, thinks awhile, and shakes his head. "No iron wagon. I leave tonight. Easy two-night ride. Meet you when train stops in Columbus on third day. You go to El Paso *mañana*, find Peach, make sure he ready for hard ride in Mexico."

"I don't doubt you're right. Take Satanas and my gear with you. If my memory serves me right, the train gets to Columbus two or three hours after sunrise. We'll meet you at the station. I'll get Peach to ask his sources where they think Villa is then, and that's where we'll head. What do you think?"

He nods, "Uhmm. *Bueno.*"

After we eat, I load Satanas with my saddle and gear and we walk over to the train station. A schedule shows the train from El Paso arrives in Columbus at eight o'clock every morning. Yellow Boy swings into his saddle, waves the Henry in salute, and says, "Columbus, three days. We hunt *loco hombre.*"

I salute him back.

"Columbus, three days."

Leading Satanas, he canters the horses out of town heading for the place where he likes to cross the Rio Grande. While at the station, I go ahead and buy a ticket for the eleven o'clock train to El Paso the next morning.

39. TRAIN TO COLUMBUS

The train rolls out of El Paso in the cold, gray light of a windy dawn, Thursday, 9 March 1916. I've stayed in El Paso two days longer than I planned. I haven't slept much worried Villa might come across the border before I reach Columbus. If, as Zack Cobb suspects, Villa comes across the border for political asylum, I can't touch him once he's in protective custody. I know I shouldn't worry. Hell will freeze over before Villa swallows enough pride to ask the *gringos* for help.

Two major unrelated stories delay Quent coming with me, but I decide to risk the wait until the day we're to meet Yellow Boy in Columbus.

The morning I arrive in El Paso, the El Paso police arrest and jail over forty men, twenty of them Mexicans, involved in a brawl with soldiers over Mexican raids along the border. They go through the jail's standard, weekly delousing procedure of a vinegar and coal oil bath and rinsing their clothes in gasoline. A fool named H.M. Cross, who doesn't hear the warning not to smoke or not to strike a match with their clothes still damp with gasoline in the fume-saturated air, tries to light a cigarette. The instantaneous roar of flames sweeping through the locked cells burns nearly all the prisoners to death. Quent's fast, accurate investigative work shows the disaster an accident and almost single-handedly prevents major riots from breaking out all over El Paso.

Villa's move north triggers an avalanche of stories requiring additional long, speculative essays to fill the front pages of the papers in Arizona, New Mexico, Texas, and Mexico. Quent's previous essays and stories on Villa also cause his work to be in demand for the front pages of the *Chicago Tribune, New York Herald, New York Times, Washington Post*, and other big-time papers covering Villa's move toward the border. Calls from major papers for Villa stories and analysis demands Quent write more every day.

I pace the floor in his office and watch amazed at how fast he turns out copy until Hughs Slater, the *Herald's* owner, editor, and publisher tells him he has enough material for a week's worth of papers and to go on with me to Columbus. With as much national interest as Villa now generates, an interview with him might easily establish Quent as a full-time, national columnist which will sell a lot of papers for the *Herald* and provide Quent with a fat income.

* * *

As the train rumbles west across the slowly brightening and churning ocean of windswept, creosotes and mesquites, Quent pulls his hat down over his eyes, slumps in his seat next to a window, and, in less than five minutes, begins snoring.

I'm wide-awake, thinking about what to do when I find Villa or have him in my sights. Conflicting desires and emotions fight in my mind like two tomcats in a grain sack. Do I kill him to avenge his betrayal of my trust and friendship? Does killing him violate my oath as a doctor? My Apache honor says Villa and Roja must die. Does Ussen want him to live? What about Camisa Roja? Am I to be satisfied with the beating I gave him? Will he come after me? The only thing I know for certain is that I won't live my life in fear. One way or another, Villa, Camisa Roja and I will come to terms… through blood, or, perhaps... However it ends, it ends during these days, not tomorrow's.

A few minutes before we're due to arrive in Columbus I notice a long, black smoke plume drifting east past the rushing train.

Quent, awake and staring out the window notices it too.

"I'll bet there's been a fire in Columbus."

"Yeah, it sure looks like it."

The fuzzy black streak, spreading out across the bright blue sky and against the golden glare of the morning sun, leave me with a sense of foreboding.

The train slows to a crawl when we're over a mile from the station.

Quent pushes out of his seat.

"Something's going on. A train doesn't slow down this far out from the station unless the engineer thinks he might have to make a quick stop. Come on. Let's take a look outside."

By this time everyone on the train stares at the black cloud and several armed men check the loads in their pistols. Quent and I step outside in the cold, biting wind. I climb up the ladder leading to the top of the passenger car to see how the tracks look in front of us.

The smoke cloud looks like it's rising from several different fires near the train station in Columbus. Off to the south, maybe in Mexico, a high rising dust cloud suggests a herd of running horses or cattle.

Quent jerks on my pants leg and yells into the wind, "Let me look."

I climb down and motion him up. In few seconds I hear him yell into the wind, "Damn!"

He climbs back down, and, shivering, we go back inside.

Men gather around us. One says, "Has Villa burned Columbus?"

Quent answers, "No. I saw only four or five columns of smoke. Most of the houses and stores look like they're still standing. I didn't see any signs of fighting. We did see a big dust cloud to the south that might be made by running horses. Just stay calm. We'll be all right."

The men look at each other and back at us, nod, and, with a hand on their guns, each sits down to wait.

Within two hundred yards of Columbus Station the train creeps along slower than a walking man. The conductor jerks open the door at the back of the car. "Take it easy, folks. We're nearly to the station and it looks like the raid, if that's what it was, is over. Anybody in the car a doctor?"

I grab my bags and walk back to the conductor, a big, beefy man whose coat and vest have a dark, wet stain that smears into red blood on his white shirt. He motions me out the back of the car.

"Are you hurt?"

He shakes his head, and without saying a word leads me back the to the caboose with Quent right behind us.

The conductor opens the door. On a bed close to a coal stove, a man babbles incoherently and begs for water, the crotch of his pants and lower waist covered in blood.

The conductor says, "That's James Milton. He was down by the tracks like that when I saw him. He's an engineer and pump man for the El Paso and Southwestern Railroad, and he lives here with his wife. I'm afraid to give him any water in case he's gut-shot. Judging from all that blood around his crotch he may be worse'n gut-shot. Might'a got his balls blowed off."

Kneeling by the bed, I begin examining Milton, looking for bullet holes and other injuries.

"How'd he get on the train?"

"I saw him as we was creepin' in, knew who he was, and jumped off and got him. He looks in mighty bad shape, Doc. He gonna live?"

"I don't know. Looks like he's been shot twice, once down here in his left leg and there's a wound that passed through his crotch and into his right leg. Help me get his pants off."

The conductor and Quent help me ease Milton's pants off. I use my scissors to cut his underwear away from the wound. The conductor's ruddy complexion turns milk white when he sees it, and Quent turns away with a deep sigh. It's a nightmare wound. A bullet hit Milton's penis and scrotum and remains in the big thigh muscles of his right leg. There's a lot of blood but it appears both bullets missed the femoral arteries. The wound in his left leg shows no exit hole, the bullet still in the wound, and with the holes in his pants and underwear so clean, there have to be pieces of his pants and underwear packed in the wound with the bullet. Left there, he's certain to get gangrene from the cloth, regardless of the bullet's location and whether it can be found.

I give Milton water and a shot of morphine, wash the wounds with carbolic acid, and pad and bandage them. The train stops as I finish.

"Get him down to the Army surgeon at Camp Furlong where he can get at the bullet and be certain the wounds are clean, and stitch up the wound in his privates. The Army will be carrying casualties to El Paso and they can take him with them. There are great wound surgeons at Fort Bliss, so he'll get much better care than we can give him here."

Regaining his composure, the conductor scratches his chin as he puts it all together.

"Thanks, Doc. I'll find a stretcher and some fellows to help me get him over to Furlong. He don't live but a couple of blocks from here. The wounded in town will need you and it's best you go. If you see Milton's wife, let her know where he's at, will yuh?"

Quent and I walk up the tracks from the caboose. Columbus looks like an image straight from Hell, dead horses and bodies scattered in the streets, wounded Villistas crumpled in the sand, no one bothering to help them, most dead, but a few still alive, some twitching in death throes, others holding their hands over terrible wounds, groaning in agony, some lie with crucifixes on their chests, preparing to meet God. Women, clenching their teeth and shaking their heads, walk by staring at their attackers with hatred. I wonder if any of the men I rode with, maybe even patched up six months ago, lie among those in the street, but see no one I recognize.

A half-burned automobile smolders in the middle of a street, wisps of smoke still drifting from its carcass covered with bullet holes, blackened blood smeared on the driver's seat, the driver dead, burned almost beyond recognition. Smoke rises from the ruins of the Commercial Hotel and several of the buildings nearby.

Kids already replay the raid in the streets, sticking their fingers in bullet holes scattered everywhere, shooting at each other with sticks and finger pistols while loudly yelling, "Bang, bang, I got you, you damned dirty Mexican." Men and older boys collect guns and swords dropped by fleeing Villistas or are still in the hands of the dead or wounded. Soldiers throw buckets of water on still smoldering fires or carry stretchers with the wounded toward the Hoover Hotel, its adobe construction making it nearly fire and bulletproof.

I see several figures, probably Army officers, on the top of the little hill across the tracks from the station. Using binoculars, they look first toward the southeast and slowly swing west, surveying the land toward the border. Several troopers behind them kneel on one knee and lean against their Springfield rifles. They appear to be awaiting orders from officers pacing back and forth.

I turn to Quent who is looking in all directions and busy making notes in his unreadable shorthand script. "I'll check in the Hoover to see where I'm most needed. I don't see any sign of Yellow Boy. He's probably staying out in the mesquite until things settle down. Go get your stories. I'll see you later."

Quent, still looking and writing, nods. "Good idea. I'll see what I can learn and meet you at the Hoover in a little while."

40. TWO WOMEN

A corporal and private carry a stretcher bearing a woman into the cool gloom of the Hoover Hotel. Holding on as if she's dangling over a fall into eternity, she clings to the hand of a young, disheveled woman. The soldiers gently set the stretcher down on the blood-red lobby tiles, and the corporal, sweat streaking his dust-covered face, sends the private, with the barest hint of a blond mustache, to fetch a hospital corpsman from Camp Furlong.

Seeing me come forward with my doctor's bag, the corporal says, "You a doctor? This here lady's been shot and needs one bad."

I kneel beside her and take her free hand. Even with her eyes squeezed shut, her teeth clenched, and her long dark hair matted with dust and tangled on top of her head, her beauty still shows.

"Ma'am, I'm Doctor Henry Grace. I'll do everything I can for you and this other lady. Where are you wounded?"

She moans, licks her lips, and croaks, "Is there any water?"

The corporal hands me his canteen and I hold her head up to help her drink. She takes a couple of long swallows before she coughs and chokes, pushing it away.

I offer the canteen to the young woman holding her hand. She smells of horse and human sweat and desert dirt. Red from sun and wind and framed by her dust-filled, banshee-like hair making her look like some wild jungle woman, her face is somewhere under dirt smudges and grease smears. Lips, cracked and chapped, curve in a smile of appreciation as she takes the canteen. Closing her gray eyes, she tilts her head back, and takes long, gulping swallows before handing the canteen back to the soldier.

From the doorway behind the registration desk across the lobby, a man, his big belly pushing out between red suspenders, and right behind him a tall, gray-haired woman with big dark eyes behind wire-framed glasses, cross the lobby to the stretcher. He sticks out his right hand.

"I'm Will Hoover and this is my mother, Sara. We own the hotel. Who's that on the stretcher there? My God! It's Susan Moore!" He nods toward my black bag. "You a doctor?"

Before I can answer, he motions toward the corporal.

"Come on let's carry her down the hall to a room so the doctor can examine her in private."

Susan doesn't let go of Jungle Woman's hand as Will Hoover, huffing and puffing like some great steam engine, and the soldier carry her down the dark hall. Sara leads the way and opens the door to a guest room. After some twisting and turning with the soldier backing into the room across the hall, they manage to get her stretcher through the door.

Jungle Woman, still holding her hand, says, "She's been shot in the right hip and leg. Ease her off the stretcher on the right side of the bed so she can lie on her left side. She'll hold on to me and I can help give her some support when we ease her off the stretcher."

I turn to Sara, "Ma'am, I'm going to need boiled water and clean towels. Can you get those for me?"

For a woman her age, she's very agile and two-steps around us to zoom through the open door, calling over her shoulder, "I'll be right back."

We manage to get Susan on to the bed without causing her much more pain.

The corporal rolls up the stretcher, leans it in a corner, and asks in a low voice, "Is there anything else I can do before I drive the ambulance over to the camp hospital?"

I shake my head as I wave him and Will Hoover out the door. Susan moans from deep in her chest, creases in her face reflecting a throb of pain. I find a morphine vial in my bag and give her an injection. It isn't long before she relaxes and passes out, finally letting go of Jungle Woman's hand, who, massaging her temples as though trying to push something out of her head, slumps down in a rocking chair, tilts her head back, drops her arms over the sides and closing her eyes, sighs.

Pulling up Susan's long dress and petticoats, I see brown bloodstains streaked down her fancy silk pantaloons and where she's ripped off enough underskirt to make a bandage around a bullet wound grazing the muscle a few inches above her knee. Well up on her hip, another round black circle oozing dark, coagulating blood shows where she's been hit a second time.

She's very lucky. There isn't any extraordinary swelling and discoloration, indicating the bullet missed her thighbone. Unfortunately, I can't find a companion exit wound, which means she has to go to a hospital where the bullet can be removed without killing her.

Sara Hoover knocks on the door and rushes in with white towels and a shiny, zinc-plated, five-gallon bucket full of steaming water. Without strain, she lowers the thirty-pound bucket to the floor. Seeing Susan's bloodstained pantaloons, she shakes her head.

"She gonna live?"

"I believe so if I can get these wounds clean. The one on her lower leg just grazed her. The one up high in her hip didn't pass through. I'll have to get her to a hospital in El Paso to get it out. The best I can do now is clean the wounds and stop the bleeding."

"Is there anything else you need?"

I shake my head, as I pull a bottle of carbolic acid out of my bag and take a towel to wash my hands in the nightstand bowl.

Sara turns to the young woman flopped in the chair.

"I don't believe I know you, ma'am. You're not from around here, are you? Is there anything I can do for you?"

The woman says in a soft southern accent, "I'm Maud Wright. My husband and I have a ranch about a hundred miles south. I've been a Villista prisoner for nine days. They murdered my husband and our friend helpin' us, and they took our two-year old son, Johnnie, and gave him to the hired Mexican family livin' with us."

Sara puts her arm around Maud's shoulders. "Dear God in heaven, I'm so sorry."

Maud sounds on the verge of tears, but there are none. She rubs her forehead between her thumb and fingers, further smearing the grease smudges and dust on her brow.

"I can only pray that by the grace of God they've been able to keep Johnnie safe and fed. I've only had parched corn to eat for the past few days, been rubbed raw riding all over northern Chihuahua on a pack mule, and my feet are torn up and swollen from walkin' through goat head stickers and cactus after Villa let me go. I've barely had enough water to drink, much less bathe, and I'm stinkin' nasty. Anything, Mrs. Hoover, just anything you can help me with, I'd be grateful."

Tears run down Sara's face as she hugs her.

"Of course we'll do anything we can for you. I'm so sorry to see and hear how badly you've been abused. You —"

There is a firm knock on the door. Sara goes to crack it open, and looks around the edge. A skinny young private, hat in hand, salutes her.

"Begging your pardon ma'am, but one of the ambulance drivers told me Mrs. Moore and the lady with her was here. Captain Smyser, who found them this morning, told me to let them know Mrs. Slocum, the colonel's wife, wants them ladies at her house. Says to tell them she has all the conveniences a lady needs, including a tub and plenty of hot water."

Sara looks over her shoulder at me, her eyebrows raised.

Looking at Maud, I nod.

"Mrs. Wright, you go ahead with the soldier to Mrs. Slocum's house and tell her I'll make arrangements to get Mrs. Moore to a hospital in El Paso as soon as possible, and then I'll come check on you."

Maud clasps her hands together and bows her head. I hear her murmur, "Thank you, dear God." She looks up at me, tears brimming at the edges of her eyes. "Doctor Grace, will you help me get my son back?"

"Yes, ma'am, I sure will. Get on up to Mrs. Slocum's and have a bath. You'll feel better. Don't worry, we'll all help get Johnnie back and he'll be fit as a fiddle. You're safe now, that's the most important thing for both of you. Go on, I'll be along in a little while to check on you."

Sara looks around the edge of the door again and says to the soldier, "If you'll wait in the lobby, I'll be right down with Mrs. Wright and you can escort her to Mrs. Slocum's. I'm sure you know the colonel only lives a couple of blocks up the street."

The soldier nods. "Yes, ma'am. I'll be waiting."

Maud follows Sara out the door and looks back at me to mouth, "Thank you."

I finish all I can do for Susan Moore and ask Will Hoover to have someone keep an eye on her, help her if she needs anything, and to tell her I'll be back as soon as I can make arrangements to get her to a hospital in El Paso. Hoover promises he'll take good care of her.

Outside, the sun blinds me. As my eyes adjust to the hard, brittle light, I see organized turmoil. Soldiers up the street are using teams of mules to drag smoldering and blackened embers from the Commercial Hotel and four or five burned stores into a grid of woodpiles on the southwest edge of town. The Army ambulance hauls bodies of Villistas over to the piles of burned wood. A few hundred yards north of the woodpiles, dust fills the air as Army gravediggers work preparing places for the caskets of fallen soldiers not being sent back home because the Army is their home.

The bank behind the hotel serves as a morgue. A soldier stands guard at the door to keep curious onlookers out, and to give the Army hospital corpsman time to ensure the bodies of the ten civilians and seven soldiers are properly identified for someone to claim or to fill a casket for one of the graves being dug.

The roads north to Deming and west to Douglas produce steady dust clouds as automobiles and wagons roll into Columbus filled with curiosity seekers and those anxious to help friends and neighbors. A photographer arrives after driving from El Paso in record time. He takes pictures of everything and anyone, including the captured Villistas and bodies in the street. Columbus is fast becoming the national center of attention.

I walk down to the Army hospital at Camp Furlong and find the officer in charge, a young lieutenant with red hair and freckles scattered across his nose and cheeks. We shake hands and I say, "Sir, my name is Doctor Henry Grace from Las Cruces, New Mexico. I have a patient that needs to get to an El Paso hospital in short order. Any idea when a train carrying wounded to El Paso might be leaving?"

He shrugs. "I hope late this afternoon, Doctor Grace. There are so many things happening at the same time right now that any and all schedules are out the window. My guess is I'll be lucky if I can get my men on a train before tomorrow morning. Can your patient ride sitting in a seat?"

"No, she's been shot twice. Once in her right leg, once

in the right hip and the bullet is still in place. She'll have to stretch out on her left side."

Shaking his head, he says, "I don't know what to tell you, Doctor Grace. If you can go with her, I'm sure soldiers will give you all the room you need, even if they have to ride all the way standing up. Why don't you plan on catching the 4:00 a.m. that comes through from Hachita? There shouldn't be too many passengers on that one."

"Good idea. Thanks." I give him a little open-handed salute, which he returns with a grin and a snappy Army hand chop.

Looking at my watch as I walk back to town and estimating Susan Moore will be sleeping for another couple of hours, I decide to check on Maud Wright at the Slocums. After that I have to eat. My stomach growls when my nose passes busy restaurants.

Passing the Hoover Hotel, I see a small crowd gathered in front of the Slocum house and wonder what's going on as I double my pace to get there.

A tall, gangly major, a captain with a Rock of Gibraltar jaw, three lieutenants looking barely old enough to shave, and six or seven men in business suits shuffle around in front of the Slocums' small yard outlined with rocks. Flowerbeds with several different varieties of cactus decorate the sand inside the outline. The captain and the major speak to a grizzled black man who looks malnourished and gaunt but laughs and grins at every joke and appears contrite and humble when answering their questions.

Off to one side, my reporter friend, Quentin Peach, speaks with a couple of the men in business suits. The corpulent one, jowls hanging over his white, starched collar, wears an expensive pinstriped suit and small-brim fedora. He constantly mops away sweat running in rivulets down the sides of his face. The other man, tall and beefy, wears a brown herringbone suit and vest. I see a shoulder holster carrying a large caliber revolver under his coat and he studies Quent's face with the unblinking focus of a cat watching a mouse. Quent waves me over.

"Henry, you're just in time."

He motions my attention to the sweating fat man.

"Doctor Grace, this is Mr. George Carothers. He's a special State Department agent assigned to keep an eye on our friend Villa, and this gentleman is Mr. E. B. Stone, Bureau of Investigation."

We shake hands as Carothers and Stone look me over and say how pleased they are to meet me.

"These gentlemen came running as soon as they heard Villa hit Columbus. After all the raids along the border by the Carrancistas, they want to be sure Villa was the leader and determine how big an Army he has. I told them we were headed down here on the train from El Paso early this morning after hearing Villa was close to the border. I wanted to get an interview and you wanted to see a friend you'd known ten years ago." I'm relieved Quent hasn't said anything about my *medico* work for Villa last year. Given last night's raid, I'd be hard pressed to explain my latest association with Pancho Villa.

Stone tilts his head to one side and crosses his arms as he studies me with a look intended to be intimidating. I have to smile; he needs to work on his look. Looking at me over half-frame glasses floating at the end of his big bulbous nose, Carothers squints in the bright sunlight and says, "So you knew Pancho Villa ten years ago, Doctor Grace?"

Rufus Pike taught me the best defense was a good offense. I don't waste anytime beating around the bush.

"That's right. I knew him back in his bandit days when I lived in Chihuahua."

Stone shrugs. "Okay...so what brings you to Colonel Slocum's house?"

"I came by to check on a lady named Maud Wright. Over at the Hoover Hotel she told me Villa kidnapped her nine days ago but turned her loose after the raid. She said Villa executed her husband and a family friend and gave her two-year old son to a Mexican family. Mrs. Wright's desperate to get her baby back. I promised I'd do all I can to help her. Maybe the State Department...?"

Carothers nods, his jowls flopping.

"Yes, yes, of course we will. We just need to verify her story first."

He thumbs towards the black man and the officers peppering him with rapid-fire questions.

"See that Negro cowboy over there? His name is Bunk Spencer. He was kidnapped, too, but managed to get away about the same time Villa released Mrs. Wright. A few ladies will step out on the Slocum's front porch here in a minute. If he can pick her out, it'll tell us they're both telling the truth and we can rely on their information."

He pauses, frowns a little, and says as if to justify the lineup, "And you can be damned sure the State Department will squeeze the Carranza government hard to get the child back. In fact, I'll wire them as soon as Bunk identifies her."

The front door creaks open for five young women who come out to stand side-by-side across the front porch. They are all dressed about the same and are about the same height.

I'm amazed at how much better Maud looks. A bath and fresh clothes have done wonders.

Buck Spencer doesn't hesitate. He turns to the major and says, "Yas, suh. No doubt 'bout it. Dat lady, second from de right, she's de one, she Miss Maud. Howdy, Miss Maud." Maud smiles and nods at him.

Stone turns to Carothers and says, "Looks like we have a winner."

41. MAUD WRIGHT'S ODYSSEY

Carothers and Stone peel off their coats as they prepare to interview Maud. They sit on one side of the Slocum's big mahogany dinner table, Maud and I sit on the other side, and Quentin Peach sits at one end like a judge in conference with competing attorneys. Carothers, who knows Quent and respects his work, has asked him to sit in on the questioning as a witness and to keep an independent set of notes. At her request, I sit with Maud to give her moral support.

After arranging his portfolio just so, uncapping and laying a black lacquer ink pen in the crease, and clearing his throat, Carothers says, "Now, Mrs. Wright, we need you to tell us your story with as much detail as you can. Any information you and Bunk Spencer can give us might very well affect how President Wilson decides to respond to this bloody, outrageous attack on the United States. Mr. Stone and I serve different masters in the government. If you don't mind, in the next day or two, we might need to separately ask you additional questions to satisfy our superiors.

"I want you to understand that we're here to help you in any way we can. I've already had the State Department contact the Carranza government about the return of your little boy and we expect a quick reply. We won't rest until your child is back in your arms. Fair enough?"

Maud slowly nods, accepting, but not reassured by Carothers' lofty rhetoric.

"Now then, ma'am, what can you tell us?"

The sunlight filtering through sheer curtains casts the room in warm yellow light and through the closed door comes the soft background murmur of the other women staying at the Slocum house. Maud stares at Carothers's eyes as he speaks and looks at her clasped hands resting on the table. She licks her lips, puffs her cheeks, and says, "Where do you want me to begin?"

Carothers smiles.

"Begin at the beginning, Mrs. Wright, always at the beginning."

She thinks a moment and nods.

"Yes, of course. My husband Ed and I own a small ranch west of Pearson, about a hundred miles south. We bought it in 1910, had to leave for a couple of years because of the Revolution, came back for a while in 1914, and then had to leave again. While we waited for the Mexican government to stabilize, we spent nearly every cent we had to build up our herds of horses and cattle. Early this year, the Carranza government told us the war with Villa had ended, and that it was safe for us to return. We weren't back more than a couple of weeks when Ed and our young friend, Frank Hayden, who was helpin' us get started again and also earnin' wages at a nearby sawmill, took a couple of pack mules over to Pearson to pick up supplies."

She stares at the gauzy curtains behind Stone and Carothers as if watching moving pictures.

"It was startin' to get dark when I heard horses and looked out the kitchen window, expectin' to see Ed and Frank. Instead I saw some kind of Mexican Army patrol. The dark, dusty man who came to my door introduced himself as Colonel Nicolás Fernández and said he needed to buy food. I told him I didn't have much, just enough for our ranch people, but I'd give him what I could.

"He pushed his way into the kitchen and looked around, saw Johnnie, and said he commanded a Carrancista patrol looking for the bandit, Pancho Villa. He asked if I knew the whereabouts of Villa, and I told him we'd just come back after a couple of years north of the border and didn't know anything about anybody."

Carothers holds up his hand, palm out to ask a question. "When you answered Fernández did you say anything derogatory about Villa or Carranza?"

"No. Livin' down there you never know who you might be dealing with. I'd lived in Mexico long enough to know to keep my mouth shut. Fernández said my cookin' smelled good and that he hadn't eaten all day. I offered to serve him supper while we waited on Ed and Frank.

"They rode into the yard while Fernández was eatin', saw the soldiers waitin' around the barn, and figured the Mexicans had us in a tight situation. Actin' like the soldiers didn't bother 'em any, they unloaded the pack mules, and came on inside.

"I introduced them to Colonel Fernández, who nodded but didn't say anything, and just kept eatin'. When Fernández finished, he said he had to feed his horse and asked Ed where he kept our grain. Ed said he'd show him and they went out to the barn.

"After waitin' a minute, both of us too scared to speak, Frank looked across the table at me, shook his head, and said, 'I'm gonna help Ed. You stay inside with the baby.'

"As soon as Frank went out, the men outside came in. They were dirty and ragged, smelled like they hadn't bathed in a month, and wanted to know where I kept our supplies. I showed 'em and they took all my canned goods, everything I'd canned, jars of molasses, salt, pepper, lard – everything – and carried it all outside. I picked up Johnnie and followed 'em out, wonderin' how we were going to eat for the next few days. Just then they led Ed and Frank out of the barn ridin' on one of the pack mules with their hands tied behind 'em.

"I panicked and ran up to Ed. 'They're gonna kill you.' Ed just looked at me like it was Saturday night bath time and says, 'We'll be all right, Maudie. It's cold out here. Go on now. Take the baby back inside before you both get sick.'

"I went back inside. By that time the soldiers had taken pots and pans, bed covers, my combs and brushes, all our clothes…" She sighs and looks at her hands, "They took everything in the world we owned, everything. When I followed 'em back outside, I was thinkin', *It's just stuff, at least I still have Johnnie.*

"Maria, the woman of the Mexican man we'd hired to help Ed and Frank work the ranch, had come out to see the commotion. When she saw the soldiers takin' everything, she stood there not knowin' what to do, a cryin' and shiverin' with her young uns hangin' on her skirt, and no doubt thinkin' Fernández was goin' to take her man, too.

"Colonel Fernández came riding out of the barn, pointed at Johnnie and said, 'Leave the baby with the woman and swing up behind me.'

"I said, 'I'm not doin' any such thing! I'm not leavin' Johnnie.'

"He pulled out a big pistol and says, 'You choose, *señora*, the *pistola* or the *caballo*.'

"I was scared and angry, and Johnnie was startin' to cry when I handed him over to Maria and whispered, 'I'll be back.'"

"Rather than ride on the back of Fernández's saddle, I took one of our mules from the soldier leading him. Fernández watched me mount and said, 'Please understand, *señora*, we are not Carrancistas but part of *División del Norte*, General Francisco Villa's army. We only need your *hombres* to guide us out of this territory and away from the trails Carrancista patrols use. When we get out of this country you will all be set free.'"

Stone holds up his hand. "Mrs. Wright, did you ever see any Carrancista patrols when you were with Villa?"

"No sir, none."

Stone nods, makes a note, and says, "Please, continue."

"We rode all night in the freezin' cold. One of the soldiers gave me a dirty, rat-holed serape to put over my shoulders and that helped some. I didn't see Ed and Frank on their mule the whole night, and my insides got tighter and tighter with worry. About daybreak we got to Cave Valley."

Stone stops her again. "How far from your ranch to Cave Valley?"

She frowns, thinks a moment, and says, "Maybe thirty miles. Cave Valley has high canyon walls covered with trees and a creek running along the bottom. It's a beautiful place. Reminded me of a Bierstadt painting I'd seen as a girl with my parents in some museum.

"When I first saw it, smoke was pourin' out of the canyon like there was a forest fire, but it was just from campfires made with damp wood. There must have been two or three thousand men camped in there. Their stock looked in awful shape, ribs showing, heads hung low, so tired they weren't even tryin' to graze.

"As we rode into the canyon, I nearly fainted with relief when I saw Ed and Frank still on their mule. I rode over close enough to speak to 'em.

"Ed said, 'We talked to Villa. Told him what we knew about the trails he needed to follow, and he said we weren't gonna be executed.'

"I shook my head. 'Don't be so sure of that.'"

I remember the days I spent with Villa, especially the latter ones watching rage change him from a friend of Americans to a mad man dedicated to killing *gringos*, and I nod in agreement. Her men didn't have a chance and she knew it.

My mind drifts back to Maud's story as she says, "We swapped ideas about how to get away but never firmed up a plan, except to promise that whoever got away first, would go back for Johnnie. During the day, I rested close enough to Ed and Frank so I could keep an eye on 'em.

"We stayed in Cave Valley until late afternoon. After we moved out, Colonel Fernández assigned a man named Castillo to guard me. Castillo made me ride off to the east and then parallel to the main column. I think maybe Villa decided to keep me in case he needed a hostage, but kept me isolated because he didn't want lust for a woman to stir up hard feelings among his men.

"I looked for a while before I finally saw Ed and Frank on their mule back toward the end of the main column. I waved at 'em, but they never showed any sign they saw me. We rode that way for a couple of hours until the sun started settin'. I looked back and thought I saw five or six men leading Ed and Frank on their mule toward a hill we'd passed.

"I said to Castillo, 'Where're Ed and Frank headed with those soldiers?'

"Castillo shrugged and shook his head.

'I don't know, *señora*. Maybe the *gringos* have to fertilize the soil because they're so full of *merde*.'

"He hooted and laughed out loud thinkin' he'd made a big joke.

"When I looked back again, the men and Ed and Frank had disappeared behind the hill. Not seein' 'em gave me a really bad feelin', but I kept hopin' and prayin' they were just guidin' the soldiers down a trail. Near dark, I looked back again and saw the men who rode behind the hill but not Ed and Frank. I felt so bad. I wanted to throw up and cry and scream, but I didn't. I'd never let those sons of...men see any weakness in me. I knew I had to get through this trial. I had to get Johnnie back. That's all that mattered then and all that matters to me now: get... Johnnie... back. You do understand that, don't you, gentlemen?"

We look at her and solemnly nod. The more I listen to Maud, the more I admire her strength, courage, and willingness to endure any trial, suffer any indignity, fight any battle to get her son back, and I marvel at the power of a mother's love.

Stone somberly says, "Yes, ma'am. We understand getting your son back is all that matters to you, and we beg your pardon for this intrusive interview. Do you want to stop for a while?"

She stares at her reflection in Mrs. Slocum's shiny, dark mahogany table and slowly shakes her head. "No, sir. I've grieved over Ed and Frank for eight days waitin' to get free and find our son. I'm ready to go on."

"Very well. Thank you for your patience. Mrs. Wright, do you remember the trail the column took? Were there any places Villa appeared to favor on the march north?"

She shook her head. "No. The trail didn't make any sense at all. It seemed totally crazy. We'd ride east for a while and then swing back west and cover nearly the same ground like we'd lost somethin' and were searchin' for it. No, sir, they didn't seem to favor anyplace.

"We did stop for a few hours one day at a small, abandoned ranch. They slaughtered some cattle and fed the soldiers there. They were starvin' and barely cooked the meat before eatin' it. They gave me a *tortilla* with meat burned on the outside and bloody on the inside. I couldn't eat it, but I saved it to cook some more and ate the *tortilla*.

"Castillo was vulgar and only had one thing on his mind. After I complained about him, a man named Juan Ruiz who spoke perfect English and acted like a real gentleman became my guard. I didn't have any more harassment from the likes of Castillo. Ruiz didn't even let any of the men swear in front of me. Said they'd better treat me like a lady or he'd know the reason why."

Carothers nods. I hear the impatience in his voice, "It must have been a very harrowing experience. Now, can you tell us when you first saw Villa?"

Maud frowns and stares at the table, thinking.

"It was the second or third day. He was wearing a straw hat like some farmer and he rode a little mule. As he passed me, he bowed like a gentleman and smiled like a rattlesnake. Much bigger than the others, he surprised me and intimidated his men. He's real thick and beefy up around his shoulders and neck. I remember his mule had the same choppy gait as those of the other soldiers, but Villa's head didn't jerk around like the others, in fact, it didn't move at all, and that impressed me. It takes a good, strong horseman to ride easy like that. I was raised with four brothers, and I can work as hard as any man in the field. Bein' around men doesn't bother me, but after he rode by I feared him. And the way the men shut up when he passed by, I know they feared him too."

Stone frowns, shaking his head. "I've always heard he rides big fancy stallions. That's what he did when Carothers here was with him down in Mexico for a while."

"Oh, yes, sir, he had several stallions, but when I asked Ruiz why he didn't ride his big studs, he said Villa only rode them to lead his men into a fight. Those horses have special handlers and are never ridden or used as pack animals. Every time we stopped to rest, which never lasted more than about three hours, they were fed grain and curried and their hooves got a goin' over. They had better care than any of the men."

Stone nods. "I understand. If his men feared him, did you see any desertions while you were a captive."

"Yes sir, I did. The closer we got to the border, the more men slipped away. A couple of days before we got to the border, desertions became so bad that five took off in a group. Villa sent a man named Candelario Cervantes after 'em. Cervantes returned in a few hours, leading their horses with their guns, bandoliers of bullets, literally everything they had, hanging on their empty saddles. What Cervantes brought back, the other soldiers divided. Seeing all five deserters apparently caught and killed by Cervantes alone in less than a day, pretty well ended any more desertions."

Stone rubs his chin, leans back in his chair, and asks, "What does this Cervantes look like and where did he ride in the column?"

"Let's see," Maud thinks for a moment tapping a finger on the table. "He has a big broad nose and square face. Oh, and his left eye seems bigger than the right and, unless he's holding his sword, he's always clenching and unclenching his fists down by his sides. He was head of Villa's scouts or some such thing because he led about eighty men who rode out in front of everybody else."

Stone and Carothers make notes and Carothers asks as he writes, "When did you realize you were close to the border?"

"On Tuesday morning we reached the Boca Grande River. Cervantes and his men reconnoitered the countryside while everyone else practically drank the river dry and collapsed, worn out from the long waterless march with practically nothing to eat. That's when they caught the three cowboys and killed 'em. The only one I saw killed, Cervantes shot, and then had the cavalry trample him to death."

She bows her head, and closing her eyes, murmurs, "Awful…awful…" before burying her head in her hands. Stone and Carothers sit back, saying nothing, eyeing Quent and me, waiting for her to compose herself. Before I can suggest taking a break, she looks up, eyes clear, sniffs, and continues.

"Late that afternoon we crossed the Boca and headed for Columbus. The wind came up and brought a hard blowin' dust storm. We rode most of the night in that wind and dust until we came to a steep *arroyo* and camped down in it to get out of the worst of the wind. Shortly after dawn, the wind ended. Grit was blasted on me from my scalp to my toes. I've never felt so dirty in my life.

"In the mornin' light, the officers, usin' field glasses found Columbus pretty quick. Without glasses, I barely made it out. It was just a little smear of dark brown shimmering in the distance, the smoke from stoves plumes giving it away. In a little while Villa and three of his officers rode over to the top of a close-by hill and spent the better part of the mornin' studyin' it and the Army camp with their binoculars."

Carothers asks, "Who were the officers with Villa up on the hill?"

Maud shakes her head and shrugs. "I only knew two, Cervantes and Fernández. Another one was named Ortiz. When they came back to the *arroyo* they were in a big argument. Villa thought the cavalry garrisoned at Columbus too big for an attack. Said he didn't want to waste his men on what he called a 'piss-ant town.'

"Cervantes claimed the garrison didn't have more than fifty men and they'd be wiped out in a couple of hours. They must have argued back and forth for two or three hours before Villa finally threw up his hands and ordered the attack, telling Cervantes to send some men in to scout the town. The rest of the men and animals rested on empty bellies. Villa probably thought they'd find plenty to eat in Columbus.

"Before sunset Fernández brought me a rifle and said he wanted me to take it and kill some *gringos* during the raid. I told him I wouldn't do any such thing, and if I got my hands on it I'd kill every Villista officer I could. I meant every word, and he knew it. He didn't give me the rifle and he only half laughed when he told the others, 'A hard woman, *señores*, very hard.'"

We all laugh and it seems to make her feel better.

Smiling, she says, "Last night was very cold, and the *jefes* roused the men around two o'clock. Freezin' and glad to get goin', I prayed I'd get away in all the thunder and confusion that goes on in a battle. Villa had changed into a uniform and sat in the saddle on his big paint stud that pranced around, anxious to go..." She pauses, staring at the day-old memory.

Carothers urges her to continue. She nods. "Sorry. Villa rode up on the side of the *arroyo* and made a speech to fire up his soldiers. I've never heard such swearin' and name callin' in any language in all my life, and I've been around hard-workin' men who didn't hesitate to cuss and swear about any and everything. He didn't talk long but blamed the *gringos* for all the starvation and poverty they endured in Mexico and for their defeats at Agua Prieta and Hermosillo.

"Then he shook a newspaper at them and roared that the *gringos* had burned twenty of their brothers to death just this past week in the El Paso jail. He said it was time for payback and finished by yellin', 'Let's go kill some *gringos*, boys!'

"I've never seen such an angry crowd of men. They were cryin' and swearin' and stampin' and slappin' the ground, and I was beginnin' to wonder if I'd live through the night.

"We mounted and rode slow and easy toward Columbus.

First, we rode east and then west through some gaps they'd cut in the border fence. We finally stopped about a mile off, behind that little hill over on the other side of the train tracks on the south side of town."

Stone raises his brows, "Any idea what time that was, Mrs. Wright?"

"I'd guess it must have been about three o'clock or so. It was very dark, just light from a fingernail moon. We dismounted and Villa and his officers looked over the men to pick out the ones who were to be in the attack. I stayed back with the horse holders. They were so short of bullets that the horse holders were told to give their bullets to the men in on the attack. One bunch started north and one went east, but I didn't see any on horses. I believe Villa and his officers rode up to the top of the little hill to watch.

"After the shootin' started, I didn't hear much except a lot of yellin' and screamin'. I knew when the Army got into it because I heard machine guns. A dimwit Villa kept around played a fiddle all the time. Up on that hill with Villa, he played "La Cucaracha" over and over.

"The Mexicans started gettin' the worst of it after they torched the buildin's. In a while bullets started landin' back where we held horses. One hit the dirt in front of my mule and one grazed him in the mane. He was kinda hard to hold there for a while.

"They started bringin' the wounded back to the horse holders. They didn't have a single doctor that I knew of, just a few boys who worked as *medicos*, and all they did was lay the wounded, most of 'em boys not over fifteen or sixteen, on their blankets to moan and cry."

Carothers asks, "Did Villa stay up on that hill the entire the time of the battle?"

She shakes her head. "No, sir, he didn't. I heard that paint of his squeal many times from several different places in town where there was a lot of noise. Then this man comes running up to get another stallion and says Villa's on foot because the paint had been shot out from under him. Near the end of the battle, the soldiers came running up with their loot to get their horses and mules. Some of 'em looked like big fat men 'cause they had so much stuff in their shirts.

"Villa came runnin' after 'em. He was yellin', '*Muchachos*! Don't run! Stand and fight like men!' He swung the side of his sword against their backsides and shot his pistol in the air tryin' to make 'em stop. A few did take a knee and shoot toward the Americans, but it wasn't long before all the horses were racing south for the holes in the border fence wire.

"We rode past the Moore ranch and Villa came chargin' up to try and get in front of 'em and stop the retreat. He emptied his pistol in the direction of his soldiers and waved his hat at 'em yellin', 'Stop! Stop!' but it didn't do any good. They were like cattle stampeding to get out of there. Yes, sir, that's what it was, a stampede. Villa didn't show any fear. I believe he wanted to fight the entire US Army.

"After we rode through the holes in the border fence, Villa came ridin' back to me. He sat the new stud like he was in a rockin' chair while it danced around, sweatin', rollin' its eyes, and snortin' like it'd been running spooked all day. Villa says to me, 'You want to return to the United States?'

"I said, 'Yes, please.'

"He says, 'You can go away. Take your mule and saddle with you.'

"Needless to say, I turned back toward Columbus, but

my mule, so spooked by the rush and the smell of blood and death, kept trying to turn back and run with the others. I finally had to dismount and lead him back, and that's when my feet got all tore up.

"When soldiers came runnin' past, some stopped and shook my hand, sayin' good-by and tellin' me how sorry they were they treated me bad.

"I hadn't gone too far when I heard a man lyin' near some creosotes. He was cryin' and groanin', '...*water... water...In the name of God, please, water...*' It was my first guard, Castillo and he looked shot-up pretty bad. When he guarded me, he had a great time tryin' to scare me and kept sayin', '*Señora*, you probably won't be livin' tomorrow unless you are a little more cooperative for me, a little more sensitive to my needs, and you know what I need.'

"I took his saddle; it was a lot better than mine. I was sorely tempted to impale him with his own sword, but instead I said, 'What do you think of American soldiers now?' He turned his head away and wouldn't look at me. I walked away, leavin' him to die, and I hope he did.

"I got back to the Moore ranch, went in the corral, and watered my mule. I took a long drink myself right out of the horse trough, walked up to the ranch house, and saw a dead man in a pool of blood by the side of the porch. I tried to see if anybody else might be there when I heard this low noise out in the bushes behind the house. I listened, tryin' to locate where the sound came from, and then I saw the troopers with Mrs. Moore.

"When I came up to 'em, she saw me. There was blood turning black on her nice dress and she was clenching her teeth in pain. She says, 'Where did you come from? I don't think I know you.'

"I said, 'Ma'am, I've been Villa's prisoner for the last nine days.'

"She says, 'You look mighty hungry. Have you had any breakfast?'

"I said, 'I haven't had much of anything to eat since I was taken prisoner.'

"She shook her head. 'Well, when we get to town you go to any restaurant and eat all you want and tell 'em Mrs. Susan Moore will pay for it. Can you please stay with me and ride into town in the ambulance and help me get a doctor?'

"I took her hand and gave it a little squeeze. 'Of course I will.'

"She didn't let go of my hand and seemed to relax a little after that, but the way she was clenchin' her teeth and squeezin' her eyes shut every once in a while, I could tell she was in a lot of pain.

"In about an hour the ambulance came. Mrs. Moore had a store in town, but believed it was probably ransacked. She decided to take a room in the Hoover Hotel so that's where the soldiers took us, and that's where Doctor Grace stepped up to look after us."

Quent finishes his notes about a minute after Maud finishes her statement, and caps his pen with a definitive click, like a soldier snapping a sword into its sheath. Carothers and Stone continue writing their notes for another five or ten minutes.

Carothers looks up as he closes his portfolio and says, "Mrs. Wright, you're a very courageous woman. I've never heard of one any braver, and I can assure you the United States and the State Department will do everything in its power to get your little boy back. I emphasize again that

Mr. Stone and I will probably need to chat with you in a day or two in order to further clarify our understanding of your story for our superiors, but we'll try to keep our use of your time to a minimum. Thanks again, you've been very helpful."

Maud nods. "Thank you Mr. Carothers. Just help me get my Johnnie back. That's all I ask."

As he and Stone push up from the table, Carothers says, "Yes, ma'am. Rest assured, we'll find him."

42. SUSAN MOORE

The interview with Maud finishes mid-afternoon. After Carothers and Stone leave, I speak briefly with her.

"Mrs. Wright, I'm going down to the Hoover to check on Mrs. Moore. I expect to be back to check on you before dark. I want you to get all the rest you can. If you need me to take you back to the Hoover or if I can get you anything, just let me know."

Her face muscles sagging with fatigue, dark circles around her drooping eyes standing out against her sun and wind-burned face, she smiles through lips so dry and cracked they nearly bleed.

"I'll stay here with Mrs. Slocum. Several of the other women and children who lost their husbands and daddies have been asked to stay with her too. Thank you for sitting through that interview with me. You've been a great help and support. Please give Mrs. Moore my best regards."

Quent and I leave the Slocum house with the intent of my seeing Mrs. Moore and then finding a place to eat. Columbus now reminds me of downtown El Paso. People and cars are everywhere, their movement kicking up dust that glows gold in the falling sunlight. The air carries the strong, unforgettable stench of burning hair and flesh, arousing old memories of days long past when I witnessed Sierra Madre Apaches torturing their enemies with fire.

Quent makes a face and points to tall wavering columns of greasy black smoke on the other side of town. "This stink makes me want to gag. See that smoke from over there on the other side of town? The Army must be cremating the Mexicans they killed last night. If they don't get those fires hot enough, all they'll have are piles of roasted Mexican. Come on, Henry, let's get down to the Hoover so we can get out of this."

I smile as we race-walk to the Hoover. Quent has seen and smelled thousands of men torn apart in battles all over northern Mexico, but he can't stand the smell of battle cleanup.

Men crowding into the hotel lobby hear Will or Mrs. Hoover patiently telling them that there are no rooms to be had in the Hoover and that they can try at houses up the street that might take in a border or two.

Mrs. Hoover sees us and comes bustling over, sweat streaming down the sides of her face as she mops her brow with a lacey white handkerchief. "Doctor Grace, I'm so glad you came. Our patient woke up about a quarter of an hour ago. The shot you gave her is starting to wear off and she may need another."

I nod and check my pocket watch. "Yes, ma'am, I'm not

at all surprised that the pain is starting to keep her awake. I need to change her bandages and give her another shot of morphine. I plan to take her to an El Paso hospital in the morning on the 4:00 A.M. train. After I tend to her, I'll try to be back around sundown and check in on her again. She'll likely be hungry if she wakes up before I return. Don't give her any solid food, just water and thin soup. Can you do that, Mrs. Hoover?"

"Of course I can. She's no trouble at all." She frowns at Quent and looks him up and down. "I don't believe I've met this gentleman."

I grimace. "I'd forget my head if it weren't permanently attached. Forgive my bad manners. Mrs. Hoover, this is my friend Quentin Peach. He's a reporter for the *El Paso Herald*. Perhaps you've read some of his columns and his stories on the Mexican *Revolución*."

Her jaw drops and she throws the flat of her left hand to the middle of her large bosom and sticks the right one out to shake hands. "Why land 'o Goshen. Of course we know of Mr. Peach. We read all his stories. He knows more about Pancho Villa and the Revolution than any reporter in El Paso. Mr. Peach, I'm Sarah Hoover. My son William and I own this hotel. It's so nice to meet a famous writer. Won't you stay with us this evening?"

Quent shakes her hand, grinning and nodding, and speaking with such a pompous gravitas, I nearly laugh out loud.

"So nice to meet you, Sarah. I'm delighted you like my work. I'd be honored to stay here tonight but I thought you had a full house."

"Well, we nearly do, but we'll find room for a distinguished gentleman like yourself."

I leave Quent to keep her company and walk down the hall to Mrs. Moore's room. Her eyes flick open when I come through the door, but she says nothing. I suspect she's still disoriented from lack of sleep and the morphine.

I change her bandages. There's no sign of infection in either wound, but it's obvious her hip wound is giving her a lot of pain. I wish I could remove the bullet but just can't take the risk that it's near major blood vessels. A probe or cut a millimeter or two in the wrong direction and she'd bleed to death. I know the pain from the bullet wounds are nothing compared to the pain she must feel in her heart over the murder of her husband.

As I examine her after changing the bandages, I see tears at the edges of her eyes.

"I'm sorry, Mrs. Moore. I'll make this as quick as I can and then I'll give you another morphine injection."

Lying on her left side, she shakes her head a little. "You're very gentle, Doctor. I'm just recalling how my husband was murdered by the raiders."

"Tell me about it. It'll make you feel better to get it out and I want to know what happened."

She pauses a few moments, sniffs and then speaks in a remarkably calm voice.

"All during the attack in town we hid in our house with the shades drawn. Just before sun-up, the road in front of our house filled with running, dirty, ragged men. Some stumbled and staggered forward wounded, blood all over their rags or brand new shirts and pants they stole in Columbus, others, on running horses, barely hanging on.

"Doctor Grace, they were so young. Most of them were just boys not more than fourteen or fifteen years old. Some of them stopped in our corral to drink and water their animals. An officer came riding up on a big white horse and ordered several of them to check our house.

"They climbed up on the porch and when they found the door was locked they broke out the window in the bedroom. John told me to go to the dining room and then opened the front porch door. He stepped out on the porch into the middle of men who all pointed their guns at him. The officer asked him if he knew where Sam Ravel was. John said he didn't know, and he didn't, he never lied.

"The officer says, 'Very well.' And then, and then… Oh God… they started stabbing him with their bayonets and hacking at him with their swords and knives, and then they shot him. The sounds of it all…his groans…their knives tearing his flesh…their yells of blood lust, it all plays like some terrible music in my head."

She sobs for a minute or two as I try to sooth her by smoothing her hair back on her forehead. She becomes very still and quiet, and from that time on I don't think I ever saw her cry again.

"John never had a chance, Doctor Grace, not a chance. They squatted by his body like buzzards and picked over him, taking his ring and watch and wallet. Then they remembered me and came in the house, saying they wanted bread and gold. They had me by each arm and I knew I was going to die at the hands of those wretched boys. I even recognized one, an officer who had come in our store during the afternoon of the day before to buy a pair of pants.

"They saw my jewelry and demanded I take it off and give it to them. As I tried to slide my wedding rings off I decided they planned to kill me any way and I had to fight back. I looked out the door and screamed at the top of my lungs. They jerked around to look at the door and loosened their grips just enough for me to snatch myself away from them, hike my skirts, and run out the back door.

"Some solders trying to start our Ford out in the garage shot at me when I ran by. I felt a stinging in my right leg and knew I'd been hit but ran on anyway. I was hit again where you're changing bandages now and it knocked me down, but I got up and kept running until I got to the barbed wire around our central lot, somehow got over it, and crawled to hide in a clump of mesquite. I passed out and don't remember much after that except the gunfire dying down.

"When I first came to, feeling my drawers sticking to my legs and dampness all over my backsides, I knew blood must be flowing. After tearing a ruffle off my petticoat and binding my wounds, I passed out again. The second time I woke up, I heard horsemen and realized it was our soldiers. I hung my handkerchief on one of the mesquite branches and called for help.

"They found me and tried to make me comfortable when out of nowhere I saw the dirtiest young woman I'd ever seen, watching me. She helped them with me and told us she'd been Villa's prisoner for the past nine days. Such a kind and caring person, she stayed with me until you came and saved us."

I again feel the fire and anger against Villa growing hot in my soul. The outrageous things he did to these people and to the *peons* he forced to become soldiers, all an affront to human decency, deserve justice, the same kind of deadly justice Rufus Pike, Yellow Boy, and I gave my father's murderers. I wish I had Villa and Camisa Roja in the sights of Little David to blow them both straight to Hell and gone. *I'll make those bastards pay.* Through clenched teeth, I say, "Don't worry, Mrs. Moore. I'm sure your husband will be avenged."

Her eyes flood, the tears spreading over her cheeks as she croaks, "I don't care about revenge. I just want my husband back." It was beyond my ken then to understand what she meant.

I pat her on the shoulder and tell her I plan to take her to El Paso as soon as I can get us on a train, maybe as early as the one at 4:00 A.M. early the next morning. I give her a morphine injection and promise to return in two or three hours as she whispers her drowsy thanks before slipping into unconsciousness.

43. YELLOW BOY TO THE RESCUE

Quent and I leave the Hoover to find a place to eat. The stink of burned flesh and hair permeates the air, carrying sparkling, golden dust motes in the long low beams of sunlight streaming between buildings. Trains rumble up and down the tracks bringing more soldiers and their supplies. The road between Columbus and Deming, filled with curiosity seekers on horses, in wagons, and trembling, gurgling automobiles, stays under a thick, brown dust plume visible for miles. A tent city grows in the creosotes and mesquite behind Camp Furlong to the east and south of the railroad tracks. Children still run and play *Raid* in the streets. Some pretend to be Villa's men while others, Army heroes, are on their knees, swinging their machinegun broom handles on tops of wooden boxes at the raiders, and yelling *bam, bam, bam, bam, bam...* The raiders flop in the dust only to get up and begin the raid again.

Telephone lines are overloaded, leaving Quent to forward his article for the *Herald* via the telegraph office. We head for the cantina Yellow Boy and I used during the El Paso trip to fetch Quent. I've seen no trace of Yellow Boy since we've arrived and I worry that maybe he's wounded and lying out in the mesquite somewhere, or that Villa's men might have caught and executed him.

Cowboys, peddlers, and businessmen surround the cantina door, waiting to get a seat. I'm ready to pass on and find somewhere else rather than wait, but Quent convinces me that we ought to stick our heads inside and look around.

The same fat Mexican with the slicked-back, greasy black hair and drooping mustache who ran the place when Yellow Boy and I were there in September, meets us with his hand up, palm out to stop us.

"*Perdón, señores*, but there ees no place for you to…" He recognizes me and says, "Ah, *señor*, your *compañeros* have your table by the window. Go join them, *por favor*, and I bring you chairs."

Quent looks at me, his eyebrows raised. I shrug. We walked around the corner of the bar where the Mexican pointed. My knees sag with relief. Yellow Boy sits at the table with a *tortilla* in one hand, his knife spearing a piece of meat with the other, and in the chair across from him sits the grizzled old veteran, Sergeant Sweeny Jones.

His cheeks puffed out like a squirrel's filled with nuts, Yellow Boy sees us, raises his knife, meat still on its tip, and waves us over. Before we manage to squeeze through the crowd, the manager appears at their table with a couple of rickety chairs.

Sergeant Jones stands as we approach and shakes hands.

He smiles as he takes Quent's hand. "I don't believe I've met you, sir. I'm Sergeant Sweeny Jones, US Army, 13th Cavalry. Me an' Yellow Boy rode together back in the Geronimo War days. Looks like we may be fightin' together again, 'cept the enemy this time is that no good sonofabitch, Pancho Villa."

Quent grins as he sits down. "Yes, sir, that might be. From what I hear, the Army's heading for Mexico."

Jones grins and nods. "Don't know nothin' for sure. But the US Army ain't about to let no Mexican bastard come in here, shoot us up, burn half the town down, an' git away with it."

Grinning, he shakes my hand. "'Member me, Doctor Grace?"

I laugh. "You're a hard man to forget, Sweeny Jones."

I turn to Yellow Boy who chews on the piece of meat that had been on his knifepoint. "Uncle, my eyes are glad to see you. Were you here during the raid?"

Sergeant Jones slaps the table and bellows, "Was he here during the raid? Hell, yes, he was here. He saved my damned bacon and then did hisself proud ridin' with Major Tompkins a chasin' Villa and his boys. Go on Yellow Boy, tell 'em what happened."

We all look at him and grin. He shrugs, swallows, and takes a slurp of coffee before he leans back in his chair and crosses his arms.

"Before sun comes, moon hides. *Mucho* dark. See light from iron wagon. Iron wagon follows iron road toward rising sun and El Paso on *Rio Grande*. I ride for iron wagon light, find iron road. See light at town where iron wagon stops. Ride beside iron road toward light. Hear many guns. Mexican *hombres* yell. Soldiers yell. Women scream. Horses squeal.

"I tie my horses in mesquite. Take rifle. Run toward battle. Stay by iron wagon road. Get close to soldiers on rising sun side of army camp. Mexicans everywhere. Many bullets fly. Watch. See Sweeny Jones by guard tent. Mexicans come. Nearly shoot Sweeny Jones. I shoot Mexicans. Rifle no miss. Sweeny Jones happy Yellow Boy comes. We move north around town. Shoot more Mexicans. No see good, stay in mesquite. Mexicans many times yell, 'Where is Sam Ravel?'

"Mexicans shoot many times, in Many-Sleep-House, what you say…hotel…many die. Mexicans go in trading posts, take many things. Mexicans burn Many-Sleep-House and trading posts. Fires give good light, Sweeny Jones and Yellow Boy shoot Mexicans. Army many-shoots guns, they shoot many bullets, kill many Mexicans. Sun comes. Mexicans leave.

"Army chief stands on hill. Use big eyes. Watch Mexicans ride away into Mexico. Sweeny Jones and Yellow Boy find Major Frank Tompkins. Major Frank Tompkins tells Sweeny Jones to find men and horses. Says Yellow Boy come. Track Mexicans. Find and kill. No get away. Sweeny Jones runs to find men and horses. Yellow Boy comes with his horses. Frank Tompkins goes to hill. Talks to big chief. Big chief says go. Pretty quick we go. Chase and shoot Mexicans. Kill many. Leave where they fall. No catch Villa. When sun makes no shadows, soldiers have no more bullets to shoot, no more water, stop chase. Come back. Take care of horses. Sweeny Jones and Muchacho Amarillo eat in this place and then Hombrecito and Quentin come. This is all I have to say."

We're sitting there absorbing Yellow Boy's description of what happened when a waitress brings us bowls of beans with chilies and *tortillas*, which is all they have left to serve. We don't complain. It's the best meal I've eaten in a long time.

Between spoons of beans, I say, "So the Mexicans were lookin' for Sam Ravel last night? I'm not surprised. Villa has wanted to cut his throat since September. Where was he anyway? Did they get him? At least they hit his store."

Quent shakes his head. "Tale I got was that Ravel was in El Paso seeing a dentist. He must be the luckiest fool in the world even if Villa did burn down his store."

We spend the next half hour speculating on what the Army will do next. Major Tompkins' chase into Mexico violated all kinds of agreements the United States has with Mexico. Quent believes the Carranza government won't dare protest the invasion of their country by a hostile force chasing Pancho Villa. He says Carothers believes his old friend, Villa, is a mad dog that needs killing, and he intends to tell that to President Wilson."

"What do you think Wilson will do?"

Quent leans back in his chair and uses his napkin to wipe salsa off his chin. "He'll send the Army into Mexico after Villa, regardless of Carranza's objections. The Mexicans will despise the *gringos* crossing the border uninvited. We might even get into a full-blown war with Mexico if we go in, but if Wilson wants to catch Villa, he has to move quick or Villa will disappear in the Sierra Madre where no one can find him. Albert Fall is already pushing the Senate to invade Mexico and make Chihuahua and Sonora a US Protectorate. He says it's the only way to catch Villa. My money says Wilson will send in the Army to catch him, but it won't go as invaders. We ought to know what Wilson is goin' to do in a couple of days."

44. OATH OF MAIMONIDES

We finish our supper in good spirits. Sergeant Jones has a place at Camp Furlong for Yellow Boy and our horses and gear. Major Tompkins impressed by the skill and bravery of Yellow Boy on the chase after Villa, told Jones to make him welcome and to recruit him for the Mexico campaign that's sure to come. Leaving the cantina I tell Yellow Boy I have to visit a couple of patients before I spend the evening with him. Quent leaves to wander the streets before writing a piece for the *Herald*.

The train station hums with activity as the Army rolls in more troops and equipment. A ticket clerk, glasses on the end of his nose, verifies that a train will stop at 4:30 the next morning on the way to El Paso, but he's not sure I can get on it. I tell him I'm a doctor and my patient, Mrs. Moore, has wounds that require I get her to El Paso fast for surgery. He nods and says he'll make room for us and to be at the station at 4:15. I thank him and head for Colonel Slocum's house to check on Maud Wright.

Smiling, George Carothers huffs out of the tiny house next to the Hoover Hotel, where the telephone switchboard is located. Seeing me, he does a double take at a note in his hand, and waves for me to stop.

"Doctor Grace," he puffs, "you've saved me trying to find you. Great news! The State Department has just informed me that the Carranza government has found Mrs. Wright's little boy, Johnnie, and will have him in Juarez the fifteen of March for her to take back. With things in such turmoil between the United States and Mexico, it could be...uh...counterproductive for me, or one of my staff, to accompany her to Juarez. We all want to ensure she and the boy are reunited and that the child arrives in good health. She'll need a doctor's support when Carrancistas return him. Might you be so kind as to..."

I smile, knowing how happy the news will make Maud.

"Of course, I'll be more than happy to do anything I can to help get her son back. I'm headed to Colonel Slocum's house now to check on her. Has she heard the news?"

Carothers' grin grows as he leans back from his belly and runs his thumbs under his suspenders. "Why, no, I just got word myself. Please give her the news for me and tell her that you've agreed to accompany her to Juarez to get little Johnnie back."

I give Carothers a little two-finger salute off my hat as I turn away to continue back up the street to Colonel Slocum's house.

* * *

As the sun kisses high twilight clouds with purple, blood red, and orange, the early spring temperature falls like a stone in a deep well. Maud sits rocking on Slocum's front porch and stares south, her shoulders covered by a thick wool shawl. Through the screen door come clinking sounds of knives and forks on plates and muted conversations over a supper being eaten by several adults and young children.

She sees me and nods toward Mexico.

"My son and husband are down yonder, Doctor Grace. Crows, coyotes, and buzzards have probably eaten Ed's body by now. I can only pray Johnnie still lives and that he's well-cared for."

"He is Mrs. Wright. You'll get him back."

"I hope so, and soon."

"No, I mean you'll get him back in six days, on the fifteenth of March, in Juarez. He's fine. Mr. Carothers just got the information from the State Department and asked me to tell you and to accompany you to Juarez to get Johnnie. If that's your desire, I'm happy to do it."

Surprise and joy fill her face, tears of relief spread over her cheeks. She dabs her eyes.

"I'd be most grateful if you came with me. It'd mean a lot. I've felt so alone and helpless since Villa murdered Ed. I have to get Johnnie back. I have to. Please help me."

My heart goes out to her.

"Of course I'll help you in anyway I can. We'll have Johnnie back before you know it."

Years of living with the Apaches taught me not to hesitate considering practical matters.

"Have you thought about what you'll do after you get him?"

She stares off into the dimming twilight and shakes her head. "No, not really. My parents and I lived in New Mexico when Ed and I ran off to El Paso, married, and headed south for the Promised Land in 1910. I still have friends in El Paso. They're very generous and I'm sure will let me stay with them until I can support myself and Johnnie."

The lady has real grit and I much admire her for it. I know in the long run she'll be all right. If she stays in El Paso, it won't be long before men will line up to court her and she'll have her pick.

"I've got to take Mrs. Moore to El Paso on the 4:30 train in the morning, and get her in a hospital. I should be back sometime tomorrow afternoon. Is there anyone you'd like me to contact while I'm in El Paso? Your friends, maybe?"

She eagerly leans forward. "Can't I go with you?"

I shake my head. "It's better if you stay here. Your feet are beginning to heal, but you can barely walk. Carothers will be getting additional information about the Carranza government's plans to bring Johnnie to Juarez for you. You need to stay where he can find you easily if I'm not here."

Tears well up at the corner of her eyes. Her words become a rushing torrent.

"Please let me go. I have to be there when Johnnie comes. What if Villa attacks again or something happens to the tracks with all the trains running on them. We might not get there if we wait too long. You wouldn't have to come back for me if I went and stayed until I get Johnnie. Carothers can send his information to his State Department representatives in El Paso. They'll probably have it before he does anyway."

Her pleading eyes lock on mine and I know my better judgment doesn't have a chance as she says, "Do you have to come back here? Isn't Mrs. Moore your patient? Won't you need to operate to get that bullet out of her hip? My feet don't hurt. I'd walk on burnin' coals and barbed wire if it'd get me back my Johnnie. If I wasn't a mother, I'd already be searching for the murderer who killed his father and I'd have me some satisfaction too. I'd have me some justice for what that lame excuse of a human bein' did killin' my Ed and Frank Hayden. I'd chop him to pieces with his own sword and wash my hands in his blood, I'd…"

I hold up my hands and motion for her to settle down, memories of my own father's murder filling my mind.

"All right, all right. I know exactly how you feel. Come with us in the morning and I'll stay in El Paso until you get Johnnie back. While we're waiting, you can talk to your friends and see if they can take you in until you get back on your feet. If they can't, I have money, and although I know what it might look like, a bachelor paying for a widow lady's hotel room, I'll do just that until you can support yourself. But after you get Johnnie, I have to come back here. I have a personal score to settle with General Francisco Villa. Can you live with that?"

She looks at me, her eyes wide. "Yes, of course... What do you mean by a personal score to settle with Villa?"

The cloud of anger deep in my soul condenses into a black gusher of venom spewing out of my mouth.

"Years ago, he saved my life, and to repay him I helped him last fall when he crossed the Sierra Madre. After listening to him, I believed the right thing to do was serve as a *medico* in his army. I believed all he told me. I believed in his war with Carranza. I believed he had only the best interests of the Mexican *peons* at heart. Now, that I've learned better, I mean to blow him to Hell and gone. If it were only me he tried to kill, if it were only me he betrayed, then I'd walk away and wash my hands of him, and call all debts even. But the atrocities he committed against a small village and the murder of their priest betrayed everything I believed about him, betrayed all the trust and respect I had for him. He and one of his henchmen, a man I wanted to kill a long time ago, deserve to die. I should have killed them both when I had the chance. Now with this raid and the outrages he's committed on good people like you, I feel it's almost my fault that it happened. I'm going after him. I'm gonna kill him."

"I pray you do. I pray you'll kill that monster, but how can you murder anyone if you're a doctor? Didn't you swear some kind of oath to preserve life when you became a doctor?"

I swore the Oath of Maimonides when I received my medical degree. I memorized it, spoke it line by line when the world was told I was qualified to practice medicine, and said it to myself often when I tried to save the life of some *peon* who had been shot to pieces. Now, its cadences flowing as though spoken, line-by-line, pass through my mind:

> *The eternal providence has appointed me to watch over the life and health of Thy creatures. May the love for my art actuate me at all time; may neither avarice nor miserliness, nor thirst for glory or for a great reputation engage my mind; for the enemies of truth and philanthropy could easily deceive*

me and make me forgetful of my lofty aim of doing good to Thy children.

May I never see in the patient anything but a fellow creature in pain.

Grant me the strength, time and opportunity always to correct what I have acquired, always to extend its domain; for knowledge is immense and the spirit of man can extend indefinitely to enrich itself daily with new requirements.

Today he can discover his errors of yesterday and tomorrow he can obtain a new light on what he thinks himself sure of today. Oh, God, Thou has appointed me to watch over the life and death of Thy creatures; here am I ready for my vocation and now I turn unto my calling.

I know the spirit of that oath, but I do what every man does who goes against his own code: rationalize. Rationalize every darkness; rationalize every error.

"The oath I swore says I've been appointed to watch over the life and health of God's creatures. Any doctor will kill a rabid dog that's attacking people and that's what Villa's become. He no longer serves the cause of justice in Mexico, and his ego and military stupidity have destroyed the best army to fight for the *peon's* rights. He serves only himself. He has to be put down, even if a doctor has to do it."

Her fingers, powerful and strong, grab my arm and she looks straight into my eyes. In a desperate whisper through clenched teeth she says, "Promise me. Promise me, Doctor Grace, swear before God and all that's holy, that, if for no other reason, you'll kill him for murderin' my husband and our friend. Swear it and give me peace in my soul."

I look into her big gray eyes, their water flooding her cheeks. The words fall off my tongue so easily.

"I swear to you, Maud Wright, I will kill Pancho Villa, kill him if only to avenge your husband, kill him to give our souls peace and satisfaction that a black evil has been cut from the world."

Her grip relaxes and she slumps back into the rocker. She sighs low and lonely, wipes her eyes with the backs of her sleeves, and looks again into my eyes. Deep inside, I feel like I've jumped into an abyss, but I don't know why. I just know that now I've sworn to kill Villa for the evil he did Maud, her husband, and their friend, or die trying.

"Thank you, Doctor Grace. With your help, I may yet survive in this miserable world. How should I prepare for tomorrow mornin'?"

"We need to be at the train station by 4:15. I have a room at the Hoover next to Mrs. Moore's. I'll borrow a horse and take you down there now if you like. You can have my room and I'll bunk with Quent. Then, Mrs. Moore, you, and I won't have far to go for the train station that early in the morning. How does that sound?"

A smile fills her face and her eyes sparkle.

"I can't ask for more."

"I'll find a horse while you tell Mrs. Slocum and the others good-by. I'll be back in a few minutes."

"I'll be waitin'. Thank you for puttin' up with me and for all your trouble."

I smile and it warms my heart to feel her joy.

"It's no trouble at all, ma'am."

She grabs my arm again in that talon-like grip of hers.

"One more request, Doctor Grace."

"Yes, ma'am?"

"Please, call me Maud."

"Only if you call me, Henry."

Her smile seals the deal.

45. STRATEGY

I decide to hire a horse for a little while from the livery a couple of streets over from the Slocums. The night is cold, cast in a haze from smoke, fog, and dust. Squads of soldiers march down the streets to take up positions around the Columbus perimeter just in case Villa returns to attack again before morning. It's like closing the barn door after the horse is gone. Villa won't be back.

The livery stable corral, filled to capacity, holds horses from riders, buggies, and wagons that arrived during the day, but the liveryman only has an old, broken down mare and a riding mule for hire.

He says, "Villa's sonsofbitches come in here last night and took ever' damned horse I had. I found these two wanderin' around late this mornin'. Don't know who they belong to, but you can rent one for a while this evenin'. S'pect their owner won't be around till tomorra, if ever."

Chuckling, he spits a long brown stream of juice from a big wad in his cheek. "Now don't take one o' these here animals out an' race 'em down the street. They're so fast they might set the town a fire again." The old boy, full of beans, and I have a few good laughs while I saddle the mule.

With Maud in the saddle, I lead the mule down to the Hoover. The night is cold but she's so happy she hums some little Mexican ditty I remember hearing years ago. Still tender, her feet appear to be healing well from thorn and cactus wounds, goat head sticker sores, and cuts from sharp gravel. I take her in my arms and carry her into the Hoover to keep her off her feet. They might be bleeding again tomorrow from all the walking she'll have to do. She smells of soap and her warm body next to mine stirs feelings I know I shouldn't have as her doctor.

Mrs. Moore, sunk deep in sleep, breathes quietly, not moving at all. For a moment I fear she's fallen into a coma, but then relax, she's finally resting like she should.

I say to Maud as I turn to go, "Try to get some sleep there in the next room. I'll be back in a while."

She smiles as she heads for the bed through the open door, "Now that I know I might have Johnnie in a few days, I might finally get a few winks. Thanks again, Doctor Grace."

I look for Quent before I visit Yellow Boy, but he's nowhere around the hotel.

Riding the mule over to a guard post at Camp Furlong, I tell the guard who must have lied about his age to get in the Army that I want to see Sergeant Sweeny Jones. The guard grins and points toward a lone tent at the far end of the horse shelters. Yellow Boy's paint, Satanas, and our pack mules are tethered in the string of horses under the long open horse shelter next to Sweeny Jones' tent.

As I approach the tent, Yellow Boy appears out of the gloom and motions me over to the far end of the shelter, where cavalry saddles hang across wooden sawhorses. A large white field of Army pyramid tents looking like ocean waves frozen in place, spread out before us in neat rows running south and east.

He lights a cigar as I dismount.

"Uncle, will you scout for the Army when it chases Villa in Mexico?"

He blows a stream of smoke toward the stars and shakes his head. "No, Hombrecito, other scouts come. Boys maybe so, but still Apaches, more better than Army scouts. Even with these scouts, Army never catches Arango. Arango knows many tricks, lives many seasons with Apaches in *sierras*. Arango hides until Army goes back north.

"Army chase, no catch. We know Arango. We like Coyote, big tricksters. Use Shoot-Today-Kill-Tomorrow and Yellow Boy rifle. Find Arango, you shoot. Find Camisa Roja, you shoot. They die, we all sleep more better. Your woman from many seasons ago walks in peace with the grandfathers. We leave tonight. Catch Arango plenty quick."

I shake my head. "My uncle speaks true. Speaks with clear eyes. But I can not go after Villa and Camisa Roja for seven suns."

He frowns and looks at the end of his cigar. "Seven suns? You not do this when we leave in season of red berries. You do special White-Eye di-yin ceremony before we go? You learn this ceremony in the place you go, the place of White-Eye healers?"

"No, there's no special ceremony. I heal, make medicine for all that need and ask for it. Two women need and ask for my help."

He takes another puff and frowns, trying to understand my point as I continue. "One woman, Arango's soldiers shot twice. One wound is not bad, the other is here in her thigh and the bullet is still there. I can't remove the bullet without maybe killing or crippling her for life. I have to take her to El Paso plenty quick and find a di-yin who can get the bullet out.

"Arango stole the other woman on his way north and made her leave her little son behind. The Carrancistas have found the child and are bringing him back to her in Juarez in six days. I promised to help her get the child back and kill Arango because he murdered her husband. I'll return to this place in seven days and begin the hunt for Arango and Camisa Roja. Will you be here when I return?"

I know the answer before he grunts, "Hmmph. I wait. Peach comes?"

"I don't know, but I'll find out tonight. The women and I ride the iron wagon to El Paso before the sun comes *mañana*. I'll look for you here when I come back?"

He nods. "*Sí*, I wait here at Sweeny Jones' camp."

We talk for an hour about where Villa might go and where we ought to begin looking for him when I return. Yellow Boy believes Arango will head south before he turns west into the Sierra Madre to hide, maybe with Rojo's Apaches or some other band with whom he's friendly. Rojo's camp, the northernmost village of the Apache lodges hidden in the Sierra Madre, puts Villa behind the Americans if they blindly plunge into Mexico after him.

Yellow Boy assures me, "This the Army will do. Army chiefs strong fighters but use cannon when a rifle will do."

We decide that when I return, we'll find Rojo's camp

and wait a couple of weeks to see if Arango appears in any of the Apache camps.

I find Quent in his room at the Hoover, a glass of Jack Daniels bourbon next to his bedside lamp, boots off, legs crossed while he sits on the bed writing a *Herald* article. He points toward the bottle. "Help yourself. You'll find a glass on the dresser."

"Thanks, a little shot of that fire water will take the ache out of my bones."

I pour a couple of fingers in the heavy crystal glass sitting on the tray by the water pitcher, and sit down on the second bed. A swallow of the bourbon burns all the way to my belly, and I feel its warmth spreading all the way to my toes.

"Medicinal! I'm escorting Mrs. Moore and Mrs. Wright to El Paso on the 4:30 train in the morning. Maud has my room. Mind if I bunk with you? I'll try not to wake you up when we leave."

He laughs. "That's amazing. Slater sent a wire a little while ago and said I needed to get back to El Paso first thing tomorrow. His friends in Washington tell him that Woodrow Wilson is meeting with General Scott, Chief of Staff of the Army as we speak and it's likely that first thing tomorrow, orders will be cut to send Black Jack Pershing into Mexico after Villa. Scuttlebutt has it Pershing will have at least a division with all the Army's latest equipment."

I frown and shake my head, "What do you mean by *latest equipment?*"

Quent shrugs.

"The old Army, the horse cavalry, is fading away, Henry. There's a major war going on in Europe right now, and it's using the same kinds of tactics, trenches, barbed wire, and machineguns, we saw used against Villa at Agua Prieta. The United States wants to stay neutral, but everybody knows it's only a matter of time before we're in the fight against the Germans. The Mexico expedition will allow the Army to try out a lot of the new stuff that's being used overseas. You know, things like automobiles, trucks, new guns and explosive shells, hell, even airplanes. I understand there'll likely be some Jennies for aerial surveillance and droppin' bombs on big groups. It'll also test the Army's ability to motorize delivery of supplies rather than use pack mules or heavy wagons. Slater wants me to go to Fort Bliss and write about what's going on. He says he'll even give me a daily column if I want it."

I'm incredulous.

"No more horse cavalry? What will they do? Drive to war in automobiles like they're going to the next dance? It'll never work. What can those generals be thinking?"

Quent scratches the stubble darkening his jaw.

"They'll probably keep their horses for a while to fight in places like Mexico, where there's little fuel. Chasing Villa in Mexico makes for a good test for motorized troops and their logistics. The Army already knows that where the roads are passable, like in Europe, motorized transportation is the only way to go. They can maneuver and cover ground much faster and carry bigger, deadlier weapons than they can with horses. And, let me tell you, if aeroplanes live up to even half their potential, well, God help us all. The enemy can bomb you while you sleep in your bed miles away from the actual fighting."

I sit back stunned at what I'm hearing, and suddenly feel very old even though I'm twenty-eight. I'm just getting comfortable in the world in which I grew up and managed to survive. Now everything is changing. Things will never be the same and, I guess for that matter, never are the same. I don't know whether to laugh or cry.

"Maybe I can go with you for a day or two when you go over to Ft. Bliss? I'd like to see the Army's new equipment."

Quent nods and smiles.

"Sure. I'd be happy for you to come with me. I'll introduce you around to some of the folks I know. You might find some of the officers useful contacts."

46. GENERAL PERSHING

I take Susan Moore to the Hotel Dieu Hospital run by the Sisters of Mercy in El Paso. When Maud calls her friends they beg her to stay with them, and, giggling with relief, she promises to be there soon. I press a few dollars into her hand, pay for the taxi to take her to friends, promise I'll stay in touch with George Carothers and the State Department, and call her as soon as I learn anything on Johnnie's status. Quent insists I stay with him and Persia at their home, and I promise to show up as soon as I can arrange for a surgeon to look at Susan's wound.

The superb nurses at the Hotel Dieu bathe Susan, change her bandages, feed her, help her into a bed, and introduce me to Doctor Rose, an old white-haired gentleman with twinkling blue eyes who specializes in gunshot wounds. After examining Susan's wounds and complimenting me for not trying to dig the bullet out of her hip, he chats with her about how she's feeling, how her hip feels when she moves her leg in opposing directions, whether she's passed blood in her urine or stool, and whether she continued to move after she was shot (she did in fact run some distance before climbing a fence to get away from her attackers after she was wounded). He takes copious notes all the while, nodding he understands or stops to ask a clarifying question. When he finishes he tells her that he wants to discuss her hip wound with his colleagues to be certain of his conclusions and he'll return to talk with her in the afternoon about her options.

Her brow rises at the word *options*. "What options? Just put me to sleep and cut that bullet out before it kills me."

Doctor Rose sighs and shakes his head. "I'm afraid, Mrs. Moore, it may not be that simple, but we'll see."

I sit in on the consultations Doctor Rose has with other doctors, one, like Doctor Rose, a former Army surgeon. They conclude that there is definitely a bullet in Mrs. Moore's hip, that it's probably .30 caliber, and that they have no idea where it is except it hasn't fractured her pelvis, touched any other bones, or punctured her colon or any vital organs. They don't think it's wise to do exploratory surgery since the odds of finding it are very small unless they know exactly where to look. Given enough time, maybe a year or two, the doctors believe the bullet will work its way up to the surface and then be easy to remove. The most important thing they can do now is kill any infection the bullet might generate and that means two or three weeks in the hospital.

Susan grimaces when she hears Doctor Rose's prognosis and recommendations. "I hate to be laid up and doing nothing, but if I have to, this place will do just fine. Doctor Grace, I feel I owe you a great debt of gratitude for all the help you've given me. I know beggars often ask too much, but please help Maud find her son. I know you will."

"Yes, ma'am, I can promise you that I'm already working on that problem with the State Department and it looks like we might get the child back sooner rather than later. You'll see, don't worry. I'll check in on you every day before I leave. Do what these fine nurses tell you now."

She smiles for the first time since I've met her. "Yes, Doctor, and I'm delighted Maud will have her little boy back in her arms soon. Tell her I'm looking forward to a visit as soon as she's able."

I give her hand a gentle squeeze. "You can be sure she will, especially when she has that baby back."

As I leave, a nurse hands me a note. Quent has called and requested I call him at the *Herald* as soon as possible. I find a telephone and put through the call. It takes a couple of minutes for the man who answers to find Quent, who sounds out of breath when he speaks into the horn.

"Henry, can you leave the hospital in half an hour?"

"I'm ready now."

"Okay!" His voice eager, full of adrenalin, he practically shouts down the line.

"I'll be by to pick you up in front of the hospital in twenty or thirty minutes."

"I'll be ready. See you then."

The late afternoon sun is warm and comforting when Quent comes roaring up in his shiny black Model T with the roof down. I toss my bags in the back seat and jump in, barely closing the door before the wheels are turning.

"What's going on?"

Quent looks over at me with clenched teeth in a big toothsome smile.

"Less than an hour ago, Newton Baker, new Secretary of War and a pacifist to boot, came out of a cabinet meeting with Woodrow Wilson and announced the United States is undertaking a Punitive Expedition against Pancho Villa in Mexico. Wilson is trying to throw Senator Fall enough red meat to keep him from stirring up a full-scale invasion of northern Mexico and at the same time assuring the Carrancistas that we're not invading Mexico, and that our sole purpose is to find Villa and his men and wipe 'em out.

"Most *Herald* reporters think that General Funston over in San Antonio will lead the forces goin' after Villa. Slater thinks Funston is too hotheaded and blunt-spoken to be runnin' around at the head of an army in Mexico, and that the Army's top commanders, old Hugh Scott and Tasker Bliss, will convince Mr. Baker that General Black Jack Pershing, who commands the 8th Brigade at Ft. Bliss, is the man for the job. Slater wants me to interview General Pershing at Ft. Bliss as soon as I can. If we're lucky we might even find out who's going to lead the expedition."

"What makes you think he'll talk to you?"

"I've already interviewed him twice and minded my manners about what I wrote. He thinks I'm a tame reporter. I just hope I don't persuade him otherwise if I get this interview."

The long shadows from the Franklin Mountains, their ridgeline glowing bright gold in the late afternoon sunlight, reach for the western edge of Ft. Bliss as we park at the commander's office. Young officers scurry in and out the doorway. Everywhere I look, everyone runs. Quent looks around, nodding. "I'd say Slater has it about right. Let's go see."

We step through the office door and confront a big, black desk behind which sits a ramrod straight lieutenant who's the gatekeeper to the doors behind him, one of which has a sign: *General John J. Pershing*. The sign on the desk reads *Lt. Martin C. Shallenberger*. We stand in front of the desk until Lieutenant Shallenberger looks up from his paperwork and says, "Gentlemen? What can I do for you?"

Quent hands Shallenberger his business card and motions toward me.

"I'm Quentin Peach, reporter for the *El Paso Herald* and this is Doctor Henry Grace, who is the State Department representative for Mrs. Maud Wright. We both know Villa well and have information that we believe will interest General Pershing."

Shallenberger raises his brow, and says in a slow, dismissive voice, as if he'd heard this line before, "I see. Well, General Pershing is very busy right now. Give me your information and I'll see he gets it."

Quent smiles at Shallenberger and shakes his head. "No, I don't think so. Just give my card to the general and tell him we're waiting to see him."

Shallenberger sighs and nods toward some chairs along the wall facing his desk. "Very well, have a seat, but you'll have to wait awhile."

We sit down in the chairs facing Shallenberger's desk as he puts Quent's card aside and returns to the paperwork on his desk. I steel myself for an interminable wait, wondering exactly what Quent thinks we know that might be of value to General Pershing.

We're not seated more than five minutes before Pershing's door opens and a lean, blond sinewy gentleman in his mid-fifties and wearing a big star on each side of his shirt collar appears. His face is lined and there's an air of sadness and loss about him that I recognize and instinctively understand. "Shallenberger! Get me the map of... " He sees Quent and smiles, "Mr. Peach, what are you doing here? I thought you'd be in Columbus with all the action."

"We've already been there and come back. General this is Doctor Henry Grace. He and Villa go way back. We've seen Villa up close and personal during the past six months and Doctor Grace is helping Mrs. Maud Wright get her little boy back. Villa kidnapped her on his way to Columbus and he made her leave the child behind. We think we can give you some information that might be of use to the Commander of the Punitive Expedition."

Pershing smiles, nods, and waves us into his office as he says, "Shallenberger, get me the map of Casas Grandes, Colonia Dublan area." Shallenberger snaps a quick salute and steps around the desk and out to the porch.

We sit down facing Pershing's big mahogany desk spilling over with maps and reports. Pershing, wearing riding boots, sits down straight in his big office chair and, looking us in the eye, doesn't waste a second getting to the point.

"What do you have?"

Quent gives him the most important information he learned from Maud during her interview with George Carothers and E.B. Stone. "Sir, according to Mrs. Wright, who Villa kidnapped from her ranch near Pearson about ten days before the raid on Columbus, Villa didn't use more than about five hundred men in the raid. She told me later that she had overheard one of them say most were from Namiquipa and initially recruited by General Nicolas Fernández for Villa's army."

Pershing, his right hand under his chin, scratches his jaw and listens intently. "Five hundred, you say? Colonel Slocum claims there were probably over two thousand men in on the Columbus raid. Do you dispute that number?"

Quent doesn't flinch from Pershing's rebuttal. "Sir, Mrs. Wright said the first day's rest she got was in Cave Valley about thirty miles from her ranch, and that there were about two thousand men there, but desertions were terrible as they marched north and she went all the way to Columbus with them. She said she stayed with the horse holders when Villa picked the men who went in on foot. She's very steady, very forthright in her statements. If anything, you'd think she might exaggerate the number of men since Villa executed her husband and a friend of the family, Frank Hayden, who was helping them get restarted in Mexico. If I had to choose, I'd believe her."

Pershing, the deep lines around his eyes growing deeper as he squints and gives a short, quick nod. "All right. What else?"

"His men are in terrible shape. According to Mrs. Wright, they're on the edge of starvation and running so low on ammunition they have to share bullets. However, I know from personal experience having covered him during the war with Díaz, that he has ammunition and guns buried all over Chihuahua, especially in the Sierra Madre, and that's probably where he'll head."

"That's consistent with reports my officers have prepared for me. Why did he attack Columbus? The reports say his men were searching for a Sam Ravel, who cheated him out of supplies."

Quent shakes his head. "Balancing accounts with Ravel was a secondary objective. Villa was the best friend the United States had in Mexico until President Wilson let Carrancistas take trains across the border to Douglas and march into Agua Prieta to defeat his forces. Villa swore after that, and Doctor Grace and I know this for a fact, we were with him at Agua Prieta, he'd never waste another bullet on a Mexican brother. He wants to use them all on *gringos*.

"Doctor Grace was with him and saw most of the remainder of *División del Norte* wiped out at Hermosillo. At Agua Prieta, anger at the US nearly drove Villa crazy. After Hermosillo, he slid off the deep end, executing anyone he thought might have connections with the *gringos*. Fortunately Doctor Grace got away and made his way back to the United States. My opinion is Villa wants to start a war with the United States that will turn the Mexicans against Carranza and put him at the head of an army to fight the invaders."

Pershing listens carefully to all we can tell him about Villa's mental state and what we think he might do next. We talk for the next fifteen or twenty minutes before Lt. Shallenberger knocks on the door with the maps Pershing wants. Pershing waves him in with the maps and then waves him out.

"Gentleman, you've given me some very useful information, more in fact than my intelligence staff has been able to provide about Villa and his capabilities in the last year. It would be very helpful if you came along with me. Doctor Grace, I can always use your medical help along with your insights on Villa. Mr. Peach, I'd trust you as my lead correspondent. What do you say?"

Quent smiles. "Sir, is it safe to assume that you've been given command of the Punitive Expedition to find and destroy Pancho Villa?"

Pershing's thin line of a mouth, reminding me of Yellow Boy's, quivers on the edge of a smile. "That is a safe assumption, Mr. Peach."

"Then, sir, I'll be joining you.'

"Good. Just be sure any newspaper reports you file, you run them by me first, understood?"

"Yes, sir, I wouldn't have it any other way."

Pershing raises his brows. "And you, Doctor Grace, can I count on you also?"

"General Pershing, I have some personal business I have to take care of first. I'll join you later in Mexico if you like."

He leans back in his chair to study me a moment. "Very well. Come when you can. Gentlemen, if you'll excuse me, I have a lot of work to do. Mr. Peach, we'll leave Columbus and cross the border on the fifteenth of March. Come by here tomorrow and Mr. Shallenberger will have papers for you and Doctor Grace that will give you access to me wherever the Army goes in Mexico. If you learn anything more before we advance, please let me know."

We shake hands with Pershing and leave the commander's office under Lt. Shallenberger's curious stare.

47. WHEN JOHNNIE COMES MARCHING HOME

Maud and I sit on a bench in the shade of the Juarez train station platform. We're practically alone except for a few pigeons cooing in the eves of the roof over us, and two men in tan uniforms who pace the station's perimeter with rifles on their shoulders. A Carrancista colonel and a squad of soldiers have come early and run off everyone in the station except a local photographer, Maud, and me.

She stares, as if in a trance, down the long, shiny steel rails curving away toward the east. Her right heel taps a rapid tattoo, reminding me of a fast train clicking off the miles as it rolls down the tracks.

The past five days have been a nightmare. The Department of State and the Carranza government haggle over every little detail of Johnnie's transfer to ensure that the Carrancistas keep their word in returning Maud's little boy, that they receive proper international recognition for their good deed, and that they won't let Villistas steal the child again. My brief service to the State Department convinces me I'll never, ever serve in the diplomatic corps.

A sporadic wind, blowing puffs of sand that land between the rails to hide oil-spattered track ties, increases the morning chill. Maud's friends in El Paso have helped her find clothes to replace the ones Mrs. Slocum lent her. Her plain wool skirt reaching to the top of her brown brogans, knee-length corduroy coat, blue turban hat with a stylish bow on the side, and kid leather gloves fit her well and keep her warm. She can walk now without limping, and the lower part of her face and neck, once red and ruddy, have faded to a nice tan.

I check my watch.

"The train's not due for another half hour. Can I get you anything? Maybe a burrito and coffee?"

The steady tap of her brogan stops. She turns her sad, gray eyes to me. "Henry, you're very kind, but no, thank you, all I want is Johnnie back."

"He'll be fine. Sit back and try to relax a little before the train comes."

She leans out and takes another look down the tracks, and, slumping against the bench, jams her hands deep in her coat pockets. Another dust devil whirls out of the far creosotes, wobbles crazily across the tracks for a few seconds and disappears. The rising wind, trying to work itself into a dust-filled, all-day blow, makes the platform roof shudder and groan as if a giant hand pulls and shakes it.

Her eyes find me again. "You said in Columbus that Villa betrayed you. How did you ever know him well enough to call him friend or to trust him?"

"I'll answer your question if you'll answer mine first."

She frowns. "What?"

"After you were kidnapped, did you see a man wearing a bright red shirt around Villa?"

She crosses her arms, and cupping her chin with her right hand, taps her right index finger in a thoughtful beat against her cheek.

"Why, yes, I did. He served as some sort of scout and, unlike most of the soldiers, rode a good horse. He'd disappear for hours, and reappear out of the creosotes and mesquite to talk to Villa while they rode along together. Villa never stopped. Somehow he kept that mule going, never stopping. When Red Shirt talked to him, I couldn't hear what was said, but I saw Villa nodding or shaking his head, and then motioning in a particular direction, and away Red Shirt went.

"I liked Red Shirt. He acted like a perfect gentleman and did kind things for me. I complained to him about Castillo. I thought he was some kind of officer. He asked Villa to reassign Castillo and he did. Yes, I remember the man in the red shirt very well. Do you know him?"

It's my turn to stare off down the tracks, thinking, *so Villa didn't kill Roja after I got away.* I wonder what Roja told him about my escape. I'm glad he's still with Villa. Hunting them down separately might have taken years.

Maud's voice filters back into my consciousness. "Henry? Are you still with us? How do you know the man in the red shirt?"

I puff out my cheeks, blow, and lean back beside her. "Ten years ago, the man his friends call Camisa Roja, Red Shirt, killed my wife and unborn child."

Maud catches her breath and puts her fingers over her mouth as she whispers, "Oh, Henry, I'm so sorry."

"I wanted to kill him, but my uncle, Yellow Boy, said I'd gain no power if I did because my wife looked like a man from the distance he shot her, and that he killed her trying to protect his *patrón's hacienda*. I thought about it for a while and deferred to my uncle's judgment, although many times in the dim light of dreams, I see her and the times we had together and wish to God I had somehow avenged her, but I left him alone.

"I came back from medical school last year and hung out my shingle in Las Cruces. One evening in September there's a knock on my door and there stands Camisa Roja bigger than life, bandoliers across his chest, the big Winchester he used to kill my wife in the crook of his arm, and having no idea what he'd done or that I wanted to kill him. I didn't recognize him at first. He said Villa wanted to talk to Yellow Boy and me and had sent him to fetch us. We owed Villa a favor, so we went."

"Why would you do Villa a favor?"

"He saved our lives."

"How?"

"He killed a grizzly bear with a Bowie knife before the monster ripped us to pieces. We knew him as Doroteo Arango in those days. When he sent Roja for us, it gave us an opportunity to pay our debt and we were glad to do it."

"What did he want you to do?" She leaned forward, looking in my eyes, eager to know.

"He wanted us to find Quent, you remember my friend the reporter in Columbus, and bring him to a meeting at Villa's camp in the Sierra San Luis just south of the New Mexico border, and to ask Sam Ravel where were the supplies he'd ordered. So, I went to Columbus and talked to Ravel about cheating Villa and to El Paso to bring him Quent for a talk."

"Why did Villa want to see a newspaper reporter?"

"Publicity. He wanted Quent at Agua Prieta to watch *División del Norte* wipe out the Carrancistas in a big successful battle and report the story in the *Herald*. Villa believed a good newspaper story might cause Woodrow Wilson to realize that *División del Norte* was the better army and recognize him as First *Jefe* rather than Carranza, or at least not publically favor Carranza.

"At that meeting, after listening to Villa tell Quent how he had to rid Mexico of yet another dictator, stop *peon* exploitation, and do what was right for Mexico, Yellow Boy and I joined the *División del Norte* march over the Sierra Madre to take Agua Prieta. Those soldiers marched through unbelievable hardships by the sheer force of Villa's charisma and their determination to stand with him.

"What that army did was truly remarkable. They started out short of supplies, barely enough to get them across the Sierras, expecting to resupply from the big ranches along the Rio Bavispe. After they crossed the mountains into the Bavispe Valley barely alive without food or water, they found nothing. The *Revolución* had already stripped the big *ranchos* in Sonora down to nothing. Villa's army couldn't live off the land like they had three years before. They probably had less food and water crossing the *sierras* than the men who kidnapped you. It didn't make any difference. They marched all the way to Agua Prieta and fought General Plutarco Calles, who sat behind his two-mile trench lined with artillery and machine guns and a forty-foot wide, coiled barbed wire barricade.

"By the time *División del Norte* marched to Agua Prieta, Wilson let Carranza ship soldiers and supplies across the southern edges of New Mexico and Arizona to reinforce Agua Prieta. Villa was outraged, and rightly so, claimed the *gringos* had betrayed him after all the support he gave Americans living in Mexico during the Díaz *Revolución*. I firmly believe Wilson as President of the United States, betrayed Villa by choosing Carranza as First *Jefe* and by supporting him after claiming the US neutral in the civil war between Villa and Carranza. Villa vowed revenge against the *gringos* and I suppose part of the Columbus raid was payback, but it's my opinion Villa hopes the Columbus raid will start a US war with Mexico where he can ride to the rescue with a new army."

Maud shakes her head. "So President Wilson's choice of Mexico's First *Jefe* and his betrayal of Villa got me kidnapped and separated from my little son, and my husband and our friend murdered?"

"I'm afraid so."

She sighs and studies the ugly brown mountains west of Juarez.

"Wars truly are things of darkness, aren't they? We blindly stumble through them tryin' to right wrongs, always creatin' new ones, killin' tens of thousands because of the passions and charisma of a few men, and vowin' revenge against those who believe they're actin' honorably. This war between Villa and Carranza isn't even a war between nations, it's a war of egos, like a couple of half-grown men fightin' over a woman, and yet it's stolen my child and killed my husband."

She turns to stare in my eyes.

"Why? Where is the right in any of it? Ed and I tried to do the right thing. We treated both sides in the Revolution the same. We fed and gave water to any man, and his animals, that came to our door thirsty and hungry. We just wanted to build our ranch and be left alone, but we still had to leave and come back. We hadn't been back a month before Villa took us. When does it end, Henry? When?"

I shrug, knowing I'll never be able to answer such questions. "I don't know. You're right: wars are things of darkness, but they can also be tools that right wrongs that have been around for a long time. Wars, like axes, are sometimes used when a scalpel ought to do, but axes have their use. Villa lost his way and betrayed the very people for whom he fought. He's murdered innocents, including your husband and friend and very nearly you and Johnnie, for no other reason than the blind hate he now has for *gringos*. I just know that even in times of darkness, debts are paid, justice is done, and wrongs are righted."

I'll never forget the desperate look in her eyes, the frustration in her voice, and the breeze flipping and shaking the bow tails on her turban.

"It has to end, Henry. Somehow, it just has to end."

Off in the distance we hear a train whistle. Staring down the tracks, Maud springs to her feet and I'm right behind her. The Carrancista colonel, smoking a *cigarro*, hears the whistle too, and struts to the center of the platform, thumbs hooked in his shiny brown belt, looking smugly pleased, the photographer standing not far behind him.

An engine pulling several passenger cars, its black smoke scattered by the shifting wind, appears in the curve of the tracks and swings down the long straight stretch, steaming straight for us. Maud, biting on her lower lip, stares at it, her hands, in front of her breasts, pressed together as if she's praying.

Five passenger cars trail behind the engine and coal tender as they slow, creeping past the station platform until the engine stops with the middle car even with the colonel. Soldiers streaming from the passenger cars, their rifles held ready in front of them, form a shoulder-to-shoulder guard detail around the platform.

Maud's eyes dart from window to window, searching for her son.

When the soldiers are in place, the colonel steps forward and waves a come-out motion toward the middle car. A conductor appears and drops a walkway between the car's back steps and the station platform.

Time seems to momentarily stand still, and then I hear Maud gasp and croak in a tear-filled whisper, "Thank you, dear God."

A middle-aged Mexican woman, a shawl over her shoulders and wearing a threadbare, faded red skirt reaching to her sandaled feet, appears on the walkway. Against her shoulder she carries a small, blanket-wrapped, child who wears a blue stocking cap and turns his head from side-to-side, curious and unafraid, as he surveys all the strange faces.

Her black, gray-streaked hair tied back in a bun, the woman, appearing old far beyond her years, looks around, sees Maud, grins broadly, and pointing toward her, whispers something to the child, who pushes back from her shoulders and twists in her arms. Seeing Maud, he lets out a squeal of delight, yells, "Mama, Mama," and stretches his arms out to her. Every man in the station smiles. I hear the colonel mutter, "Every *niño* knows his *madre*."

Maud, crying and saying, "*Muchas gracias*, Maria," over and over, takes giggling Johnnie and hugs Maria. She leans back, looking at him in her arms, and hugs him close as he throws his arms around her neck. The colonel turns to me and says in respectable border English, "*Por favor*, Doctor Grace. Take the *madre* and her *niño* inside the station and verify he is healthy and well-cared for so we can take the *fotograpía* to satisfy our governments that they are happily reunited."

We go inside the station waiting room. I examine Johnnie while Maud and Maria watch, whispering to each other, laughing, and making Johnnie giggle with their happiness. He's in perfect health and I tell that to the colonel, who smiles and nods. He motions the photographer to set up his camera. In a few minutes, he takes several exposures of Maud with Johnnie in her arms, both with big smiles. The colonel and I give the photographer instructions about where and to whom to send the pictures on both sides of the border, and then pay him. Maud and I sign several documents for the colonel, releasing Johnnie into Maud's care and certifying he has been delivered to her on the day promised and in good health.

The colonel shakes hands with me, clicks his heels and gives a quick, little bow from the waist like some European martinet.

"*Muchas gracias, Señora* Wright and Doctor Grace. The government of Mexico wishes for you a long and productive life. *Adiós*."

He turns to step out the door when Maud says, "*Colonel, un momento, por favor*."

He turns to look at her, a now-what frown on his face.

She steps over by the colonel and speaks Spanish near his ear in a voice so low only he can understand her. He nods, and when she finishes, says, "*Si, señora*, it will be done." With that, he salutes and steps out the door, ordering his men aboard the train, yelling, "*Vamos, hombres!*"

All this time Maria sits on the bench where Maud and I had waited for the train. Maud walks out to the platform with Johnnie, hugs her again and has a few words with her. Maria breaks into a big smile and hugs her, saying, "*Oh gracias, señora, muchas, muchas gracias.*" The colonel motions her to hurry. She tears herself away from Maud, waving good-by, and climbs on the train as it begins creeping out of the station.

I offer to carry Johnnie as we walk to my borrowed Model-T, but Maud just laughs. "I've waited on Johnnie too long to give him over now."

Curiosity circles my brain. "It's none of my business, and don't feel obligated to tell me anything, but what did you tell the colonel just before he left?"

She scrunches her shoulders and says, "I don't mind telling you, just don't spread it around. There's nothing left for me in Mexico except Ed's bones. I told the colonel I wanted Maria and her family to have what was left of our ranch. When Fernández kidnapped me I gave Johnnie to her, and she brought him safe and sound back to me. I told the colonel where to send any papers that needed signing and I'd sign them. You saw him assure me that he would see to it. You're my witness."

I laugh, feeling better than I have in a long time at such a fine act of generosity. I open the T-Model door for her and say, "Yes, ma'am. I'm your witness any time you need one."

I drive Maud and Johnnie back to her friend's big Victorian house just off Stanton Street in El Paso. They've fixed her a room and told her to please stay as long as she can. At the curb I help her out, we hug good-by, I swing Johnnie, giggling, high in the air before giving him a kiss on the cheek on the way to his mother's waiting arms. I promise to come for a visit when I return from Mexico.

Maud's eyes are sparkling and happy as she says, "Henry, that's a promise I'll expect you to keep."

I stop by Hotel Dieu Hospital to visit Susan Moore. Her wounds are healing, but with the bullet still in her hip, she finds it very hard to walk and she's still having nightmares about her husband's death and her narrow escape. Based on my experience seeing my father murdered and escaping by the thinnest of margins from being murdered myself, I know she's going to have bad dreams for a long time.

She asks, "When will you return to visit me again?"

I shrug my shoulders. "I don't know, maybe a long time. I have debts to pay and I may have a long ride to pay them. I promise I'll check on you as soon as I can when I return."

Nodding, she says, "I'm planning to make a go of what is left of the store John and I ran in Columbus. I know it'll be hard because I can't move around too much, but if I can find some good help, maybe I'll make it." There are tears at the edges of her eyes as she says, "Thank you again, and please take care of yourself, wherever you go."

I give her hand a little squeeze. "I will. Good luck with the store. I'll be back as soon as I can. *Adiós.*"

She smiles and waves as I leave.

By the time I brief George Carothers on Johnnie's return and tie up loose ends with the Department of State, it's late afternoon. I take a cab to the train station, expecting to wait several hours before I can catch the next train to Columbus, but the Army is shipping so much materiel west, a train leaves nearly every hour. I manage to get a seat on the next one. Exhausted, I ask the conductor to wake me at Columbus and pulling my hat over my eyes, spiral into the depths of sleep unbothered by ghosts or jaguars.

48. PELO ROJO'S CAMP

I first look for Yellow Boy at Sweeny Jones' tent. From the sentry's guard post, I can see Satanas, Yellow Boy's paint, and our two pack mules under the Army horse shelters near the tent. Finding Yellow Boy after sundown will be easier than I expected. In the lights around the camp there is a sense of abandonment. No other horses and mules crowd under the shelter with our horses and mules, and no men except the sentries move anywhere.

The guard lets me pass and not fifty yards from the horse shelter, I see a figure wrapped in blankets by the coals of a small fire. I smile. If he's sleeping, it's a golden opportunity to pay back my uncle for those times he made me jump by appearing like a ghost out of nowhere. I creep forward, careful not to scrape by a bush, kick a pebble, or step on a stick. I'm within ten feet of him when he sits up in his blankets, his old single-action Army revolver cocked and pointed at my middle. I freeze, hold up my hands palms out to show they are empty, and hear the hammer on the revolver ease down.

"Hombrecito! You sound like wild horses thundering through the camp. Take coffee and meat for your belly and warm yourself by the fire. Come."

He stokes up the fire, puts on the coffee and stew pots, and sits back on his heels waiting to hear my story while I go for my gear I left with the guard. When I return, I speak of meeting the big *gringo* Army chief and of what happened to Maud Wright and Susan Moore in El Paso.

Yellow Boy nods. "Hmmph. Some warriors carry bullets in legs many years. No walk good. Bullet no kill or make loco, makes warrior stronger, power greater." He pauses and looks at the weave and woof of the flickering fire. "Some die. Some live."

He tells me about the Punitive Expedition leaving.

"This day many soldiers go to Mexico. Many horses, many iron wagons, soldiers call 'em *truck*, go into Mexico. Man birds, soldiers call Jenny, they fly into Mexico. Many guns go into Mexico, all after Arango." He shakes his head. "*Gringos* waste many days. Arango too smart, too long live with Apaches. *Gringos* no catch. Maybe Hombrecito and Yellow Boy no catch. We Apaches. Know desert. Know *sierras*. No lose tracks. Maybe still no catch Arango."

I take a swallow of his hot bitter coffee and say, "Do you still think it's best to stay at Pelo Rojo's camp until we learn Villa's whereabouts?"

Studying the fire, he nods. "*Sí*. Wait in Pelo Rojo's camp. Find Arango more easy if we wait there. Maybe we lucky, maybe Arango come to Pelo Rojo, maybe not. Pelo Rojo scouts find Arango and army pretty soon now."

Excitement stirs in my core. "When do you want to go?"

"Go now. Better ride night time, easier miss *gringo* army."

Confused, I frown. How can we run into the *gringo* army when it's already left and heading south for Casas Grandes when we'll be riding west?

"Peach say *gringo* Star Chief has two armies. One leaves this place today. Another leaves maybe tonight from Culbertson *rancho* off to west. Columbus army joins *rancho* army at Casas Grandes. Peach goes with Star Chief. He leaves tonight."

When I frown at the name Star Chief, Yellow Boy rubs the edge of his coat collar between his thumb and forefinger. I think, *Ah, yes. Pershing, a brigadier general, wears a big gold star on each side of his collar.*

Yellow Boy says, "Before he leaves, Peach tells me come quick. Help Army chase Villa to ground. I say to Peach, 'Hombrecito comes today. We go to Sierras, keep promise he makes then find army, all go home.' Peach, he laugh. *Comprende* what I mean."

I eat while Yellow Boy packs the mules with the load of supplies he's brought from Mescalero for Rojo's camp. The cold night air makes every breath look like a puff of smoke and makes me shiver and stand close to the fire while changing clothes. In an hour we head west. A waxing, gibbous moon fills the rolling desert with soft white light and paints inky black shadows around the yuccas and mesquite. Yellow Boy closely following the same trail that leads to Hatchita, points us toward the dark mountains in the distance, barely outlined against the stars in the moonlight.

We ride all night, stopping at ranch tanks to water the

animals and near dawn find a place in a mesquite thicket to rest in the shade for the day. The second night Yellow Boy picks his way up familiar canyons on the Bonito River, and, just as the sky turns to a delicate shade of gray, we ride up a familiar trail to a plateau on top of a ridge in the middle of the Sierra Espuelas.

The eastern sky is turning an angry red, and far to the north we can barely see the tops of the Animas Mountains just above the rolling mountains surrounding us. Yellow Boy, raising his rifle over his head three times, stops in sight of a tall rock outcropping that looks like some gigantic finger pushing out of the earth, surrounded by boulder size marbles. A nightjar answers *tup to to tu tu ti ti trridip* in sharp chirps that rise to a flourish out of the trees on the eastern side of the ridge. Yellow Boy waves me forward.

Memories from my first trip to the top of this ridge when I was about fourteen flood my mind: the sun floating up over the horizon, a big, blood-red ball squashed down at the top and bottom; mountains spreading out around us in every direction; the Animas Mountain tops in the distance; a line of trees crowding up slope on the far side of the ridge; and the thin rawhide rope running from the top of the rock finger into the brush and trees on the other side of the ridge. Yellow Boy stops when we're directly under the rope and speaks Apache in a low, but easy-to-hear voice. "Who watches? Muchacho Amarillo and Hombrecito bring gifts to our brothers in Pelo Rojo's band."

Long auburn hair so dark it's nearly black in the new sunlight frame wide doe-like eyes peering over the rock finger top. "I am Ojos Verde, daughter of Rojo. It has been many seasons since Muchacho Amarillo and Hombrecito find Rojo's camp. Rojo's heart will be glad when he sees you." Ojos Verde waves her hand toward the trees on the eastern side of the ridge. "Go!"

Yellow Boy waves his rifle in salute. "You guard the camp well, daughter of Rojo!"

We follow the rope on a path off into thick Emory and blue oaks, pines, juerga trees, and squawberry bushes. A large corral from the old days, hidden well back in the trees, still stands. The first time I saw it, fourteen or fifteen years earlier, it held maybe ten horses and mules, and there were the three smaller pens connected to it holding several cows and a few calves. Now it holds nothing and it doesn't appear to have been used for a long time. The leather rope we follow passes across the tops of brush and trees and ends tied to the flapper of an old church bell hung between two notched posts. It's a clever warning system. If the lookout pulls the rawhide rope when intruders approach, the bell rings and gives the villagers at the bottom of the canyon warning to scatter or prepare to fight.

We follow the trail through the trees down the side of the ridge, and can hear the faintest sound of water flowing at the bottom of the ridge. The air near the canyon's bottom is moist and chilly. Water burbles over rocks in a wide, slow creek strewn with big, smooth boulders, reminding me of giant eggs. Wisps of ghostly morning fog float across shafts of sunlight, beaming like searchlights through the tops of the trees. A sunbeam passing through a notch in the ridges reflects off the creek to cast random spots of yellow light that dance on the trees and canyon cliff walls.

We splash across the creek, turning downstream for a couple of hundred yards until we reach a bench covered with trees and brush a few feet above the creek, its surface a lazy mirror moving with barely a ripple. The bench is maybe three hundred yards long and fifty yards wide, reaching halfway across the canyon from the eastern wall. Sycamore and cottonwood trees and heavy brush line the edge of the shelf, making it look impenetrable. We ride up onto the bench, following a narrow, hard-to-see trail at its far end.

The trail up on to the bench leads past sycamore, ash, walnut, and maple saplings until we come to the edge of the camp, all but invisible from only a few yards away. Even smoke from the cooking fires can't be seen in the morning mists, and it's eerie not to hear any village sounds. No dogs bark. No children yell at play. No mule brays or horse snorts. You don't hear nor see anything suggesting human activity until you literally walk into the camp's clearing. Women prepare meals at fire pits that hold beds of glowing hot coals producing little smoke. A few men lounging near the doors of their lodges speak in soft voices to visiting friends. Brown-faced children with jet-black hair play without making a sound. Babies, waiting to be fed, strapped to carry boards, take in everything around them without the slightest complaint.

Ten brush wickiups, just like fifteen years before, form an outer perimeter closest to the creek and blend perfectly with the surrounding brush. Six appear to have occupants. They face five small cabins with walls five or six feet high made of flat river rocks mortared with mud. They cluster together toward the back of the nearly vertical canyon wall on the eastern side and near the center of the camp. Two circular cabins, the largest one was about fifteen feet in diameter, the other maybe twelve feet in diameter, stand out from the other three stonewall lodges, rectangular and about six feet wide by eight feet deep.

I remember the first time I saw them I thought they looked strange. It took me a while to realize that their walls didn't have sharp, ninety-degree corners. Each wall literally curves into the other, making them harder than normal to distinguish from the natural rock and brush background. In both the circular and rectangular lodges, the walls support a roof of poles tied together and covered with canvas, hides, brush, or some combination of all three. These lodges stand as solid as any adobe house.

Everyone stares at us. Several groups of two or three men each approach. Some wear classic desert moccasins with rawhide soles and leg shafts long enough to reach their knees, long white breechcloths, shirts, and vests. Others wear pieces of Mexican Army uniforms the women have reworked to be more comfortable. Most of the men pull their smooth black hair back with red and blue patterned bandanas, but two or three wear ancient cavalry hats and one or two dusty, brown Stetsons.

I scan their faces, wondering if Villa or some of his men have arrived already, but see no Mexicans or Americans. On my first trip fifteen years earlier I was surprised to find them here; now it seems odd without them. There were three Mexicans in the camp that first trip, and they reminded me of lean, hungry wolves. Two armed with old trap-door rifles also carried two or three revolvers each, and the bandoliers across their chests held long, buffalo-gun cartridges. The third Mexican stood taller than the other two. He wore a short jacket over an old-time, blue gambler's vest and shiny, black cavalry boots polished until they reflected light like mirrors. A long-barreled revolver in a plain holster carried on a belt filled with cartridges hung from his hip. When he smiled under his big black moustache, his eyes sparkled with welcoming good humor. His name was Doroteo Arango, the same man now called General Francisco Villa.

The Americans in those days, like the Mexicans, hid from the law or wanted to buy stolen cattle from Pelo Rojo. Two Americans were camped here the first time I came and one of them, Rafaela, a woman dressed like a cowboy, became my wife. Her former lover, who brought her to the camp, turned out to be the craziest man I've ever known, but he truly loved her in his sick, perverted way.

The Sierra Madre Apaches then were a mix of Indians, Mexicans, and Anglos, all hard men living a hard life, and it took a strong man to keep them together, the redheaded Apache, Pelo Rojo, more commonly called, *Rojo,* or depending on how bad your Spanish was, sometimes, *Roja.*

When we enter the camp, Rojo stands up from his place in front of the largest circular stonewall lodge and comes to meet us. His long red hair shows streaks of gray falling from under an old, battered pork pie Stetson pulled down to his eyebrows, but he still dresses in the classic Apache style of long breechcloth and knee-high moccasins. I'm surprised at how much he's aged.

Average height for an American, but tall for an Apache, and though he's in his early fifties, his big, corded muscles still make his shirtsleeves ripple when he crosses his arms. Nothing escapes his brown eyes that study everything about you and stare at your soul. It never takes long for all who meet him to grasp his potential for being a bad enemy or a strong friend.

An American child, taken as a baby, Apaches kidnapped Rojo during an eighteen-seventies raid on a miner's camp near Pino Altos in New Mexico. Juh, Geronimo's close friend, raised him. Juh's women thought Rojo's red hair was very beautiful, a special gift from White Painted Woman, and they took special care of him. The Mexicans called him *Pelo Rojo*, Red Hair, but Juh's wives, not the best of Spanish speakers, called him Roja because they thought it sounded better, and some still called him that. Juh, a great warrior, taught him how to make war, hunt, find strength from his heart, and to be a good leader who always put the needs of the People before his own. Rojo grew to be strong and powerful among the Sierra Madre bands and led many raids against Mexicans and Yaquis, but he never raided north of the border, never fought his own people.

Rojo steps up to our horses and spreads his arms, speaking in Apache with a big grin covering his hard face slashed with many wrinkles. "Welcome Muchacho Amarillo and Hombrecito. Many seasons pass since you are here. Hombrecito returns a grown man, his arms strong, his eyes clear. Our camp is your camp as it has always been so and will remain."

Yellow Boy slides off his pony and raises his rifle in salute. "Rojo, friend, it is good to be back in your lodges and again with the People. We bring gifts and supplies from your brothers in Mescalero. Hombrecito has studied the medicine of the White Eye. He brings healing power to the People. We will help the People while we stay. Is there a lodge for Muchacho Amarillo and Hombrecito?"

Rojo speaks more for the crowd's benefit than for us. "We feast your return and presents and supplies. The women will prepare a lodge for you and the young men will take care of your ponies and mules. Come! Let us eat and speak together."

The men return to their smokes and conversation; children begin new games, and the women return to their cooking fires, scooping up their babies as they go. Boys unsaddle and unload the horses and pack mules and lead them to a small corral at the southern end of the camp. Yellow Boy asks the boys to feed our animals from the grain sacks on the pack frames and to rub them down with handfuls of grass.

A young woman leads us to our lodge, one of the little rectangular stone cabins a couple of places down from Rojo's lodge. The roof is covered with canvas, and, like the other lodges, it stands in excellent condition. We store our gear, and then bathe in the creek, its water cold and bracing.

Rojo lights his pipe with a twig from the fire when Yellow Boy and I sit down with him. His wife gives us bowls of meat stew she has bubbling over the fire pit. She fries thin patties of corn meal bread and flips them for us to catch with our fingers and stuff in our cheeks while we eat, the hot grease running down our chins. I've never eaten better anywhere.

We eat our fill, belch our appreciation, and sit back, studying the camp and sipping a cup of strong jojoba coffee. Cool, morning breezes sweep down the canyon and sunlight filtering through the trees makes our shirts feel warm and pleasant on our shoulders.

My head fills with questions, anxious to learn what Rojo knows about Villa. But sly Yellow Boy takes the indirect way and breaks the easy silence to ask a more obvious question, "Where are the camp's warriors? On a raid? Hunting for meat? San Carlos trading for horses?"

Rojo, taking a long draw from his pipe and blowing the smoke toward the treetops, leans his head against a hand and looks at us with sad rheumy eyes. His forearm and hand, palm down, swing an arc parallel to the ground.

"Gone, wiped out. In war between the Mexicans the great *hacendado* herds disappeared. Both sides wanted the meat and took the cattle at every opportunity; the *hacendados* gave every *peon* a rifle and taught him to fight, to shoot other Mexicans, to shoot any Indian. Meat became harder and harder to find, and the *peon* soldiers defended the remaining cattle well. The warriors wanted and needed bullets in the soldier wagons.

"I tell the warriors to wait and watch, wait and watch like a hunter for the deer. They do not listen. Soldiers on the wagons, especially the iron wagons, have shoot-many-times guns, very fast, one gun like fifty soldiers. We cannot raid these wagons without losing many warriors. Hunger in the eyes of a man's woman and children makes him a fool. Shoot-many-times guns wipe out many warriors who do not listen to Rojo. Now we stay in the mountains, let the Mexicans kill each other. We only hunt for our meat. Many women who lose their husbands go to San Carlos, sit in the dust and eat the weevil-filled bread the White Eyes give them. Other women ask to be warriors like Hombrecito's woman. Now we have little. It is the time before the season of many leaves. The supplies you bring help us much."

Yellow Boy crosses his arms and looks around the camp. It has the same number of lodges when we were here before, but fully half the men are gone and maybe a quarter of the women. "*Americanos* and Mexican *banditos* no longer come to join you?"

Rojo draws deeply on his pipe, making its coal glow bright. "Sometimes maybe a few of Arango's men come. Want cattle. We don't have them. Want to trade ponies. We don't trade." Yellow Boy frowns. Rojo explains. "Arango ponies not even fit to eat. Covered with sores, ribs show. No meat." Rojo looks to one side and spits in contempt. "Good horses now hard to find. Arango's men ruin many. Ride too far, too hard, don't rest, and give little feed. No feed horse, soon no horse, no ride, no meat."

Yellow Boy scratches his chin and says, "Hombrecito and Muchacho Amarillo want to find Arango. You see him since one moon?"

Rojo shakes his head. "No. No see. Scouts no see since time of falling leaves. Remember Runs Far?"

Yellow Boy nods but says nothing.

"Runs Far and two women scout south in season of falling leaves. Return after two moons. Runs Far says Villa moves army through El Paso Púlpito toward Oaxaca. Runs Far and women say Villa army has no supplies. There is nothing to take except worn-out horses. In south they find nothing, no cattle, no mules, no horses. Runs Far even loses own horse, returns on woman's horse."

Yellow Boy purses his lips and asks, "Where is Runs Far now? No see in camp."

Rojo takes a puff from his pipe. "Runs Far and women scout east and south of *sierras*. Return in maybe ten suns. Maybe bring news of Arango when they return."

Yellow Boy nods. "Maybe so. Arango runs south from big *gringo* army. Needs supplies, place to hide. Maybe comes here, maybe attacks and takes supplies."

Rojo shakes his head. "Arango will not attack camp. We

sit together one day at Colonia Dublan moons after Mormons leave. I ask if he will attack the camp of Rojo. Arango laughs, says no. No attack any Apache camp as long as the Apaches leave his army alone. He says he needs scouts for his army. He pays with guns and cattle. I say each warrior can decide. Arango, he says he understands. We are friends for many years. He says to stay clear of Mexican army soldiers. They kill Apaches or make slaves. Arango speaks true.

"Now warriors spend many more days hunting than scouting. I keep close guard of camp. I hear many stories of Arango fights with other Mexicans. The stories say he loses many men. In last season of falling leaves I worry. Maybe he tries to wipe us out, take our winter supplies, use Apache camps in season of the Ghost Dance, use Rojo's camp. Maybe he speaks lies at Colonia Dublan. We watch close. Stay ready to fight, but Arango does not come.

"Muchacho Amarillo and Hombrecito, why do you look for Arango?"

I know Yellow Boy will not lie, but with the treaty Rojo has with Villa, I don't think it's prudent to tell him we're after Villa. Rojo might decide we have to leave to ensure we don't endanger his camp. Villa might very well try to wipe out Rojo's camp if he knows we came after him from here. *It's better*, I think, *to only tell Rojo that I'm after Camisa Roja and not Villa too. Isn't half a truth better than a complete lie?* I've thought like a White Eye for too long.

Yellow Boy looks Rojo straight in the eye. "Hombrecito and Muchacho Amarillo look for Arango and the *hombre* Camisa Roja. There is a debt of blood and they will pay it."

I think, *Oh, no. This is going to get ugly.*

Rojo doesn't blink. "What is this debt?"

Yellow Boy takes his time, pulling a cigar from his shirt and lighting up. When the cigar's ash is glowing orange-red, he says, "Rojo remembers Arango saving Muchacho Amarillo and Hombrecito from the great bear. We owe Arango our lives for many seasons. Arango sends Camisa Roja to find Hombrecito and Muchacho Amarillo in the last season of falling leaves. Arango asks our help. It makes our hearts glad to at last pay this debt of life and we do as he asks. The debt is paid.

"Hombrecito and Muchacho Amarillo see Arango needs men and supplies. We tell him we will help in his fight with the other Mexicans. Hombrecito helps Arango's medicine men. Arango is glad for our help. We are like his brothers. He moves army over Sierras through El Paso Púlpito before snow. This you know from Runs Far."

Rojo nods, never taking his eyes off Yellow Boy.

Yellow Boy takes a long draw from his acrid black cigar and blows the smoke toward the fire pit.

"Arango army goes to Agua Prieta on border west, beyond Valley of San Bernardino River. He thinks taking Agua Prieta will be easy, but the *gringos* help his Mexican enemies. At Agua Prieta, Arango is a fool. He does not think. Arango tells his warriors to charge ropes filled with thorns in front of shoot-many-times guns. Same guns kill Rojo's warriors. Many Arango soldiers are wiped out. Arango goes loco. Blames *gringos* for every loss. No more thinks of his warriors. His pride kills many. My belly fills with this foolishness. I leave. Help Arango no more. Hombrecito stays. He will not leave Arango's soldiers. Arango loses nearly all soldiers. Same thing happens in every battle; soldiers charge guns and thorn ropes. Many soldiers and horses die. Arango grows more *loco*.

"No more soldiers, no more fights, Arango returns east over mountains with only a few warriors. On way east Arango kills men and boys and Mexican priest protecting their village. Hombrecito tries to stop Arango. No good. Arango tells Hombrecito to leave. Tells Camisa Roja to kill Hombrecito out of sight of his soldiers. Hombrecito gets away. Hombrecito swears debt of blood against Arango and Camisa Roja. I come with Hombrecito to pay this debt. Before we come to border, Arango attacks *gringo* town, Columbus, north of border. Now big *gringo* army chases Arango. Arango and warriors maybe come to Pelo Rojo Camp to hide. We find Arango and Camisa Roja first?" He makes a slashing movement with his fingers across his throat.

Rojo crosses his arms and leans back to study us. He takes a few more puffs on his pipe and then knocks its ashes against his palm before tossing them into the fire pit. "Arango is a *tigre loco*. You kill. I help. The word of a *hombre loco* is no good. Today I send out more scouts, find Arango and this *hombre*, Camisa Roja. Wait until they find him and come back. Then you go."

Yellow says, "*Muchas gracias*, Rojo. We will collect this debt of blood. The camp of Rojo will be safe. We will help the People of the camp. Yellow Boy hunts, brings meat. Hombrecito brings strong White Eye medicine."

I nod when Rojo raises a brow and looks at me. I feel a sense of elation I've not felt for a long time. My hard-earned medical skills might help these people while I await the satisfaction of killing my enemies.

49. RUNS FAR RETURNS

That night Pelo Rojo holds a council to discuss using my power for the People. The round lodge, lighted inside by soft, flickering yellow light from oil lamps hung on the center post, and a large clay pot glowing with red and orange coals driving off the night chill shelters the men in council. Rojo sits opposite the blanket-covered door, a wool Pendleton blanket covered with classic geometric designs over his shoulders. Yellow Boy and I sit to his right. The men from the camp, solemn, eyes glittering with curiosity, sit around the wall, blankets over their shoulders, waiting, all eyes on Yellow Boy and me. Nothing has changed from what I remember of the councils ten years earlier.

Pelo Rojo nods toward us.

"Yellow Boy and Hombrecito have been many seasons north with our brothers on the reservations. Men of the camp, Hombrecito returns with the power of a White-Eye di-yin, a White-Eye medicine man. He followed the tracks of White-Eye di-yins many seasons to find this power. The People do not know his ceremonies of power and medicine. He offers the People his power. The People's di-yins have their ceremonies and our women know medicine that comes from plants. In Rojo's camp no di-yin stays with the People. We heal ourselves unless our medicine has no power, then we call a di-yin from the reservations or another camp in the Sierras to help us. We follow this way since before the days of my father. Today Hombrecito tells me of his power and offers it to help us. I ask Hombrecito to speak to the council now so that we can all understand his power and decide if we can accept his offer to help us. Speak, Hombrecito, and we will listen."

I look around at the solemn faces framed in flickering light and shadow. I still don't speak Apache well, but use it anyway.

"For six circles of the seasons I work to learn White-Eye di-yin power. White-Eye di-yin say I am ready to use this power. I have used it to help White Eyes and to help Arango and his soldiers. Now I offer this power to help the People. Rojo speaks true. White-Eye di-yin power looks different from that of the Apache di-yin healing power, but stands strong against the hidden enemies of the People. My power can take away the power of sickness. Many times, I can find the source of the sickness's power if I can put my hands on your bodies, look in your eyes, your ears, and in your mouths. When I find the source of this sickness power, I know how to take it away. Rojo says the council must make the decision to let me use my power for the people. I will do as the council tells me. I have no more to say."

An old man, his arms crossed, sits by the blanket covering the door way, his long, gray-streaked hair tied back with a blue bandanna, tilts his head to one side and speaks in a voice cracked by age and hard times.

"What does Hombrecito ask of us for using his power? How many rifles? How many horses? How many cows?"

I shake my head.

"I give my power to the People. I ask nothing in return."

There is a long silence as an understanding of my offer begins to sink in. Another man speaks. "Can Hombrecito use his power for children? Can he use the White-Eye di-yin power for our women and old ones as well as the warriors?"

I nod.

"I can use it for all the People. I will do this for your children and your women and your old ones. My power is not afraid of a woman's power even in their moon time. Their power cannot make me sick. I help the warriors. I help the women. I help the children. I help old ones. I help you all."

Another asks, "Must we accept the White-Eye god for this power? Ussen is the Apache god."

"No. I will not speak of the White-Eye god."

One asks, "Where will Hombrecito use his power to perform his healing ceremonies?"

I raise my brows, look at Yellow Boy and Roja, and shrug. I haven't thought about where to practice my medicine. Rojo speaks up.

"We will build a wickiup for this work by the river, away from the camp, so the powers Hombrecito drives off follow the water down the canyon and do not return to camp. Hombrecito knows the ceremonies to make it his place of power. He will need a woman to help him. Lupe knows the power of many plants. I will ask her to help Hombrecito in his work."

The council asks every imaginable question. I answer them all. The pot of coals grows black and our breath can be seen in the lamplight when the council agrees to let me use my power in the camp.

The next morning a young woman in her early twenties comes to Rojo's fire during the morning meal. She waits at a respectful distance until Rojo motions her to come sit by the fire. I remember seeing her in the crowd the day we arrived. Exceptionally tall and angular for an Apache woman, her thin, oval face, high brow, long nose and high cheek bones makes her, by Apache standards, ugly.

As soon as I see her, I know that the light in her kind bright eyes comes from an old wound to her soul. Her shiny black hair cut short, her arms showing scars where she cut herself in a time of mourning, speaks of a widow not yet taken by a new man. If none of the other men in the camp take her, she might agree to become second or third wife to a warrior Rojo chooses for her.

Rojo says, "Lupe, you remember Hombrecito from many seasons ago?"

She stares up into the trees and nods, saying nothing.

"Hombrecito comes to help the People."

She looks at me and says, "I remember Hombrecito and his warrior woman. I did not yet have a husband. He knew me only as a child. I saw him make Apache Kid look like a fool when they shot at Massai's hat."

"Yes, it is true you did not yet have the Puberty Ceremony. He was a young warrior skilled far beyond his years. He took the *gringo* woman living here. You know she is no more. Now he needs a helper when he uses his power in his curing ceremonies. You have no man. You have no child. You are di-yin with the power of plants. I ask you to help Hombrecito use his power for the People."

Lupe folds her hands in her lap, and turns her bright bird-like eyes to study me. I don't think I need a nurse, but I won't argue with Rojo and his concern that I have a helper. The way she looks me straight in the eye, an insult to any other Apache, doesn't bother me at all. I stare back at her. Rojo clears his throat, ready to tell her not to be disrespectful. Yellow Boy understands she intends no offense, grunts, and when Rojo looks at him, gives a nearly imperceptible headshake. Rojo waits.

She turns to Rojo, her chin up, after seeing what she sought in my eyes.

"What does Hombrecito want from me?"

Rojo doesn't hesitate.

"You will do all the things a woman does. Today you will help the other camp women build Hombrecito a lodge where he can use his medicine power. Use your power to make it safe for his ceremonies. He will bless it to make it a place of power, of wisdom, and of healing. Every day you will light the medicine lodge fire, carry the water, bring your power with plants, make your medicines, make his medicines, and perform the ceremonies he teaches you. When Hombrecito leaves, maybe he will leave some of his power with you."

She stares in my eyes again.

"He has no woman here. Does he expect to sleep in my blankets?"

My face turns red, and Yellow Boy looks away, a grin playing at the corners of his mouth. Sleeping with Lupe is the last thing on my mind. I shake my head.

Rojo shrugs.

"No man calls you his woman now. It is for you to say if he comes to your blankets. Hombrecito honors my word and eats at my fire with his uncle, Yellow Boy. Hombrecito will not force you. What is your answer?"

Pulling away hair that had fallen over one side of her face and looking at her moccasins, she sighs. "For the People, I do the things Hombrecito asks of me and learn the ceremonies of his power. I will build a medicine lodge and help him."

Rojo grunts and nods. "Uhmmph. Good."

Saying nothing more, Lupe returns to her mother's lodge.

Later that day Lupe and several of the camp women finish a large wickiup they build down the creek, not far from the main camp. They weave a brush cover over a hemisphere–shaped framework of poles, and finish just as red, orange, and purple light from the setting sun lights the canyon and blesses the new medicine lodge with power. As twilight falls, Lupe carefully wanders through the brush collecting firewood. She's an expert at using an axe without leaving any sign that the surrounding brush has been disturbed.

The next morning as gray light creeps above the canyon edge, I sit with Lupe by the fire at the medicine lodge. Water boils in a big pot. Her freshly washed hair in the firelight glistens, shiny like a raven's wing, pulled back out of her face. Her head cocked to one side, left ear turned toward me catching every word, eyes narrowed in a squint of concentration, she reminds me of a bird listening to an insect crawling in leaves and grass.

"Lupe, I use this ceremony before and after I see each

one who comes for my medicine power. I wash my hands in water that is boiled and use soap from the yucca plant three times in separate washings and rinses before I touch anyone. I use only boiled water for this. You must do this also. You must wash again this way after you return from relieving yourself. When I find signs of sickness power, I decide then what must be done. You must help me remember what we did for each one when we perform my ceremonies. Can you do this?"

She nods. "I can do this. How do you find where the sickness powers hide?"

I pull the stethoscope out of my doctor's bag. "One ceremony uses this to listen for the wind powers in their lungs and the rhythm of their hearts. I can hear when the wind powers are attacking or a heart grows weak. I feel their bodies for powers that should not be there."

I show her a thermometer. "I put this shiny stick in their mouths to hold under their tongues. Reading the signs on it tells me the strength of the sickness power. When we find signs of sickness power I will show you how to make the medicines I know and I will listen to your power when you show me the ones you know. With your medicines you also have the powers of a di-yin. We must be sure you do not have the wind sickness powers inside you before we begin. Hold this on your chest inside your shirt where I point. When I tell you, breath slow and deep."

Modest, she lowers her eyes and opens her shirt to reveal well-formed breasts. I give her the end of the stethoscope, point where to hold it, and tell her to breathe slow and deep. Her heart and pulmonary functions sound perfect. I put the earpieces in her ears. The demure modesty in her face is replaced by a quizzical look.

"The sound you hear like flowing water over rocks in the creek is your wind power. The sound of the drum is your heart."

Handing it back to me, she nods and buttons her shirt.

"Hombrecito has much power. He lets Lupe use this power also? Lets Lupe listen for the wind powers in others and the strength of their hearts?"

I nod and she smiles for the first time since I've met her.

The People come to us unbidden. Word spreads that my ceremonies will begin this day and the news, like telegraph clicks down a high wire in the desert, follows all the fast paths through the camp. With Lupe's help I do ceremonies for everything from minor lung infections to constipation to bad teeth. I pull a few teeth, and set a broken bone or two on the first day we use my power. Men show us wounds and cuts that don't heal well. A warrior bears his pain and doesn't complain. I practically have to make them tell us their problems, and they say they feel better before the medicine can possibly do any good.

In the evening I begin to show Lupe how to check for serious diseases in the old ones, children, and women, and what medicines or procedures to use if they're found. For the most part, Lupe already knows which plants to use for most common ailments.

A few days glide by. Yellow Boy goes out every day to hunt or to scout the trails. Lupe learns fast, becoming an excellent helper, and we work well together. In the evenings Yellow Boy and I sit and smoke with Pelo Rojo and speculate how Villa will hide from the *gringos*, the best places to hunt, and where best to steal guns and ammunition from the Mexicans and *gringos*.

A week passes, then two. No scouts return with any news. I'm losing faith in our strategy for finding Villa.

One afternoon a young boy runs to the medicine lodge. He says between puffs to catch his breath, "A scout returns…Pelo Rojo asks for Muchacho Amarillo… and Hombrecito."

We're in the middle of boiling my surgical instruments and I pause to consider how long before I can leave. Lupe smiles and waves me toward the camp. "Your helper can do this work. I know the ceremony. Go."

Pelo Rojo sits by the fire outside his lodge with Yellow Boy, Runs Far, and the two women who ride with him. They smoke, Pelo Rojo his pipe, Yellow Boy a cigar and Runs Far and the women a Mexican-style corn-shuck cigarette.

It surprises me to see the companions of Runs Far smoking. Apache women don't smoke in public until they're beyond their childbearing years, but these women, hard though they look, are still young enough to make babies. I suppose they've decided that if they can make war like men, they're entitled to smoke like men.

Runs Far, no doubt wondering if Yellow Boy has told Pelo Rojo about their fight over taking *División del Norte* boys captive, sits with his arms crossed, eyeing Yellow Boy who pays him no attention. Pelo Rojo motions me over to sit with them.

When I'm seated and have my pipe started, Pelo Rojo says, "Runs Far and his women return from a long scout. They see the *gringos* who chase Arango. Speak, Runs Far, tell us what you see, what you hear."

Runs Far blows a puff of blue smoke from the side of his mouth and licks his lips.

"The *gringo* army rides far south of the *gringo*-Mexico border. Many horses and wagons come. *Gringo* soldiers ride in long lines on Mexican wagon trails. Some iron wagons, move by spirits, use no horse, no rail, no steam. Spirits inside iron wagons try to get out. They make *mucho* noise and smoke. *Gringo* soldiers guard their supplies well, hard to raid."

Pelo Rojo nods. "Arango, now called Villa, you see him?"

"Villa rides fast south. Maybe three hundred soldiers follow him. Takes *mucho* supplies in Galeana fight with other Mexican army. Villa leaves men who are shot and takes new soldiers at El Valle. Fights Mexican army at Namiquipa, wins battle, takes many guns, many horses. Prisoners he frees. Goes to Rubio, warriors rest, take more supplies. Leaves Rubio, goes to Guerrero, fights again with Mexican army. Mexican army runs away…"

Runs Far pauses long enough to focus our attention. Impatient, Yellow Boy says, "Speak, *hombre*."

Runs Far takes a draw from his cigarette and lets the blue smoke curl slowly off the faint smile on his lips. "Villa shot in leg…from behind with bullet like one from Hombrecito's Shoots-Today-Kills-Tomorrow rifle. Makes big hole. Villa can no ride horse. Carried in wagons with other chiefs. Villa loses his power. He cries and moans. Sounds like woman birthing big baby. *Gringo* soldiers nearly catch Villa at Guerrero."

Pelo Rojo frowns. "Where goes Villa?"

Runs Far sticks out his chin, shakes his head, and flips his cigarette butt in the fire. "We last see Villa in wagon on trail south of Guerrero."

I sit listening, my teeth clenched in disgust. Villa, nearly helpless, still gets away. Now, after waiting more than two weeks, all I know is that he was shot south of Guerrero. All I can think is, *damn, damn, damn*. I hope he's still alive when Yellow Boy and I find him.

I say, "Did any of the men around him wear a red shirt?"

Runs Far nods. "*Sí,* one with Villa wears a red shirt."

Yellow Boy and I sit alone by the medicine lodge fire, daylight nearly gone, discussing how best to find Villa and Camisa Roja. Yellow Boy says, "Best to wait until other scouts come back, use what they see, hear, and then decide where to find Arango."

Impatient, like a hard-ridden horse smelling the barn, I shake my head.

"Already we wait too many days. Pelo Rojo's scouts will not find much watching from long distance. We need to talk to Army scouts, hear what they know, maybe talk to Mexicans on the road, then we will find where Villa and Camisa Roja hide. We'll never find them sitting in camp waiting. Anything is better than sitting and waiting."

A smile crosses Yellow Boy's lips. "Hombrecito still does not have the patience of the hunter. Remember ride we take many seasons ago because Hombrecito does not wait?"

I grin. "Yes, years ago I ought to have waited to go after Jack Stone, but it worked out didn't it?" It occurs to me that the man who raised me, Rufus Pike, died because I'd made a fool kid's mistake.

Yellow Boy sees the clouds of regret in my eyes and shakes his head. "The man who raised you no die because you hurry, Hombrecito. The grandfathers called him. He lives a long time before he goes. Great warrior. You honor him. You di-yin. We think on these things, decide after we eat from Pelo Rojo's pot. Si?"

I nod and we go to Pelo Rojo's lodge.

50. SEÑOR ROOSTER

The Mexicans believe they've been invaded by the United States. Chihuahua is a tinderbox needing only a spark to become a roaring fire of outrage determined to drive the Americans back across the border. Villa has disappeared, leaving no indication where he hides, and no Mexican willing to say he knows. The Americans with their scouts and money to pay informers continue to search ranches and houses in the vicinity of Parral south of Ciudad Chihuahua.

The day after Yellow Boy and I talk, scouts report seeing a few of Villa's men passing through mountain villages south of El Paso Púlpito. Some groups continue south toward Durango, and some, shot to pieces after fights with *gringo* army patrols, want to stay and rest a while. After hearing the scout's report, Yellow Boy and I agree it's time for us to find Villa and Camisa Roja, and prepare to leave Pelo Rojo's camp the following evening.

Pelo Rojo and I discuss how best for Lupe to use the skills I've taught her. He agrees with my suggestion that she live in the medicine lodge and continue to help the People, and I agree that when we finish our business with Villa and Camisa Roja, I'll come back often to help her.

Before we leave, I spend the day with Lupe going over my ceremonies, watching her make medicines, and ensuring she understands she must follow my strict hygiene ceremony. The Apaches, very clean people, bathe often using chopped yucca root boiled to make shampoo and soap. Teaching Lupe that she must strictly follow how I've taught her to wash means only that she has to learn to wash even when she doesn't think her hands need it.

As we've worked together from day-to-day, I can feel the tight fist of long-buried grief around my heart loosening. I admire and respect Lupe, learn from her, draw closer to her, dream in my midnight fantasies of taking a woman again, of being a lover once more, of knowing the pleasures of life with a woman. With her, my thoughts of Villa no longer fill me with sour rage, and my desire to rid Mexico of a mad dog and myself of a blood debt weakens. I'm learning that life and living are not driven by ideas of sweet revenge.

The canyon's western ridge glows in retreating sunlight, a low twilight lingering in the canyon as frogs by the burbling creek tune up and crickets begin their songs. We end the day sitting in the medicine lodge reviewing my notes on who we've treated and how. Lupe sits beside me and verifies or supplies new details about each patient as I go down my list.

We finish and I check my bag to ensure I have a basic supply of medicines and instruments. I want to leave as much medicine and as many instruments as I can with Lupe and empty my medical bag of all but its bare essentials.

When we finish, she goes to the door and pulls its blanket door down, a sign telling visitors we want privacy. She turns to me, looking into my eyes, the light from the fire reflecting in hers. Inside I tremble as she cups my head in her hands.

At first she speaks in a shy, halting voice but it grows stronger with each word, "With you gone, the days will be long, Hombrecito. All the village will miss you, but no one more than me. White-Eye di-yin make powerful medicine. Your hands have a gentle touch. Your heart understands and values kindness. Every day I thank Ussen for sending you to help the People. Every day I thank Ussen for sending me to help you.

"Once I had a good man. He was a strong, powerful warrior. Now he walks with the grandfathers and I am a widow, free to choose a man who wants me."

I'm not such a fool that I don't know where these words are leading. A longing and desire for her fill me, but I'm not ready to take a wife again. I stand, gently hold her shoulders, and say, "You honor me with your words, your help, and your heart, Lupe. You have shown me many fine medicines I did not know. I am proud to help the People with you, a fine woman, full of life, knowing much. I've lost a good wife and you a good husband, but I have much work to do in hard days to come. I must use my power beyond the People's lodges. I'm not ready to take another wife."

"Do you desire me as a man desires a woman, Hombrecito?"

I stare into the little oil lamp fire and see the flame moving sensuously. I feel my pulse race and I whisper, "Yes."

"I do not speak of marriage. I am free to choose who I want. I want you. Lie with me that I can know you when you lose yourself to Ussen in the pleasure of our union. Warm yourself with the fire in my heart. I give you fire stronger than the jaguar's fire, fire stronger than the blind rage that burns in a man's heart."

I'm stunned. I haven't told her of my dreams. "How do you know of the jaguar's fire?"

"My power shows me many things. It tells me it will keep you safe. It tells me to keep you in my heart. This I do. Take me as a man takes a woman. Lose yourself to Ussen, know my fire."

She blows out the oil lamp. In the darkness I hear her shift fall to her feet and I'm stirred in a way I've not been in years. I feel her arms surround me as she lays her head on my chest and my hands feel smooth warm skin down her back as I pull her to me.

Yellow Boy and I use the same narrow trail up out of Rojo's canyon and across the Sierra Espuelas we used ten years earlier to chase the man who kidnapped Rafaela. It winds south and east along the ridges of the Sierra Madre and leads to the eastern entrance of El Paso Púlpito near where Rafaela is buried. Out of El Paso Púlpito, we ride across the great, rugged Chihuahuan *llano*. Always pointing toward the southeast, always toward Colonia Dublan and Casas Grandes, always in the night, always passing far around the campfires of Punitive Expedition patrols, Carrancista Army patrols, small groups of bandits, and even a few remnants of *División del Norte*.

In the middle of the fifth night, we find the large camp

General Pershing established on the outskirts of Colonia Dublan. Rather than risk being shot by a nervous sentry, we decide to rest the three or four hours until sunrise and then show ourselves. We find a place in a thick willow and cottonwood bosque along the Rio Casas Grandes south of the Punitive Expedition headquarters, make camp, dig a deep fire pit to keep the firelight from giving us away, unsaddle and rub down the horses, and make coffee to take the chill off our bones. I wrap in my blankets and lie down next to the fire. Yellow Boy, as usual, stays out of sight nearby.

I'm weary, but it takes a while before I pass into fitful sleep.

My eyes snap open. Darkness, coals in the fire pit barely orange. I hear the click of a pistol's hammer pulled back, start to rise and feel the pressure of a cold steel barrel pressed against my forehead. Against the stars I see the outline of a dark figure above me with waist-length hair, and in the dim glow from the fire coals I can make out a US Army uniform shirt.

The figure holding the gun barrel against my forehead motions me to stay still and says in heavily accented, guttural Spanish, "Who are you? Who are the others in the camp behind you? Speak before *mi pistola* blows off your head."

Before I can answer we hear the hammer on Yellow Boy's Henry click to full cock. "*Buenos días, Señor* Rooster. He is Doctor Henrique Grace. The Mescaleros call him Hombrecito. So you join the White-Eye army? Wear their uniform? Speak before *mi* rifle blows off your head."

The cold steel on my forehead vanishes and I hear the pistol's hammer ease down before the weapon slides into its flap-covered, army holster. Rooster squats down by the fire, rocking back on his heels, and lifting the coffee pot, throws a few sticks on the coals, saying, "*Buenos días,* Muchacho Amarillo. *Sí,* I track for the Army. The soldiers search for Villa, but cannot find him. They will welcome you and Hombrecito in the soldier camp to help them. Why sleep here? Is it because of your friends in the other camp?"

Yellow Boy materializes out of the darkness, comes to the fire, and squats down. "Guards nervous in the night. Shoot first, and then ask who is dead man. We wait until light so guard sees us. Where is this other camp you think belongs to us?"

"Ha, Muchacho Amarillo makes two camps of Apache brothers rather than one. Cannot catch all if one camp raided. Waits here for light while others sleep. Wise choices. Hard to find small camps, *gringo* guards always nervous. You come to scout for the *gringos*?"

"No. I scout only for Muchacho Amarillo and Hombrecito. Why are you here and not south with the *gringo* army looking for Arango?"

"I carry Big Star Pershing paper tracks to the *jefe* of this camp."

Yellow Boy tosses Rooster a cup. "Have coffee. I will speak with you."

Rooster sits down next to the fire and crosses his legs, pours his coffee, takes a swallow, and smacks his lips. "Humph... Hot. Strong. Good. You join Big Star Pershing's scouts. His army gives warm uniforms, *pistolas* that shoot many times without reloading, belts to carry supplies, and windows to keep dust from the eyes." He pulls his goggles off his headband and shows them to us, sticking out his lower lip, nodding in obvious satisfaction. "Very good supplies." He taps his wristwatch. "*Gringos* even give time on wrist."

Studying Rooster, Yellow Boy leans back on his left elbow, the Henry on a blanket beside him. "Where does Arango hide?"

Rooster shrugs his shoulders.

Yellow Boy rephrases his question, his eyes narrowed to a squint, staring at Rooster. "Where does Rooster think Arango hides? Speak."

Rooster first eyes Yellow Boy, then me, and returns to Yellow Boy. He shrugs again.

"I don't know. The *gringos* go no further south than town of Parral. Soldiers search between village of La Joya and Parral. *Mi jefe*, he says Villa must stay in one place until leg heals or he loses it. I hear Mexicans tell Mexican Army *jefe* they see Villa. They say leg bad, very bad. Black here to here to here and white stink leaks from bullet hole." Rooster marks off about six inches on either side of a place below his knee. "Mexicans say he cries like a woman having baby, say he wants to kill self. Villa's power gone. You gain no power if you kill him."

I'm stunned by what Rooster says. Villa's power gone? He can't take the pain without crying? In an Apache's eyes, any man who can't take pain has no value.

Rooster empties the cup with a long swallow and pours a little more. He looks at Yellow Boy and makes a one-sided grin. "If I look for Villa on my own? I go south of La Joya between San Jose del Sito and Parral. Mexicans in villages nearby say Villa hides near Santa Cruz. Me? I don't know."

Yellow Boy nods as Rooster swallows the last of the coffee and hands back the cup.

"*Gracias,* Rooster. How far to Santa Cruz?"

Rooster tilts his face toward the tops of the trees as he thinks, and then looks down into the fire.

"The village lies southeast, near San Jose del Sito. It is seven, maybe eight days hard ride if you have strong horses and grain for them. I know you always travel at night. Good. Ride with care. Many *gringo* and Mexican patrols also travel at night. Many Villistas still roam free looking for horses, rifles, and bullets. *Gringo* cavalry goes fast, goes far. Soldiers wear out horses, take extras, and keep riding. Glad they no chase me."

Yellow Boy sticks out his lower lip and nods he understands. Rooster stands up and stretches. "I go to find *jefe* of the camp. Give him talking paper, eat, sleep, carry paper with *jefe's* tracks back to Big Star Pershing. *Adiós.*"

Yellow Boy says, "Rooster, answer my question."

Rooster frowns. "What question?"

"Where is the other little camp of Apaches?"

"Ah, so you play games between you, eh? Ha. The camp is a rifle shot south in the bosque. They make no fire. Maybe they are only passing by Casas Grandes. Then I find you and think maybe you and these Apaches come to scout for or steal from the *gringo* army. This is so, Muchacho Amarillo?"

Yellow Boy frowns and nods. "*Si.* Apaches come to the *gringo* army."

He starts to leave but I stop him. "*Un momento, Señor* Rooster, *por favor.*"

"*Si?*"

"*Señor* Peach, Quentin Peach, rides with Big Star Pershing?"

Rooster frowns as he thinks, and then grins. "*Sí, Señor* Peach rides with Big Star Pershing. Makes many tracks on paper. Asks many questions."

"When you return to Big Star Pershing, tell *Señor* Peach you see Hombrecito in Colonia Dublan and that he and *Señor* Yellow Boy ride south to search for Villa. Will you speak those words to *Señor* Peach?"

"*Sí*, Hombrecito, I will speak those words."

"*Gracias, señor, muchas gracias.*"

51. JESÚÚS

Rooster disappears into the darkness, a ghost filled with information drifting over the land. He leaves us wondering about the other Apaches he saw and how best to find Villa far to the south, hiding like a wounded animal at the edge of the Sierras, gaining strength, readying to slash and burn and kill again when the *gringos* leave.

Faint gray begins outlining the edges of the mountains to the east, bringing with it the call of awakening birds and the first whispers of icy morning air stirring into a breeze that later grows into a dashing spring wind. I throw more sticks and driftwood on the fire and see Yellow Boy staring at the flames. I know in his mind's eye he tests one strategy against another, searching for the best way to find Villa.

"What do you think, Uncle?"

Yellow Boy looks at me from under his brows. "Arango hides far away. Trail south very rough, no see trail since I am a young warrior. *Mucho* changes." He taps his forehead with his rough and calloused finger. "*Mucho* of the way south not here, no more in my head. Need tracks on paper, what the *gringos* call map."

He pulls a cigar out of his coat pocket and lights it with a stick from the fire. The light blue smoke catching the morning breeze, the red-orange coal at its tip glows as he thinks, drawing on it, puffing it to life.

"Who do you think the other Apaches are that Rooster saw?"

He smiles. "Runs Far and his women. He will not let pass me taking his horse and making him ride on a woman's horse. He will have his revenge.

"Maybe he tries to take our horses. Leaves us to take long walk across *llano* with no water. Maybe try to kill."

"Lets go take care of Runs Far now."

He shakes his head. "No, not now. Let them follow. We watch. Maybe ambush. Runs Far and his women follow Yellow Boy and Hombrecito no more. Follow no man no more."

"*Bueno*. What will we do now?"

"Rest horses today. Ride when the moon comes. Stay close to Galena road, watch for *gringos* and Mexicans, stay out of sight. Watch for Runs Far; make him think we not know he is there. There is still *mucho* fighting. *Villistas* fight *Carrancistas. Gringos* fight *Villistas* and *Carrancistas. Banditos* take anything, run. Too much war, too many raids, *peons* starve. They take your rifle, coat, horse, anything they can trade for food, keep *niños* warm. Do what they have to do to live. This land kills you quick if you no watch. We must be like Coyote, trickster. They no see us come, no see us go."

"Sí, Uncle, you speak words of truth."

* * *

The sun, at first appearing squeezed into a shimmering, oblong blood-red balloon slowly inflating into a fuzzy golden ball, floats in the morning mists above the tops of the mountains, filling the sky with feathered turquoise, changing the gray outline of the eastern mountains to a brilliant, blinding ribbon of gold. We cover the fire pit and give the horses their morning grain. Yellow Boy says he'll take the first watch while I sleep.

Near the horses I find a huge, ancient willow, its long limbs covered with new green leaves, forming a natural wall that passes only a few narrow beams of sunlight that paint drifting dust motes with gold. I spread my saddle blanket on the dry, crunchy leaves gathered in piles around the big trunk roots and stretch out, trying to relax, wanting to sleep as much as I can before my turn comes to keep watch. Across the fields and river I hear the clank and rumble of men and their machines at the big Army camp. Thoughts that we will finally set things right with Villa and Camisa Roja and memories of my last, sweet hours with Lupe and the thirst for life she stirred in me keep my eyes open.

Dreams finally come. Dreams filled with fleeting images that flick back and forth in my mind, images of Villa killing the grizzly with a Bowie knife; of thousands of horses and men flying apart in bloody pieces as they charge over and over into machine guns and barbed wire; Villa, bug-eyed and crazy, shooting the priest; like a black fog passing, Maud Wright appears, smiling, holding Johnnie, waving good-by; and then Lupe, tall and angular with bright, bird-like eyes and a good heart, leading me to her blanket in the medicine lodge.

A tapping on the bottom of my foot by the barrel of Yellow Boy's rifle makes the vision of Lupe in my arms vanish like thin vapor on the wind. Yellow Boy points toward the sky with his Henry. The angle of sunbeams filtering into my dark den show it's at least an hour past noon and my turn to watch. He waves his hand palm down to indicate all is well, points toward his guard spot in a bamboo thicket next to the river, and we swap places. It's a luxury to go to the riverbank and splash water on my face to wake up.

From Yellow Boy's spot in the bamboo I have clear lines of sight into the Army camp and up and down the river. To the north there seems to be a constant dust cloud along the road as Army trucks loaded with supplies, their engines puttering and gears grinding come south, their loads increasing the growing supply dump near the center of the camp, and trucks rumble back north, most empty, some carrying wounded soldiers and sacks of mail. Idly watching them, I try to think of how best to find Villa, tossing every idea that comes to mind into the void as unusable.

I turn my attention to the camp across the river. A tent serves as a barbershop. It has a chair tilted back twenty or thirty degrees that is nothing more than a stump sawed off at the same angle relative to the ground with packing crate planks nailed to it for a backrest and seat so the customer can rest his legs on a hitching rail. Tents serving as pharmacies or soldier messes have nearly constant streams of men in and out. Entrepreneurs, doing a thriving business, dressed in clean pressed shirts and pants, probably local Mormons allowed past the guards as the result of deals made with the camp commanders, sell everything from vegetables to enchiladas to baked goods. The camp's soldiers unload trucks or march and train in infantry or cavalry formations. I don't see Rooster anywhere and assume he's crawled off somewhere to sleep or maybe has already left.

Near the center of camp stands a tall woven wire fence like that used for stock pens. It surrounds a rectangular area maybe a hundred feet on a side and eight heavily armed guards, two to a side, pace back and forth, meeting at the middle, doing a smart half turn, then marching back to their respective corner post before snapping around again to pace toward the middle.

Inside the pen, at least thirty or forty dirty, ragged men, obviously prisoners, some wearing *peon* straw hats, most bareheaded, shuffle about, stirring the dust into little clouds around their feet. I retrieve my old field glasses from my saddlebags and study their faces. I jerk back in surprise when I see the emaciated face of Jesús, my young helper on the march to Agua Prieta. My heart sinks in despair at seeing him in the custody of the *gringos*. Not yet sixteen years old, marching or riding across burning deserts and frozen mountains, filthy rags his only protection, never having enough to eat, his body covered with sores, he worked to exhaustion bringing me men who might survive after being shot to pieces in Villa's foolish charges against trenches and barbed wire.

I curse Villa for leading such a fine young man and thousands like him straight into Hell's jaws fighting *hacendados* and corrupt government, their reward slaughter in raids and foolish battles or being herded into pens like livestock waiting for slaughter.

"Oh, God," I moan, "where is the justice in all this? Where is the justice?"

I'm a useless guard. I pay no attention to anything or anyone except Jesús. I conjure how to get him out of there, measuring every guard's move, noting where we can hide after I steal him, wondering if we have any chance of getting away without killing soldiers or being killed ourselves. The sun is no more than a bright glow in a cloudless sky behind the western *sierras* when I feel Yellow Boy squeeze my shoulder before he sits down beside me. "You see Jesús?"

"*Sí*, Uncle. I've spent all afternoon trying to figure out how to get him without killing soldiers or our being killed. He might be a big help guiding us to Villa, but I don't care if he can't or won't help, just so we get him out of there. I can't abide him being kept like an animal ready for slaughter. Will you help me free him?"

"*Sí*, we free Jesús. I have plan."

I grin. I should have known he wouldn't leave our old friend to the dogs of war. "*Bueno*. Tell me."

He points toward the north edge of the camp where the troops keep their mounts tied to long ropes, feeding and grooming them after the afternoon drill. About three hundred yards west of the horse lines is a supply dump, smaller than the big one near the prisoner pen. Heavily guarded and covered with large pieces of canvas, its supplies are stacked on a wooden floor of some kind.

Yellow Boy says, "I watch the place where soldiers guard supplies under canvas. Watch soldiers put boxes in pile." Hefting his big, brass telescope, he says, "Big eye show boxes of bullets, many bullets. We take Jesús? You shoot pile. I stampede horses. Many soldiers chase. Soldiers forget prisoners when they chase horses and dodge own bullets. You let prisoners go. Take Jesús, ride for Galena. I find you on road to Galena."

It's a good plan, far better than anything I dreamed up during my watch, and it might work if it draws the guards away from the fence. I can only hope it doesn't get us shot or behind the wire ourselves. In the falling twilight we work out the plan's details, my crawling as close as I can to the fence before shooting the ammunition dump, Yellow Boy waiting just long enough to free the horses in order to make it look like they've broken the rope line in fright because of the explosion and bullets flying in every direction, and Yellow Boy grabbing a horse and meeting us in the south pass on the Galena road between Colonia Dublan and Casas Grandes. We strip off our shirts in the chilly air, cover our bodies and faces with bacon grease, and fire charcoal to make our skin black against the night.

We want to get into position before the moon rises over the mountains and be ready to move as soon as twilight dissolves into cold, black air. The wind dies. The air is still. Frogs croak and night birds call. Across the river the camp relaxes, men going to mess tents, lanterns inside creating eerie golden glows across acres of tents. We can hear occasional laughs or curses from poker games as we saddle our horses and ready our gear. Satanas still strong, watches the camp, smelling the Army horses, his ears up, ready to run, while Yellow Boy's paint nibbles grass.

Wading into the river, we're halfway across when Yellow Boy stops and points toward the prisoner pen. Two lights six or seven feet apart on the front of a truck, its engine chugging, transmission grinding, move toward the pen. We retreat back across the river and I frantically pull out my field glasses to stare at the lights heading for the prisoner pen. There isn't enough light to see much of the truck except that it looks like some kind of motorized covered wagon and there are two soldiers with rifles riding in the back with their legs hanging off the tailgate.

The truck makes a big swooping curve and backs up to within twenty feet of the pen gate. A number, 1079, is painted in white figures about a hand width high on the front bumper. The driver hops out of the open cab and gives the guard some papers. They chat a couple of minutes and then stand around as if waiting for someone.

Soon a line of soldiers with rifles on their shoulders carrying lanterns marches down an aisle between the tents. They march to the pen gate, their leader salutes the guard who has the trucker's papers, and orders his men, rifles at the ready, to form a double row about four feet apart and facing each other between the gate and the truck.

The guard with the paper unlocks the gate and is followed inside by soldiers with rifles at the ready. We can hear names being shouted inside the pen: Gomez…Padilla…Muñoz… Soon after we hear a name, a man or boy appears at the gate and walks escorted down the aisle between the soldiers and climbs in the truck.

My mind races to understand what's going on. Are the soldiers taking the prisoners somewhere to execute them? They obviously can't take all of them in one truck. I remember Peach telling me the objective of the Punitive Expedition will be to kill or catch Villa and as many of his men as possible, or, bring them back to the United States, give them a trial, and hang them, everyone, with Villa to be last. This must be a load of prisoners heading north, heading for a trial and a hanging. I pray that Jesús won't be part of the group. How in creation can we stop a truck, this thing Runs

Far calls an 'iron wagon moved by spirits'? On a good road, they can probably drive all night, faster than a horse can run for a few miles. They won't need to stop and rest. They can be in Columbus by sunrise.

Something deep in my guts tells me it's going to happen and it does. The man calling out names yells, "Avella!" Soon Jesús appears at the gate and walks with his escort to climb in the truck.

Frowning, Yellow Boy looks at me. I raise my arm and hold my hand above my head like I'm holding a piece of rope and cock my head to one side like I'm being hanged and then point north. He jerks his head toward the horses. I take a last look at the truck but don't see anything that distinguishes it from any other we've seen that day except the number, 1079. I take a long look at the driver's face, swing up on Satanas, and race after Yellow Boy, already low in the saddle, galloping north up the trail by the Rio Casas Grandes.

52. THE RESCUE

We put the horses into a fast gallop hoping to get far enough ahead of the truck carrying Jesús to set up an ambush. Luckily, no trucks are rolling on the road now and the very bright moon makes it easy to see the land. The dusty caliche hardpan out of the Army camp runs due north out across the *llano*. After eight or nine miles, our horses tiring, we come to a big, reddish rock on the right side of the road just before it drops down into an *arroyo*, its sides showing twisted shelves of rock that look like some gigantic thumb has flipped the pages of a stone book.

Yellow Boy reins in his paint and carefully follows the road down into the *arroyo*. He stops and stares back up the road's ruts to the edge of the *arroyo* and then up and down the *arroyo* filled with mesquite bushes deep in shadows. He says, "We stop iron wagon in this place. You kill iron wagon with Shoots-Today-Kills-Tomorrow?"

I shrug, not knowing much more about trucks than he did. I knew if I hit the motor or the radiator in the right place, it might stop. "Probably not, unless I'm lucky."

He dismounts, and pulls his nearly empty grain sack off the back of his saddle. He points toward the top of the rock on the right side of the *arroyo* road.

"Tie horses behind big rock. Climb on top of rock. Watch for iron wagon. Call like nightjar if you see. I come soon."

He walks down the *arroyo* toward a mesquite thicket. I lead the horses up the road and around behind the big rock, tie them off on a mesquite, and climb to the top of the rock which slopes back toward the *arroyo*. I find a spot to stretch out that gives plenty of cover, pull out Big Eye, Yellow Boy's big brass telescope, and look down the road. A point of light twinkles in the distance. Seeing it doesn't surprise me. The truck is coming, but so far away the lamps on each side of the truck appear as one. Ten minutes pass, fifteen. The single point of light becomes two.

Yellow Boy appears, carrying his grain sack tied off at the top. He points down the road. "Iron wagon comes." I hand him Big Eye. He looks for a moment and hands it back to me. "*Bueno*, only one."

"Uncle, what's in the sack?'

He drops it at my feet. Instantly the sack heaves, a loud distinctive rattle filling our ears.

"A rattlesnake? How are you going to stop a truck with a rattlesnake?"

He laughs. "Ha! Watch, you see."

"What do you want me to do?"

"Iron wagon stops at bottom of *arroyo*. Take guards and driver prisoner. Free Jesús. Let other prisoners go. Tie guards and driver. Leave in iron wagon. Sun come, iron wagons from north or Casas Grandes find guards and driver. Sun come, we south with Jesús."

"Where do you want me to wait?"

He points toward a shelf of rocks about halfway down the side of the *arroyo* and about five yards off the side of the road. I offer him back his telescope before I leave but he shakes his head and points at his eyes. "Sees enough. Go now."

I get a rope off Satanas, take the position where Yellow Boy wants me, and he takes a spot in the big rock's shadow by the side of the road just as it starts down the *arroyo's* bank. We wait in the cold still air. Soon we hear the puttering truck motor and the whine of its transmission and see occasional flashes of light on the roadway as it runs up and down over the shallow, rolling hills.

Yellow Boy opens the sack and tosses the snake out on the ground by the road. Thinking it's free to crawl off, it heads for cover. Yellow Boy is on it like a bird on a grasshopper. He grabs it behind its head and at the base of its tail so it can't rattle. It's the biggest rattlesnake, at least six or seven feet long, its head the size of my palm, I've seen since I was a boy helping Rufus Pike on his ranch. The snake, enraged, twists and turns to free itself, its jaws spread, fangs bared to bite anything, all of which Yellow Boy wants as he steps back in the shadows to wait.

The truck draws closer and above the mutter of the motor and whine of the gears we hear the driver singing "Camp Town Races" at the top of his lungs and one of the guards yelling, "Shut up! Shut up, you fool, and give us a little peace and quiet back here."

Just as the truck reaches the top of the *arroyo* and starts down the bank Yellow Boy steps out of the shadows and tosses the snake directly into the truck's cab. There's a large thumping sound as it hits the cab floor rattling.

The driver's singing instantly goes from, 'Doo dah, doo dah' to 'Oh doo dah... What the ... Oh, damn!" He's out the far side of the truck, moving like his pants are on fire, scrambling up the road's ruts to the top of the *arroyo*, yelling, "Snake! Snake!" Without the driver's foot on the brake, the truck gains speed rolling down the *arroyo* bank. With the snake in the truck's cab rattling for all he's worth, the four guards come flying out across the tailgate, scramble up the bank behind the driver, and leave the prisoners to fend for themselves.

When the last guard reaches the top of the bank gasping for air, they gather around the driver to watch the truck roll to the bottom of the *arroyo* and start up the other side, but the engine, not getting enough gas, coughs, sputters, and dies, leaving the truck stopped, starting to advance up the far side of the *arroyo*.

Yellow Boy steps out of the shadows, a ghoulish specter shining in bacon grease and charcoal black, and levers a shell into the Henry to catch the attention of the soldiers who turn toward the sound, their eyes big and round. Yellow Boy says, "*Señores,* drop your guns, raise your arms." All but one instantly throw down their rifles and pistols. The one who hesitates feels his campaign hat fly off his head as he and the others are momentarily deaf and blind from the thunder and flash of Yellow Boy's Henry. The last rifle and automatic pistol instantly hit the sand as the last pair of hands reached for the stars. "*Bueno, señores.*" He calls to me, "Bring, your *reata pronto*." To the soldiers, he says in a commanding voice, "Sit down!"

The deadly rifle stays pointed at them until I appear with the reata to tie each of them together with their hands behind their backs. When I finish, Yellow Boy nods for me to go to the truck and let the prisoners go.

I walk down to the back of the truck and say in a loud voice, "Jesús! Come out!"

There are sounds of chains being dragged across the bed of the truck. He reaches the tailgate, grabs it with both hands and swings over it to the ground. His hands and ankles are manacled and attached to a long chain that feeds back into the truck. He doesn't recognize me in my bacon grease and charcoal. "*Sí, señor?*"

I call to Yellow Boy, "Keys!"

He herds the soldiers down to the truck, pats them down until he finds the one with the keys, and gives them to me. I remove Jesús's manacles, tell him to put them on the guard who had the keys, to go to the top of the *arroyo*, and stay by the rock with the horses. As the prisoners climb out of the truck, we unlock their chains and put them on the soldiers, chain them together, and then make them climb back into the truck. Three of the men don't want anywhere near the truck, afraid the big rattler, now long gone with the cab doors left open, is still around, but Yellow Boy's Henry convinces them the snake is the least of two evils. When they're all inside, we lock the end of the chain to the truck, and bid them *adiós*.

Off to one side, out of the soldiers' hearing, I ask the prisoners if any of them can drive the truck. Two of the men say they can. I tell them they can walk away or drive the truck to Janos, which I guess is about twenty-five miles, and that they should be in Janos well before midnight. I say that if they take the truck, they are under obligation to me not to harm the soldiers, and to leave it with the soldiers near the road the supply trucks from the north use. An older man who knows how to drive promises to do all I ask. The driver and one of the other men crank and start it without a problem, and slowly drive it up the bank and disappear into the night.

When Yellow Boy and I reach the horses, Jesús is grinning from ear to ear and pacing about slapping his arms and stamping his feet trying to stay warm in the cold air.

"Doctor Grace, I did not recognize you and our *amigo*, *Señor* Muchacho Amarillo. *Muchas gracias* for saving me from the *gringos*, but why are you in Chihuahua?"

The adrenaline that had me ready to fight is fading away. I'm so cold from the icy night air with nothing on my torso that I begin to shake before I can answer.

Yellow Boy sees me tremble and says, "*Agua* down the *arroyo*. I find snake there. Come. Make fire. Make coffee. Wash before we ride and talk."

Jesús makes coffee while Yellow Boy and I rub our bodies with sand to take off most of the charcoal and grease, and wash the dust and sand off in a small standing pool. It feels good to be clean again and to feel my shakes disappear into the warm glow of the fire and cover of a shirt and coat. I give Jesús my change of clothes and tell him to wash as well. He's been in the prisoner pen for so long we prefer to stand upwind from him.

The coffee is strong and hot, something we all need as we listen to a thousand coyotes singing in the distance under the cold, bright moon and shimmering stars. I say to

Jesús, "You asked why we saved you from the *gringos*. The *gringos* take you to Columbus to put you on trial and hang you for the Columbus raid. We cannot let this happen to our *amigo* and *compadre*. Did you ride with Villa in the raid on Columbus?"

He stares at the cup, slowly nodding his head, his mouth pulled to one side that speaks volumes of regret.

"*Sí*, I was at Columbus. I held the horses and worked as a *medico* when they brought in the wounded. The general did not want to risk his best *medico* being shot. That says a lot, does it not Doctor Grace, that I was his best *medico*? Me, a kid who barely knows what to do for any *medico* problem except boil water or carry a stretcher."

I take a swallow of coffee.

"At least he did something right, protecting his *medico*. How did the *gringos* catch you?"

He shakes his head, makes a clicking noise, and taps his temple with his forefinger. "I have no brain. After the fight at Guerrero, the general says for me and other *hombres* to go home, hide our arms and wait. He says he will call us after the *gringos* get tired of chasing him and leave Mexico. This I do.

"Soon the *gringos* come. They search all the houses in my village. They find a dress a raider at Columbus gives me for the *señorita* I want for my wife. The *gringos* they arrest me and other *hombres* who have such things. They take us to the camp at Colonia Dublan and I wait in that pen for over seven days before they load us on the truck. You are right, Doctor Grace, they plan to give us a trial and hang us. The guards tell us this and laugh. I am very thankful you save me from the *gringos*, but Doctor Grace, I ask again, why are you here? It is very dangerous and I do not want *mi amigos* shot."

It's my turn to stare at the fire. I glance across the flames at Yellow Boy, and then at Jesús. "We have come for the general. Do you know how to find him?"

Jesús speaks the truth, not understanding what I mean when I say we've come for the general, and I don't try to clarify what I know he must be thinking. He says, "No, not exactly. I can guess from what I have heard. It is a good thing you seek him. I have heard stories that he was shot just below the knee in the battle at Guerrero and hides in a cave nearby. My *amigos* say he has great pain, pain so great he tries to kill himself. I have also heard he is at a *rancho* south of San José del Sito. I do not know where he is, but I will help you find him if you want."

I nod. "*Sí*, Jesús, we want your help. An Army Apache scout Muchacho Amarillo knows says the *gringos* believe the general hides south of San José del Sito. We ought to look there first."

Jesús smiles, his teeth showing bright against his brown skin. "*Bueno,* Doctor Grace. *Sí,* I will help you find the general. It is my great honor to ride with you...if I have something to ride."

We all laugh and I say, "Didn't your namesake, Jesus, who walked all the time, ride an ass into Jerusalem? You'll ride your own pony into San José del Sito."

We eat the bacon and drink the rest of the coffee before covering the fire and mounting up. Jesús can't weigh much more than a hundred pounds and Satanas easily carries us together. We return back down the Colonia Dublan road and ride for the foothill pass outside of Casas Grandes and near the road to Galeana.

53. TRAIL TO LAS CRUCES, MEXICO

Leaving Rojo's camp, Yellow Boy and I expected to live off the land and not pack supplies around in the middle of a war where they might be confiscated or, more likely, stolen. Now Jesús rides with us, making a group of three, far more noticeable and easier to spot even in the dark than two fast-moving shadows. Although Jesús has known hunger and thirst on long marches with his mount, if he has one, starving, ready to collapse with the next step, I don't think it's necessary to travel that way unless we have to. I wait for daylight in Casas Grandes to buy supplies while Yellow Boy and Jesús ride on to make a camp in the south pass off the road to Galena.

At a livery stable, the Mormon owner, Burklam Jones, looks me in the eye and gives me a good, steady handshake.

He makes and I accept a reasonable offer on a sturdy roan mustang, a well-worn saddle, and a new bridle, its leather well-oiled and flexible. As an afterthought I buy a little brown jenny with excellent confirmation and a pack rig for her to carry all our gear.

When I give Burklam Mexican silver for the animals and equipment, his ancient, wrinkled face cracks with a big smile and he writes a note for me to give his brother, Emerald Jones, who operates a mercantile store a couple of blocks down the street. The note says I paid for my animals and gear with *hard money* and that Emerald is to give me a twenty percent discount on anything I buy in the store. Emerald comes through with the discount and is generous in the weight of supplies he apportions for the price. Since I have three animals and relatively little weight in personal supplies, I buy twice the grain I normally would, a Dutch oven, and a sack of corn meal, all luxuries on a rough trail. For Jesús I buy pants and shirts, boots, a sombrero, underwear, a cup, pan, and spoon, and a long-used but serviceable Winchester '73 with a hundred cartridges.

Outside of Casas Grandes, I see a glint several times, far off near the top of the north side of the main pass. Someone is using field glasses to watch the traffic down the main road toward the north pass. I smile and wonder if it's our friends Runs Far and his women looking for Yellow Boy and me. I tell myself vigilance is its own reward and to stay alert.

The sun stands nearly straight overhead when I find Yellow Boy's camp hidden next to a spring in the south pass. Yellow Boy and Jesús have just swapped guard duties, Jesús to watch and Yellow Boy to sleep. I unload the horses after Yellow Boy silently gives me the all clear signal from where he lies and nods approval when I show him the jenny.

Jesús, teary-eyed, says, "*Muchas gracias*" many times when I give him the roan and gear I've bought. I find a place under a juniper, the tart smell of cedar sap filling my nose, unroll my horse blanket, crawl up under its deep shadow cast by myriad limbs letting in small dots of deep blue sky, close my eyes, and collapse into deep sleep.

Leaving the pass while the moon glows brightly behind the mountains to the northeast, we ride out on the *llano* parallel to and about a mile south of the road that runs from Casas Grandes to Galena, tracking southeast toward a few twinkling lights in Galeana ten or twelve miles away. American trucks, their lantern headlights filling the rough roadway, continue hauling supplies south to some new, unknown logistical supply point Pershing wants beyond Colonia Dublan. Among the trucks, an occasional automobile chugs along, probably carrying businessmen, reporters, photographers, members of Pershing's staff, or even Carranza government officials running errands.

Within a couple of miles of Galeana, we hit the Santa Markí, a wide, shallow river running south. Jesús says we can travel much faster and probably avoid American and Carrancista patrols if we stay between the river and the road running from Galeana to Buenaventura. The riverbed is dry in a few places and then shows long, slow stretches of water that become deeper and wider as we approach Buenaventura.

At Buenaventura, a village at the head of a valley three or four miles long in front of a deep canyon from which the river flows, we swing west around the village, and southeast into the rapidly narrowing valley as the sky begins to turn dawn gray. An hour later we're near the entrance to the canyon that Jesús says leads to Las Cruces and then to Namiquipa. He says he heard Villa fought a couple of successful battles at Namiquipa with Carrancista troops he'd caught by surprise, and took much needed supplies and a number of forced recruits. The tall ragged mountaintops in front of us are outlined in brilliant gold when we ride up a small creek feeding the river. We've covered a lot of ground, by my estimate maybe as much as forty miles, and we need to eat and rest.

Over a cup of coffee I say to Jesús, "Why do you think I left the general at San Pedro de la Cueva?"

Staring at his coffee, he shrugs and looks at me from under his brows.

"The general, he tells the *hombres* with him you had to go. We are surprised the general does not speak of putting you in front of a firing squad for attacking him. We think it is because you are old *amigos*. The way he says you had to go, it sounds like you have very important business at your village. Was there a bad problem, at your *hacienda*, that you had to leave, *Señor* Grace? You must have been in a great hurry. None of us, your *amigos*, saw you to say *adiós*."

Yellow Boy's stoic face never changes, but I see him squint at Jesús studying the honesty in his eyes. I say, "*Sí, mi amigo*, I am sorry I had to leave pronto and not tell *mi amigos, adiós*. There was important business I had to settle in my village. I didn't even tell *mi amigo*, Camisa Roja, *adiós*. When did you see him last? Is he still with the general?'

Jesús nods. "*Sí*, he was with the general when I left for home. I saw him a few days after you left. He was beat up bad. He said he was ambushed and nearly killed by San Pedro de la Cueva men who escaped the general's execution orders and were hiding in the mountains. He looked lucky to be alive."

"What did you think of the executions in San Pedro de la Cueva?"

He stares at his coffee cup for a couple of minutes, listening to the fire hiss and pop, the morning birds sing, feeling the cold air on his back, the fire's heat on his face and hands, hard and calloused, the result of hard labor and war far beyond his years. He sighs and slowly shakes his head. "Those villagers, they just made a mistake. It was not right for the general to execute them. You ask me what I think? I'm still a kid, not old and wise, I cannot even write my name, but the general went a little loco. The priest, Doctor Grace, the priest, *mi Dios*, he shot a priest. That was a bad thing for all of us. *Mi madre*, she says *Dios* will strike us all because the general murdered a priest and we did nothing. It was a bad, bad thing. What do you think Doctor Grace?"

"Your *madre* is right, Jesús. God will strike him for murdering a priest. Maybe *Dios* will strike us all because we were part of the general's army and did not stop him. Killing those people wasn't war. It was murder. I believe there is hard justice in this world. We all get our due and none of us have clean hands. *Comprende?*"

"*Sí, comprendo.* Still I am glad you go to help the general. He is a great man."

I see Yellow Boy cut his eyes to look in my face. I say nothing, only nod.

As the sun slips behind the western mountains, we head up river into the long winding canyon with sides a thousand feet high and the trail so black with shadows from moonlight blocked by the high mountain ridges, we have to pick our way along the river trail very carefully. I doubt we could have made it without Yellow Boy's cat-like night vision.

It's nearing dawn and very cold when we see white adobe buildings and a tall church tower in Las Cruces. Three or four miles up river from the village, we make our day camp in piñons up a creek that runs into the river from the west. Jesús has an uncle who lives in Las Cruces and after we camp, he leaves to learn news of Villa and the *gringo* army chasing him.

Returning at mid-morning, Jesús brings a basket full of *tortillas* and a pot of beans seasoned with fiery red chilies from his aunt. His uncle learned from a peddler just the day before that Villa was seen outside of San Francisco de Borja and that there is a *gringo* cavalry squadron no more than a day behind him and gaining. There is also news that some Carrancista soldiers northwest of Guerrero mutinied, intending to join the Villistas.

Jesús shakes his head. "*Señores*, we must be very careful who we palaver with from now on. I have no more uncles farther south."

54. FINDING GENERAL PERSHING

More than half the trail to Namiquipa is through rough, hilly country that gradually smoothes out into open fields along the river. Yellow Boy often pauses to survey the countryside, looking for shadows that should not be moving, looking for Runs Far and his women, looking for any mounted horses. We pass Namiquipa and later pass east of Santa Ana de Bavícora. Desert bushes are reclaiming the land that once supported huge croplands of the *hacendados*, and off in the distance in every direction, we see the trembling light from orange fires where potential enemies gather to ward off the night's chill.

Jesús thinks a cluster of lights off to the east must be Rubio. We camp for the day two or three miles past Rubio in a grove of cottonwoods and willows by the river. The animals hold up well through the long nights of hard travel. Even the little jenny, carrying the heaviest load, shows no signs of sores on her back or of not being able to keep up when we put the horses into a steady gallop.

The next evening we ride through San Jose Pass and stay on a straight line across miles of what might have been, at one time, fertile fields and might be so again when the Mexican politicians stopped trying to kill each other. Near dawn we see stars reflecting off a huge lake in front of us, and ride around its western edge toward the lights of Anáhuac.

I'm a little nervous. There's no apparent place to hide a camp and daylight is coming fast. However, we cross a small river that feeds the big lake and, following the river, soon come to long stretches of trees that can hide us very well.

The gray light of dawn is coming quick, crows roosting in the trees begin to fly out toward the hills on the other side of the lake, and birds are beginning to call as light pours golden and bright out of the outline on the mountain ridges. While Jesús makes a fire, Yellow Boy and I climb up the creek bank, careful to stay hidden in the dark shadows of the trees, and survey the countryside. Yellow Boy thinks he may have seen someone behind us, but looking down our back trail in the dawn light sees nothing.

I say, "If they're behind us out on the flats won't we see them when there is enough light?"

He shakes his head.

"No. Old trick. Make horse lie down on side and stay. Man searching for riders never see rider and horse when they lie down in grass or near bushes."

About a half mile south I see glints off something sitting in a field near the lake. The light is too poor to tell if it's a man with binoculars, farm machinery, some kind of vehicle, or maybe a shed with a new roof. I pull out my binoculars and the first thing I see makes me take steps farther back into the shadows. A man moves around in front of field machinery. I nod for Yellow Boy to use his telescope in that direction. He sees the man, but recognizes nothing else.

Shivering in the cold gray air we wait for good light and the revelation of who and what we've seen. As the sun finally pops over the mountains, I recognize the mechanical thing as three automobiles and a truck parked to form a square. The man, tall and thin, maybe middle-aged, looks familiar. He puts on a shirt after he finishes washing in a zinc bucket sitting on a stool. There's something about his carriage and the thin face with a mustache I've seen before… "That sorry woman, Fate, loves us today, Uncle."

"You see woman, Hombrecito?"

"Take a look with your Big Eye. You're looking at Big Star's camp. The tall thin one outside the cars and truck is General Pershing, Big Star. I'll bet you beans on a plate that Quentin Peach is sleeping inside the area formed by the cars and truck. Come on, let's go have a look."

We tell Jesús what we've seen, that we'll have a look, and for him to stay by the fire and wait for us in case someone in the group might recognize him. I tell him to watch us with my binoculars, and if he sees anyone coming to check our story, to say that he's our guide and cook.

Saddling the horses, we ride up the bank and out on to the pool-table-flat field between where we've camped on the creek and the motorized fort by the lake. We aren't a hundred yards out of the trees before someone points at us and yells to the others. We let the horses casually saunter across the field toward the little fort, and see at least ten rifle barrels level down on us. Pershing casually finishes buttoning his shirt, stuffs its tails in his pants, and stands watching us, arms folded across his chest. Several curious, protective men soon join him. Off to his left, with a Cheshire cat grin, Quentin Peach appears from behind the truck.

Running to our horses, he reaches for our hands for a hardy shake.

"Gentlemen, this is a pleasant surprise. Glad you could drop in today. General, this is Doctor Henry Grace and his Apache uncle, Yellow Boy. You met Doctor Grace when we stopped by your office at Fort Bliss four or five days before you left for the Culbertson ranch."

Pershing squints up at me and extends his hand.

"Why, yes, I believe I remember Doctor Grace. Tell me gentlemen, why are you in Mexico when there's a good chance you might get shot by the US Army, Villistas, Carrancistas, or just plain old bandits? These are deadly times. Swing down and join us in an Army breakfast. It's not much, just hardtack, beans, and coffee."

Yellow Boy and I both grin at the invitation.

"Thank you, sir. We've been riding all night and hadn't even lighted a fire to cook anything when we saw you in front of your auto fort."

We dismount and are handed eating utensils out of the truck's supplies. Squatting by the warm little fire inside the protective automobile and truck circle, we eat the hardtack and beans and drink strong bitter coffee, glad to have it.

Hat pushed back on his head and a new Army .45 hanging on a web belt, Quent sits down beside us, delighted to see fresh faces and hear news about what's been happening in the rest of the world. I see him exchange glances with Pershing and know Pershing wants him to get as much information out of us as he can. Out of Pershing's sight, Quent gives a little conspiratorial wink and I give him a tiny nod camouflaged with a shoulder stretch.

"How'd you boys come? See anything interesting?"

I take a slurp of coffee and scratch my chin and Yellow Boy keeps his poker face, not revealing the first hint of interest in Quent's question. I tell him our story and give him as much detail as I can so it won't look like we're trying to hide anything.

"After we came out of the Sierra Madres we passed by Colonia Dublan, which is gettin' a mighty big stack of Army supplies from all those trucks drivin' back and forth from Columbus. I've never seen so many motorized vehicles on the road at one time–not even in San Francisco.

"I stopped by Burklam Jones' livery in Casas Grandes and bought some supplies from him and his brother Emerald who runs a mercantile store. They gave us a pretty good price on our trail supplies. Then we rode over to Galeana and on up the river to Buenaventura and down that long, deep canyon that the Santa Maria River passes through. We camped just outside of Las Cruces for a night and went on to Namiquipa, camped outside of Rubio, and then came on over here last night."

As Quent listens he nods and doodles in the sand with the point of a bayonet he's been given along with his Army '03 Springfield.

"Where you headed today?"

"We're gonna make camp down by the creek over yonder. That's where we left our guide and supplies. Remember Yellow Boy and I traveled at night when we took you to Villa's camp last September? Well there's a whole lot more reason to travel at night now and that's what we're doin'."

He pulls a pack of Camels, the first packaged cigarettes I've ever seen, all ready rolled, ready to light up, from his pocket. He offers them to Yellow Boy and me and then takes one himself. Yellow Boy and I aren't quite sure what to do with ours but imitate Quent tamping the tobacco on one end for our mouths and then lighting ours off his match. It's a good smoke, one of the best I've had in a long time.

Taking a long, lazy draw from the cigarette, he lets the smoke curl over his lips and out of his mouth before he blows the remainder into the air above his head.

"Some drummer gave me a box of these in Columbus and asked that I pass them around to the soldiers to see what they thought. It's a pretty good smoke. It doesn't satisfy like a good cigar or pipe, but I can see where just the sheer convenience of having a smoke any time you feel like it without having to roll your own will be addictive. So where are you headed? Must be important if you're willin' to risk getting your tails shot off by virtually any passerby."

I take a deep drag and blow the smoke into a little cloud that slowly drifts away in the cold morning air. Although Pershing has his back to us, and is using his binoculars to scan the country around us, I can tell he's listening.

"We're headin' south; we hear that Villa is somewhere south of San Jose del Sito, but still north of Parral, and we're gonna find him."

Quent grins.

"Yeah, well get in line. Seems like most of the northern hemisphere wants *to find him*, as you say. Mind if I ask why you want to find him?"

"Let's just say there's a personal matter to settle between us and I also made a promise to Maud Wright to set things right when I found him, not that it's anything I hadn't already planned to do anyway. You remember her, don't you?"

"Yeah... yeah, I remember Maud Wright very well. I hope she and Johnnie are doin' well in El Paso."

He buries the cigarette butt in the sand as he blows the last of the smoke out his nose and spits a stray piece of tobacco off his lip and shakes his head.

"Damn, Henry, it seems like I've been away from home forever."

We relax for a couple of minutes, saying nothing, sipping coffee, watching the sun's reflection floating like a golden bowl, move across the smooth lake's surface. Pershing lowers his binoculars and calls to his executive officer.

"Mr. Patton, I want a meeting with the staff in five minutes."

The officer, a tall blond lieutenant not yet thirty, wearing a fancy nickel-plated .45 caliber revolver with ivory handles, jumps to his feet, salutes. "Yes, Sir!"

After Lieutenant Patton strides off to gather the officers and is out of hearing, Pershing turns to me.

"Doctor Grace, if you find Villa before I do, and you survive settling your business with him, I'd very much appreciate you giving me his body. It'd prove we didn't need to be down here any longer and I could send my boys home."

I squint at him, swallowing to keep down the bile, and chew on my lip a moment before I answer.

"I'm sorry sir, but I'd never let you treat Villa's body like a scalp, like some kind of Roman spoil of war to be hung from the city gates. Villa and these people deserve better than that. I'll bury him in a respectful grave and let his *dorados* know where it is so they and the *peons* he fought for can come to pay their respect or hurl their curses, but I'll never hand him over to you."

Pershing, stares at me a moment, sticks out his lower lip, and nods.

"I can respect that. You're an honorable man, Doctor Grace."

We shake hands.

"Sir, my uncle and I will be leaving for our own camp shortly. I expect you'll still be with your staff when we leave. Thanks for breakfast. *Adiós*."

"Good luck finding Villa. If our success is any indication, you'll need all you can get. Remember to come join me when you finish your business."

I smile and snap him a salute as he joins his officers.

Kneeling on the ground, surrounded by his staff, Pershing rolls out a battered map covered with military shorthand for troop and materiel locations. The officers kneel down by it or sit where they can see it as he talks, tapping the map with his riding crop as a pointer, discussing his latest intelligence on Villa and the movement of his four squadrons of cavalry.

Hands in his back pockets, Quent follows us as we walk over to the horses and prepare to mount.

"I hope you boys make it and don't get filled with Mexican lead. Pershing's intelligence corps believes Villa is somewhere near Santa Cruz de Herrara, about fifty miles northwest of Parral. It's at least a long three or four-day ride south through very rough country. Chances are you'll be too late to get any satisfaction, even if you do find him."

I look at him and frown.

"What are you talkin' about?"

He shakes his head and looks disgusted.

"Villa and several Japanese peddlers who rattle around down here selling everything from pots and pans to rifles and bullets are friends. Pershing's intelligence staff found a couple who claim to know Villa well, made a deal to give them a promissory note for several sacks of gold up front, with more to come if they slipped Villa some poison the Army intelligence staffers gave them."

I laugh out loud.

"Are they crazy? You know and I know, everybody in Mexico knows, Villa doesn't touch his food until somebody samples it before he ever takes a bite or a swallow. Besides, they have to know that if they're successful, the *dorados* will drag them all over the desert and turn them into greasy spots riding over them with horses. It's a miserable way to die."

"Delayed reaction."

"What?"

"The Japanese said almost exactly the same thing. The Army boys say the poison has no taste and is odorless, but most important, it doesn't do anything until three days after it's taken. That's supposed to give the poisoners time to get away and death looks like it's from a heart attack or stroke. The Japanese gave a small dose to a dog that was hanging around camp and waited around to see what happened."

"So what happened?"

Quent makes this sly, Br' Fox grin.

"Three days after running off with some meat they poisoned, the dog gives this long mournful howl, gets stiff-legged, starts shaking all over, and falls over dead as a hog hit between the eyes with a sledge hammer. The Japs were impressed and agreed they'd try it on Villa."

"How long ago did they leave?"

Quent flips through his notebook and looking at me from under raised brows, says, "Two days ago."

55. BLIND MIND'S EYE

Back in our camp by the creek, Jesús cooks and Yellow Boy eats a second breakfast of *tortillas*, seasoned meat, and coffee. I tell Jesús what we've learned about the Japanese poison plot and how they're two days ahead of us out of Ciudad Chihuahua, looking for Villa. Jesús's eyes grow round and his jaw drops like a surprised child's before it snaps shut against clenched teeth.

I stare at him for a moment, wondering what must be going through his mind as an angry red thundercloud frown begins to gather around eyes narrowed to a squint and a thin, straight slash mouth. He shakes his head, as if to gain his balance and clear his mind.

"Those men, the Japanese, they were good *amigos* with the general. He is always fair with them and treats them like brothers. They take *gringo dinero* to murder him with poison? Who needs bastard *amigos* like these traitors? They deserve to die. I hope he catches them and the *dorados* drag them for miles through the cactus and trample them to pieces. Where did the *gringos* give the Japanese this poison?"

"Somewhere near Ciudad Chihuahua. Why?"

Jesús stares off down the creek, thinking, scratching his jaw. "They will be in their peddler wagon. That means they will take the road to Parral and turn west where it forks to Valerio, go across the mountains to San Francisco del Sito, and over the mountains on a very rough road to Valle del Rosario. From there the land is mostly flat and the road follows the river past Balleza and finally cuts across country to Santa Cruz de Herrera. Maybe it takes these peddlers six or seven days to reach Santa Cruz de Herrera this way.

"If we go cross-country past Cusihuiriachi to the San Pedro River, the ride will be very hard but we can be in Santa Cruz de Herrera in four nights. Maybe we can get there at about the same time or before they do and stop them, without riding the horses to death. We can go faster if we take the roads and probably catch them in the mountains between San Jose del Sito and Valle de Rosario, but we will wear out the horses and the mountains will be filled with Carrancistas and Villistas looking for a fight. It is better to take the way along the San Pedro and Concho Rivers. There is time. The Japanese, they will stay a day or two before they leave. They will not poison the general before we find him."

We look at Yellow Boy, his cheeks puffed out like a squirrel's stuffed with nuts as he wolfs down his second breakfast. He nods and holds up his hand for us to wait, his mouth too full to speak. He swallows and says, "Jesús speaks wise words. Go by way of Cusihuiriachi." Jesús's idea makes a lot of sense to me too.

I shrug when he looks at me for agreement with Yellow Boy. "*Bueno*, we will do as you say."

We ride out of camp up into the fields on the south side of the river as the sun kisses the land *adiós* with a cloud bouquet of reds and oranges and purples. Yellow Boy, staying in the lead, rides straight as a bowshot for Cusihuiriachi, only a few miles up the road.

The whitewashed doorways in the long adobe buildings with bars on the windows at Cusi, as Jesús calls it, are shut tight against the night and no lights show anywhere in Cusi as we ride up the valley, following a rough trail around low mountains and over a low pass down to the winding San Pedro River that leads to San Francisco de Borja. The land is quiet and still and feels totally empty. There is no light from fires or lights from lanterns anywhere, only moonlight, bushes, and sand. We wrap our blankets around us as we ride to shield against the freezing night air, looking like dark cocoons adrift, floating across the land, and we only stop three or four times to rest the horses and the jenny.

Just before dawn Yellow Boy turns up a large creek coming down a valley out of the western mountains. We ride around a bend dodging bushes and small trees hanging over the banks, and within a few hundred yards of the river, stop for the day.

While Yellow Boy keeps the first watch, Jesús and I make beds in a thicket of piñons filled with inky shade. The cold air rapidly disappearing with the rising sun, it's warm and toasty wrapped in my blanket and soon the dream comes like it always has in the last year, a ghost following me, haunting me, refusing to go away.

* * *

The jaguar, flames roaring and whistling like a mighty, red wind, digs its claws in the creek's flat, limestone bottom, dragging its paralyzed hindquarters forward, expending all its strength and roaring its rage, strains to reach a paw forward to hook me with its awful claws and drag me into its snarling fangs and the fiery burning wind consuming it...

My eyes snap open, my heart pounding. I lie there a moment knowing Yellow Boy will soon come to tap on my foot for my turn to keep watch. Sitting up in my blankets, I feel sweat pouring off my face like a downpour from the black anvil clouds of summer. Jesús is on his back, still asleep, mouth open and snoring. Waiting for my pulse to slow, I ask myself why I keep dreaming of my fight with the jaguar and why he's consumed with fire like a meteor burning itself to oblivion, about to take me with him before I wake up.

The air is hot and still in the thicket, my throat dry, my body begs for water. I find a canteen and take a couple of long pulls. The cool trickle never felt so good going down. Wiping my mouth with my sleeve, I try once more to understand what the dream is trying to tell me. Staring across the mid-morning, shimmering heat waves, I study the mountains, their patchy red, steep cliffs, piñons near the bottoms, tall pines near the top, and recall the real jaguar that tried to kill me ten years ago. Is the dream just an over-active imagination elevating a true memory into something more? My mind struggles but just can't see the dream's message.

I see Yellow Boy rise out of the tall gra'ma grass up on the hill, where he's kept watch up and down the river and across the valley. He waves me forward to take my turn at guard in his nest. I point toward where I slept under the piñons. He nods and disappears as I walk forward in waist-high grass. When I reach the trampled down grass, I look back and he's already asleep on my blanket.

56. THE HIDING PLACE

Yellow Boy studies the valley, north and south up and down the river and across the valley to the Sierra El Alamo Mocho Mountains, always looking for signs of movement, and of men, dust clouds, light or smoke from fires, reflections off glass or brass or silver, but he sees nothing.

I ask Yellow Boy, "Do you think Runs Far has gotten in front of us and waits in ambush?"

He shakes his head. "They must follow. Don't know where we go. Hang back and follow tracks. Wait for mistake. Maybe he makes mistake and we ambush him. Watch close for Runs Far."

A smooth, sandy trail stretches over most of the way to San Francisco de Borja, and there is plenty of water for the horses from occasional pools that have not yet disappeared in the sandy bottom of the nearly dry San Pedro River. The stars are out and the moon still a bright yellow glow behind the northeastern mountains when we see twinkling lights in the village of San Francisco de Borja, and turn east off the river trail to follow a road that swings around the mountains standing behind the village.

As Jesús and I ride on, Yellow Boy sits his horse and watches our back trail from the deep shadows of a bridge in front of the village. He catches us three or four miles down the road and nods when my eyes ask.

"*Sí*. Runs Far follows with his women. Time for them to leave. We send them back to Pelo Rojo pretty soon now."

A big, bright yellow moon floats above the tops of the eastern mountains as we ride through Santa Ana, just a few adobe houses, doors bolted, and pigs and chickens hidden from prying eyes, clustered around an ancient small, adobe church built with a clear view of the river and the mountains on the other side.

Crossing the river on Santa Ana's little wooden bridge and following the trail south for a mile or so, Jesús leads us east into the mountains. He follows a wide, juniper-lined *arroyo* that passes many smaller *arroyos* that, during monsoon season, make small rivers, draining the valleys and canyons leading up into the mountains. We climb steadily until, looking back down the trail, I guess we're at least a thousand feet above the valley.

Jesús leads us up a high-walled canyon. The trail isn't bad, but it's steep and bathed in icy gray light as it leads us up to a small lake with maybe six hundred feet left to climb to the top of the ridge. Yellow Boy points toward a grove of trees in a sheltered niche at the south end of the lake, near where the trail begins for the ridgeline.

"Rest horses. Eat. Ride over pass when sun goes away. Maybe fix Runs Far."

I'm tired and ready to stop and there's no argument from Jesús.

The lake water is icy cold and as high as we are, the swirling wind, desperately cold, blows nearly all the time, making our hands shake as we try to light a fire several times until, hunkering down together, and using our bodies to shield a wavering flame from a Redhead match, finally get the tinder lighted and kindling aflame.

Looking back down the trail we have a narrow view between the canyon's walls of sunlight on the western mountains as the shadow line creeps across the valley and up our trail until we're bathed in bright, soft light. It's been a long, exhausting night ride, and wrapped in my blanket near the fire, the unconsciousness of sleep takes me, swift and sure.

The fading light from the western sun pouring through the canyon is like a spotlight on the trail before us. Yellow Boy has explored the canyon while I slept and thinks it's a perfect spot to ambush Runs Far. A large boulder balances precariously on a ledge on the south side of the canyon. He wants to roll it off on Runs Far. If we kill him that way, there will be no blood feud between Yellow Boy and the relatives of Runs Far. They'll never know if the boulder fell on its own or not. If it doesn't kill Runs Far, he'll likely think we're on to him and either leave or hang so far back he won be any threat at all anymore.

We take Yellow Boy's telescope, give the horses and jenny to Jesús and tell him to lead them to the top of the ridge and wait there for us. The way up the trail is clear as we break camp, and Jesús leads the horses forward while Yellow Boy and I walk down the trail to the canyon entrance and climb the steep wall to the shelf where the boulder sits.

We try rocking the boulder a little to determine if, between the two of us, we have enough strength to get it started off the shelf edge. When we put our shoulders to it, it rocks a little. There is only a couple of feet between the boulder and the canyon wall. It'll be close hard work with little room for leverage, but Yellow Boy thinks we can move it and sits down on the edge of the ledge to study the trail down the canyon with his Big Eye telescope.

A half hour passes and the moon glow behind the eastern ridges increases. In an hour the canyon is bathed in moonlight and shadow but there is no sign of Runs Far and his women. I'm worried. If we spend too much time waiting on Runs Far we may not get to Villa before he's poisoned, and, for some inexplicable reason, that's important to me. I don't understand why. Yellow Boy and I are here on the ledge ready to push a two thousand pound rock down on the member of our own tribe and aren't giving it a second thought. As I shiver in the cold dark shadows, I marvel at the vagaries of the human psyche.

In a little while Yellow Boy smiles, hands me the telescope and points to the shadows near the north side of the entrance to the canyon. I see nothing until one of the shadows moves. I look closer and watch a few seconds. It's a horse moving up the canyon. Yellow Boy takes the telescope and speaks softly near my ear.

"Roll rock now."

By my estimate we have less than five minutes before Runs Far, his women, and their horses are past us. Yellow Boy and I strain to give the boulder a good strong push using our shoulders. It rocks back and forth a little, but doesn't budge. We get lower and try again. The rocking back and forth increases, but still no joy: the rock isn't going anywhere this way. Run's Far will be by us in a couple of more minutes. The night air is freezing cold but sweat pours in torrents from both of us.

Yellow Boy scrambles to gather a few fist-sized rocks. When he has four or five, he gives them to me and whispers for me to put one as far under the boulder as I can when he pushes it forward. He braces himself between the cliff and the boulder, and pushes with all the power in his legs. The boulder tips forward. I put a couple of rocks under it before it can tilt back. I hear the horses in the wash gravel as they approach us.

Yellow Boy takes a deep breath and pushes with all his might, and I push hard against it, too. The boulder suddenly tips over and goes crashing down the canyon side in an instant starting a minor landslide and nearly taking Yellow Boy with it. I manage to grab his arm and hold on long enough for him to steady and not slip over the edge.

From below we hear, "Wah! Run, sisters! Run!"

Moments after the explosive cracks from the boulder bouncing down the canyon side and taking other rocks with it, we hear horses screaming but no human voices, none at all.

A thick cloud of dust hovers in the canyon, hiding everything under it. Yellow Boy nods toward ridgeline. Time to leave.

Up the trail we stop by the lake for a few swallows of water before climbing the rest of the way to meet Jesús waiting on top of the ridgeline.

"Do you think we killed them, Uncle?"

He shrugs.

"Maybe, maybe not, but horses are no more. They go back to Pelo Rojo now. Forget Yellow Boy and Hombrecito. After Villa, we return to Rojo's camp. Know then if they live. Go now. Burning moonlight. *Vamos.*"

I have to smile. I've heard cowboys use, "We're burning daylight." I've never heard anyone use 'burning moonlight' before Yellow Boy.

We soon find Jesús on the ridgeline and head down the other side of the pass in deep shadow darkness that makes for slow going getting down to the river canyon below us. After a long rest and grain for the horses at the river, we set off for Ojitos. Once out of the river canyon we cross long rolling ridges that, from their tops, look like an angry, frozen ocean in the white moonlight. It's as rough a country as I've ever seen except high in the northern Sierra Madre and the horses and mule work hard to get us across it.

Reaching San José del Sito we ride around the village and down the Conchos River trail toward the low, rough mountains covered by moonlight and shadows in front of us. The river soon branches off toward the west into a narrow valley with the Sierra Azul Mountains on one side and high hills on the other. As we planned, we follow the river branch rather than take the road we suspect the Japanese follow.

About a mile down the river we come to a hard ride between cliffs in a quarter mile of rocky, boulder-strewn canyon, the horses having to swim a hundred yards or so when the trail disappears at the canyon edges. Leaving the canyon we pass another village, La Joya. It looks much like Santa Ana with a big adobe church surrounded by several small adobe houses. In the cold gray light of a disappearing moon and stars, no dogs bark, no rooster crows, and no pigs snuffle. La Joya appears abandoned. Like Santa Ana, there are no signs of life anywhere.

We follow the river until there's good light, and make camp in the trees on a small bench above the river.

Jesús believes we might reach Santa Cruz before dawn the next day. I hope so. I want to finish my business with Villa and get on with my life. My time with Lupe makes me think more about living than killing, and of using my medical skills on others besides men and horses shot to pieces in battles led by a narcissistic murderer.

We leave our camp on the little bench by the river while there's still light. The river is wide and shallow with wide sandy banks that make for easy riding. Finally leaving the canyon, we ride east along the river, which is used to irrigate broad fertile fields already planted. Passing Valle del Rosario we see a few lights after an hour or so from, what Jesús says, is Balleza.

Stopping to rest the horses and jenny, Jesús smiles. He's been studying any landmarks he can see.

"*Señores*, I am glad to say Santa Cruz is not far. It is an easy ride and we ought to make it before the daylight."

Yellow Boy looks down the road and the river running beside it.

"Many use the road, and in the night, army patrols ride. Is the river trail any good?"

"*Sí, señor*. It is not bad but it takes maybe half again

longer than the road because we have to cross the river a few times."

Yellow Boy stares down the road and looks up and down the river again before saying, "Hmmph. More better we take river trail, less chance of meeting *gringos*, Carrancistas, or Villistas."

We take the river trail. The river is wide and shallow with wide sandy banks, and it's easy to follow until it narrows into a canyon with high, nearly vertical, striped sandstone walls, but even then the narrow trail is clear and we don't have to get in the water like we did as we approached La Joya.

The lights from Santa Cruz not more than a mile away and a nearby ranch house not more than a quarter mile away are easy to see as we leave the river canyon. My heart races as I realize we're close to finding Villa, and if I'm very lucky, I might also find Camisa Roja with Villa and take care of business with both.

We find a small canyon back off the river that gives us a clear view of Santa Cruz and good tree cover to keep us out of sight. I'm a little uncomfortable being so close to the ranch house across the river, but all things considered, we're safe enough, and the little canyon leads into the Sierra Azul Mountains giving us a back door getaway.

We make camp and Jesús volunteers, "*Señores*, when the sun comes, I will ride into Santa Cruz and ask the old men at their coffee where the general hides."

Yellow Boy nods and I shrug "Okay" as we unload the horses and jenny and give them their end-of-ride rubdown.

Jesús makes coffee and as he cooks a meal, we slurp the hot, precious brew, enjoying it warming the inside of our bellies, and the fire's warmth on our faces. Listening to the homey scrape and clank of Jesús's pots and pans, we're quiet, tired from the long night ride and pushing a rock weighing at least a ton off a cliff on to Runs Far.

Staring into the flames I try to imagine how to get close enough to Villa to stop the Japanese and still settle accounts with him. I turn to Yellow Boy and ask, "How is the best way to approach Villa's camp and the *dorados* guarding him, without getting shot?"

Before Yellow Boy can answer, Jesús says, "Let me go in first. I was a *medico* and horse holder at Columbus. The *dorados* with the general know who I am and they will welcome me back when I tell them I have brought our friend Doctor Grace to help the general with his wound."

I feel like a deceitful traitor coming all this way and not telling Jesús what I plan to do.

Yellow Boy says nothing and his poker face shows nothing as he listens to Jesús, but I can tell he's not happy that Jesús doesn't know our plans, that he thinks we're betraying Jesús with a lie. I think, *I ought to tell Jesús what we're planning, but I can't risk him telling Villa. Whatever it takes to settle my score, to settle Maud's score with Villa, even if it means betraying a trust, means telling a lie, I'll do it.* I remember when I told Quent I'd rather die than lie and marvel at how easy it's been for me to forget that principle.

I nod. "What you say is probably the safest thing to do, but there's still a chance they'll shoot first and ask questions later. Are you sure you want to risk it?"

"*Sí*, Doctor Grace, I want to risk it. They will not shoot me, and the sooner we can help the general with his leg the better off we will be."

He grins appreciatively when I reply, "You're a good man, Jesús."

"Gracias, Doctor Grace, and so are you and *Señor* Yellow Boy."

My head scrunches lower into my bandana with the full weight of my deceit made clear by Jesús's compliment.

The stars are bright in the dark before the dawn. Jesús and I nap by the fire while Yellow Boy takes a blanket for the first watch, and finds a hiding place at the edge of the trees where he has clear lines of sight up and down and across the river.

At first light I'm up and drink some leftover coffee while I use my old field glasses to study the nearby *hacienda*, not more than a quarter of a mile away across the river. I have to look through the trees surrounding the place and that makes it hard to see much detail. There are a couple of men who look like some of Villa's *dorados* I remember from last December. Can it be possible to have come so far and have the luck to camp next door to Villa's hiding place?

A wagon carrying two men rattling down the road running by the *hacienda* drives through the gate on the fence surrounding the *hacienda*'s yard. The men who remind me of *dorados* I know saunter over to the wagon, rifles in the crooks of their arms. Words are exchanged and one of the men reaches in a vest pocket and hands a brilliant white scrap of folded paper to one of the *dorados*. He unfolds it, looks at it front and back, and walks into the *hacienda*. A man on the wagon pulls off his hat and wipes the sweat off his forehead with a shirtsleeve. I think, *I don't believe it*. The man is Japanese.

I motion Jesús over and hand him the binoculars as I

point toward the wagon. "Who do you think stays there?" He barely puts his eyes to the soft rubber eyepieces before he breathlessly says, "Japanese! Those men on the wagon are Japanese! I'd bet a hundred pesos they're trying to get in the house to see the general. I don't think I need to go into Santa Cruz to find General Villa, Doctor Grace. He's just across the river."

We jump when Yellow Boy silently comes to stand behind us and says, "*Sí*, Arango is in the *hacienda*."

57. THE GAMBLE

The white-washed adobe *hacienda* surrounded by beds of blooming desert plants, its yard fenced by a combination of posts and rails and a stone wall that keeps horses in and cattle out, projects a sense of timelessness like it's been there since before the *conquistadores*. It reminds me of a big sculptured white rock, part of the natural landscape.

After a long delay, the Japanese peddlers are led into the *hacienda* through a door near where several *dorados*, alert and vigilant like cats waiting for a foolish bird, smoke cigarillos, clean their pistols, or nap with their sombreros pulled over their eyes.

Studying the *hacienda*, I try to think through what's awaiting us across the river. Since Jesús doesn't know Villa tried to have me murdered, it's likely the *dorados* won't know either and they'll welcome a *medico* and his assistant who rode with them at Agua Prieta and Hermosillo. Villa is vain enough to ask me to come inside thinking I've forgiven his betrayal. I'll need to be alone with him to kill him. Maybe I can claim I have a private message for him. Regardless of how I kill him, he's going to know it's coming and that I'll be doing it. If we can get out of the *hacienda* alive and back across the river, Yellow Boy can make it look like we've disappeared into thin air. The *dorados* will never find us. Camisa Roja is the wild card. If he's in the house and sees me, it'll only be a question of who shoots first. If, by some twist of fate, I'm lucky enough to execute him too, and escape, I'll never need to return to Mexico.

I shake my head. Rationally, there are too many "ifs" to survive killing Villa in the *hacienda*. Trying to wait out the situation isn't an option either. The longer we wait, the more likely one of Pershing's squadrons will find Villa and his *dorados* or we'll be discovered. I decide to let the chips fall where they may. I won't live my life in fear, without honor, without power. It's my life or Villa's.

Staying out of sight from the *hacienda*, Jesús and I ride down river into Santa Cruz, cross the bridge, and return back up river on the road by the *hacienda*. Yellow Boy crosses the river upstream and comes back to hide in the trees behind the yard fence in case we need covering fire when we try to escape. He knows I'll have to drag Jesús with me to get him out of there.

I feel like Judas for lying to Jesús about what I intend, but since the deception has been cast, it's my only opportunity to take Villa, and I have to kill him regardless of the cost. Jesús riding up to the *hacienda* door with me makes him an innocent part of my assassination plot. If the dorados catch him after I try to kill Villa, he'll be lucky if he's only dragged and trampled to death, his crushed remains no more than a bag of broken bones hung in a tree to rot. I'm fast learning assassination is nasty business, both in its objective and the taint it leaves on every innocent associated with it.

Turning off the road and passing through the fence gate, we ride past the peddler wagon, and stop near the door where the *dorados* watch us with poker-faced indifference, cold black eyes staring at our faces, fingers wiggling to stay loose, palms casually resting on the butt ends of their revolvers.

Jesús and I advance up to the door, stopping six or seven feet from two *dorados* who stand to face us. Tension fills the air like the dry, electric calm before lightning falls out of an overheated summer sky.

Jesús holds up his right hand, palm facing the *dorados*, and says with good cheer, *"Buenos días, muchachos.* Remember us? We marched with you over El Paso Púlpito and fought by your sides at Agua Prieta and Hermosillo. I drove a wagon to pick up the wounded and Doctor Grace here dug out bullets from some, sewed up what was left of others, and fought for the general. Remember how he shot out the spotlights at Agua Prieta when the Carrancistas and *Americanos* used them against us?"

I recognize the tallest *dorado* facing us. He has a coarse, straggly beard, hooked nose pushed to one side, and yellow, crooked teeth his lips stretch to cover when he closes his mouth. He exclaims, "Ay-ya-yi," slaps his cheek with his gun hand and nodding like a goose in a mating dance, says to the others, "*Sí, sí*, this *hombre* he was with the general when we came across El Paso Púlpito. He is a *medico*. And, the young one with him, he drives the ambulance wagon during the fighting at Agua Prieta and Hermosillo... he held horses at Columbus, but the other *medico* was not there." The other *dorados* relax a little, but their hands never leave the butts of their revolvers.

A muscular, dark-skinned man, probably a Yaqui Indian, hat pulled down over his eyes, a *dorado* bronze medallion pinned squarely in the center of his hat's crown glinting in the sunlight, flips away a corn-shuck cigarette he's been smoking, and stands up from squatting against the *hacienda*. Approaching the other two, he hooks his thumbs in his gun belt. Head cocked to one side, he ambles over to Jesús, and stares up at him. I see him casually slide his hand around a bridle strap near the bit rings of Jesús's roan, making sure Jesús can not whirl the roan away and charge off. He says in a smooth, almost feminine voice, filled with whispery threat, "Why have you come to this place, *señor*?"

Jesús grins and says, "We heard the General suffers from a bad wound. Doctor Grace comes to help his old *amigo*."

The man holding Jesús's horse shakes his head, clearly irritated, and the tone of his voice is pleasant but deadly.

"I say again, *señor*, why did you come to...this... place?"

Jesús shrugs his shoulders. "It is what they say in the village, *señor*. General Francisco Villa recovers in this house."

I hear the *dorado* mumble under his breath.

"Someday, I will burn down that damned whorehouse."

He lets go of the bridle on Jesús's roan and steps over next to my saddle. He starts to take Satanas's bridle like he did with Jesús's roan. I say in a soft tone, barely loud enough for him to hear, "I wouldn't do that, *señor*. If I tell my black devil to run, he will drag you until your hand rips off trying to hold him."

His hand pauses an instant, and looking at Satanas, reaches over and scratches his jaw below the bridle strap.

"Your stud, *señor*, he reminds me of one *Señor* Comacho owned before the *Revolución.*"

I nod.

"*Sí*, he is one and the same horse, *señor*. He was left in the Comacho barn after an Apache raid when all the *vaqueros* and *hacienda* servants ran away. I took him."

The Yaqui sticks out his lower lip and nods.

"He is magnificent, a very lucky find, *señor*. So you come to heal the general's wound?"

His tone changes from one of admiration to an instant challenge.

"Tell me, *señor*, how did you learn that the general was wounded? Perhaps you are a spy and you learn these things from the *gringos*, *sí*?"

The best lies are those mixed with truth.

"No, *señor*, I am no spy and did not learn of the general's wound from the *gringos*. I was in an Apache camp in the Sierra Espuelas when word came from their scouts that the *peons* were saying the general had been shot in the leg, a very bad wound, and was heading south. As soon as I can leave my work, I left to find him and offer my help. Along the way I found my young *amigo*, Jesús, and he guided me as we followed your trail south. We asked the people along the way about the general who disappeared near Rubio, but they seemed to know little. We crossed trails with the *gringo* general and with him was my *amigo*, the *reportero*, Quentin

Peach. He was with us at Agua Prieta. He told me privately of the rumors that General Villa hides near Santa Cruz de Herrera and so we come here."

The Yaqui's eyes study mine as I speak. When I finish, he slowly nods. "I believe you speak true, *señor*. And the Apache, Muchacho Amarillo who rode with us to Agua Prieta, I don't see him with you. Where is he?"

"Ready to shoot you, *señor*."

He laughs, a knowing chuckle. "*Sí*, I'm sure he is. He was angry when he left Agua Prieta. Tell him when you see him, perhaps I will come to visit him one dark night and then he can shoot me. Climb down from your horses, *señores*. The general has visitors. I will let him know you come. His leg smells of infection and I have to lift him out of bed or he moans and clenches his teeth in great pain. The local *medicos* know nothing of wounds such as his. He needs your *medico* skills and will be glad to see you. The tree over there provides a little shade from the sun."

He makes a quick jerk of his head toward an old man, who disappears into the *hacienda* as Jesús and I dismount and lead our horses to a big, tall cottonwood. I scan the tree line behind us, but see no sign of Yellow Boy.

My mouth feels filled with dust, and my heart pounds. My face-to-face with Villa finally comes down to my gamble on his vanity and that Camisa Roja doesn't know I'm here. If Villa thinks I've come to kill him, we won't live another ten minutes.

58. EPIPHANY

Ten minutes tick by, fifteen, twenty, forty-five. The whitewashed side door opens slowly, letting bright sunlight into the dark, cool interior of the *hacienda*. An ancient, bent over, old man totters out of the darkness and speaks to the big Yaqui. It takes all my discipline not to put my hand on my revolver and to continue looking relaxed.

The Yaqui waves us over and says, "The general is glad you have returned. He asks you to come sit and talk with him awhile in the left bedroom at the end of the hall. Go on in, *señores*."

We step through the doorway and move a few slow steps before our eyes adapt to the dark. Wide doorways, the doors painted bright white, line both sides of the hall, its length running the full width of the *hacienda*. The last door on the left at the end of the hall is closed. I knock in the middle of the door and step to one side in case Villa fires through the door.

From behind the door, a familiar, smooth voice, "*Sí?*"

"General, Hombrecito and Jesús, the *medico* assistant, come to help you. May we enter?"

"*Sí, amigos, por favor, entre.*"

Villa, fully dressed, wearing his flat-brimmed porkpie hat, sits in a big, straight-backed ornate chair from the time of the grandee sons of the *conquistadores*. Next to him on a bedside table lies his gun belt and revolver, and crutches lean against the wall on the other side of the chair. His wounded leg stuck out straight, wrapped in a massive bandage running from four or five inches above the knee to nearly his ankle, rests on a stool. A light stain shows on the top of the bandage a few inches below his knee. A bottle of gin and a glass, two-thirds full of clear liquid sit on the bedside table next to the revolver. I'm surprised. I've never known Villa to drink. His once full face is thin to the point of emaciation, and his big, proud mustache looks like it's been dragged through the weeds and tried to come back as a full beard.

Barely lifting his hand off the chair's armrest and curling his fingers, he motioned us through the door. "So *muchachos*, you come to help me or kill me?"

Jesús frowns at the question, but says nothing.

I say, "We are *medicos* General. We come to help you, not put you out of your misery like a horse with a broken leg."

"There were times coming over the *sierras*, Hombrecito, my leg hurt so bad I wished someone would shoot me."

We walk over and shake his hand, his grip still firm but not vice-like as it was last fall. He watches me carefully as I sit my bag on the bed, open it, and find a pair of scissors to cut away the bandage. I say as I sit down on the bed and dangle the scissors from my fingers, "We're going to need plenty of hot water. Jesús, why don't you go boil us some?"

Villa waves his hand toward the bedroom door.

"The kitchen is on the other side of the *hacienda*, down a hall through the door across the hall from this one. A couple of Japanese friends are making coffee, they can help you."

Jesús turns to go, saying over his shoulder, "I'll be back *pronto*."

As I watch him leave, I think, *This is almost too easy.*

As soon as the door closes, I hear the hammer on Villa's revolver click twice to full cock. I turn to stare at the black hole at the end of its long barrel and see the ends of the bullets in the cylinder.

"So you little bastard, you did come back as you wrote on the paper. You came back even though I let you live after you nearly beat Camisa Roja to death. Now I have you, you little son of a bitch."

"*Sí, Jefe*, I came back. You know me too long to think I wouldn't. Jesús knows nothing of my plan to kill you. If I die, he is innocent, let him go."

My nervousness vanishes, and all I feel inside is astonishment that he believes he let me live.

"What do you mean you let me live? On your orders, Roja was about to murder me."

Villa shrugs, his haggard face winching in pain from the movement. "I sent no one after you when Camisa came back across his horse. I should have killed him for letting you get away, but he is too good a man to die because of the likes of you. You were not chased or killed on the way back to the land of the *gringos*. No one tried to kill you after you returned to Las Cruces. I left you alone even though I should have had you shot like the traitor you are."

His audacity is stunning. He let me live? I'm a traitor?

Cold, focused fury begins growing in my gut at the insanity and narcissism that fills his mind, and I feel a peculiar joy that I'm so close to killing him and ending thoughts in his crazed brain forever.

"*Jefe,* you know that every man you might have sent after me would have died, never hearing the shot that killed them, and yes, I tried to stop the outrageous murders you committed in San Pedro de la Cueva. That, *señor,* was not betrayal. You were *loco*… like…like you were on fire and out of your mind, you, who the *peons* call *El Jaguar Indomado,* a crazed jaguar on fire, a crazed tiger consumed by flames of hate and insanity."

Instantly all the pieces fall into place and I realize what I'm saying is what my dream has been trying to tell me for months.

"Oh, *sí,* you were *el tigre* on fire, a burning, crazed jaguar, who after seeing *División del Norte* slaughtered, became *loco* because the *gringo presidente* betrayed you, *loco* after being beaten by Carranza and Obregón, and in your roaring insanity, you murdered those you swore to protect, not Carranza, not Obregón. You murdered *peons,* you murdered a priest, and then you tried to murder me, your *amigo.* You are the traitor, *Jefe,* not me."

Leaning forward, he levels the gun to kill me, his face twisted in a snarl of pain, his eyes filled with thundering rage, the heavy weapon wobbling in his hand as he struggles to focus through the fog of pain and pull the trigger. In a rage myself, faster than a rattlesnake strike, I coolly snatch the pistol's barrel, effortlessly twisting it out of his hand before his trembling finger can pull the trigger.

He slumps back against the back of the chair, staring at

me with fever burning in his eyes, panting through clenched teeth. "*Loco* am I? Then shoot me you son-of-a-bitch. Satisfy your thirst for my blood. Put me out of my misery you little bastard."

"Not yet, *Jefe,* we'll wait until Jesús returns with the boiling water so he can leave the *hacienda* and won't be blamed for what I do. Make your peace with God, it won't be long before you'll see him."

He spits in disgust.

"To Hell with you, Hombrecito. You and the pup won't live through the day. Go on and do it, kill me now, and we'll be seeing God together before we burn in Hell."

I smile and shake my head. There's a knock at the door and a low man's voice with a Japanese accent, "Coffee, general."

I give a quick nod toward Villa and mouth. *Answer.*

"*Bueno, entre, amigos.*"

They come in with quick, short steps, thick black hair tied back in twisted buns, their slanted eyes flicking about the room, taking in every detail, and smiling as though the upward turn of their mouths is permanently etched on their faces. One carries a big blue and white speckled coffee pot and one three heavy clay mugs.

I pretend to examine Villa's pistol. They bow and smile, placing the pot and mugs on a table against the wall on the far side of the room. The one with the mugs says with almost no accent, "*Buenos tardes*, Doctor Grace, your assistant will be bringing you boiling water *pronto*. We brought plenty of coffee for the general and you, too. May I pour you both a cup?"

I shake my head.

"No, *señores*, none for me or the general. You drink it."

They smile and bow, quickly shaking their heads.

"Oh no, *señor*, coffee is far too strong for us. We drink only green tea."

Villa watches this little exchange, curiosity filling his eyes.

"Hey, *amigos*, I will have a cup of your coffee. Pour me some coffee in that blue cup, with the bird on the side."

The one who speaks almost perfect Spanish reaches for the cup.

"General, drink that coffee and you'll die in three days. It's poisoned, part of a *gringo* plot to kill you."

I knew several Japanese at Leland Stanford's college, but none were ever as pale as those two when I say they poisoned the coffee. They shake their heads, and hold up their hands, palms out.

"Oh, no, no, no. No plot. No plot. No poison. No."

Villa's eyes narrow and become thin, sharp blades slicing through their deception.

"Traitors! I ought to make you drink the whole pot. I am surrounded by traitors."

He clenches his teeth and speaks in the same guttural growl I heard with Thigpen and Miller at Agua Prieta and with the priest in San Pedro de la Cueva.

"Leave now, *señores*. Never let me find you in Mexico again. If our trails cross, I will kill you on sight. *Comprende?*"

They bow, stepping backwards out the door, their hands pressed together in steeples pointing at their chins, and saying, "*Sí,* general. We understand. *Adiós,*" We hear their shoes slap a fast tattoo against the hall floor tiles as they run for the door at the end of the hall.

Villa laughs, his eyes crinkled in pain. "How did you

know, this Hombrecito? Why didn't you let them poison me?"

I close the door, seeing the flash of light from the door opening and closing at the end of the hall as the Japanese leave. "Quentin Peach told me privately four days ago when our trail crossed the *gringo* general's. I didn't think they could poison you, you are too careful, but we pushed hard to get here to stop them just in case you let your guard down. You deserve to die like a man General, not like some coyote killing sheep."

Saying nothing, clenching his teeth, his hands trying to make fists, but failing, he stares at me, unblinking. I admire his courage.

A light tapping at the door, I say, "*Entre.*" The door swings open and Jesús, surrounded by a cloud of steam, carries in a half-full, five-gallon galvanized tub of steaming water. He raises his eyebrows questioning where to set it, and I motion toward the table against the far wall. He sits the tub down, seeing me with Villa's revolver and the expressions on our faces, he frowns as he steps back to close the door.

"What goes on?"

"Sit down, Jesús. I have a confession to make."

He sits on the edge of the bed, his eyes flicking back and forth between Villa and me. Villa turns his head away and stares at the wispy cloud of steam just above the tub.

"What?"

"I've deceived you. I let you think I was hunting the general to offer *medico* help, but that was not true, I planned to kill him."

His eyes grow round. "Why? Why do you do this, *señor*? You are a *medico*, not a *pistolero*. General Villa is your *amigo*. Why?"

"Remember the executions of the village men at San Pedro de la Cueva? Remember how I tried to stop General Villa after he murdered the priest, and then how I left the same afternoon with Camisa Roja? Do you remember? What did you think of those things?"

"*Sí*. I remember all of those things. I did not want you to go, but it was a good thing. *Hombres* who don't respect the general face the firing squad. All understand in *División del Norte* his authority is *absolutamente*. Because you were his long-time *amigo*, he let you go, even sent Camisa Roja to show you the trail. We all thought that was a good thing, *señor*, and besides the general he says you have important business at your home. All of the soldiers, we think it is a good thing for the general not to execute you because of your disrespect and attack on him personally."

"You don't think he was wrong murdering the priest and all those men for their understandable mistake?"

"War, Doctor Grace, we all make mistakes in war. Always men die; most deaths in war are not just. The night you left, General Villa, he cries in his wagon, cries like a woman, sorry for what happened, sorry he sent you away. Old Juan, his cook, he told me so. Why do you ask?"

"Because, General Villa told Camisa Roja to kill me, and he nearly did. That's why. I sent Roja back tied across his saddle, with a note stuck on his red shirt saying I'd be back to repay his betrayal of me and of so many in the *Revolución*, and I came back. I would have come back crawling across the fires of Hell to repay blood for blood as my Apache father taught me."

Jesús looks at Villa and then me. He slowly shakes his head, looking at the floor.

"But, Doctor Grace, you lied to me to find General Villa. You betrayed me to find the man who betrayed you."

"I am very sorry, Jesús. I never intended to deceive you. I had to find General Villa to set things right for betraying me, for betraying all those men in senseless charges against machineguns in trenches and barbed wire, for those murders at San Pedro de la Cueva, for betraying women and children like Maud Wright and her little son, Johnnie, for a thousand betrayals no one will ever mention, but will never forget. I had to have your help to make things right, even if I didn't tell you. Don't you understand why I deceived you? It was for justice. It was to give Villa what he deserves."

He stares at me, his eyes clear, honest.

"Your hands are not clean to deliver the thing you call justice, *señor*. You must not commit this murder. You are a better man, a bigger man than this one, but you and the general, you are only men, and men make mistakes they wish they never made. We never get what we deserve for our evil. Even I, a boy, know this."

There it is, like a flash of lightning, like the instant sting from a slap across the face, the dream fulfilled, the metaphor completed, the epiphany clear. Villa, the jaguar, the tiger on fire in my dream, tearing at my soul, and the unseen shadow coming to pull me from its claws; it's Jesús, as if he were his namesake, rescuing me, rescuing me from becoming a cold-blooded murderer, rescuing me from being bound forever to the dark side of life because I killed a tiger, a tiger burning bright.

I sigh and relax and ease down on a chair feeling a peace I haven't known in a long time and knowing without doubt that now I'm doing the right thing.

Jesús and Villa stare at me, puzzled, uncertain what to think, wondering what I'll do next, wondering what they'll do next. I let the revolver's hammer down to safety, flipped open the loading gate and began punching the shells out of the cylinder into my palm. Villa watches, frowning, confused. But Jesús knows what's happening and smiles.

"*Gracias*, Doctor Grace. *Muchas gracias*."

The last cartridge falls into my palm. I look up at Jesús and shake my head.

"No, Jesús, it is I who ought to be saying *muchas gracias*. Help me get the general on his bed and let's see if we can't fix that leg."

59. ESCAPE

Villa shakes his head and holds up his hand to stop us from helping him on to the bed. "Call Gamberro. He's strong enough to move me without driving me insane with the pain."

Jesús passes through the door and charges down the hall to bring Gamberro. Villa stares at me with hooded eyes, still not believing I won't kill him. "So, Hombrecito, you lied to the *muchacho* to find me? I know you. You won't give up so easy trying to kill me, but try something with this leg, and Gamberro, he will shoot you where you stand."

"I no longer have a desire for revenge, *Jefe*. Today I finally understand a dream I've had many times since I returned to New Mexico from medical school. Until now I did not understand it was warning me against killing you. It was trying to tell me how killing you would pull me into the fire consuming you. Burn me, haunt me, drive me crazy for the rest of my life. I am a *medico*, trained to heal. I swore an oath to heal all who need my help. I will do my best for you now and never return. This part of my life is finished. I give you the rest of yours; use it as you choose."

Villa snorts, shakes his head and rolls his eyes, saying nothing more as Gamberro, the big Yaqui in charge at the side door of the *hacienda*, strides into the bedroom, Jesús right behind him.

Sighing, Villa says, "Ah, Gamberro here you are. Help me on to the bed, *por favor*. The *medicos* need to look at my wound and maybe can help make it better. You stay here too and help look after them, eh?"

Gamberro flicking his eyes first at me and then at Jesús, says, "Certainly, General. Here, let me lift you out of the chair and on the bed."

Gamberro is one of the strongest men I've ever seen. He walks over to Villa's chair, slides one arm under his shoulders and the other under his legs, and, with no more than a small grunt, effortlessly lifts Villa out of his chair, carries him the three steps to the bed, and with a splay-legged squat, lays him in the center of the bed. Villa, over six feet tall, is at least two hundred twenty pounds of pure muscle and dead, awkward weight.

After putting him on the bed, Gamberro pulls the chair around in which Villa had been sitting so he has a clear view of us while we work. Gamberro puts his big pistol in his lap where it's easy to reach, takes the makings for a cigarillo out of his vest pocket and nods at Villa.

"Doctors, the general is waiting. Proceed carefully, *por favor*, I hate to shoot you if you make a mistake, but I will."

We say nothing, put some pillows under Villa's

lower thigh and heel to help support his leg, and begin unwinding the dirty bandage showing infection seepage. After several turns of the bandage, we find two large mallow leaves separating the flesh around the wound from the bandage cloth.

Mallow leaves can be used to make a good soothing poultice that reduces pain and inflammation. Whoever used the leaves had a clear idea of what would cut down on inflammation and infection, but raw leaves external to the wound probably aren't doing much good except to keep the cloth from sticking to the infection. Before I remove the mallow leaves, I pause to take some soap out of my bag and use some of the boiled water in a hand bowl to wash up and pour carbolic acid over my hands.

As I lift the leaves off the wound, Villa clenches his teeth and desperately sucks in air as pus and small chunks of matter flow out of the open sore. I let it drain while I look at the rest of his leg. The bullet entered from the back about six or seven inches below the knee joint, and passed straight through apparently passing between the tibia and fibula, probably nicking both and making many small bone fragments but not shattering either major bone. The entrance wound has closed and apparently healed on its own, but the exit wound on his shin is a mess. It's closing with a pus hole just above it. Villa moans as I gently touch the area around the pus hole and feel bone fragments.

"General, you're at risk of losing your leg below the knee if I don't clean the wound and open it up to pick out the bone fragments. Once I do that, it ought to heal in a month or so and you'll feel a lot better. How about it?"

He eyes Gamberro, who sits impassively watching,

cigarillo smoke drifting from his nose. Gamberro shrugs and takes another puff. Villa's feverish brown eyes study my face and he slowly nods. "Go on and do it," his voice churlish, "No *hombre* lives forever. But, if I die, so will you. Show us your skill, Doctor Hombrecito."

I take a bottle of chloroform and a gauze patch out of my bag, holding them up for Villa and Gamberro to see. "This is chloroform. A few whiffs and you will sleep so you feel no pain while I work."

Villa shakes his head. "I can stand the pain. I do not want to be asleep."

"You have to be still while I work or I'll make the wound worse and you'll be longer healing. If not the chloroform, then drink the gin in that bottle on your nightstand."

"No. It makes my head hurt when I wake up after I drink it."

Petulant, it's his way or nothing.

"Very well, then have Gamberro hold you down while I work. You can't be thrashing around when I start picking the bone fragments out of that pus-filled wound."

Jesús, standing at the foot of the bed ready to assist, says, "*Por favor*, General, take the chloroform. It is the best thing. Gamberro will watch over you with his *pistola*."

Villa looks at Gamberro, Jesús, and, finally, me. He stares at the ceiling for a few moments before puffing his cheeks and blowing, sounding like a steam engine starting. He looks me in the eye.

"Very well, Hombrecito, do your work. I hope you live until the end of the day, because it means I'm still alive. If I live, Gamberro, you take good care of our guests."

It takes over an hour to clean the wound. I have to reopen

the healed exit hole and find the bone splinters, making the wound a running sore. After I finish, I flush it out with carbolic acid and put a poultice of yerba mansa on it. With Villa snoring, all that's left to do is wait. If the fever breaks, we're in time to stop a major infection and Villa will, at least, keep his leg. If the leg doesn't show signs of healing, then, we have to figure out how to get out of Gamberro's tight hold and far away from the *hacienda* sooner rather than later.

I leave Jesús to clean up and motion Gamberro out into the hall. With the door to the bedroom closed.

"*Señor*, I believe I found all the bone splinters and General Villa will recover soon. When he wakes up, he will be very thirsty; give him a little water at first, and then more as he becomes fully awake. Jesús and I will camp outside and…"

Gamberro shakes his head, a sarcastic sneer twisting his lips. "Oh, no, Doctor Grace. As the general recovers you will need to give him quick attention in case your medicine does not do so good. You and the *muchacho*, you stay in the room next to him. It has a connecting door. He calls, you answer. *Comprende*? We have already put your horses in the corral and take good care of them. You stay here and look after the general, eh?"

I smile. "*Sí, comprendo.*"

As I explained to Gamberro, Villa awoke about an hour after we finished desperately thirsty and groggy from the chloroform. His thirst satisfied, he wants to sleep more, and tells Gamberro to reload the revolver I emptied. He goes back to sleep with his arms crossed at his chest like a body ready for burial, the pistol in his right hand ready for instant use. As we watch, Villa sleeps the rest of the afternoon and well into the night.

Gamberro opens the door between the bedrooms and motions us to follow him inside the adjoining bedroom.

"Doctor Grace, this door stays open. You only go to the hall through the general's door. An *hombre* guards the way. I tell him to kill you if you try to run. I have business outside. Take good care of the general when he calls."

"*Sí, señor.* The general is my patient and I am his doctor."

Gamberro locks our bedroom door to the hall from the outside. I hate being trapped like this, a mouse being toyed with by cats, praying that Villa awakens feeling better and in a good mood, otherwise he'll probably decide we're charlatans deserving of the firing squad.

I don't sleep well. Expecting to be called at any time, I awake from a shallow, fitful sleep as the grandfather clock down the hall strikes twice. My eyes pop open. Something doesn't feel right. I start to sit up, when a powerful hand forces me back down on the bed. I say nothing and strain to see in the pitch black.

A faint whisper fills my ear, "Hombrecito, we go now?"

Relief washes over me like a plunge in a cold winter river.

"*Sí.* First I speak with Jesús. Where will you be?"

"Go out the kitchen door to the garden behind the *hacienda.* You can wade across the river. There I wait with the horses. At the door of Arango, guard sits but is no more. Move *pronto*."

The whisper and the hand's weight on my chest disappear. A shadow floats through the half-opened doorway to Villa's room and out the open door to the hall.

I kneel by Jesús's bed. His short, excited breaths tell me he's awake. Next to his ear I whisper, "Yellow Boy waits across the river. We go now, *pronto*."

I feel him staring at me. His hand finds my shoulder and pulls my ear close as he whispers. "No, Doctor Grace, I need to stay here. The general needs me."

"He's liable to kill you if you stay and I'm gone."

"*Sí*, this I know, but there is nowhere else for me to go. *Vaya con Dios y muchas gracias*."

I'm tempted to cold-cock him and carry him with me, but as the Apaches taught me, he's a man and it's his choice to make. I find his hand and shake it. "*Adiós*, my good friend. *Vaya con Dios*."

I grab my doctor's bag from the foot of the bed, take my hat off the bedpost, slide out through the bedroom doors, and glide down the hall. I grin as the snores from Villa's room fade into silence and think, *the last thing I ever heard from Pancho Villa was a loud, saber rattling snore*.

Out the kitchen door, I stay in the shadows, slide under the last rail of the fence, step on rocks scattered on the long, sloping banks of the river and find an exposed rock shelf that lets me step off into the water without making a splash. Yellow Boy's right. The river is not much over knee deep. The current is very slow and the burbling water and thousands of frogs croaking along the banks make it easy to wade across without making any noticeable noise. I come out the other side in dark shadows and stay in them until, nearing our camp, I hear a horse snort and Yellow Boy whisper, "Here."

Never so glad to see anyone, I find him in the shadows under the pale light of a fingernail moon. I whisper, "Uncle, you save me again in the middle of the night. How did you get the horses?"

"Humph," he grunts, "Am I Apache? Villa lives? Jesús stays?"

"*Sí.*"

"Before moon rises above *sierras*, Camisa Roja returns. Yaqui tells him you here and Villa lets you live. Camisa Roja full of fire. He says he knows what Villa wants and swears he kills you *mañana*. Leave now. *Mañana* Camisa Roja follows. Maybe you get lucky with Shoots-Today-Kills-Tomorrow."

Camisa Roja. Will I ever be rid of him? Will I always be looking over my shoulder? Will I always wish I'd killed him when I had the chance? I clench my teeth and tighten my grip on Little David. "Lead the way, Uncle. *Si*, maybe I will be lucky."

60. A CHANGE IN TACTICS

We cross the river about three quarters of a mile north of the *hacienda*, follow a dry *arroyo* to the main road, and set the horses on a pace that eats up the miles.

The morning sky is turning a light, gauzy turquoise blue as we splash across the Concho River at the little village of La Joya. Its silent, scattered adobe houses and church stand cold and somber against the contented gurgle of the river. We ride into a canyon on the far side of the river, picking our way up a dangerous, loose gravel trail, twisting and turning up the south side of the canyon until we gain a ridge overlooking the village. We need to give the horses and mule grain and time to rest after pushing them hard since we left the *hacienda* and we make camp in the shade of a grove of large piñons on the other side of the ridge and about thirty feet below the top. While I roast meat and make coffee,

Yellow Boy climbs to a jumble of boulders on top of the ridge, where he nests down with his Big Eye telescope to watch our back trail out of the mountains behind La Joya. Carrying a pan of beans and meat up to eat with him, I know he must be disgusted with me for riding over three hundred miles into Mexico and not killing, or even trying to kill Villa or Camisa Roja, as I swore to do as a son of Yellow Boy.

Watching the sun brighten the shadowed places in the big *arroyos* and valleys in the mountains we've just crossed, we eat in silence, the gnawing hunger from the night ride fast disappearing. Finishing, Yellow Boy belches his appreciation, and keeping his eyes across the valley says, "I watch. You sleep."

I return to the fire, pour us coffee and carry it back up the hill. Yellow Boy nods his thanks and takes a few sips while I sit using my cup to warm my hands against the still chilly morning. I wait for him to speak first, wait for the lesson I know is sure to come, wait to learn how far I've slipped in his respect. At last he turns his eyes to me.

"You no kill Arango or Camisa Roja. Why? They try to kill you. You a son of Yellow Boy. Why you no take their lives? You have right. You leave them, you take no honor. You leave them, you take no power."

"A dream told me I must not."

He purses his lips, takes a long slurp of the black, steaming brew. "A dream? Dreams are powerful medicine. Tell me of this dream, my son."

I describe the details of the dream that's haunted me for months as he drinks his coffee and studies my face. I tell him how I came to understand the dream was about Villa when I was about to kill him, but still didn't know how to interpret it until Jesús brings the boiling water and I tell him the truth about why we've been searching for the general.

"Jesús looked me straight in the eye and said I was as bad, if not worse, than Villa, for betraying his trust."

"Hmmph. Jesús speaks true."

"I know. The wisdom of his words filled my ears like a flash of lightning fills my eyes in the blackest of nights, and let me see the truth clearly. Then I understood Jesús is the one I never saw in my dream, the one who rescues me from the burning *tigre*. Villa, wounded like the burning *tigre,* was pulling me in, ready to burn what soul I had left, consume me for the rest of my life with the memory of his killing. He laid in that bed a weak, sick, old man who had no power. There was no honor, no power in killing such a man.

"Uncle, this is how I understand the dream and what it means for me. The White Eye di-yin promise I made before I returned to you requires that I heal. I will not kill this man, even if he tried to kill me. Years ago Villa gave us our lives by killing a bear that almost tore us both to pieces. Giving him his life back, for he was as good as dead before Jesús returned, made me feel like a great rock was lifted off my shoulders. I was free to walk away without his blood on my hands. My dream spoke true. Jesús, unseen in my dream, pulled me away from the teeth and claws of a burning *tigre*, a *loco tigre*, one that nearly had me. Do you understand these things, Uncle?"

Yellow Boy stares out over the valley for a long time slurping his coffee, and I tremble inside wondering if he'll disown me and think I'm crazy.

"Same-dream-comes-many-times powerful medicine, Hombrecito. Man is a fool who no listens to their voices.

Sometimes man waits long time to understand what dream tells him. You wise. You listen. You wait. By and by you hear the speaking of your dream. You keep your honor. You keep my honor. There is no better thing than to live a straight life. Arango lives, still on fire, still *loco*. No honor now. No power now. Maybe power and honor comes again. Maybe he dies, no honor, no power. He sends no one after you but he stops no one. Camisa Roja, man you cannot kill, and big Yaqui, they come, Villa no stops. What you do?"

"If they come under the sights of Little David, they will die. They chase death. Can we wait here and stop them before they make an ambush on the trail or try to find Rojo's Camp or cross the border to Las Cruces looking to kill me?"

Yellow Boy slowly shakes his head.

"Roja and Yaqui no ride sun trail. Ride moon trail. *Muchos gringos* and Carrancistas ride under sun, not under moon. Mostly *gringos* and Carrancistas fight. Villistas hide. You are not one of them? They shoot first and ask your name when you dead. Camisa Roja and Gamberro know this. Stay out of sight. Not know the trail we take. Camisa Roja uses Jesús. Learns we return to Apaches in Sierras and Las Cruces and Mescalero north of border. We say so in front of Jesús. He knows. Camisa Roja knows we use trails out of El Paso Púlpito to Apache camp. Few *gringos* or Carrancistas west of Casas Grandes. Ambush in Mexico more better than across the border. Roja and Yaqui ride to El Paso Púlpito before we do and kill us. I watch our back trail now. Think maybe we might have luck; maybe they big fools, but they no come this way. They take faster trail to El Paso Púlpito."

Everything he says makes perfect sense. If we don't make El Paso Púlpito before Camisa Roja and Gamberro, they'll be waiting for us when we try to go through the pass, and in the game they're playing, if you don't shoot first, then the odds are high you'll die.

"My uncle is a great warrior, he speaks wise words about our enemies. What must we do? Stay away from El Paso Púlpito? Go around the mountains? Use another trail through the Sierra Espuelas?"

He slurps his coffee and stares at me, his black flint eyes glittering. "*Sí*, we can hide. They never see us until we let them. They no see? Cross border; wait in Las Cruces; try to kill you from ambush. Better to kill them at El Paso Púlpito when they fall under the sights of Yellow Boy rifle and Shoots-Today-Kills-Tomorrow."

"But, Uncle, if they take the fastest roads they will be ahead of us in two or three days and we'll be the targets at El Paso Púlpito. How can we stay ahead of them?"

"Old Apache trick…"

"Which is…?"

"Surprise enemy. No do what he expects."

Waving my hand in a circle I say, "Which for us is…?"

"Ride soon. Ride in daylight."

My jaw drops and I know I must look like a man without good sense. Yellow Boy laughs at me.

"Hear me, my son. Now we lead Camisa and Gamberro by maybe half a day. Camisa Roja knows we ride under no sun. He rides under no sun. We leave pronto. Ride rapidamente. Roja stays with Villa and rides tonight. We ride today. Stay maybe day, two days ahead. When he camps at daybreak, we lead maybe by a sun but gain maybe a sun while we ride and they sleep. *Comprende*?"

I nod, "*Sí*, Uncle, *comprendo*. What about the *gringos*,

Carrancistas, and Villistas? It will be hard to avoid them in the daylight. Even villagers living off the main trails will be hostile to a *gringo* and an Apache. The animals need some rest or they'll never get us there ahead of Camisa Roja and Gamberro."

He takes another slurp of coffee.

"*Gringos* use Apache scouts. I am scout in my jacket. You be *gringo* officer. Stay away from villages. Stay away from all who know us. Stay away from patrols; let *gringos* and Mexicans fight. We stay away. Now, we give animals a little rest. We rest. When sun makes no shadow we ride. *Sí*, ride now, today, animals suffer. They strong and can rest all night. We win race to El Paso Púlpito, Camisa Roja and Gamberro lose bet. Pay with life. I say try."

I stick out my lower lip and nod. "*Sí*, we will try. It is time to end it."

61. RETURN TO EL PASO PÚLPITO

From La Joya the ride north back to El Paso Púlpito takes six days; it took almost fifteen days to cover nearly the same distance riding south. If we hadn't taken detours or had to wait out *gringo* patrols or Carrancistas passing us while we hid in *arroyos* or brush, it's likely the ride might have taken less than five days.

Yellow Boy approaches El Paso Púlpito with care, ensuring we don't ride into an ambush. Out on the *llano* we continue riding north past the canyon entrance and then turn west up an *arroyo* to follow the back of the ridges forming the north side of the pass entrance. About three miles up the *arroyo*, Yellow Boy leads us up to a saddle between two high hills and there below us is the trail to Rafaela's cairn.

Without a sound, we drift down out of the saddle to the trail, stopping often to listen for anything out of the ordinary. By the time the long shadows disappear into dusk, we reach the spring and cliffs where Rafaela is buried and find no signs or tracks of passersby.

We water the horses and mule, let them rest a bit, and ride down the canyon to the main trail leading through El Paso Púlpito. Crossing the main trail we climb a steep ridge and make camp just below its top on the other side to stay out of sight from the main trail through the pass. Even in the low early evening light, our location gives us a perfect view down the canyon to the *llano* and the trail Roja and Gamberro will use to approach the pass. I breathe a sigh of relief. We've won the race to El Paso Púlpito.

Our animals are worn out. Even Satanas, the strongest, looks gaunt. They're glad to get the cool spring water, the extra ration of grain, a long grass rub down, and a good roll in the dust. We hobble them to graze on the western side of the ridge, where I build a small fire in a deep pit to keep down any signs of light and cook beans, *tortillas* and coffee. Yellow Boy makes a place in the stunted piñons on the top of the ridge so we have a clear line of sight down the trail from the canyon entrance, maybe four miles away, all the way up to our watching post and west toward the pass.

We eat and watch the moonrise from behind the mountains throwing inky, black shadows in our direction and casting parts of the trail in patches of brilliant white light and impenetrable darkness. While we watch the trail up the canyon and slurp our coffee, I ask, "When do you think they'll come?"

He looks at me through the steam from his old tin cup, a twisted half-smile on one of his cheeks. "Maybe they are already here and we have not seen each other. Maybe tonight, maybe tomorrow night they come." He shrugs his shoulders. "Who knows? Soon now."

"Maybe they're already here? Tonight? Why? We've ridden long and hard to stay ahead of them and we started with a day and a half lead."

"They know all hidden trails; they know how to travel fast because they fight wars; and they have friends in villages we have to ride around. Wait. You see. Rest. You watch from half way in the night to the morning sun."

After I lie down by the warm glow of the fire pit, it seems only seconds pass before I feel the familiar tap of Yellow Boy's rifle barrel on the bottom of my foot to awaken me. Yellow Boy's shadowy outline in the dim light makes a horizontal wave with his hand parallel to the ground. All is well.

From the star positions and where a nearly full moon hangs high in a twinkling, diamond filled sky, I know it's past midnight. I take my blanket, binoculars, Little David, and my cup, pour some coffee, reduced to thin black syrup from the pot sitting on the dimming fire coals, and climb up the ridge to Yellow Boy's aerie.

I find his nest in the piñons, and wrapping the blanket around me, sit down cross-legged to slurp the steaming black brew in the freezing air. With the moon high overhead, the trail down the canyon out to the *llano* is easy to see, brightly lit in the moon's icy white light, the piñons and brush look like black ink blots scattered down the canyon. Starting at the canyon entrance, I begin a systematic search of every possible hiding place along the trail toward us until I reach the place where the trail north to the spring branches off the one leading west to the pass. I see nothing.

It occurs to me that the jaguar-on-fire dream hasn't visited since I left Villa in the land of the living. I know I've rationalized letting Villa and Camisa Roja live using an interpretation of the dream, but, truly, I still don't fully understand why I didn't kill them. I believe it was *the right thing to do*, but it put Yellow Boy, Jesús and me at risk of being killed. I wonder if my years at medical school have made me too soft to survive in this hard land, too soft to live as my Apache father taught me.

As I sit musing on my fate and life's strange twists and turns, my binoculars return again to the canyon entrance and I realize something has changed. It takes a minute, instantly awake and alert, adrenaline filling my veins, thinking in the back of my mind to stay calm and clear, to realize a small dust cloud, pale and ethereal in the moon's white light, is approaching from the *llano*.

I throw off my blanket to get Yellow Boy. Before I can tap his foot, he sits up from his blanket perfectly alert and raises his brows to ask what was happening. I jerk my head toward the nest at the top of the ridge and hold up the binoculars.

"Come and see."

He grabs his old brass telescope and joins me to study the little dust puff approaching from the *llano*, dust filled with death and destruction.

It hangs in the cold, still air for maybe five minutes. Then it begins to fade away, never reaching the canyon entrance. The riders making it aren't moving. I can see some black specks that weren't in the scene before the cloud and might be the riders, but the power of my glasses is too low for me to tell in the dim light.

Yellow Boy's telescope has about twice the lens size of my binoculars and four times the magnifying power and Yellow Boy has the best night vision of any man I've ever known. He stares for a couple of minutes before he says, "Five *hombres*. One on horse at the canyon door uses big eyes. He looks for signs of firelight. Others climb off horses. Make water on mesquite."

"Can you tell who they are?"

He shrugs. "Still too far."

"What do you think we ought to do?"

"They wait. Watch. No see firelight, come in canyon, camp in piñon shadows on south side of canyon, eat, rest. Maybe wait for sunrise before scout canyon looking for sign. After they make camp, then learn they war with Apache. We go to their camp, take horses, water. Pull them into canyon, look for horses, look for water. They walk. Need for water grows." He reaches out and grabs a handful of air. "We pick off one by one, take their power one by one."

I nod.

"*Bueno*."

In half an hour, the *dorado* using the glasses is satisfied no one is staring back at him and leads the others up the trail toward the pass. Maybe three hours before dawn they stop to camp at the third canyon on the south side of the trail.

Yellow Boy and I take only our knives and pistols, ease down our ridge over to the ridge of low mountains forming the south side of the canyon, and begin running along the south side of the ridges toward our pursuers' camp. I haven't run in weeks. Cold air filling my lungs and my body warming from our long, fast strides feels good, very good. Two-thirds of the way down the south side trail, Yellow Boy turns to run up the slope to the top of the ridge. When we reach the top, we run along the ridge crest toward the east until we reach the top of the ridge above the canyon where the *dorados* camp. Sure enough a small fire blazes and men eat.

We study them with our glasses. I see Camisa Roja and Gamberro sitting cross-legged off to one side of the fire. There are two others I don't recognize and the fifth one by the fire...I whisper, "Oh, no. Damn it, I told him, I told him..."

They have Jesús, his face bruised and swollen, his hands tied. I point at him and Yellow Boy nods, whispering, "When they sleep, I take their horses, ride for our camp. You empty their water barrel and canteens, free Jesús, climb back to top of ridge and follow way we come back to camp. If they follow you they will die by my rifle, this I promise you, my Son."

The old proverb says that it's always darkest before the dawn. It is. I have to use every skill I've learned from my Apache mentor to get down the ridge to the *dorado* camp without being heard. Their fire has burned down to yellow-orange coals glowing beneath gray ash, and the sentries are dozing for a few seconds at a time before their heads nod over and they jerk awake. Yellow Boy creeps to the rope where their horses are tied, introduces himself to each one by letting them sample his breath and he theirs, and then cuts and holds each end of the rope as he swings up on the middle horse. The horses are ready to run when he's ready to spook them.

Jesús, exiled from the fire, sleeps in a fetal position shivering in the freezing air, without blankets, on the bare ground. I ease my hand over his mouth. He jerks in surprise but I feel him smile when he recognizes my smell and outline in the feeble light from the fire's coals. I hold a finger to my lips signaling silence and he nods. I cut the rope that binds him and look around for their water cask while he rubs circulation back into his hands and wrists.

The cask is with the saddles, pack mule harness, and their meager supplies. Slowly I ease it over on its side and use my knife to pry the bung out to let the water dribble into the dry, thirsty sand. I empty all the canteens I find with the saddles and figure that even if I've missed one or two they'd all be thirsty by midday.

Faint gray is on the eastern horizon when I crawl away with Jesús. A hundred yards up the canyon from the camp I'm whispering the plan to him when one of the *dorados* staggers up from his blankets to water a piñon. Wobbling back to his blankets he stares in the direction where Jesús slept. Jesús wants to run. I hold him by the wrist and hold my finger to my lips to signal silence, mouthing, "Wait, wait."

Looking over all the camp, the *dorado* finally realizes Jesús is gone and roars, "Damn!" Yellow Boy answers with an ear splitting, angry scream and drives the horses straight through the middle of their camp scattering hot coals in all directions. All the *dorados* hide in their blankets except one, the one in the red shirt who rolls to his feet and fires in the direction of the horses disappearing into the soft gray light filling the freezing air.

In the confusion, Jesús and I scramble to the top of the ridge and start down the other side. I can't believe how lucky and successful we've been to steal the horses, free Jesús, and destroy their water supply. We could have killed them all, but I suspect Yellow Boy plans to make them wish that we had.

When Jesús and I reach camp, Yellow Boy sits in the piñons watching the *dorado* camp with his Big Eye telescope. He looks at Jesús's battered face and grunts. "Hmmph. Why does Camisa Roja and Gamberro bring you to hunt us?"

Barely able to see out of his puffy eyes, Jesús, still trying to catch his breath, leans over, hands on his knees, and says, "Bait. They believe I planned to kill the general. They believe Doctor Grace will not let them kill me. If I look bad enough, they think they can draw him out to help me."

"Did Villa send them?"

"I do not know. I did not hear him tell them to do it. Roja says he has a personal score to settle with Doctor Grace. Gamberro says if he kills Doctor Grace, Villa will make him a general. If they can kill him, they believe there is much to gain for them both. The other two *hombres* come for the promise of *dinero*."

Yellow Boy motions toward his chest.

"Do they know I'm with Hombrecito?"

"They never speak of Muchacho Amarillo."

Yellow Boy shows one of his rare smiles.

"Now, they know."

"Uncle, what will we do now?"

"Camisa Roja knows spring in rocks up canyon where your woman's bones rest. Arango gets water there when *División del Norte* cross El Paso Púlpito. They come for water by and by. They no find if Hombrecito shoots straight."

I smile.

"They will not drink."

While Yellow Boy keeps watch, and I take care of the stolen horses, Jesús, like a starving man, eats the leftovers of bread and meat from our supper. When he finishes I do the best I can for him, washing away the dirt and treating infections beginning on his face and upper body.

The sun fills the canyon with golden light and the cold night air turns warm and pleasant. Yellow Boy watches through his telescope. The shadows are still long when he says, "They come."

I watch the four specks through my binoculars as they spread out on either side of the main trail and begin carefully to move toward us. Yellow Boy points where the main trail branches off up the canyon toward the spring. "Hombrecito, use Shoots-Today-Kills-Tomorrow. No pass to spring."

I nod. "They will not pass. Uncle, I claim Camisa Roja. Do what you will with the other two and Gamberro."

62. A GOOD DAY TO DIE

For a few minutes we watch the *dorados* advance up the canyon, staying low, scrambling from bush to bush for cover, scanning the ridges on both sides of the canyon, and occasionally glancing down the trail to our distant ridge. Their advance, slow as they run from bush to bush, makes Yellow Boy yawn and stretch.

"Hombrecito watch *dorados*. Keep all in sight. I smoke then take your place."

He pulls a cigar from his coat and disappears below the top of the ridge. I watch the *dorados*. At the rate they're coming, it'll be another two or three hours before the fireworks begin. All we have to do is to keep them in sight, making sure they don't set up an ambush of their own.

I keep track of all the *dorados* but I pay special attention to Camisa Roja. He stays low in the wash that twists down the middle of the canyon. At least if shooting starts, he'll have real, bullet-stopping cover, not just a mesquite bush to hide behind. I have to give him credit. He's a smart, deadly fighter, a worthy opponent, and, a man close to breathing his last.

Smoking his black, acrid smelling cigar, Yellow Boy motions Jesús over to sit with him.

"*Señor*, what trail did you ride to El Paso Púlpito?"

Jesús shrugs and shakes his head.

"Gamberro, he leads us on trails through the mountains, trails the general never used in all the time I am his *soldado*. Gamberro says they are trails the Yaquis use for centuries and only a few know."

Yellow Boy nods, takes a few more puffs.

"You come after us with these *hombres*?"

Jesús hangs his head.

"I am a fool, Muchacho Amarillo. The General, there were tears in his eyes when he asks me to go with the *dorados* and convince Doctor Grace that he is very sorry for his treatment of his old *amigo* and beg him to return as his personal *medico* until the *gringos* leave Mexico. I believed him, I wanted to help him, and I agreed to come with the *dorados*. I saw the *dorados* talk together before we leave. I was tending the general's leg and do not know what was said. It was not something they wanted me to hear, and now I believe I know why."

Yellow Boy inhales deeply and blows a long puff into the wind.

"Why you beat in face? Ribs blue? Sleep on ground, no blanket, like dog?"

"The second night we stopped to rest the horses. Gamberro wanted to know if Muchacho Amarillo rode with Doctor Grace. By this time I'd heard the other two *dorados* laughing about how Doctor Grace might have an accident, maybe trampled by horses after he was found, and I understood I made a bad mistake coming with them. I say to Gamberro, 'No. Muchacho Amarillo is not with him. Muchacho Amarillo is north of the border in Mescalero.'

"I do not lie good, *señor*. They did not believe me, and Gamberro tried to beat what I knew out of me. I tell them nothing. Camisa Roja made Gamberro leave me alone. He said the general might shoot them if I died and they did not find Doctor Grace. Gamberro, saying I might run to warn you, tied my wrists and me to my horse and kept it on a lead rope. I wished for my knife many times to slit the throat of that whore son."

Yellow Boy nods, but says nothing more as he smokes. We wait an hour, two, maybe three as the *dorados* approach where the north trail splits off for the spring. The cold, still air, fast disappearing, is replaced by a warm updraft toward the tops of the ridges. When the *dorados* approach within three quarters of a mile of us, I start using Little David to take sight pictures of each one using the smallest aperture on Little David's Soule sight. With the bright sun I can see each man through the sight's smallest rear aperture, but given the updraft in our faces, any shot that hits anything at that range will be a very lucky one. We wait. In a while I guess they are within nine hundred yards, a little more than half a mile. They keep coming. Yellow Boy and I watch their moves, Jesús occasionally taking a look through our glasses.

Watching men I know I might have to kill, my mouth grows dry and I ask Jesús to bring me a canteen. My heart begins to race, making my sight pictures wobble all over the *dorados*, who are within four or five hundred yards of the north trail and maybe seven or eight hundred yards from our position. I take a couple of deep breaths to steady up.

The memory of Rufus Pike's words to me when I was a boy drift by on the currents of my mind, "*Henry, ye gotta be cold and cakilatin' to survive in this here country.*" I smile. I wasn't more than fourteen when I first heard him tell me that, but the old man's wisdom still sticks with me. A swallow of water, a few more breaths, and everything I do thereafter becomes calculated, measured, and steady.

The *dorados* finally reach where the trail forks. They are smart enough not to bunch up as they hide behind their brush covers, trying to work up the courage to run out in the open through the fire of a potential ambush.

I pull six .45-70 cartridges out of a full box, slide three in my right vest pocket, put one in the breech of Little David, and hold the other two in the fingers of my right hand ready for fast use. Rufus Pike trained me to shoot the big, heavy Sharps and taught me to hold the spare cartridges between my fingers and flip them into the breech with minimal hand motion so the entire shooting cycle became one, fast, continuous motion. I can fire the Sharps for those three rounds faster than most men can fire three shots with a lever-action Winchester. I pick the spot carefully for a warning shot for the first *dorado* when he tries running up the north trail. If he stops and turns around, I won't waste another cartridge, but if he keeps on running, he'll be a dead man with a hole in him big enough to ride a horse through.

Yellow Boy levers a shell into the chamber of the Henry and slowly lets the hammer down to safety, waiting, his eyes glimmering, black flint behind a narrow squint. I sit resting my elbows on my knees, holding Little David snug against my shoulder, sighted on my warning shot target, a place in the middle of the trail. Jesús watches in rapt attention, waiting for the drama to unfold.

One of the young *dorados* is up and running, rifle across his chest, big sombrero bouncing on his back like a rider on a bucking horse, dust exploding in puffs like splashed water as his boots pound the trail, his mouth gaping open, gulping more air against the strain of his dash. I don't hesitate pulling the hammer and set trigger back on Little David, and taking no more than a couple of seconds to line up on the spot before I fire.

The ancient thunderboomer roars, sending echoes of eternity down the canyon, kicking me in the shoulder, flooding my body with adrenaline, as I automatically bring the hammer to half cock, lever the breech open to flip out the spent brass, slide in a new cartridge, raise the breech, and find the line of sight for the running man's point of no return.

When the trail in front of him suddenly explodes for no reason, the running *dorado* jerks to a stop, confused, his jaw dropping, his chest heaving. He hears the Sharps' thunder rumbling down the canyon and instantly understands what's happened. He freezes in place for a couple of seconds and looks back at his friends hiding in brush, a pale sickly look on his face.

Yellow Boy is watching with his telescope and exclaims, "Fools! They wave him on!"

The runner looks up the north trail and his legs start churning again. The men in the brush yell at him, encouraging him, telling him to run harder, run faster. He passes the point of no return.

No man has ever outrun one of my bullets. My sights, smoothly tracking his motion, follow just in front of him. I fire again. The bullet hits him a few inches below his armpit on the left side and passes out about half way down his right side. I hear Jesús gasp in disbelief at the damage a shot from my old rifle does to the human body. The *dorado*, thrown sideways from the impact, blood spraying from his mouth, collapses in a heap, dead before his body hits the ground in a cloud of dust that slowly settles to cover him in white powder, making him look ghost-like.

His blood pooling in the sand turns black, leaving a spot the size of a spittoon, reminding me of how my murdered father looked when I was eight. I want to vomit but swallow down the bile. Jesús, who has seen men torn asunder in Villa's battles, sits down and puts his head between his knees, muttering over and over, "*Cristo…*blessed *Cristo*."

Yellow Boy, watching the other *dorados* says, "Others no move, stretch out, stay close to ground, hide, pray they are brother to the mesquite. They wait. *Mucho* thirst comes. We wait. They run pretty soon now. You see by and by."

I'm deciding how best to adjust my Soule sight for the updraft when Yellow Boy says to Jesús, "*Muchacho,* saddle horses, load the mule. Lead them and the *dorado* horses to the *arroyo* behind us. Go quick. Wait there. No move."

Jesús nods. "*Sí, señor. Rapidamente.*"

I wonder why Yellow Boy wants Jesús to move the animals. He points toward the mesquites in the draw near where Camisa Roja hides. Through my glasses I see a faint wisp of smoke rising in the breeze and disappearing. It's so thin I almost miss seeing it. It's April, two or three months before the monsoon season. Everything is tinder dry.

Yellow Boy looks at me, eyes glittering, filled with fight, today is a good day to die.

"Fire comes. Makes smoke. Shoot where you see their smoke. Soon now they bring fire to this side of wash. Wind blow fire up this ridge. *Dorados* run for water behind smoke. I go to spring. You and Jesús follow *dorados*. No let 'em turn back. I go now."

I nod my understanding without taking my eyes off the increasing whiffs of white smoke below us.

Yellow Boy runs to the horses Jesús holds in the *arroyo*, mounts his paint, and rides off across the road and into the hills where he can reach the spring unseen by the *dorados* and set up another ambush. I send a few rounds into the mesquite and piñons where the *dorados* hide but the smoke grows.

A wand, its tip flaming, shoots out of the mesquites and lands in a patch of gra'ma grass just across the main trail from the branch heading to the spring. The grass blazes up instantly, fire jumping from patch to patch like the boots of a giant marching up the side of our ridge. I'm dumbfounded that one of them has a bow and arrow or can made them on the spot strong enough to shoot from behind the mesquites all the way across the road, a range of maybe sixty or seventy yards. Camisa Roja told me later that Gamberro had made the bow from a piece of mesquite, the string from threads in a sash he wore, and arrows split from wood plank they found in the wash. However they did it, it's time for me to join Jesús.

As the wind carries the fire up the front side of the ridge, I scramble down the backside. Jesús is having a hard time holding the horses, wild-eyed and prancing around, trying to get off the lead rope. They smell smoke and want out of there. I help him quiet them down while we wait for Roja, Gamberro, and the remaining young *dorado* to run up the canyon for the spring and its cool, sweet water.

They wait until the fire is near the top of our ridge before dashing up the north fork for the canyon and the spring where Yellow Boy waits. They run right by the man I'd killed, only Camisa Roja momentarily taking a knee and rolling him over to be sure he's dead. Jesús and I wait until they're out of sight, and then we ride up the trail behind them.

When we're about a hundred yards past the body, we dismount and walk surrounded by the *dorado* horses and our own mounts. I'm not taking any chances. The three we're chasing will likely make their own ambush for anyone following them up the trail.

We're half a mile up the canyon wash when I hear Yellow Boy's Henry bark followed by five or six shots from a Winchester. We pause to listen as the echoes die away, only to see a dust plume from a bullet landing right in front of us and hear the rifle shot echo follow the first ones across the hills. Jesús and I don't have to coax the horses into the piñons on the east side of the wash. From the way the dust plumed and the report echoed, I have no doubt the shooter hides on the west side of the canyon. In the piñons covering the east side of the canyon, I use my glasses to study the cliff rocks, talus, and each little cluster of piñons below the cliffs on the west side.

I finally find what I'm looking for in one of the piñon groves next to the talus, a glimmer of red showing in the branch shadows. Camisa Roja has fired a warning shot to go no farther, and I'm content to wait for Yellow Boy to take care of Gamberro and the other *dorado* before forcing Roja out of his piñons. We wait.

Up the canyon there's a brief tattoo of Winchester rifle fire. As the echoes fade away, the Henry barks again and its echoes are followed by screams of mortal agony that lower to desperate, grunting moans that soon stop, leaving the hot still air silent. I stretched my neck as much as I dare, look up the canyon, but see nothing.

Camisa Roja leaves his cover and runs along the edge of the cliff talus up the canyon toward the spring. I fire my own warning shot in front of him, a ricochet into the talus that sprays his face with tiny pieces of stone that luckily doesn't blind him but cover his face with a hundred scratches, each oozing its own few drops of blood. Looking like a teenager with a sudden case of terrible acne, he turns back for the piñons and I fire again in front of him. He gets the message, sits down where he is, wipes the blood from his face and pulls the makings of a smoke from his coat pocket while he tries to see what happens between Yellow Boy, Gamberro, and the young *dorado*.

I'm consumed with worry and curiosity about Yellow Boy but I dare not leave a boy to do a man's job, and my job is ensuring Yellow Boy is not in danger of being flanked by the man I cover. The screams and moans we hear from near the spring tell me Yellow Boy has mortally wounded, if not killed, the young *dorado* with Gamberro. Gamberro would have died in silence and excruciating pain before ever screaming like a woman in childbirth.

Gamberro is twice the size of Yellow Boy, half his age, fought in some terrible, bloody battles, and is a Yaqui. Yellow Boy has twenty more years of fighting experience, knows every trick in guerilla warfare, and most importantly, is an Apache warrior who asks no quarter and gives none. Gamberro is at a definite disadvantage.

I pull the hammer back on Little David, ready to fire, and say to Jesús, "I have Camisa Roja in my sights and can kill him instantly. Step out where he can see you, raise your arms in a surrender sign and motion him in this direction, and sign he's to leave his weapons."

Jesús sticks out his chin and nods, determined to prove he has as much courage as anyone else in this fight. "*Sí, señor.*"

It takes him a couple of minutes, but Jesús finally gets the message across to Roja. He very deliberately holds up his empty right hand, and with his left lays down his rifle and pistol where we can see them. He stands with both his hands up, and slowly walks, making a switchback path down the side of the canyon, to the wash immediately in front of us. The only sounds are the breeze rustling through the piñons and the occasional rock his feet dislodge that bounces and rolls down to the wash. If groans still come from the wounded man, we can't hear them for the breeze gently shaking the trees and brush.

I say, "Jesús, get the reata from my saddle, and when Roja gets to the wash, sign for him to stop. If he does, tie his hands behind his back and search him well, even his boots, for knives or guns. When you have him tied, sit him down cross-legged and I will come claim the prisoner."

He smiles and says, "*Sí, señor.*"

Ten minutes later I walk up to Camisa Roja, hands tied, sitting straight, his jaw stuck out defiantly, his legs crossed in the sand. Holding the end of the rope, ready to jerk Roja back in place if he attacks or runs, Jesús squats nearby, rolling a smoke from the makings he took from Roja's pockets.

"Very good, Jesús. You've saved an *hombre's* life."

"*Muchas gracias*, Doctor Grace. Here is your prisoner."

I look at Camisa Roja, his grim face expecting the worst. "*Buenos tardes, Señor* Roja. It is a good day to die, no? Tell me, *señor*, why did you run from your cover like that? Did you not think I'd see you?"

Roja smiles the grimace of the damned. "I couldn't see you or your horses and thought you'd gone farther back down the canyon where you couldn't see me. It was a foolish boy's mistake. I deserve to die. Take your vengeance, Hombrecito. You have traveled many miles to spill my blood."

"*Sí*, I have traveled many miles to settle a matter of honor. I have traveled many miles with a dream trying to speak to me, haunting me like a ghost. Before anything is settled, we will speak of this dream and then you will make a choice for life or death."

Roja squints at me from under his brows, curious, defiant. "Life or death, you truly give me a choice Hombrecito? I will make it. You know I am not afraid to die. Sometimes death rotting your bones is better than living in Hell –"

We hear a horse pounding down the wash toward us and instinctively move to one side to get out of its way. Yellow Boy, having killed Gamberro, must be hurrying to join our fight and end it before Roja can slip away. The horse rounds the bend, stretching its neck out in a dead run down the middle of the wash, throwing small clods of dirt and pebbles in looping little arcs high in the air, raising waist-high puffs of dust each time its flying hooves hit the ground. Yellow Boy's paint sweeps by us, Gamberro urging it on with whacks on the pony's rump from his Winchester and swearing in a scream, "I'll be back. You bastards will die."

I've never seen anyone take Yellow Boy's paint in all the years we've been together. My heart sinks, caught by the belief that the only way Gamberro can take the paint is to put Yellow Boy down, maybe even killing him.

I turn and drop to one knee, pulling the hammer back on the Sharps, snugging it against my shoulder, trying to see Gamberro, rapidly disappearing in the center of his cloud of dust. I'm fearful a wild shot will hit the paint. I decide that if I can't hit Gamberro, I'll have to take the paint or I'll never have another chance at Gamberro. My finger is closing on the trigger when I hear running feet behind me and look up to see Yellow Boy stripped to the waist, sweat streaming down his body, race up to Jesús and take the reins for Satanas. He shakes his hand at me, palm up, a signal to wait, and says only, "Mine! Back *pronto*."

I sit back, relieved beyond words, and laugh. Jesús and Roja look at me like I'm crazy. Roja, on the edge of a smile, says, "Gamberro escapes, Hombrecito. Muchacho Amarillo can never catch Gamberro with a long head start on a good horse. Why do you laugh?" The look on Jesús's face shows he's thinking the same thing.

I shake my head smiling.

"*Señor* Roja, you have a very short memory. Nearly twelve years ago, Muchacho Amarillo took my horse, the one left at the Comacho *Hacienda*, the one *Señor* Comacho called *Espirito Negro*, Black Spirit. He gave it to me and I called him Satanas. Working with me, it took Muchacho Amarillo nearly a day to convince Satanas to let us ride him. In those days there was not a horse three hundred miles north or south of the border that could outrun him. Now there might be a few, but the paint is not one of them. The remainder of Gamberro's life can only be measured in minutes to hours at the very best. Gamberro's bones will soon bleach white in the *llano* sun and coyotes and buzzards will have a belly full of him. Muchacho Amarillo will return this night. Get up. We go to the spring, water the horses and have a little talk."

63. THE RECKONING

Between the horses and our own thirst, we practically drink the little cliff tank dry. It's a peaceful, pleasant place and I'm glad I can see the top edge of Rafaela's cairn on the cliff ledge above us. Camisa Roja sits with his back against a large juniper and stares at the cliff's crags and crannies. Jesús naps under a juniper near where he hobbled the horses. The canyon fills with long shadows from the falling afternoon sun.

I sit with my back against a large boulder and study the man I've wanted to kill for ten years. I've ridden hundreds of miles to take my revenge for their attempt to murder me but let him and Villa live. Roja couldn't believe, couldn't accept my flash of insight. He followed me to this place to kill or be killed. Everything I learned as a child and young man about justice from Yellow Boy says I have every right, maybe even duty, to send Camisa Roja to the grandfathers. I no longer have a desire for his blood, but I won't spend the rest of my life looking over my shoulder either, waiting for the man in the red shirt to come north again. Whatever happens here will end our trails twisted together. Fate makes me judge, prosecutor, jury, and executioner. *How ironic*, I think, *that* Rafaela's *killer stands in judgment before her grave.*

In the canyon's falling light I point toward the cairn. "Can you see the burial place of the woman you murdered, *señor*? The woman I took as a wife, the only woman I've ever loved and will probably ever love, the woman who carried our child in her belly when you murdered her?"

Roja frowns and shakes his head. "Murdered her? I did not murder her. *Sí*, I killed her. I freely admit that. She was with Apaches who tried to wipe out my *patrón*. She dressed as a *hombre* and she was running away after searching the pockets of a dead man in the road. *Sí*, I can see the place of the stones you say is her burial place. I am truly sorry if I killed an innocent woman, but I did not murder her. Will you murder me now?"

"I will have justice. I owe you debts of honor for my woman's death, for trying to kill me at San Pedro de la Cueva, and now you come here to murder me even after I decide not to kill you and Villa in Santa Cruz. You told me at San Pedro that you were just following Villa's orders. Are you now just following Villa's orders when you came after us this time?"

"No, *señor*, not Villa's orders. Gamberro and I did what we thought was right to protect the general."

I'm astonished.

"How can you believe murdering me and my friends in an ambush is the right thing to do?"

He shrugs his shoulders a little and grimaces.

"I learn you come to Santa Cruz when I am in the mountains. Sitting by the fire, deciding what must be done to protect the general, I consider all the miles you rode to get to Santa Cruz, all the hardships you must have suffered riding in the cold at night on trails you do not know while avoiding *gringos*, Carrancistas, and Villistas, and the great thirst you must have for avenging the way Villa treated you, and the even greater thirst you must have for killing me. I know that whatever happens in Santa Cruz, you will not rest until you have satisfaction. Your desire for revenge must be branded on your soul.

"You did not kill the general in Santa Cruz and did not even look for me. The general, he says you tell him of a dream that haunts you, pull the bone splinters out of his leg, stop his suffering, and leave. Even though he says you save him from the *gringos*, Jesús stays to help the general.

"I am amazed when I return and find you have not killed him. Why didn't you kill the general? I know. You are a man of honor. You will not kill a wounded, crazy man until he can defend himself, he…"

Roja sees the surprised look on my face and grins. "Oh, *sí*, Hombrecito, I know very well the general is crazy, he blames the *gringos* for everything, even dry rivers and hot sun that have been here since time starts. I know, after you leave Santa Cruz, a man with a scar on his soul such as yours, you will come back when the general is strong again, you will finish what you came to do this time, and Jesús, still a boy, will be there to open the door for you whether he knows your intentions are good or not. The general cannot, as you say, spend his life looking over his shoulder, and I will not spend my life that way either. I came to end it, one way or the other. I kill you or you kill me. Your vendetta, it ends here.

"Gamberro? He doesn't care who is right or wrong, he is like Rodolfo Fierro, *el carnicerro*, the butcher, he likes the killing and the smell of blood, he will use any excuse to satisfy his thirst for killing. The other two *dorados*, they come for the *dinero* we think you carry. We failed to kill you, failed to protect the general because of this Apache, Muchacho Amarillo. We are not the warriors you are. So, tell me, *señor*, why did you not kill the general or try to kill me? How am I wrong in my thinking?"

I stare at his eyes and see no guile. I pull out my pipe, stuff the burl bowl with tobacco and light it. The smoke hangs in the still air above us.

"I want to tell you a story. Twelve years ago I lived with the Apaches. The woman you killed, Rafaela, and another woman and her little brother and I hid from a Díaz army division. We were in a canyon on the Rio Bavispe south of Colonia Oaxaca. The biggest jaguar I've ever seen carried off the little boy and slaughtered his sister when she chased after them. Rafaela and I made a pact to kill that jaguar, and we did, but not before it almost killed me. I live only because Rafaela took a rock and smashed in its brains before it tore me up after I shot it."

"I much regret that I killed such a fearless woman, Hombrecito, but as I..."

"You regret it far less than I do, *señor*, just listen."

He grimaces and nods.

"I have learned many things since Rafaela's death. Chief among them is that undiscerning eyes rarely see the truth.

Things are never as they seem. I went to the university for many years to become a doctor and returned to Las Cruces where you found me last fall. Almost from the day I returned, even before you came, I began having a dream, a dream that relived my fight with the jaguar and how close it came to tearing away my life. But this dream was different from what happened in the canyon. The jaguar was on fire…"

Roja frowns. "A jaguar on fire, what does this mean, a jaguar on fire? How…"

"I didn't know what it meant, and I always awoke before I saw Rafaela finally killing it before it took me. In the dream, I never saw who killed the jaguar. The dream came often, maybe two or three times a week. I didn't understand it, but I came to believe that maybe it was trying to send me a message.

"Finally, when I was alone with Villa in the *hacienda*, ready to kill him, he drew his pistol to shoot me. So weak he can't steady it to pull the trigger, I snatched the *pistola* away from him leaving him defenseless. Before I can kill him with his own gun, I realize that the jaguar in the dream is a symbol for Villa. Many call him *El Tigre*. He is *loco*. His anger is like a fire consuming him and making him *loco*.

"Jesús walked through the door bringing me hot water for use in treating the general's *leg*. In that room I told Jesús that I deceived him in order to find and kill the general. I want him to leave so the *dorados* will not kill him if I am caught after the murder. Jesús will not leave and tells me that if I betrayed his trust to find Villa, then I am no better than Villa who betrayed me. All things from the dream were suddenly clear. The burning *tigre* in my dream is stopped from taking me by the one I cannot see."

"I do not understand. I hear none of this at the *hacienda* in Santa Cruz."

"In all the times I dreamed the dream, I never knew how or even if I escaped the jaguar in flames, the burning *Tigre*. I know now that my killing Villa for his betrayals and murders would have reduced my ability to know the difference between good and evil. Losing my way, I'd become no better than the crazy hypocrite Villa was then. Jesús stopped me from killing Villa, stopped me from losing my soul, and ultimately stopped me from becoming like Villa. Villa will crawl away and die on his own someday. I don't need to help him get there sooner. In fact, I won't help him die at all. He must live with the consequences of his mistakes. Perhaps that is worse than dying because of them.

"You, *señor*, presumed too much when you left Villa to kill me. Two of your *compañeros* are no more. Gamberro joins them soon if not already. Now, I must decide if I can let you live or you must die."

Roja, his dark eyes fixed on me, nods, takes a last puff from his cigarette and grinds it out in the sand beside him.

I sit smoking my pipe and thinking about what to do with this man who killed the love of my life and has tried to kill me twice. Jesús awakes and sees Roja and I facing each other. He keeps his distance, not interrupting two men speaking of life and death, and leads the horses to water as the crickets begin their songs in the lingering dusk.

As the dusk turns black, Jesús digs and lights a small fire pit, puts a pot of coffee on to boil, and starts meat, potatoes, and chilies cooking in a stew.

In a while I hear stones click together down the trail and cock Little David after signaling Roja to keep silent. The sounds increase from something or someone coming up the canyon.

Minutes pass. Satanas appears in our circle of firelight and snorts, his ears rising as he stares toward the cliff. He has no rider, just the reins tied loosely at the saddle horn. I smile. It's a favorite trick of Yellow Boy, who stands at the tank behind us, watering his paint.

Jesús jumps up to lead Satanas to water, but I let the hammer down on Little David and signal I'll do it myself, saying, "Just keep an eye on our guest."

I take the reins and lead Satanas to water. Yellow Boy's paint, ridden hard and played out, hangs his head and drinks slowly, unable to go any further without rest. Satanas isn't in as bad a shape as the paint but needs water and rest.

As the horses drink, I look Yellow Boy over, and don't seeing any bullet wounds or broken bones.

"It is a good thing for you to return now, my uncle. Are there wounds I need to see? Our *amigo* cooks for us. Soon we eat."

He doesn't waste any time getting to the point. "No wounds. I see Camisa Roja. You kill him?"

"No…not yet."

He looks at me with raised brows for a moment and nods. "Your prisoner. Do as you want."

We rub down the horses and give them a big ration of grain. The paint lies down, too weary to eat. We leave grain for it, knowing it'll be on its feet in two or three hours, and it will be at least two, maybe three days before it can carry Yellow Boy across the mountains. Even Satanas will not be ready to ride tomorrow.

We sit down with the plates of stew Jesús gives us.

We're all hungry. Roja, like a starving man, eats two full plates. After acknowledging Jesús's outstanding stew, we sit drinking coffee.

"Uncle, tell us of Gamberro."

He takes a long slurp of coffee and answers.

"I am at spring, Gamberro across wash. We shoot. No see, no hit. Paint sees snake, rears to get away. Breaks tie line, runs for wash. Gamberro runs between the paint and me, grabs his bridle, swings up on him, and rides for *llano*. I take Satanas. Gamberro rides paint too hard. I see him falter two, maybe three times. I no shoot, no hit paint. Gamberro shoots back at Muchacho Amarillo and Satanas many times, wastes many bullets. When I see him start to reload, I push Satanas hard, hold rifle from barrel like war club, ride up close, swing back toward his face, and crack him across forehead. Gamberro flips off paint backwards, lands on head in road. I catch paint, ride back to Gamberro. No move. Neck broke. Gamberro is no more. I drag body off road. Take clothes. *Mañana,* sun cooks plenty quick. Buzzards, hawks eat good. Maybe coyotes have full bellies tonight. That is all I have to say."

I see Roja slowly shake his head. I can imagine what he must be thinking.

Yellow Boy, Jesús, and I divided up the night watches. I have the last one before dawn.

I can't sleep before my watch. My brain runs at high speed considering what I should do with Camisa Roja even as I hear him snore across the fire that's turning to gray ashes. He knows, and I know, I won't murder him in cold blood. How do I assure myself that I'll never need to worry about him coming after me? Why do I no longer feel any anger for him killing Rafaela and for twice trying to kill me? By all I've been taught by Yellow Boy and Rufus Pike, he deserves to die.

It occurs to me, *Wanting to kill Roja is like trying to take revenge against the wind when it blows down your house or fire when it burns you. He's a force of nature. He had no personal passion when he killed Rafaela or when he tried to kill me on Villa's orders or came after me to protect him. It was nothing like he claimed to feel when he killed Elias and Kid. With Rafaela and me it was just...being a soldier, just protecting the tribe, just doing a job like branding cattle.*

My mind wanders across all the times we crossed paths during the last year and settles on that last terrible day in San Pedro de la Cueva when Villa was ordering lineups for the firing squads and threatening the priest. I got there just as he kicked the priest, begging on his knees for the lives of the village men, backwards. In a fury, I nearly jumped him then but a hand in a red sleeve reached out and grabbed me and held my arm like it was in a steel trap. I couldn't get near Villa, and didn't jerk away from Red Sleeves tight hold until Villa murdered the priest. I pounded Villa a few good licks until someone in a red shirt rang my bell with the butt of a Mauser. Whoever it was probably saved my life because those *dorados* were prepared to kill anyone attacking the general. In my case Red Shirt knocked me out before they could shoot or hack me to death with their swords. It's the first time I've realized someone in a red shirt saved my bacon that morning. Of course, I know instantly who it was even though I hadn't consciously made the connection before... funny how our minds work...I suddenly feel much more relaxed. Come first light, I can settle a debt for which I wasn't aware...and feel reasonably certain Camisa Roja and I will never cross swords again.

When the jagged eastern mountains turn blood red just before being outlined in fiery gold, I saddle a *dorado* horse, fill a canteen from the spring, and tap Roja on the bottom of his boots with my rifle. He jerks up, instantly awake. I cut the rope around his feet and motion with my head for him to go to the horse tied in the wash. When he takes the reins of the horse, I nod down the wash for him to start walking. Little David and my pistol ready for instant use, I walk to the left side of Camisa Roja and the horse. Birds in the trees begin to chirp, as the cold morning gray turns to light gold.

We reach the trail from the pass into the *llano* stretching toward Casas Grandes.

"Stop here, *señor*. I give you life and cancel all debts we hold with each other. It is the right thing to do for me, maybe a foolish thing for an Apache. If I see you again, one of us will die. Go to Villa. Serve him well. Serve him as you always have. I seek no more revenge. Life is too short to have the bitter taste of revenge on your tongue, and I now realize I've owed you a debt.

"Some say life is like a card game. We have to play the cards dealt us. Most of my cards have not made winning hands. Perhaps, someday I can say I won a hand that makes it all even, but I will never know unless I play the game. Do you understand what I have told you?"

"*Sí*, Doctor Grace. I understand very well."

"Hold out your wrists."

I cut the cord that ties his hands. As he rubs circulation back in his wrists, I put his pistol back in his holster, drop six cartridges into his coat pocket, and say, "It's a long ride from here to Casas Grandes. There is enough water in the canteen to get you and your horse across the *llano* to the next well. You know this country. You lived in it in your vaquero days. Now ride to your general and hope you never see me again."

He starts to mount, sees his rifle scabbard is empty, and motions to it. "A soldier without his rifle is –"

I shake my head. "You will get another fine one from the general's stash. Be gone."

Mounted, he smiles and gives me a little, snappy salute with his finger tips off his sombrero. "*Muchas gracias,* Hombrecito. *Adiós,* and good luck."

He gallops off down the winding canyon road into the morning light, a shadow disappearing in the distance against the rising sun.

64. THE TIGER

El Paso Púlpito, Chihuahua, Mexico, 1952

The jeep sat idling on the winding dusty trail between the canyon walls of El Paso Púlpito, framing the *llano* stretching toward Casas Grandes.

Henry relaxed and turned off the engine, smiling as it coughed, knocked, and at last died. They've listened to its complaints for the last ten days, but it always got them where they wanted to go. Fishing his pipe out of his vest, he stuffed the bowl with long, thin strands of golden tobacco, and using his thumbnail snapped a match to life in a bright flash that steadies into orange flame. With a few good puffs, a reddish-orange coal under a thin veneer of gray ash formed at the top of the bowl. Leaning back against the seat, he contentedly puffed small, blue smoke clouds that slowly drifted away, diffusing into the nearly still air.

Roberta looked at the old wagon road with new eyes. So much living and dying in this place. So much life lived in a year, so many men who marched or rode down this trail over the pass never to return, dead from accidents, starvation and thirst, hail storms of bullets and exploding shells, and betrayals.

"This is where it ended, Roberta. The canyon out to the *llano* looks just like it did thirty-five years ago when I let Roja go. Even the sunrise coming over that little mountain to the left with the stars still in the background looks the same."

Ten days on rough dirt roads across Mexico are barely gone. They've driven hundreds of miles across northern and central Mexico. She's never ridden so many miles of rough roads or gathered so many bruises bouncing in a car seat. Vast *llanos*, dark, brooding mountains, steep passes, high forests, blue-green lakes, and deep canyons in brilliant sunlight formed the canvas on which Henry painted the story of his friendship with and his betrayal by Pancho Villa, and how he came to release Camisa Roja, who killed his wife and tried to kill him twice.

Lighting a Lucky Strike, and taking a deep draw, Roberta studied Henry's face, questions filling her mind. Henry looked over at her, gave her knee a little squeeze and smiled.

"Mrs. Grace, it's been a long ten days, but having you in my blankets made it all worthwhile. At least in a night or two we'll be back in our own bed and won't be bouncing around most of the day in this old buggy."

She smiled.

"Henry, I'll never forget this trip. I know it's been hard for you pull up those old memories, but I've learned a lot… "

"Probably more than you ever wanted to know."

"No, I'll always want to know more about the man I married. It's just that… your story leaves more questions than it answered."

Henry frowned and scratched his chin. "Oh? For instance?"

Roberta took a deep drag and blew the smoke into the crisp air.

"In all the miles we traveled, in all the stories you've told me, I've tried to get my mind around your friend, or enemy as the case may be, Pancho Villa. I still don't understand who or what he was. It sounded for a while like he was a patriot to the Revolution. He had enough charisma and spoke with enough passion that he recruited you and Yellow Boy to march with him to Agua Prieta and to lead ten thousand men over the Sierra Madre. Even then, you thought he was starting to sound and act like a brutal tyrant.

"You said he went crazy after Wilson's betrayal, that he just couldn't face facts rationally. You told me how he murdered that priest and all those men at San Pedro de la Cueva, but had the will and courage and fortitude to lead starving men on an attack of Columbus in the United States and evade capture while being chased by a US Army division, and did that with a festering bullet hole in his shin.

"You said you had all those dreams of a jaguar on fire attacking you. You told me how you wound up interpreting your dream, but it really doesn't help me understand how he could be a great man and a fiery devil at the same time."

Henry shrugged and puffed his pipe while they stared down the canyon. "I've thought about that for a long time. Had all sorts of ideas about it and thought when I read

Churchill's speech about the Russians and their alliance with Germany he had pretty well described Villa. You remember that, don't you?"

Roberta smiled and shook her head. "No. What did he say?"

"Churchill said Russia was, '…a riddle, wrapped in a mystery, inside an enigma.'"

"So that's what you think Villa was, a riddle, wrapped in a mystery, inside an enigma? That's just saying he was nearly impossible to understand. Is that what you mean?"

"Yeah, in a way. But the same thing can be said about anybody. It's a great mystery how we're made one part tiger, one part lamb. Some are just more tiger than lamb and others vice versa. Villa was one of those rare types where it was easy to see both. It wasn't long after I returned to Las Cruces and I saw William Blake's poem, *The Tiger*, that I realized he had captured what I thought about Villa."

Roberta blew her cigarette smoke in the air in front of her and watched it slowly disappear. "William Blake…I remember you mumbling a line of poetry and saying then it was from a William Blake poem when we were first here. Is *The Tiger* what you were quoting?"

"Yeah. You have a mighty good memory."

"Can you recall the whole poem?"

"Yes, I can. Do you want to hear it?"

She smiled and nodded.

Henry, stared down the canyon for a moment, closed his eyes, and began.

> "Tiger, tiger, burning bright
> In the forests of the night

What immortal hand or eye
Could frame thy fearful symmetry?

"In what distant deep or skies
Burnt the fire of thine eyes?
On what wings dare he aspire?
What the hand dare seize the fire?

"And what shoulder and what art
Could twist the sinews of thy heart?
And when thy heart began to beat,
What dread hand and what dread feet?

"What the hammer? What the chain?
What the furnace was thy brain?
What the anvil? What dread grasp
Dare its deadly terrors clasp?

"When the stars threw down their spears,
And water'd heaven with their tears,
Did He smile His work to see?
Did He who made the lamb make thee?

"Tiger, tiger, burning bright
In the forests of the night,
What immortal hand or eye
Dare frame thy fearful symmetry?"

Lost in their thoughts for a long while, Roberta at last said, "The poem really does say it all doesn't it?"

Henry nodded. "Yes it does. I was lucky enough to see

and understand a little about the fire and anvil and hammer that made Villa the tiger he was."

"Did you ever see him again?"

"Never did. I followed the newspaper stories about him and I knew Quent had pretty good sources in Mexico sending him reliable information, and he kept me informed of what he knew. After Villa struck a deal with *Presidente* de la Huerta around 1920, he basically became a *hacendado*, and retired to the *Hacienda* El Canutillo, about fifty miles from Parral. Jesús and I talked about going down there to see him, but decided it was best to let sleeping dogs lie and not tempt fate.

"I first heard about Villa's assassination from Quent. He rang me up from El Paso. You know how you remember every detail about what you were doing on days when you hear shocking news. It was Saturday about noon, the twenty-first of July 1923. I had just finished setting a kid's broken arm when my nurse told me there was a telephone call from Mr. Peach in El Paso. He was excited and didn't waste time, as usual, with polite amenities.

"Henry?"

"Yes it is. That you Quent?"

"I just got word that our friend Villa was assassinated yesterday and is being buried today."

"I was stunned but not surprised. I said, 'I knew it! I knew something like this was bound to happen. Where was he killed?'"

"Parral. Evidently ambushed. He was driving, had his secretary and three bodyguards with him. My source says he was hit nine or ten times and died instantly. One bodyguard got away, but the other two and the secretary were killed too. It was a set up all the way."

"Do they know who did it?"

"No, not officially, and Obregón swears he had nothing to do with it. None of the actual shooters were identified. The story goes that after the ambush, they casually got on their horses and rode out of town. My source says General Calles, you remember him, he was the Carranza general that smoked Villa at Agua Prieta, is behind it. If I get anything else firm, I'll let you know. Got to run. Adiós."

"Quent passed along what he learned as the months went by, and it became clearer that Villa's murder was a political assassination. Obregón was implicated, but no one was ever convicted of the murder."

Roberta stubbed out her cigarette on the bottom of her boot, and crossing her arms, shivered in the cold. Henry peeled off his jacket and laid it over her shoulders. She smiled.

"Thank you, dear. I've always been thin-blooded. I remember when my family got word of Villa's assassination. My male friends who had gone off to fight with him, looked like they wanted to cry. My parents shrugged it off. There was nothing they could do. My sister and I shrugged it off too. We didn't know anything about the great Villa except he was a bandit to some, a general to others. We really didn't care that he'd been killed. You said you and Jesús talked about paying Villa a visit before he was killed. What happened to Jesús after you let Roja go?"

"He rode with Yellow Boy and me back to Las Cruces. Jesús assisted me in my practice for several years and I paid him well. I felt guilty as Hell about deceiving him when I had to find Villa and tried to assuage it with money. It's strange how guilt sticks to your soul, even when the one you've offended forgets about it. Jesús saved every penny he could of that guilt money and about 1925 married Tina Flores who worked in a cantina down the street from my office…"

Roberta knew from Henry's pause, his story had a surprise and he was waiting for her to ask, 'And…?' but she just looked at him with raised brows and her ear cocked toward him.

Henry grinned. "You've caught on to my tricks. Jesús left my office about a year before you came and he and Tina opened their own restaurant."

Roberta's jaw dropped. "You mean the *Tina's Restaurante*, where we eat two or three times a week, is owned by Jesús and Tina? Tina's Jesús is the same one in your story? Of all the gossip that goes on in Las Cruces, I'd never heard that."

Henry laid his arm around her shoulders. "Small world, isn't it?"

Roberta crossed her arms and shook her head. For a while they watched the morning light come and felt the chill of the night begin to warm as the sun rose higher over the mountain. She turned to Henry and said, "Two more questions and then I'm ready to go home. What happened to Maud and Johnnie? The way you said you admired Maud, it sounded like you were a little sweet on her, but then you spent time with the Apaches and maybe Lupe changed all that?"

Henry looked at her, raised his brows and shrugged. "Maud is a wonderful woman. I guess if I'd let nature take its course, because there was a mutual attraction, we might have wound up together. But, by that time I had decided that there was some kind of curse on the people who loved me because they always died before their time. I kept in touch with Maud, but afraid of what might happen, I kept my distance. She remarried about a year after I returned to Las Cruces and lives in Mountainair. She had eight more children, five girls, and two surviving sons. Her husband hated what had happened to her and thought talking to reporters about it or even testifying at trials for the Mexicans who were in the Columbus raid would just call up bad memories for her. He didn't let her talk to any reporters or testify at any trials.

"I saw Johnnie in Las Cruces four or five months ago. He's a good lookin' man and owns a ranch not that far from Maud's place. He said she's doing all right and still rides. Chatting with Johnnie there on the street for a few minutes is what made me decide to go on and show you Mexico and what happened the year I rode to battle with Villa and then planned to kill him.

"And Lupe? You've got good intuition. She brought me back to life as far as women were concerned. I visited Rojo's camp two or three times a year to help her with the People."

Roberta smiled and raised a knowing eyebrow. "Being a doctor does have its perks doesn't it?"

Henry shook his head. "No, it wasn't like that at all. She was so independent and seemed so powerful with her medicines, no man in the camp wanted her. Yeah, I was in her blankets when I was there, but we were like two lost souls holding on to each other just taking a little comfort when we could find it.

"About twenty-five years ago, not long before you came to work for me, I made a trip to Pelo Rojo's camp. It was my last trip there and not long after the turmoil started over Apache Juan and some of his women murdering Francisco

Timbres' wife and kidnapping his three year-old son. Pelo Rojo's camp had fewer people every time I returned. Some went to San Carlos. Some were killed off during raids, and some just disappeared. Pelo Rojo told me the People left in his camp, including Lupe, were going south with him to live with the Pima People. He said he believed that the camp had too few men left for its children to survive.

"I asked him where these Pima People were and he said in the mountains east of Sahuaripa. I was dumbfounded. Sahuaripa is a village within thirty-five miles of San Pedro de la Cueva. As you said before, it's a small world.

"I gave all the People a final checkup and told them good-by. I had a tender moment with Lupe, gave her all the medicines I had, and promised I'd come anytime, anywhere they needed me. She said not to worry, and that as long as Pelo Rojo led them, they would do well. After I left, I never went back and neither did Yellow Boy. I thought that last trip was the end of the Sierra Madre Apaches, but it wasn't."

Roberta frowned. "Oh? What happened?"

Henry looked out across the *llano* and smiled. "That's another story for another time."

Roberta laughed as he cranked the engine, pushed in the clutch, and grinding and scraping, found first gear to roll down the trail toward the rising sun.

~Finis~

Additional Reading

1. Harris, Larry A., *Pancho Villa and the Columbus Raid*, Superior Printing, Inc., El Paso, Texas, 1949. Reprinted from the original publication by High Lonesome Books, Silver City, New Mexico as: *Pancho Villa, Strong Man of the Revolution.*

2. Katz, Friedrich, *The Life and Times of Pancho Villa*, Stanford University Press, Stanford, California, 2003.

3. Tompkins, Colonel Frank, *Chasing Villa, The Last Campaign of U.S. Cavalry*, High Lonesome Books, Silver City, New Mexico, 1996.

4. Torres, Elias L., Translated by Sheila M. Ohlendorf, *Twenty Episodes in the Life of Pancho Villa*, The Encino Press, Austin, Texas, 1973.

5. Welsome, Eileen, *The General and the Jaguar, Pershing's Hunt for Pancho Villa, A True Story of Revolution and Revenge*, University of Nebraska Press, Lincoln, Nebraska, 2007.

About the Author

W. Michael Farmer lives and writes in Smithfield, Isle of Wight County, Virginia. Living for nearly fifteen years in Las Cruces, New Mexico, immersed in the region's rich history, living in its culture, exploring its deserts, mountains, and ranges he learned much of the rich story life of the southwest. A physicist by training, as an author he has published short stories in two anthologies, won awards for essays at the Christopher Newport University Writers' Conference, and published essays in magazines. Hombrecito's War, won a Western Writers of America Silver Spur Award for Best First Novel in 2006 and a New Mexico Book Award Finalist for Historical Fiction in 2007. The sequel, Hombrecito's Search, was released in July 2007. Treble Heart Press published his third novel, Conspiracy: The Trial of Oliver Lee and James Gililland, in 2009. Tiger Tiger Burning Bright: The Betrayals of Pancho Villa, his fourth novel completes the Hombrecito's Legacy Trilogy.